A BRAVE MAN

A NOVEL

MAN

WILL CHANCELLOR

SEVEN

STOREYS

TALL

HARPER

www.harpercollins.com

A BRAVE MAN SEVEN STOREYS TALL. Copyright © 2014 by Will Chancellor. All rights reserved. Printed in the United States of America. No part of this book may be used or reproduced in any manner whatsoever without written permission except in the case of brief quotations embodied in critical articles and reviews. For information, address HarperCollins Publishers, 10 East 53rd Street, New York, NY 10022.

HarperCollins books may be purchased for educational, business, or sales promotional use. For information, please e-mail the Special Markets Department at SPsales@harpercollins.com.

FIRST EDITION

Designed by Pat Flanagan

Library of Congress Cataloging-in-Publication Data has been applied for.

ISBN 978-0-06-228000-8

14 15 16 17 18   OV/RRD   10 9 8 7 6 5 4 3 2 1

ONE

THE RUPTURED GLOBE

—I'm gonna close with a quote from Dr. Johnson: "The certainty that life cannot be long, and the probability that it will be much shorter than nature allows, ought to awaken every man to the active prosecution of whatever he is desirous to perform. It is true that no diligence can ascertain success; death may intercept the swiftest career; but he who is cut off in the execution of an honest undertaking has at least the honour of falling in his rank, and has fought the battle, though he missed the victory."

The whole idea of a pregame speech seemed kind of meaty for a water polo team. Looking to an Enlightenment figure for a battle cry? Questionable to quite questionable.

The underclassmen missed the quote, thinking every word was Owen's. To them, he was indestructible and elect, Athens-bound, senior, and capable of saying such things. They knew the Owen profiled on websites, had read his capsule summary in

magazines during the run-up to Sydney, and thought he'd com-
peted like a veteran, not a teenager, in those two minutes he
churned Olympic water.

To the players who had been around Owen longest, to those
who had faced him in the pools of Burbank, Woodland Hills,
Riverside, and Van Nuys, to those who also made the Under-16
National Team and bunked with him in dorms all over the Eastern Bloc, to those who had grown up under constant pressure
to perform and knew the inner walls of an Olympic pipeline—
which is to say, to those who knew him best—he was inscrutable,
aloof, and mystic, which was why he was a *co*-captain, and why
his choice of source material wasn't all that surprising.

Never before in his collegiate career had he given a speech or
had more than a few words for a teammate. This three-minute
meander, his coach's idea, had cost him last night's sleep and made
him skittish. His co-captain was just about to start a round of pity
claps when Owen added one last salvo, one last farewell to college
sports:

—Fuck Dr. Johnson. This is my last Big Splash, and this is a
victory none of us is gonna fucking miss.

At Owen's profanity, each player stopped stretching his shoulders, flapping his arms, twisting his neck, and fell silent. It took a
moment, but Owen's words began to register on their faces. The
freshmen, whose college personalities were only a few months
old, caught the mood and began shoving each other, moshing
around the locker room until the trainers had to intervene. The
melee grew so loud that the fans outside grew quiet. Now Owen's
co-captain brought everyone down to a hush and then asked in
his most resonant growl:

—Whooose House?

The team cinched their robes, knotted their cardinal-red caps,
and exited with their hands held high, applauding the spill of fans

on the bright green slope. Blankets, quilts, and towels covered the damp grass from poolside to chain-link fence. Half the crowd was solid red, the other blue and gold. Students' biology textbooks were closed, highlighters marking places. Most fans were standing. Someone even had a sign: a woodcut print of the Stanford head coach over the single word OBEY.

While a warbled karaoke version of "The Star-Spangled Banner" played from the blown-out stadium speakers, Owen pulled at his lapels, studying them. He turned to his co-captain.

—I've felt like an asshole in this thing all season.

The terry-cloth bathrobes were a remnant of days before the advent of wrap-foil blankets and heated benches. The robes were simple, and they worked. This year, however, a sophomore from Orange County, the unofficial social chair, had ordered something the team hoped would come across as ironic but feared would be read as vulgar. When the players unboxed the updated game robes, cardinal velour with satin trim, the manager asked everyone to check the jetted pockets for Hugh Hefner's missing pipe.

In robes loosely belted, Owen and his co-captain took one step forward and waved. They stepped back from the applause.

—Everyone feels like an asshole in these things. But give him some credit. He managed to make guys more comfortable wearing Speedos than robes.

After the home team was announced, it looked as if the crowd might scatter and recline on the grass on this bright November morning, open textbooks, check phones, remember that water polo is a minor sport with minor implications. Before this could happen, an engineering student pulled the starter cord to a gas-powered blender and twisted the throttle to a roar. Students turned in alarm, then laughed, then sidled up for drinks. On the other side of the fence, a fan in board shorts and a bright red cape, wearing a cut-up Mikasa ball as a hat, sprinted into the stadium and started a cheer of "Go! Big! Red!" that lasted until tip-off.

High-knee jumps and an effort to land with menace. Each player cleared the lane line feet first, resurfaced, and took a few strokes of butterfly before slapping the water.

Seven on each side swam to their end and rested their necks on the lane line, treading water until the whistle blast.

Stanford won the sprint.

The first trip down the pool, Owen was met on the perimeter but backed down his man until he had established position in the hole. He squared up to the wing, fought off a foul to take a wet ball, and swept a shot to the far-side net before the wing defender could collapse.

Half of the arms in the crowd went straight into the air. A Cardinal roar swept across El Camino and echoed to the Bay.

Stanford's second possession was more turbulent than the first. Water boiled in front of the goal as players drove at each other, shoulder to chest. The hole defender chinned Owen's neck with his Balkan stubble, then a cheap elbow to the base of the skull. He gripped down on Owen's suit and was called for a foul, but not an exclusion. Owen kicked the ball out to the driver, who one-timed it right back at Owen's chest. For a full second the ball bobbed a little more than an arm's length from Owen. Hard step-out, creating space. Ball cupped against his forearm in a backhand coil. Now the defender was trying to get called for a foul, elbow points two pestles mashing down trapezius. Owen shrugged off the defender's weight and arched back his neck, face to the sky. The guard slapped and clawed. He was lower in the water and beat. Sprawled and tackling, now pulling at Owen's shoulder. The goalie barking two other defenders to the hole. Owen rose high, elevating to the hip, wound tight as a discus thrower, a galvanized chain ready to loose the shot that made every goalie duck. He led with his chin, whipped his head—

Red water. Blue caps. Bodies.

Then all went white.

The clinic's parking lot, intercut with clean arcs both yellow and white, both solid and dashed, belonged to a tarmac and not to this private facility that saw no more than a dozen patients at any time.

Professor Burr had parked his white Volvo in the shade of a ponderosa where he periodically glanced up from his book review to scan the clinic entrance and sip coffee from his aluminum thermos. He had been debating going inside, contrary to his son's instructions, for the past half hour and had finally decided he couldn't sit here any longer when he caught sight of Owen, knees near his chin, being wheeled through the parting glass doors. Wheelchairs aren't designed for people that tall, Burr thought. Owen leapt from the chair, quick to show everyone that wheeling him to the entrance had been a ludicrous formality.

Owen had two walks: a confident kicking gallop bridging meters with each stride, and a flip-flop shuffle that whittled down his great height until he was almost merely tall. Walking out of a hospital called for his full-heighted stride. And he strode to his father's car kicking pity, paperwork, and whatever else floated in the salt-stained air to the aether.

Even though the entire left side of his head was bandaged, Owen shone that morning, and his father was a few seconds stunned. The door lock rattled and spun as his father leaned over to let him in. After Owen slid into the cracked leather seat, he failed repeatedly to mate the buckle and clasp. When he lost his left eye, he'd lost his depth perception. Each clash of metal with plastic grew louder than the one before. His father's hand hovered, almost helping, but wavered as if it would be batted away. Owen jabbed the buckle home at last with a sharp snap.

He heard his father's mouth open. Close. Open. He heard him chewing on the words that another man might have spoken outright. Words rarely passed the barrier of his father's teeth without coaxing.

Professor Burr tasted the air a few times with a dry tongue. He never could summon those paternal banalities that sports dads spit out like sunflower seeds.

Burr fiddled with the Volvo's gearshift as they waited for a stoplight. He jerked the knob from first to neutral and back again, all the while wanting to place his hand on Owen's knee and say fatherly things about how he was going to be fine, how he needed to be extra careful with his good eye. Instead he bit his lip and fiddled with the gearshift again. Fatherhood requires too much authority. How do you comfort a statue?

A driver in front of them was slow off the line, distracted. Burr only moved one car forward, missing the protected turn. He took one deep breath.

—So I gave my talk in English, actually. Italians value fluency much more than effort, you know. Even in a place like Padua you're better off briefly apologizing for your lack of culture and getting on with it.

With the barrier broken, the words undammed, Owen eased back in the seat and closed his eye. They talked about Galileo and were nearly home when Burr asked his first topical question.

—Did any of your squad drop by?

—The team came while I was still in surgery. They had to drive back to Palo Alto.

—Why didn't they just take you to the university hospital?

—The surgeon has his own clinic, so he doesn't have to deal with anyone.

—It really doesn't look bad.

—It looks like . . . nothing.

—I suppose that's right.

They sat in silence from the last note of Burr's *hmph* until the rubber squeak of the tires turning on the concrete driveway. The garage door was open. The garage door was always open.

When Owen's father still believed in his dissertation, recent academic trends being no more than a rehabilitation of Parmenides, he had taken their front door off its hinges so their house would be open at all times. It vexed him that the Home, protective only by its closure to the outside world and useful only in its open inhabitable space, denied its humble origins in the Cave—a cave being proof that one could live both inside and outside, that one could exist in a sustained liminal state. The upshot of all this theory was that Owen had lacked a front door from 1992 to 1993. And even in coastal California that meant that small rodents, enterprising birds, and all manner of bugs eventually made their way inside. This was Professor Burr's open-door policy—a policy a colleague in the Classics Department had mocked by bringing over a fluorescent orange sign reading OPEN HOUSE. The sign was now sun-bleached, but still staked into the lawn. When one of Owen's friends suggested they just remove the garage door, Owen was relieved. He was tired of hearing about dichotomies as false consciousness, but he was more tired of squirrels at his feet during breakfast.

This was the house—or theoretically cave, since the garage door had never been replaced—that they pulled up to. It technically belonged to the university, but belonged to the Burrs in practice. Owen's mother had been the only daughter of a pivotal university president. To commemorate them both, the trustees voted for the house to stay in the family, even though Owen's parents never married, choosing to remain in the liminal state of engagement. It was two storeys, mossed, fenced by giant eucalyptus trees, and far more accommodating than the homes of other tenured faculty.

Owen picked up the plastic-wrapped newspaper at the front curb. The morning's glare knocked him off the long stone walk and into the lawn. A few firm steps righted him. He ducked in the front door.

This Japanese modernist home was the storehouse of Owen's memories. And just like a memory, the home was built for a century of patinated glow before a slow dissolve back into the ground. There could have been sliding paper doors, but there weren't. There could have been a wooden outhouse, but there wasn't. Instead, there were two downstairs bathrooms with a tremendously unhygienic library of university journals, a year's worth of folded *New York Review of Books*, the *New Yorker*, the final issues of *Antaeus*, and quite a few volumes from a German classics encyclopedia. Owen and his father reshelved what was valuable and discarded the rest of the musty collection every few years when someone came by to photograph the interior for books with titles like *Holistic Architectural Design* or *Sacred Geometry in Mid-Century California Homes*. The house's spiral footprint was roughly nautiloid and the windows followed the golden ratio. Though the proportions were golden, the windows were small. The house was dark most of the day, shafts of light here and there. A ramp of sunlight, almost solid enough to bear weight, beamed on the stairway when they walked in.

—How about some soup? You should eat with those pills.

Owen clutched the wooden rail and climbed the stairs. He dropped his duffel at the foot of his bed.

This bed, this pillowless bed, the one bed in the world built specifically to accommodate Owen's great height, had ended up being too short. His ankles spilled past the end. He pulled at the mattress with his heels, looking to his feet and waiting for Procrustes to lop away the remainder. *Tendons. The stretching soul . . .*

psukhe . . . The word drifted away, bounding down the halls . . . and Owen was asleep.

A tug on his toe brought Owen back.

—I thought it better to let you sleep. How are you feeling?

Owen sat up. His father was at the foot of the bed, flipping through an illustrated book.

—They recommended this in your discharge packet. It looks pretty worthless.

Burr showed the laminated cover. Owen read it aloud.

—*Coping with Changes in Sight.*

—By Dr. Thomas Friedlan . . . MD.

—I haven't read in a week. I'm not going to start with that.

—Did they give you a paper at least?

—*USA Today.*

—I'm sorry.

The first unqualified apology he could remember from his father, ever, and the man was talking about a newspaper.

Burr unpalmed two pills: a painkiller and an antibiotic. Owen took the glass of milk, swallowed both pills, and wondered if *painkiller* was an oxymoron. Burr made prayer hands and drummed his lower lip. Owen tried to break the trance.

—I found something in Johnson when I was looking for a quote for my pregame speech—

—"The life that is devoted to knowledge passes silently away . . .

This was Burr's Faculty Dinner Toast. In dining halls, he stood and clinked his glass, certain that the words would edify and failing to notice that his colleagues, who had heard this before, were thumbing the hem of the tablecloth, wondering why they hadn't taken that job at Goldman.

— . . . wanders about the world without pomp or terror, and is neither known nor valued but by men like himself."

—That's everybody's problem, not just scholars. I found this place where Johnson says every man wastes half his life displaying talents he doesn't possess.

—Remember, Johnson's aphorisms are too true to dismiss as mere entertainment.

—That's what I'm saying. Which half of my life am I about to waste? Which talents do I not really possess?

—Luckily, you can do anything.

Owen looked for a concrete answer in this reply.

—That doesn't help. Which half of my life will I waste? Would I have wasted?

His father moved from the foot of the bed to the desk chair.

—Well, I suppose anyone who plunks down his chips and makes a commitment will have at least half a life—which is more than most. It will sort itself out. Johnson speaks to his dried-up ambition as a poet. But had he devoted his light to poetry, the world would have been robbed of its greatest critic.

—I'm giving back my scholarship.

—Getting injured wasn't your fault. It was in the line of duty, as they say.

—I'm giving back my scholarship and stopping out.

Owen watched his father decode Stanford's euphemism for student sabbaticals. Burr looked as if someone had taken something from inside him. As if he were now missing some hitherto unnamed organ that was nonetheless essential.

—What are you going to do?

—Art.

Owen had no idea where that came from, nor why it appeared as upper case: *Art*. He was a dilettante at best, someone who'd taken a few years of drawing. Sketches of classmates littered the margins of his high school notes. His drawings looked real enough, but the art teachers never said he had talent. They picked their words carefully to encourage students like him, but not too much. Owen had no claim to the clutch of students who'd pledged their lives to art before adolescence. Still. If he wanted to do something significant before he turned thirty, it was art, music, or sports—and he'd never learned an instrument. He recognized this immediately for what it was: grasping at straws so his hands wouldn't be empty. And his expression betrayed vague ambitions, emboldening his father.

—That's not how art works, I'm afraid. You don't just declare yourself an artist at twenty-one.

—I'm going to be an Artist.

—And I'm going to be an astronaut!

—If I devote the next twenty years to studying art . . . I've got to know which is the wasted half, and right now that means plunking down my chips for art.

—That's not an option. You'll only have a few months to go from the time your prosthesis is ready until commencement.

—I'm sure as hell not going to have a glass eye.

—The medical literature says the best ocular prostheses are acrylic.

—I'm not getting an artificial eye.

—Well, what? You're just going to wear an eye patch forever?

—Yes.

—We can talk about it while you recover.

—There's nothing to talk about. Have you ever seen someone with a fake eye? It's uncanny. People can't help but examine. The best-case scenario is no one noticing. Which is another way of saying that I would be lying to everyone. No. I had an eye. Now I have an eye patch.

—It's just so . . . I don't know . . . cartoonish.

—James Joyce wore an eye patch.

—Not by choice! These options weren't available to him.

—I can't do anything about that. And you're not helping.

—If nothing else, you'll need a prosthesis to get back in the water. I'm sure Coach Rudić will want you to train your replacement in Colorado Springs and travel with the team to Athens. Who knows, you may even be able to contribute in certain situations.

—Like total darkness? In-the-land-of-the-blind type of thing? I'd just be a distraction. You know what they call a particularly effective distraction?

—What?

—A mascot.

Owen's father withered. He had no response. He looked at his feet.

—I have no idea about your sport. All I know is that you can do anything.

—Except art.

—That's not fair. I just mean that if anyone can overcome this much adversity . . .

—This is not a comeback story, Dad. And I refuse to become an ex-athlete, especially at twenty-one. I'm not going to sit on a bench in street clothes, turn and wave graciously to a crowd shaking their heads at what a pity this all is. I'm traveling with whatever's left of the insurance money.

—What insurance money? Your grandfather's estate is all tied up in maintenance on this house, and there's not more than a thousand dollars left from the other settlement.

—I'll work abroad and come back for the rest of my senior year later—several years later, if they let me.

—They won't.

—Then I'll have to adapt.

—Adapt? You have no idea what kind of world it is out there. The barbarians are at the gates! You're talking about serious engagement with the real world, but unfortunately you carry an academic's passport. Have you been in the company of Vandals? You can visit, but to think you can adapt is just too . . . Lamarckian.

—Well, I guess we'll see if I can really do anything.

Owen turned on the bathroom light. Pale blue chlorine—once from his pores, now from bleach on the tile—flared his nostrils. He gripped the cold slab counter, thick enough for a real grip, and faced the mirror. After a few confidence breaths, the same breaths he took each morning before leaping through the morning steam and crashing into the practice pool elbows-first, Owen unhooked the metal clips and unrolled the bandage around his head. The gauze pad over his left eye was a washed pink, brick red at the edges; Owen picked at the bottom, using his thumbnail as a trowel.

He braced for the tug of coagulated blood, but at his first prod the pad fell limply into the sink. Instead of a black crusted mess, Owen found a little yellow, a little blue, and a drooping—as if too much eyelid had grown in his sleep. Without thinking, he closed his right eye to compare. He would never see his right eyelid again.

That was something.

The water scalded Owen's hands. He clutched his fists, fanning out the burn. Then cold. He tilted his head and took in a side-mouthful of water, washing a Vicodin into the walls of a throat stripped raw by intubation. He set one bottle and one tube by the sink, unthreaded the cap of the bottle, and shot a saline spray into his left upper lid. It surprised more than hurt, like the puff of a glaucoma test. He put the bottle aside and uncapped the antibiotic gel. Holding his eyelids apart, Owen found something softer than he had expected. Muscle and vasculature leapt forward to fill the vacuum, heaping pillow-flesh hiding sutures that were never going to heal.

Fuck.

In pre-op the surgeon had explained that if his eye didn't improve, they would be attaching the ocular muscles to a Ping-Pong ball—not "something the size of a Ping-Pong ball." Was the surgeon serious? Owen had been too drugged to ask. Now he unspooled a ribbon of gel into his lower lid, fluttering his eye instinctively and looking away too fast. A jolt rang the center of his skull, and a world-altering headache was born. Each peal of the bell tightened his temples but made everything else expand. How had people done this before painkillers? Maybe they hadn't. If they hadn't, maybe he shouldn't.

He dug through his water polo bag for an eye patch. The elastic band bit into his brow. Stretching it did nothing.

Owen crumbled onto his bed like a tower toppled by ropes and horses. He shaded his eye with his arm. It had been three years, but Owen still saw the ink from his tattoo bleeding and leaving five interlocking rings on his forehead: red, green, black, yellow, blue. *Fucking tattoo.* Owen read a few lines of Burton. His saccade was off. The gears ground every time he came to the end of a line, jarring, like hitting the right margin on a typewriter during a breathless thought. He took another painkiller before drifting off with the book open on his chest. He woke. Nothing. Read the same sentences again, put the book on the nightstand, and fell out for days.

Three months passed with no improvement in Owen's vision. On the few occasions he tested it, his eye, if you could still call it that, took a soft impression of light. He was aware of light, as a magnet is aware when the wrong pole enters its field. He turned from the sun with the same gentle but steady repulsion. Burr agreed at last that it was time to move on, and drove him to the clinic for the final outpatient procedure.

Four days after his second surgery, in his undersize bed, Owen woke with resolve. He glanced to his clock, hoping for a single digit. A six, an eight, even 9:59 would do. One. The wrong single digit. But it explained the light. Thin winter blue through empty air, not even a dust mote dancing. Or possibly it was just because he needed his left eye to get the oblique angle. He slowly rotated his head, rolling into the thick of a radiating headache. He swallowed a painkiller and went outside for air.

All it took was a nudge of the aluminum frame to open the screen door, stained with salt-wind and hinge-sprung. The sharp dry squeak, a call to the gulls. An onshore breeze held the door closed after Owen passed through.

If he would be going anywhere, this sand would have to go with him.

Owen staggered down the cliff behind his house and over the shale, pooled by the low tide. He crabbed along the rocks until he found his familiar ledge. Leaving his sandals behind, he leapt to the wet sand.

Large dark grains, lifted and crushed by winter's northern swell, swallowed his toes. At the tidemark Owen poured a cupped hand of ocean onto his brittle yellow hair. A kayaker in the kelp forest, beyond masses of water crumbling at the point, waved a yellow paddle. Owen filled an empty mason jar with dark pumice sand.

And pumice from the shore, the dry porous stone of the sea.

He was used to finding Athene here. Ah-tee-nay, as Owen

pronounced it, to his father's chagrin. She was always around these rocks. Whenever he jumped from the rocks into the cold Pacific, he resurfaced to find her waiting. When she was present, Owen remained submerged to the neck, gripping the rocks to resist the current. She advanced his thoughts farther and along routes that he would not otherwise think of exploring. Dispersed colors condensed until everything cast a shadow of ultramarine. When she was present, everything peripheral vanished. She absorbed it all into her hyperchromatic blue.

That one shade was the text of his private religion. First he saw the color and then he gave it a face and a name. But it was the color that mattered. He met the color here, and it stayed with him for days.

It took Owen years to realize that this belief invited ridicule. In his household, the name Athena, the name Zeus, the name Apollo, were far more common than the name God. When he was very young, his religion had just been a way of matching strange colors to all the stuff his dad was going on and on about. At seven, he thought the gods were something his peers knew existed—because they too knew the names—but couldn't comprehend, like algebra. At ten, he conceded that faith in the Greek gods would be preposterous, but faith was never the issue. His religion was inductive, grounded exclusively in colors he routinely saw, all with very consistent frequencies. At thirteen, he had faith that the rest of the ancient gods existed, even though he had only seen four. And, yes, he knew he was ridiculous to believe in gods who were extinct.

Respecting his absurd belief was too much to ask of both his peers and their parents. Adults who caught a whiff of Owen's strange private world thought him fair game because of all his natural advantages. They joked in carpools. They joked in the stands. When his homeroom teacher presented his father with the brewing scandal of Owen qua pagan at third-grade parent-teacher conferences, Burr's only response was "Of course he's being ironical. I think we should applaud his sense of humor and knowledge of history." Owen would never volunteer his idiosyncratic faith to his father, and Burr never raised the issue. Their conversations were limited to calligraphy, Latin, and the injunction to "be a leader, not a follower."

Still. There was a moment every few days when the light would change, and Owen felt the presence of divinity. Most of his days were steeped in one of these hues, the shades that shouted for a name.

As far as pantheons go, the gods in Owen's world remained surprisingly few. His palette held four distinct colors—each unique to a divinity, never blended, never diluted, never confused. He experienced one of four precise chromatic shifts. Each bias would last for days. After a decade of collecting paint cards from Home Depot, memorizing a hefty portion of the Pantone scale, writing to everyone from entomologists to geologists to a pen pal in Uttar Pradesh, he had found the conventional, albeit esoteric, names for these colors: peridot, gamboge, carmine, and ultramarine.

But even after that exhaustive chase, the names he'd invented for the colors were the ones he trusted. And ultramarine was Athene.

Athene had watched over his mother, more or less approved of his father, and was the blue mist that surrounded and protected Owen. Before the accident, she raised him above every decision, giving him a privileged topsight.

Now he couldn't see beyond immediate impediments, and every decision dwarfed him. This nameless world was colorless, collapsed.

The old colors had stained him for days. Nothing could wash one away; it reflected deep into the empty space of his cells. He likened it to a suntan: the light came in, and his body responded. But he kept the experience to himself as long as he could. At age eight he'd watched *One Flew Over the Cuckoo's Nest* and learned that words can only hurt you when someone's questioning your mental health.

It's tempting to say that Owen was an empty vessel waiting for whatever he chose to call divinity to fill him with heightened thoughts. But no. Light has no volume, and he was no vessel. He was not filled. Light can exert pressure, however. It can lift. And in these washed moments, Owen was lifted to a different height. His body was strengthened, engrafted new. His hands stronger and wiser, his vision clearer.

Christmas 1992 he told his father about it. And that's when the psychoanalysis started.

Owen's first therapist was Lacanian. Why Lacanian? His father called psychotherapy "palliative care in drag," but thought there was real value in learning about Jacques Lacan, the subject of half the dissertations being defended at Mission University. When Burr examined his darker motives, he feared that he was using his son to take lecture notes.

They had trouble locating a Lacanian analyst at all, then trouble finding one willing to take on a preadolescent. Santa Cruz had the man for the job.

In his first session, Owen told his therapist about one of the Gods.

—A flash of peridot at sunset means that Hermes is there. The other colors happen gradually, like the shadow on a sundial. Hermes is like a bomb blast that happens so quickly the walls bend like saw blades and snap back with a warbling like this: *wa wa wa waaah.*

—What color is peridot exactly?

—It's exactly peridot. That's the whole point. It's a grassy green. Peridot.

—Continue.

—The peridot days are like sculpture or buildings. Like when I see a building in an architecture book, I can put thoughts inside my mental map of the building. Everything fits. But I'm not sure what fits with what; whether the idea comes first or the building. I just sort of let it happen.

—Do you know what a metaphor is?

Owen couldn't brook condescension even when he *didn't* know the answer. He was silent, snarling in the way that only a ten-year-old can snarl.

—Are you using the peridot as a metaphor for your feelings?

—No.

—Would you say you are perturbed during these peridot days?

—No. Everything falls into place. It settles. I'm not perturbed.

—Is today one of the peridot days?

—Yes.

—Does this remit? I mean, do you ever have days or parts of days that are not peridot?

—There are other colors too. But once the color starts, it stays that way for a few days.

—What stays that way?

—Everything shifts slightly.

—Do you want to draw this for me? I have several green markers. I'm not sure if peridot is in there. But you can probably make do.

Owen couldn't hide his reaction to the therapist's condescension. He might only be ten, but he knew what *remit* meant, and he didn't want to draw.

—I'm going to wait out front for my dad.

—It's that I'm treating you like a child, isn't it? I invite all my patients to draw, to play, to explore. Your Hermes is fascinating. Let's follow him and see where he goes.

Owen went out the front door and waited in the sun.

Professor Burr revealed to Owen several years later that this first therapist considered Owen actively psychotic and wrote out a prescription for chlorpromazine. He thought Owen was in severe danger of becoming "stuck there," and advised a medicated future in order to manage these delusions.

That single experience was enough psychiatry for the Burrs. Mission School District, however, insisted that Owen continue to seek professional help. They recommended a psychologist of mixed lineage who was loosely Adlerian. He had succeeded with several troubled children. Because the phrase *troubled child* had enough potency to pluck a talented athlete from the Olympic Development Program, Owen agreed to a full year of sessions.

The first three months were a standoff. The therapist didn't hide the fact that he viewed religiosity—any religiosity, much less idiopathic religiosity—as neurosis. He told Owen that Hermes, a name appearing over and over in the previous analyst's patient notes, was certainly an attempt to rationalize the absence of his mother—which certainly wasn't his fault.

Every session was the same: "Talk to me about your mother. Do you feel her death was in any way your fault? What do you associate with mothers? What do you associate with women? Do you know what labor is?" Throughout therapy, Owen refused to say a word.

On the day he knew would be his last session, as a Parthian shot, Owen told the therapist about the gamboge days, the days of Apollo. How time slowed, nearly stopped, and allowed him to realize his visions. How the color pulled ideas together in a thick resinous current. How he shot far ahead and found the mark.

The Adlerian refused to let go of the idea that Owen was being metaphorical. The therapist wouldn't even go so far as to call gamboge a mistaken belief. Owen couldn't get into his story without the therapist insisting that they talk about his relationship to his mother and father. That conversation wasn't going to happen. After ten minutes of Owen refusing to answer direct questions, the therapist offered an astute analysis of the impasse.

—I ask you about your parents and you stonewall me. Instead you talk about gods as if they're real. Maybe you're putting me on. Either way, it's not a problem. I think you're a really interesting young man, Owen. What you need, and what I'm going to tell your father that you need, is a good Jungian.

They never found the Jungian, which, as Owen would later reflect, was probably a shame. And thus ended Owen's brief experience with psychotherapy. His father convinced a colleague in the Psych Department to sign any paperwork from the school district. A taboo concerning psychology fell over the Burr house.

As a sophomore at Stanford, Owen broke the taboo by registering for Professor Philip Zimbardo's survey course. To pass, each student was required to participate in fifteen hours of grad student experimentation. The sign-up form for paranormal psychology was at the top of the bulletin board in the hallway outside the auditorium. He scheduled himself for the maximum of three hours. It was just enough time for him to tell the story of Ares.

The psych grad students, in part due to the pioneering work of Zimbardo, typically designed observational experiments that posed little risk of warping the precious minds of their subjects. Gone were the days of getting psych credit for MKUltra projects at Menlo Park Veterans Hospital. Gone were the days of Ken Kesey and Perry Lane. These were the days of a microphone, a tape recorder, and the invitation to tell your story. Owen pulled up a chair in the windowless room and hit record.

"Ares is the heaviest of the Gods to bear. His color is carmine. The word itself is as violent and beautiful as days under this influence. It comes on slowly, like mist filling a thimble. The effect lasts only a few hours, whereas the other light lasts for days. Ares only comes for big games—and at the higher levels, he comes for other people too.

The iron air descends, and the player's blood darkens. The heavier carmine air forces the inspired to breathe deeply through the diaphragm. Here. Well, you can't see that. But the player breathes from the diaphragm. His back is wider than the other athletes' backs. His eyes, this is the most important thing, are whiter than the other players' eyes. These are the all-white eyes you see in ancient sculpture. The player breathes in the carmine, and the cornea overtakes the iris and the eyes assume a fearsome whiteness. The artists knew this. It's the nonbelievers who said the eyes were painted.

I first saw these white eyes in 2000, at the Summer Olympics in Sydney.

I was sitting second from the end of the bench in the Team USA bathrobe. The inside of my left arm still itched from the Olympic ring tattoo I'd gotten after the opening ceremony— most of the athletes get their rings after the Games are over, but I wasn't going to play anyway.

Wolf's the reason this whole thing happened. He helped me get a scholarship here and helped me get a spot on the national team roster. So I was watching Wolf's game on the perimeter instead of studying how the Hungarian defense was collapsing on the hole. If Coach called my name, it would be me struggling to create enough space in the hole for a kick-out pass or a half-assed shot. But watching hole play against the Hungarians is like watching a bird with a broken wing try to fly. Each possession, our guy jerked his neck back to create space and elevate, only to have his efforts stuffed and his head submerged to the chin.

Water only churns like that when something is dying. Wolf's matchup was another matter altogether. He beat his defender twice in consecutive trips down the pool, first turning him and nearly walking the ball in, then swimming straight over the top of his man. Wolf batted away the desperate grip at his suit, dug two deep paddles, scissored high in the water, and ripped a shot off the upper right corner of the goal for a bar-in. The Hungarian coach saw our guy doing to his team what they do to the rest of the world. He wasted no time replacing the field player with someone who wouldn't have the same problem.

Uroš—I'll keep his last name off the record, but you shouldn't have a hard time looking him up—has a rosary beads tattoo, amber eyes, a thick mat of chest hair, and a fuck-off gut. He's the only player on either roster who isn't in shape. He calls his gut his "deep taper." Other than that one joke, which only swimmers would get, Uroš has little sense of humor. He has the sort of languid violent look that comes from prison. And Uroš did come close to getting locked up after a Greek player, his opposite, was stabbed during an international game, and a glass shiv was subsequently found on the bottom of the pool. But nothing was proven. And he was only twelve at the time. Uroš now looks so bored with violence that players, coaches, fans, psychologists wonder why he doesn't embrace different aspects of the game, like passing or even shooting. His shoulder was in shreds and he couldn't shoot for shit, but he would tear off a player's junk for even thinking of swimming over the top of him. His ten years on the national team are most notable for a host of atrocities committed above and beneath the water. Nice guy.

Uroš crashed into the pool and surfaced an inch from Wolf's face. Not nice. Wolf drove the heel of his hand into Uroš's chest then pulled out a patch of hair. Uroš smiled and threw his hands up to show the ref that, yes, the water was turbulent, but he wasn't the one fouling. Of course, as he raised his hands he caught Wolf with an elbow to the chin. Wolf pretended to make a break for the goal at the whistle. With Wolf's hard crossover stroke came a right elbow to Uroš's teeth. The double whistles meant Wolf would have to wait out twenty seconds, or the possession, from the exclusion area. Rather than flopping around after the ejection and skulling the water, Wolf sprinted to the other side of the lane line and treaded high with his palms in a Gable grip.

I could see Wolf's eyes getting whiter and whiter the deeper he breathed the carmine air above him.

Twenty seconds passed. Wolf sprinted back into the field of play just in time for Uroš to rip a shot three feet over the top bar in front of Wolf's outstretched arms. Tough to know if Uroš shot only so he could swing his arm or if he really was trying to score. But this much is certain: on his follow-through, Uroš tore a bandolier of flesh from Wolf's chest, leaving claw marks from shoulder to hip. Wolf smiled.

Coach Rudić called a time-out and I dove in to pull Wolf back to our side. They both looked at me. Their eyes had grown completely white. And their faces were a perfect calm. I had seen the carmine before, in games, but I had never breathed that deeply. That was the end of aggression. Wolf held my gaze as the color bled back into his irises. He put a finger to his lips, dropped to the pool floor, and swam to our side underwater with three giant pulls.

We've never talked about it. It's one of those things. Paranormal.

That was my experience with the paranormal. My name is Owen Burr. oburr@stanford.edu. Psych 1. Ted Lin's section."

Owen wasn't positive that anyone ever listened to that tape. No one called for a follow-up MRI. Maybe the cassette was buried in a steel filing cabinet in the basement of Jordan Hall. Maybe they were interested in stories of ghosts, not Gods.

And the pumice from the shore. No God today to see him off. There was no iron air, no bending, no monochrome. Just memories in the aether. So Owen returned home. Once back inside, he added a few slugs of olive oil to his jar and stirred the sand with a knife.

Upstairs, Owen emptied his game bag quickly, throwing chewed-up suits in one pile and mildewed shirts in another. Goggles yellow. Goggles blue. He gripped the signed game ball his coach had brought to the hospital; he spun it in his palm and read his teammates' well wishes, then placed it on a shelf. Scores of molded trophy-men, split at the center with a golden plastic scar, kept the ball from rolling away. Behind the trophies, a graphite sketch on a sheet of hundred-pound paper. Owen pulled it over the trophy men. This was the pride of his AP Art portfolio. It looked exactly like a polar bear. Still, Mr. Estrada had made a point of *not* telling Owen's half of the class that they had a duty to follow their passion, wherever it might lead them. Instead, he gave them all A's and said they were excellent people.

Owen packed bars of soap into the corner of his bag, housed the mason jar between black and white T-shirts, and slipped his passport into the breast pocket of his suit. Corduroy, the caned cloth, wide-wale, *durus*, but tailored because his dimensions couldn't be found on a rack. Owen wore a light blue shirt that could go well over a week without showing it. After adding a black roll-neck sweater, he still had room for books.

The holes Owen left in his father's bookshelf were more alarming than missing teeth. He excised books with a matter-of-fact cruelty. His father would instantly name the lacunae: Mayakovsky, Auden, Wordsworth, Hölderlin, Hollander, Yeats, Milton, H.D., Cavafy, and Sappho for an even ten.

Owen shouldered his sixty-pound bag and walked to the door. Poetry's density of thought made it good travel reading. These ten volumes should last him a year. But as his hair tickled the doorframe, he changed his mind. Owen took out the books he had gathered, set them on the floor, grabbed a pair of green volumes from the center of the bookshelf, and then waited—as if he had unstoppered the universe and the house itself would suck into that two-book gap.

But he heard nothing. He stood outside, his father's Loebs in hand, thinking that some Rube Goldberg had been set in motion once the two volumes of the *Odyssey* left the shelf. Perhaps the axe was swinging, he just couldn't see it. Half the world he couldn't see. *For our mind's eye sees sharply when our bodily eye withers away: Tum sane mentis oculus . . .*

The town car cut short his reverie. He directed the driver to the Amtrak station, looking all the while for his father's Volvo driving the other direction.

Dripping, steaming, hissing, the Southwest Chief waited for Owen and other passengers ringed around him to stomp up the rubber steps and begin the two-thousand-mile climb to Chicago. Right now Owen needed distance from the sinking California sun. And though the Chief's hisses and drips appeared to hold his attention, and though his gaze never wandered from the coach door where the porter leaned, pedestal in hand, and though it looked as if Owen was studying the train, in truth his attention was directed behind him. Owen sifted through each murmur of the crowd at his back: a father explaining to his son that height wasn't enough, you needed depth perception to play basketball; an old woman to his left saying, "That's a real shame"; a few approaches, but the tread was a shuffle, a stutter. Owen felt the glances, the lazy stares, but there were none of his father's steps:

no sloshing middle-aged exertion; no stumbling thunder; no father intent on stopping a son.

The porter climbed down at last and set his step stool at Owen's feet. And so Owen was the first up those rubber steps, heeling deeper all the gravel bits embedded in the furrows, until he settled in the farthest aisle in a seat that amazingly had more than enough leg room. He could even recline before his knees hit the seat in front.

With his duffel at his side, Owen sat and waited for his father to come running down the asphalt. The potpourri powder sprinkled onto carpet seats and vacuumed into the trapped air had already risen through Owen's nose and blossomed, swelling his temple until the veins were finger-wide. Dry color in the car, chalk flowers and migraine rising. Leaning his head on the cool window helped. He could use a rainstorm, but outside was bright and glareful. Other passengers slanted closer to him, but never fell in his row. Owen took a painkiller and looked through the scarred acrylic window at California slipping away.

The train skirted the Los Angeles River, glided past culverts and concrete banks, and counted Owen to sleep with a thousand rolling clacks of distance. He woke to unbalanced washing machine rumble and fell back asleep in the comfort of being inside a train whistling in the night. He woke to the *psoph* of air between car and rail. He swallowed another painkiller and passed out until they were on the other side of Victorville in the Mojave Desert.

Of course you just say I'm going to be an artist.

This forty-hour train ride from Los Angeles to Chicago was supposed to be a somber meditation on the life-altering decision before him: fly to Berlin with severely limited funds and only a vague plan to establish himself as an artist, or . . . or what? There was no Plan B, which had to be the first step in making it as an artist. The second step, if every photograph of a painter he had ever seen was accurate, was smoking. That was going to take resolution.

Rather than answer the truly difficult questions that his choice of a life in art presented, Owen chose to read Homer on Vicodin—a pretty good way to limit encounters with the waking world to five-minute intervals. He slept through the majestic countryside, thinking his pilgrimage would have been more complete had he just started walking for Chicago. He woke for five minutes every hour for the second day. Near Topeka, Kansas, he stumbled to the dining car and washed another painkiller down with a gin and tonic.

His head was draped in purple polyester curtains, mouth agape on the rubber window seal, hands still marking an early page in that little green book, when the conductor woke him at Chicago Union Station.

—Time to go, son.

Owen guided himself down the aisle from chrome rail to chrome rail until he was alone in the depot. He walked through spheres of blurred March lights until he found the escalator to the station. Inside, he wandered around to make sure there wasn't another plan. Not finding one, he boarded a train to O'Hare. At the United ticket counter, he redeemed an old $500 seat-bump voucher, charged the balance, and booked a seat on the 10:00 p.m. to Berlin. Wedged into his seat, everything stored overhead except his two remaining Vicodin and the first volume of the *Odyssey*, Owen popped the lapels of his corduroy coat and tried to fold in on himself. He'd trade anything, even the remaining Vicodin, just to disappear in that damned cardinal robe.

TWO

NO MORE LIFEGUARDS

The *Argos*, his first remote-controlled boat, buzzed into the concavity of a kickboard, bumping it through the Mission diving well, nudging it under the shadows of concrete slabs, five, seven, ten meters high, while divers waited in the bright sun, wicking their arms with aqua shammies, yoking their necks, and stretching on the platforms above until the white-haired boy piloted boat and board away.

And Owen, eyes full of chemicals, explaining on the drive home that he needed two boats to pull the kickboard through the aerated diving well, the roiling deep he and his father called Charybdis. He thought that if the boats could make it across that cauldron without sinking, they could surely cross the entire Pacific and make it to her island.

The second RC boat, the *Mentor*, had been for his first report card, not the swim meet. No. It was for the swim meet. Already bored with the six-and-under thrash across the deep end, Owen begged the coach to let him swim up an age division. He won the race, a full lap, by body lengths.

A week later Owen coupled both boats to his boogie board and steered for the white water of the diving well, water sparging to cushion thirty-foot falls, compressors birthing cloudheads that plumed from the bottom of the pool and misted into the thin blue sky.

Owen dug up an antique ring buoy from the supply closet and set it on his foam board. Then he rolled out a medicine ball that weighed about as much as he did and balanced it in the ring. By now, Owen's machinations were far more interesting than the review Burr had brought to the pool.

The divers shut off the bubbler to practice entries on smoother water. Jet spray riffled the surface, breaking the reflection so they could spot the water precisely and enter with a rip. As the divers held chrome rails and dialed in tension with their feet on large white cogs, Owen sat on the padded lip of the pool, running more engine tests and breaking the quiet rhythm of their approach. Bound—*bzzz*—rebound, then the warble and clatter of lumber tossed from the bed of a truck.

Charybdis returned. It was the women's turn to practice new dives. Early in the season, when they were still setting their programs, they kept the stakes low by bubble-wrapping their misses with the upwelling air. Owen focused on the turbulence. He sat behind a veil of thunder and burbling, like sitting in the cave behind a waterfall.

The senior in Burr's Homer seminar stopped mid-stair to talk with her coach. High-cut suit and hair glinting like a swirled gallon of gold-flecked paint. She noticed Owen's fascination with the boats, how he smoothed the cordage and pulled as tight as he could. She clapped a few times and yelled down, "Let's go, Owen!" whooping until he blushed.

Leash woven between the catamaran hulls, Owen set the board and boats in the pool. He stacked the two remotes back to back in his hands, turning the bottom joystick in the opposite direction from the top. At first, he was able to pull everything— kickboard, buoy, and medicine ball. But once the boats hit the blister's edge, the rig pitched, sputtered, and drowned.

The team groaned with Burr. But Owen was undaunted.

He spent the next hour yoking the boats like plow oxen, then linking them to the board. But it did nothing. Side by side they stalled. Burr tried to help. Owen glared.

—I'll get it, Owen snapped.

Owen, a four-foot Ajax. That was the moment Burr understood heroic stubbornness, the Sophoclean refusal to relent, as something real rather than rhetorical, something Owen had inherited from his mother's side of the family.

Still. Owen never managed to drag the medicine ball more than a few feet. He sat on a towel in the passenger seat, totally shattered that his plan had failed. Burr tried to bring him back through bribery.

—Is there anything you'd like for your birthday?

—A remote-controlled boat.

—You already have the *Argos* and the *Mentor.*

—Not a toy boat. I need a stronger one, a real one.

—You mean an RC yacht? Those don't come cheap.

—It would be a present from you *and* Mom.

Before the afternoon was up, Owen was unboxing the ship, christened *Zebulon*, and Burr was left to wonder why two pounds of molded plastic needed eight D-cell batteries in its hull.

The night of Owen's sixth birthday, they were reading a condensed edition of the *Odyssey.*

—Where exactly did Mom go? Owen asked.

The picture on his nightstand was her new-discovery smile.

—Beyond the setting sun.

The phrase was imprecise, but it sounded fatherly—a pipe-smoking answer, his best Gregory Peck.

—The sun sets in different places, though. That's why we have time zones.

—No. It's always in the west. And your mother is waiting for us beyond the west.

Burr let the words linger and hoped they'd gather weight in the silence.

They were Division III, but Mission University's diving team took their practices seriously and quickly grew tired of their un-official mascot zipping his boat over aerated water while they summoned enough confidence to turn a handstand into a back double. Owen's first boats, the smaller boats, were cute peripheral distractions that cut the tension of divers pushing the limits of their abilities. *Zebulon,* however, was louder than the bubbler and made it to the center of the plume, right under the ten-meter plat-form. After a freshman landed on Owen's kickboard and sprained her wrist, the head coach asked father and son to take their after-noons to the beach.

First Pfeiffer Beach, then Sand Dollar Beach, then the coves of Point Lobos, but there were never any other kids. The drive was the most enjoyable part of their beach trips, so they soon ventured farther afield to Zuma Beach and Point Dume. Burr only owned one pair of shorts, orange-sherbet corduroy, and wore them on their monthly outings to Zuma. Legs strong and tan, not yet var-icosed and dead-fish blue. He sat on the southern outcrop in the shadow of rock climbers, correcting papers while Owen swam past the basking crowd. He was reviewing a dissertation on Non-nos the day Owen's rude engine cut the chatters.

While Burr edited from the rocks, Owen coiled the rubber

leash around *Zebulon*'s twin hulls, coupling boogie board and battery-devouring boat with a Velcro wrist bracelet.

Owen of outlier height, six years old, white-blond hair he certainly didn't inherit from his father, behind a kickboard and toy boat, scissor-kicking his mom's old swim fins due west. Beyond where the sun sets. To Caroline.

How many minutes wasted from when Burr first looked up and thought Owen was swimming out too far until even the thought of action arose? *Yes, I should definitely do something. I should do something before things get out of hand.* How much idle contemplation as the word *riptide* became real. Finally, *Help?* Then choking out, *help!* Finding knees strong enough to stand and stumble for the water. Now yelling, *Help!*

Burr wasn't the first, not even the fifth, to respond. Those minutes of failing might still be won back. But the sting of that engine, a hornet fighting the wind that blows it out to sea, would always remain. On most days the wasping stayed in the background, but on some days the wasp dove straight for Burr's ear and he could hardly look at his son. Hard to bear, and harder to be rid of.

Wall of memory. Wave rising on the skin of the sea; misting away as it gathers and towers down; surging up-shore until it cuffs your waiting wrists with foam. Water slips through scooped fingers, no matter how tight you bowl them; first it's droplets, then it's driplets, then only whorls of brine in your fingertips and salt chains in the lines of your palm. When attention returns, saturating a memory that was finally dry and salting away, what then?

Swim for that floating remote control while your son drifts out to sea, because this gift was a quarter of your paycheck and who knows if you can replace that joystick without buying a whole new boat. Drift down the beach, showing no more concern than the rest of the Sunday crowd, biting your lip rather than answering anyone's question: *Where are the boy's parents?* If you weren't holding that neon-orange remote control, no one would be staring. Drop it. Pick it up. Yell to your bobbing son with the crowd . . . Pass the yells, the brave yells, on to others.

They have it under control.

There he is.

Then, get ready. This is the best part. Cave to the underemployed twenty-something sirs on the skiff. Wrench your hands in supplication even before they return your son to the shore. Volunteer your failings as a father, a single father. Nod and apologize to someone no older than one of your students as they hand you Caroline's old fins.

But Owen came back smiling. Boat and board in one hand, high fives for all the lifeguards. He marched through ovation, a son returned.

But not returned by you.

He didn't want to read the *Odyssey* that night. He grabbed an illustrated *Iliad* and announced that he was no longer a kid. From now on he would read by himself.

It took Burr a week to realize that reading had been the last thing they had left.

Professor Burr asked a grad student to deliver the lecture on the *katabasis* and left campus early to take Owen to the beach. Owen had been sleeping off the trauma of his final procedure with the surgeon when Burr drove off for his morning seminar. By now, he would be awake and feeling restless. Burr hoped the trip to Zuma would show him that no one wanted to keep him packed away. He could even *stop out* if he wanted. If things went well, they could hash out a plan for 2004 and have him back at Stanford next year.

Burr opened the door and called for Owen.

Silence.

Empty. A tumbleweed word, rolling, thirsty, thorned. *Empty.* And whenever *empty*, also *alone.* These words snagged Burr as he gripped the kitchen counter and read Owen's Post-it farewell. He peeled off the note and thumbed through the rest of the yellow pad in search of the real note, the reluctant good-bye from his son that must be here somewhere.

He called upstairs again. The gravity of the house had changed, as if he'd come home to find half of his possessions packed up and moved away. He scanned the living room, taking inventory of chairs and lamps as if he'd been robbed. Had to remind himself that each bare patch of wall had always been empty, never held a mirror, never held a painting. Some emptiness was always there.

Burr stumbled over a stack of books on the floor of his study. Spines bruised and hyperextended, dust covers unflapped and tore as the column crumbled and Burr took a slipping step over the rubble. With a thick thumb he undented the corners, rejacketed the hardbacks and replaced them on the shelf, leaving a two-book gap where his Loeb *Odyssey* should have been, which was fine, but he could have asked.

After surrendering to the scooped-out mitt of his leather chair, Burr toggled through a twelve-disc carousel. He gritted his teeth and pressed the small remote. Each CD sounded hollow. Bill Evans, Getz/Gilberto, Miles, Mingus, Weather Report, Brubeck. All empty.

He thumped his knee with a rolled-up magazine. Then back to the Post-it stuck to his left index finger:

DAD,

I'm going to Europe to find out which half of my life I'm about to waste. After I figure this out, we can talk about graduating.

~Owen

He peeled the note and pressed it into the molding of the doorframe, above pencil marks of Owen's height, taller than his father at eleven, six-foot-eight at age fifteen, but still standing on tiptoes, trying to get that extra quarter inch.

Raising Owen had taught Burr the beauty of being marginal. The vain side of any father wants to be Atticus Finch, but what could be worse for a boy than a father impossible to outgrow? Better to let your son know he's the center of your life and you are one of many moons. But this wasn't that. This was Owen telling him he was irrelevant. And, when he was honest with himself, it pissed him off.

The Volvo ground into gear and skidded into the street. The Burrs lived exactly halfway between the airports, but always flew from LAX. He figured today would be no different. But there was no point to any of this if he couldn't beat the pretraffic traffic and clear Ventura in the next half hour.

He rolled through a red light. In front of his neighbors and with kids walking home from school, Burr ran a red light and then another. Not orangish-red. Burr ran through lamps minutes hot. He glanced at the windshield and read his inspection sticker in reverse. It had lapsed in late '03. He almost wanted an officer to lead him away in handcuffs, just for the moment of concern when a door would be opened for him and he'd be pushed in the back with a "Watch your head."

Traffic hit long before Ventura, shattering the glassy calm of Rincon and Solimar. He was caught in a static mass and had to suffer the sight of frontage-road drivers whizzing away north and south, making him another nameless roof on Highway 101, a die-cast toy for the news helicopters to beam. He peeked over his shoulder to see if there was any way he could get right and roll down the embankment to the frontage road. A highway patrol car was parked half a mile ahead, blocking his escape.

Cars continued to rush by on the one-lane road to his left and Harbor Boulevard to his right. He was stuck. The empty space at the middle of two lines; the trapped zero in the 101.

By Ventura proper, people were thumbing silver buttons and sliding transmissions to neutral or even park. He fiddled with the gearshift and looked at the analog clock on his rubber dashboard, then at the yellow arrow of In-N-Out, pointing away from the highway to a trafficless side street where families shared French fries on concrete tables.

Traffic crumpled behind him. Burr found second gear, only to round a curve and discover thousands of red taillights. Several of his fellow motorists had given up: one leaned against the window and grinned into her cell phone; one propped a paperback on the steering wheel; one yelled at his windshield and thrust a finger at the dark-tinted windows of a pickup truck rattling license plate frames with its bass. Burr, pinned against cement sclerosis, could do nothing but redden the shadow of the overpass.

The cloverleaf, a maze of misdirection, spun traffic to all four compass points—but not the fifth, the omphalos, the only defined point of a compass, the director of direction.

He tried the radio. NPR helped. But then they started asking for money, not understanding that even though he had tenure, he had no savings account. He squirmed.

He depressed the clutch for second, then the brake lights washed back over him and he came to a full stop. A gash of metal, which he took to be a discarded fender, rocked with the wind, tickling the cement barrier and catching the setting sun. *Fire, the process we mistake for a thing. Traffic, the thing we mistake for a process.*

He lurched in his lane then aimed straight for the front tire of a bumper-hugging Infinity. The driver clucked his pointer finger. At that moment, Burr's Volvo could have been a tanker. Burr was moving right. And then right and right again, over the rumble strip, straddling highway buttons and whistling the raked asphalt.

Down the spiral ramp he drove. Thrown from the great clog and breezing past telephone poles and cypress-tree fences, green lights yellowing in his wake. Only when he was nearing Highway 1 on the two-lane road through the canyons did he realize that this was the pass for Point Dume, for Zuma.

He had stayed away for fifteen years, knowing that what he found would be bolted in tighter than the yellow bollards of the car park. Now he parked, fender inches from the trailhead.

He unlaced his boots, kicked off his socks, and walked tenderly over loose gravel to the sand below. His feet were pale, frozen, senseless things that molded to the rock bits. The beach was deserted except for a lineup of surfers.

The ocean breathed up and sneezed down on the shore. Windswept sand soon anchored the cuffs of his trousers. He looked at the sky, a washed peach smear where the sun snuffed into the thick. A steady salt-wind carried him back to the safety of his car.

He sat on the hood of the Volvo, tired arches of his pale feet on the hard plastic bumper. A young woman knocking water from her ear recognized him from campus and nodded. She had one of the few spaces. She asked him how he'd ended up at a trailhead two and a half hours from Mission.

—Bested by traffic, I'm afraid. I was headed to LAX. If there's any way I could borrow your phone, I might be able to justify this excursus as a shortcut.

She coiled the leash around the tail fins of her surfboard and handed Burr a phone.

He called LAX Terminal Services and pawed through an automated directory while she folded her wetsuit, snapped it into a Rubbermaid bin, and poured a plastic jug of water over her head.

Burr repeatedly apologized for eating up her minutes. An agent finally told him that without a court order, there was no way to access the manifests of every flight out of LAX with connections to Europe.

Thanks for that, Owen. No flight number. No airline. Not even the qualifier *mainland*. Just *Europe*.

Burr thanked the student profusely and gave her twenty dollars for the minutes, striving to make the gesture appear breezy and avuncular rather than—what's the term—sketchy.

—Wait. Here. I want you to have this.

That doesn't sound any better.

Burr opened his trunk and grabbed a book from the two dozen in a cardboard box. She held it with the hem of her beach towel, looked at her friends lashing the boards on the roof rack, and thanked him with a squint that asked if this was going to be on the final.

As they drove away, Burr watched planes rattle the skies westward, then loop around and trace the shore. He wondered if he was supposed to infer some hidden meaning in "Europe." When Owen was eight, Burr had sent him a postcard from Stonehenge reading "The World's Meeting Spot"—but the chances of Owen recalling that were slim.

Before sunset, Burr wound back to Mission along Highway 1. The narrow meander to Big Sur took lives every year, so he never chanced it after dark. The mountains were just as deadly as the cliffs. Two copies of his book slid across the backseat. On sharp turns he heard the box shift in the trunk.

Three years ago Burr had finished his grand dictionary of *hapax legomena*, words occurring only once in the written record of an ancient language. The professor assured his university press that the standard library-bound hardcover run of a thousand copies would be woefully insufficient. They bought his pitch and doubled the run to two thousand, assuring him the book would be everywhere. And everywhere it was.

The first sign should have been when they failed to get a blurb from any scholar of note or so much as a response from the generalists. Burr averted his eyes when he passed a copse of trees, seeing the forests that died for a book that would most likely be pulped. He deluded himself that a future archaeologist would confuse *Hapax* for a holy relic: so sacred was the Book of Burr that all discovered copies were untouched, immaculate. The epitaph would read, "*Hapax*: Everywhere, and Everywhere Pristine." Copies of the yellow book lined two rows of his office bookshelves, giving a false impression that he was up on modern design. These weren't the free author's copies; these were personal online purchases he'd hoped would generate some momentum. A grad student, candid from boilermakers, described how a hundred copies of *Hapax* were bricked together in the bowels of the university bookstore to form the Igloo of Burr. Here the employees got high and invented stories of narwhals and sled dogs. When he heard this, Burr laughed until he cried; thus far, this was the only application of his *summa philologica*.

Burr's hands were loose on the wheel as he wound through the Central Coast on Highway 1. To his right, purple floating in the air like a dandelion's parachute seeds. To his left, white foam underlit with the pink and green of the flame in a votive candle. Almost warm against the black slabs. Twilight, urchin purple, gloaming life to his nail beds and making his hands a moment young.

Burr's first work, his thesis work, was long on conjecture and short on scholarship. At twenty-four he found something wondrous in analyzing the cult of Hekate and the stelae of Hermes. They were slippery twilight gods, Hermes and Hekate. Bringing their lens to the modern world cast warped, original aberrations. The work began with his translation of Hesiod. Several insights came to him during his reading: phenomena are more often than not both true and false; twilight, "two lights," needs both sunlight and moonlight to exist—it is precisely the time when there is both day and night. In this twilit space, paradoxes present no problems. An adjunct in the Germanic Languages Department learned of Burr's newfound mysticism and pointed him to the Old Norse rune Dagaz,

Once he had a symbol to write in his margins, Burr began seeing these liminal spaces everywhere: a cave both inside and outside; the shore both land and sea; the present a twilight of past and future; love, like any transitive verb, an intermingling of two things formerly alone; life, a blur of birth and death—birth and death being the only two moments of life in which we don't exist.

Caroline Dennison had been looking up from her reading every few minutes to watch him scribble and sweep back his hair. Burr trying to get down on a legal pad the flood of insights, thinking himself a little dangerous, even though he was translating Greek. He upset his coffee as he turned the yellow page, and she stifled a laugh at the clatter. He put down his pen and stood.

Caroline blew on her tea and pretended to be flattered when he called her *kallisphuros*, she of the lovely ankles. The line worked well enough to earn him a seat at her table. She looked down before meeting his eyes, like a diver taking a deep breath.

The world stabilized on their parallel that afternoon. While everything else drifted into blur, the clarity between their eyes remained perfect. At some point she must have stood and left, because at some point she wasn't there. There was neither betwixt nor between with Caroline. She was there. She was not. And because his mind refused to process anything purely binary, he looked like a lost boy to the café staff who told him they were closed and it was time to go. He tried to remember her gait, but could only imagine her gliding. He tried to remember how she left. But when exactly does day leave us in night?

The next morning, Burr was at the café thirty minutes before they opened. After a bagel and three coffees, he decided that he would not be leading a study section and kept his table free all afternoon. By three, she returned. They talked about the courage of the ancients to trust that the sun would continue to rise. He said he was not a man of faith and would need her phone number.

When the summer sun brought an archipelago of freckles to her nose and cheek, he named them the Caroline Islands and committed each one to memory: Ulithi, Tonoas, Oroluk, Pohnpei . . .

He thought he could make her fit into his view of the world. But within a week of living together she had become the map, rather than something mappable. He dotted every coordinate into the aqua field of Caroline. They folded up together, perfectly aligned and protected, burying their world from the light of others. And just as an open map's twenty-four folds can seem impossible to unpuzzle and neatly pack away, their convergences were inscrutable, leaving others to trust blindly that the relationship worked.

They blazed through the reception halls of deans and department heads. Young and old faculty alike buzzed around them wherever they mingled—not because she was the only Oxbridge grad in the room, not because this young couple radiated love, not because her father was the university president, but because wherever they went they carried with them a world.

For two years they ate little more than canapés. Most of the reception room guests began conversations with, "I have something to confess," which was never an indication of being in that person's confidence, but did make them feel like junior clergy. The phrase became a punchline between Burr and Caroline. By the next spring, the sum of all these confidences made Burr's academic advancement inevitable—she would have been climbing the rungs ahead of him, but had put continental philosophy on hold to learn how to paint.

His work was inspired, but the search for relevant texts was proving to be fruitless. In all of recorded history, only two partial inscriptions supported his reading of Heraclitus and the Eleatics.

Rather than switch to anthropology or wait on the archaeologists to dig up something to analyze, he grew increasingly creative with his source material until his work hit almost New Age levels of *mysto*. Fellow department members, nonplussed at the camaraderie between Burr and Mission University's elect, thought he was on drugs—and probably supplying them to senior faculty.

A new continent began to emerge in 1982. It was unexpected but welcome, like a new Hawaiian island. As this landmass burped from the deep, they traded booze and fritters for macrobiotic staples. They danced through their junior apartment as her belly grew. He sang the only song about Odysseus he knew, "Beyond the Sea," with a real longing for her, even though she was still there. She wove through the second verse like Penelope, thinking of the globe-trotting that would accompany his unfinished, but surely forthcoming, book *Liminality*. Whenever he translated the song into Greek— πέρην ἁλὸς ἀτρυγέτοιο . . . —which repeatedly failed to impress her, she countered with Charles Trenet's original, "La Mer." Violins and harps and floating, until the instruments fell.

The map hissed orange and began to singe. It was easy for Burr to dismiss the dark edges as something fundamentally unrelated

43

to a fire, something reversible that he could fan away, clap out, or smother, something they could fix together, until the edges crackled in flame.

On August 21, 1982, their map was lost in fire.

And there's not much to say about what happened next.

Islands became ashes.

Owen took a life before he took a breath.

He very nearly took two lives. His father bobbed between drowning and drowned. Their map was the Logos that held his world from flying apart. When it burned, every thought broke to atoms and jittered into the sky.

What was left of Burr was driftwood, silvered still, empty. Each morning saw a lifeless husk wash up on the floor near his bed. He rolled against the jagged bed frame, rolled back until his head wedged against the nightstand and his body curled up fetal. Lifted up, dashed down, bobbing and unable to decide if it was yet time to sink. There is nothing more heroic than the glowing eyes of a vibrant soul inside a body that has given up, the marathon runner who crawls the final mile. Burr was the opposite: dead eyes in a capable body, or a body formerly capable and rapidly depleting. Water was too sweet to drink; lips to throat to lungs parched and cracked. Even when inhaling, his chest seemed to cave in. When he tasted anything, it was ash.

He surfaced briefly to change a diaper, warm a bottle, drink a bottle. He hung a mobile over Owen's crib. He called it a marionette, but it was really a Christmas ornament on a string. Burr duct-taped it to the ceiling, but every week it fell, strings dropped and tangled in the bends of the marionette's knees. In dreams, Burr looked around and found knots and snags in his own joints, tripping up each step, each step a taut and tangled fall. Waking, he couldn't even look his newborn son in the eyes for fear of being pulled out of his loss. Her loss.

He initially refused help. Threw both telephones in wicker wastebaskets because recounting what had happened once, just once, shattered a day, and there were at least fifty people who needed to be kept in the loop. An elderly neighbor, widow of a cosmologist, came through the garage door and announced that she was taking over. Owen's eyes widened when he saw her, and his screaming stopped.

By the time Burr returned to work, the academic articles written the prior year were just hitting the press. He was taken to task in journals for his prior gambols and given a wide berth in a basement office where he could read the scorching reviews of "Classical Liminality," the paper he had naively supposed would be the first chapter of his groundbreaking book, with amusement and whisky. He marveled at how far over his head the critics were aiming. He was sprawled on the floor while scholars shot at ten-foot phantoms. Had the mandarins only known how much pride they gave him by caring, something he had long since stopped doing, they might have dismissed him in a word.

Years passed with fewer and fewer offers to go out for a drink. And then strong encouragement from his mentors to do anything other than drink. His last remaining drinking companion was Bill Dennison, Caroline's father, who was in the process of being managed out of his role as president by the trustees.

In her life, Bill had been bronze and absent. With Caroline's death, Bill's gaze dropped a few degrees every day. During their bourbon-soaked afternoons, he kept his chin to his chest as if he were trying to prevent someone from choking him. When Burr looked closely, he could see a fist knuckling at the man's wattles, a phantom hand prying up that once-proud chin.

President Bill Dennison quickly grew old, pale, and clatty. He said his office was the only place he still felt free because it was a place he *knew* was about to be taken away. His hands, always curled in near fists, shook with fear and with pride, like a child holding a cicada. He looked Burr squarely in the eye for the first time in their relationship. And when he did, Bill found a man on his level.

Owen eventually did take two lives: his mother's and his only surviving grandparent's. In hindsight, Bill had given a few months' notice, but he never said anything specifically about his plan.

Mountains take. Cliffs take. Dennison's car was found off Highway 1 by a team of rescue divers a month to the day after his last drink with Burr. He left behind a letter on his desk stressing to the trustees that Burr, nepotism aside, was his natural successor.

Once Burr caught wind of his father-in-law's last request, he asked to be removed from consideration. Burr suggested his best friend and fellow young luminary Gerard Gaskin for the post. The board, who'd had Gaskin, MBA holder and faculty senator, in mind all along, congratulated themselves on an amicable transference of power. The trustees extended a ninety-nine-year lease to Burr on his father-in-law's residence, thinking that it would be fitting that Owen grow up in the home his grandfather had a hand in constructing.

With Bill's death came the realization that Owen would have no one else's account of Caroline. The portrait that would hang in Owen's mind would have to be painted by Burr's shaking, foolish hand. He would have to sing the lullabies, her songs, even though he couldn't force out a note.

Burr spent his first month in their new house scavenging for photos, dangling Bill's books by the spine in case a portrait of Caroline was marking a page, then dropping them to the floor. Caroline was only smiling in two pictures—crushing, because she had dozens of smiles that would now fade and disappear, impossible for him to recover and for his son to learn.

Burr's academic career had run aground. He was called before a committee tasked with managing the transition of administrations, certain he would be negotiating severance and extended benefits for Owen.

Rather than talk about his drinking or read disgruntled letters from his seminar students, they framed the meeting as early tenure review. Later he would realize that no one had any intention of promoting him to associate; tenure review was merely a polite pretext for them to illustrate his downfall. In the words of the provost, "Institutions cannot invest in speculation." They said his thinking was undisciplined, code for not publishing in peer-reviewed journals. They said the liminality work lacked focus. He blurted out, "That's the point!" Which was when they suggested he stop drinking with the adjuncts in the Poetry Department.

He was given three years to shape up. Burr surprised himself at how industrious he became following their censure. During his three-year probation he trotted out significant textual analysis in the biggest journals—the *Journal of Hellenic Studies*, *Classical Quarterly*, *Hermes*, *Classical Philology*, and the *American Journal of Philology*—thereby moving from the fringes of classics to the center. Joseph Burr was now the authority on Homer's use of the aorist middle, which is to say, as mainstream as classics professors come.

The black carry-on he wheeled into his next committee hearing buckled under the weight of peer-review journals. He stacked them high in three ecru columns and then sat with his hands folded before him, conscious of looking a bit too much like the chip leader in a poker game. The university didn't mind the swagger; it was publish or perish, and he had published. On the day he was promoted to associate professor, he had a following of eager grad students compiling several words per day for the ill-fated *Hapax*. Gone were the days of even the slightest excursus. He was scrubbed of liminality and academically sober.

But the drinking still came in waves. Burr waited at a neighborhood stoplight, looking at the passenger seat, tracked back to fit Owen's knees and reclined to make room for his head. He wondered how many months would pass until someone else would adjust it back. After today, no one could blame him for needing a drink. Once the Volvo was docked in his garage, dripping oil on the concrete slab and panting, Burr shuffled to his local.

He wrote on napkins while boisterous kissers and fancy handshakers bubbled around and jostled his bent elbow:

> Our ground is birth. Our death is sea. Two things our mind will never know, birth and death, things that are uniquely ours yet things we never have, things we are not there to inhabit, define the mind before we are given the chance. This curling throw, ripped back at once. We are the liminal. We are the wash. But he. His birth set stakes, two stakes, birth and different death implied. Always tightroping those two spikes in the ground. He jumped. And when he landed, it's no wonder he ran.

THREE

IT'S BERLIN, WE'RE ALL MONSTERS HERE

Through a wet March, Owen breezed across Berlin on his hostel's beach cruiser, pedaling the one-speed bike with firm unhurried strokes, leaning into turns and sidewinding from Ostkreuz to Charlottenburg. Over the rain-slicked roads of the Tiergarten park, asphalt dolphin-smooth, he skimmed quarter miles of cosines with broad sweeps from curb to curb.

Each morning at the Tiergarten he joined images, paired words, and left with something glazed and sharp, more pottery shard than poem. With a handful of shards he pieced a bright mosaic of memories against the grey Berlin sky: lurid storefronts splashed with ancient yellow; Helvetica shouts in stoplight red; stockinged women stenciled to walls in dripping royal blue; canary-yellow bugle calls of the Postbank; kiosk green and construction orange on every corner; a full spectrum of brick from red to brown; Army-Navy stores spilling seaweed wares to the curb; consignment shop employees with purple-red bob cuts sitting on molded plastic chairs; the plumes of squinting smokers; the expired green of shutters climbing to roofs and tiling the sky.

He was the metal comb, and Berlin was the music box—his fingers extended to plink each note of color and spin the day's melody. Everything was becoming clear except his vision of himself as an artist. He wanted to play with memory and maps, but had no specific plan about integrating them into an artwork. In art libraries and bookstores he studied Richard Long and Hamish Fulton. He fasted for a week to afford a student membership at the Hamburger Bahnhof museum and spent entire afternoons in front of the Anselm Kiefers.

One March day, in front of Kiefer's enormous lead airplane *The Angel of History (Poppy and Memory)*, a man with shoulder-length hair and a scholarly bent caught him jotting down an observation on Mnemosyne, goddess of memory, underneath a rough pencil sketch. Shy, suspicious, Owen folded from attention. But the man persisted.

—People get too hung up on Kiefer's scale and miss the mud, the materiality, the lead to silver to gold.

—The thin blue of the lead and ash under these skylights, the filter is . . . familiar.

—Are you a student or an artist?

—I'm an artist.

This was the first time Owen had declared it publicly. The real artists he knew in high school never felt the need to declare anything, they just acknowledged they were artists—the way someone else might say, "I'm adopted." Embarrassed blood pooled up.

—Are you with a gallery in Berlin?

The blush ran across his cheek, almost to his nose, and his ears turned red.

—You're too young to be making work anyway. Once you put something into the world, you can never take it back. You'd have a hard time finding an artist who doesn't want a pass on the first five years of his career.

The slight tremble in the man's paternalism made Owen suppose he was talking with a professor. This was the tone Owen usually tuned out. But what he was about to hear, in front of a creased felt blanket, beside a chair made of fat, was real, not academic, and struck him dumb.

—This artist, Joseph Beuys, was in the Luftwaffe, you know. His plane was shot down over the Crimea in the thick of winter. He would have frozen to death had a group of Tartars not greased him up with lard and wrapped him in felt blankets. So it's not as random as it might first appear that he makes a chair of fat or protects himself from a coyote, a totem of raw nature, with a felt blanket.

—Protecting yourself from a coyote is art?

—It is when you do it like a shaman. Beuys flew into New York in May of 1974. An ambulance met him at the airport and transported him directly to the René Block Gallery where he attempted to lift collective trauma by locking himself up with a wild coyote.

—What was it called?

—*I Like America and America Likes Me.*

—Good title.

—The materials are what you should be focusing on: felt blanket, shepherd's staff, coyote, the *Wall Street Journal* spread out on the floor for it to piss on. There are only two questions for an artist: first, What do I exclude? A king is he who determines the state of exception. And every artist must be a king. The second question—How do I import the most meaning to what I include?—however, is why artists outlive kings. I wish contemporary artists focused more on achieving a sense of inevitability in their work, an elegance that borders on the mathematical.

Blanket, staff, coyote. Beuys is Pythagoras, and everyone else is scribbling in sand.

After his discussion with this professor had percolated for a night, Owen saw the possibility of combining the two genres he was most interested in, Land Art and minimalism, into something he would call Laminalism. Thus far, Owen imagined his art pieces, laminates, would be an overlay of memories and moods onto landscape; he would light the world with the colors of the Gods and pin down his memories with minimalist shapes like rock cairns and runic tangles of twigs. He had a name for the work, but his new blend of art was still too inchoate and immaterial to justify fasting for studio space.

Still. In the distance he could see himself as a successful artist, selling Berlin to a young American romantic: "Here an artist can afford studio space and make a name for himself before he turns thirty."

In the past two months he had overheard the same conversation dozens of times, in English, German, French, Danish, and Italian. People told him he was in the right place. Everyone here was jostling for a name. In that respect, Owen was common. He looked around at the turbid layer of young creatives floating above him. None of them had lost a name, which separated Owen, like sediment dropped out of suspension.

The Winerei, a wine bar near his hostel, served as library, living room, salon. Idiosyncrasy defined the bar in a way that reminded Owen of his childhood in a cave. Patrons borrowed glasses at the Winerei—technically nothing was bought or sold there, all payment was voluntary. For one euro, Owen was handed a glass and invited to fill it with any of the half dozen wines they chose to uncork that night. Before shambling off to his hostel, he dropped money, on his honor, into a glass jar. Owen, now broke, paid a rounded-down wholesale April estimate of his drinking, rather than the magnanimous estimates of March, and washed glasses when it got busy.

After a few drinks, the Winerei glowed cloudy pastis green and Owen became ensnared in the nets of candlelight bouncing off mantel mirrors and dispersing through the stems of all the playful glasses. Because the wine was free, glasses were handled with a light touch and gestures were wedding-reception wild, meaning there was always someone rubbing a paste of club soda and rock salt into the hem of her blouse. He had learned to wear a black shirt if he was going to stay past sundown.

Locals had their own spots. His was a salmon-colored armchair with a great wound sliced through the seat, spilling dried yellow foam that broke off like lemon cake and clogged the wells of his corduroy pants. He sat in the disintegrating chair and read Homer, glancing up several times a page to watch passersby walk vintage bikes with a slow spoke rhythm through the first sun of spring or strut by with purposeful hips that made him blink hard and consider the possibility of discos.

Early April, Owen was sitting in his crumbling chair, looking out the window of the Winerei with this very thought. He felt someone to his left, hovering at his blind side and eager to interrupt his reading. A stream of smoke fogged between his face and his book. He kept reading, but then a voice interrupted:

—That's not gonna work here.

Owen raised an eyebrow, turned, and found legs braced in the chrome of a wheelchair, a wine bottle wedged in a crotch, and a bright blue flannel shirt unbuttoned aggressively. Beside the wheelchair, another young man swirled a glass and swept back the itch of hair at his forehead. Owen set his book on the table. Now the standing one spoke.

—Between the two of us, we've tried just about every conceivable way of picking up girls in a bar. But sitting alone and pretending to read in what, Greek? That's new.

—Or *really* old.

—Let's get real. They have the *Sports Illustrated* swimsuit issue here somewhere. I bet we can find it if we look.

—My dad's a professor, Owen responded. I grew up reading this kind of stuff.

—Does it work?

—Does what work?

The young man in the wheelchair put a hand in front of his friend's chest.

—Hey. In all seriousness, tell me something.

—What?

—Where's your parrot?

The two young men laughed. Both leaned in too close. The standing one sloshed his glass with a toasting *Arrr!* The one in the wheelchair put his hand on Owen's leg. Owen suspected they were high.

Owen exhaled slowly and loudly.

—Why does everyone go for the pirate joke? Hannibal the Great had an eye patch. Why not "Where's your elephant?" I hear a bad pirate joke every day. You guys are better than that. Assholes.

The guy in the wheelchair snapped back his hand.

—Testy!

They left Owen to scan his text and rub his temples. Over the course of the next week, they reappeared to deliver one-liners that made Owen think that his universe was both small and contracting.

Two weeks to the day after he called a disabled person an asshole, Owen saw the man's picture on the cover of *Die Welt*. He learned that he had been mocked by Kurt Wagener, a twenty-seven-year-old artist with work in the Pompidou and a forthcoming exhibition at the Guggenheim Bilbao.

April 29, 2004. The Italian managing the hostel recognized Owen's patter down the stairs and slid his computer monitor to the far end of the desk to confront Owen with the shocking image popping up all over the Internet.

Owen caught sight of something gruesome and possibly pornographic in his periphery. He decided to walk past the clerk and not mention it.

—Hey! No no no. Take a good look at the screen.

A man in a hood balanced on a cardboard box. Rigid woven plastic rose to a sharp fin. A snarl of exposed wires ran from the ceiling to the fingers of his outstretched arms. A tasseled blanket around his shoulders looked like a cut-up prayer shawl. The scene was violently overstaged, offered up to the world with the admission *Hey, you're all behind the hood.* Owen chewed his cheek.

—Where is this from?

—Your prison. In Iraq.

—I'm Canadian.

—Don't lie to my face, man. I saw your passport.

—That's . . . that's just plain fucking crazy. I'm sorry. But you think I voted for these guys? You think anybody you'll ever see at a hostel in Berlin voted for these guys?

Owen walked away, positive that the man behind the desk was gesturing for him to fuck off.

—Do you want me to leave this door open?

—I want you to leave, but it's not my hostel.

Owen passed four newsstands on his way to the Winerei. It's a raw morning when the all-caps headline of every paper reads the same thing: *FOLTER!* He didn't need to know what the word meant because from here on out, the word meant *that.*

A handful of morning coffee regulars at the Winerei would confront him, since they had already asked him to defend familiar evils like the dropping of bombs. By eleven, the two knitters and the flirtatious Brit who always sat at the round table with the Tiffany lamp had accused Owen of perpetuating the fraternal mentality that would allow these events to transpire. At five, the co-owner unwound his conspiracy theory of horrors: What must the CIA be hiding if they allowed this picture to leak?

That left pinball with Kurt Wagener and his sidekick, the two flippers who would bat Owen into the light show and then watch him roll into the drain. They would wait for the evening crush to gather before pulling the plunger.

Sure enough, the artist and his friend showed at nine. Owen had been apologizing all day. He fretted the cover of his passport until the gold-foil letters disappeared into the navy field. Apologies only. He was ready for Kurt. The artist rolled for Owen's chair with two firm strokes of the push ring. He unstoppered a bottle of red with his teeth and filled Owen's glass before taking a swig.

—Today couldn't have been an easy day to be American. You're fine?

—I'm not the one being tortured.

—Look, I understand what it means to suddenly lose degrees of freedom you previously took for granted. I understand what it means to be attacked. Unfortunately, in my case, it was a literal attack that put me in this chair.

Kurt and companion waited for Owen to respond. Kurt put the bottle back between his legs, locked the brakes, and shook Owen's hand with his cut-fingered gloves.

—Kurt Wagener. This is Hal. And tonight we've got reason to celebrate.

Owen looked at the wine as if it might be drugged.

—What're we drinking to?

Kurt raised the bottle and toasted loud:

—To another dashing American. Now the neighborhood has someone else to vilify.

—I assumed you guys were German.

—I'm Swiss, but I grew up in Greenwich, Connecticut. Hal's Swedish.

—With a student visa that expired four years ago, but don't tell anybody.

At arm's length, Kurt poured the last drops of the bottle into his mouth. He looked around as if he might throw it, but settled with holding it aloft. After a minute, Hal replaced the bottle and then helped himself to a seat at Owen's side. Owen glanced at the blue-green scribbles on Hal's arms and the one professional tattoo of a tarot card: THE TOWER. A yellow lightning bolt struck the top of the inked-in tower, setting it ablaze and throwing two figures forward toward the ground.

—We saw you in the park yesterday.

—I go there in the mornings to write.

—You attract attention. Have you ever acted?

Owen studied the speaker. Eyes like faded denim, uneven and almost yellow in places. When Owen looked closer, he saw an erosion in Kurt's eyes that suggested he had witnessed some horrible things and caused a few more. He wore his hair shaved at the sides and long on top, as did Hal. Hal looked up from the cigarette he was rolling on Owen's father's Loeb edition *Odyssey*, vol. I.

—Still reading that? You'd probably get more girls if it was in German.

—I read the verso. The Greek.

—What?

Kurt answered for Owen:

—He means he doesn't borrow his opinions.

—My father's sort of Greek.

—Americans are all "sort of" something, Hal muttered.

Owen thought of explaining that were it not for his mother's intervention, he would have been named for a dictionary: Liddell Scott Burr. A moment's hesitation, and Hal was up trailing a girl out the front door. Kurt rolled closer, until his face was inches from Owen's.

—Hal pretends he's an asshole sometimes.

Owen remembered their first encounter. The word stung.

—What else does he do?

Kurt pinched his nose a few times, sniffed.

—What does he do? Why divide who you are from what you do? That's an American schizophrenia that'll go away if you live in Berlin long enough. Berliners define themselves with verbs, not nouns. Hal plays music, but he's not a musician. He throws parties, but he's not a promoter. He takes pictures, but he's not a photographer. Well, he would say he's a photographer, but his real contribution is his presence, you know.

—He acts, Owen said.

—That's closer to the truth. So who are you, Owen? Why are you in Berlin? What do you want to accomplish?

Owen finished his glass of wine, giving Kurt time to ask another question.

—Are you an artist?

—Yes. Well, I'm trying to be.

—Perfect. I'm looking for an outsider artist to collaborate with.

—What's an outsider artist?

—In Berlin, anyone who asks that question!

Kurt laughed hard at his own joke and looked around for someone who might have heard it. Not finding anyone to connect with, he continued,

—A young outsider artist is someone who doesn't have connections. If we're talking about someone over forty, "outsider art-ist" is just a euphemism for "crazy person." And you can't really collaborate with those guys. They'll bite your hand, literally, and sue for all sorts of made-up shit. But someone like you, if you're any good, brings something new and vital to a project.

Owen squinted.

—Look, you can be another one of these mopey guys who has a "show" in a coffee shop, or you can get serious. Collaboration is the best way to make connections. It's kind of the only way. No curator is going to include you in a group show until you have a platform. Unless wrinkled balls are your thing. In which case, I see the birth of a bright star.

Kurt smiled and hit Owen's leg.

—So let's talk alternatives. I've got a booth to myself at Art Basel.

Kurt saw that the name didn't register.

—It's like the Super Bowl. And I've got seats in the owner's box. So. Are you in?

—I don't have any real works yet, just some ideas.

—Let me explain. This is all brand-new work, not a bunch of shit that's been touring London, New York, and Shanghai. I only do new. Anything that doesn't sell at an opening gets destroyed. What I'm looking for is a collaborator who can make choices. There are going to be some difficult decisions, and I'll need you to make those decisions. To a large extent, I want to be absent from the composition, or if not absent, only there in a reduced capacity—like an invisible hand.

—Yeah, but specifically . . .

—*Specifically* needs to wait until we've signed the contracts. So what do you say?

Owen raised a glass as a why-not. Kurt clanked it as a hand-shake. Hal returned just in time to offer a toast:

—To the Cripple and the Cyclops—at least you'll get their attention.

They drank. Kurt spoke sotto voce so his words would be noticed by a nearby table of girls.

—Don't underestimate being noticed. A little bit of pressure and the sense of an audience are essential to molding an artist. You know, if a few museums in London, or New York, or whatever, exhibit your work.

Kurt lit a cigarette, continued.

—Or if you're collected by some really big names. I know right now you just want to sell work, sell something to anyone, but you're better off starving. It's not how much you sell, it's who you sell to. Guard your work. Set the prices high, then prove them. The goal is to get to a point where you can't make enough work to keep the most serious collectors in the world happy. Whatever. I mean. The only thing that matters is that your friends are taken care of. You know, people come in to see my art or whatever and then maybe see a picture of Hal's and think, "Shit, if Kurt thinks he's good, I should buy this guy while he's cheap." When you're around successful people you get noticed, and maybe you pick up some of the habits that made them successful in the first place. Whatever it is you're trying to do in Berlin, I can guarantee that from my platform more people will hear the message.

Owen, young and allergic to any sales pitch, answered:

—I'm more concerned with the quality of the message than the volume.

—You don't need to pretend to be noble. This is Berlin. We're all monsters here.

Kurt now got Hal's attention and pantomimed lighting a pipe. They stopped at the table of girls. Kurt said something that made the prettiest one blush.

Owen returned to his book. Previous Kurt sightings had done

much in the past month to undercut his romantic notions of being an artist, but he also wasn't prepared to back out—if for no other reason than to figure out if art was the wasted half or his real reason for staying above the ground.

Kurt and Hal came back with red eyes, surrounded by a cloak of tobacco. Kurt locked his wheels. Hal stooped over the table and began sketching a map of Prenzlauer Berg and Friedrichshain on a napkin with his felt-tipped pen.

—If you follow Saarbrücker Straße, Kurt said, through Prenz'l Allee, it will change names, but stay on the road. Eventually it hits our park.

Kurt took the napkin and added several trees, a triangle, and a cylinder. He squinted, pinched his cigarette, and admired his work.

—This is the *Wasserturm*, he said, adding a star to the top of the cylinder. Do you know that word? It means "water tower." You'll see it when you get in the park. It's on the top of a hill. You can stay with us as long as you like—a month at least.

—I can't really pay you anything.

Kurt cocked an eyebrow.

—I'd never expect you could.

Hal tried to find an earnest expression:

—You're lucky you came here tonight.

—You live in a water tower?

—The big *Wasserturm* is in Kollwitzplatz. Our *Wasserturm* was built for a brewery.

Kurt explained:

—These kinds of things would never be possible now, even with colossal sums of money. Hal and I were in East Berlin at the beginning, and now we have my gallery to take care of all the paperwork—because of the wheelchair or whatever. We've been living in the water tower since the mid-nineties. When this shit happened, we converted the stairs to a big ramp, like the Guggenheim.

Hal finished his wine then clapped Owen on the shoulder.

—You'll see for yourself. Go check out from your hostel or whatever and meet us at the tower tonight. The door will be open. First floor's yours.

Kurt stabbed out his cigarette.

—European first floor. American second floor. You'll see.

Kurt shook Owen's hand and turned away when the young woman he had been performing for walked over. Owen bussed wineglasses. Hal followed him to the sink.

—Come tonight. It will seem too awkward tomorrow. But trust me, this is a good idea. I know better than anyone that Kurt can be . . . abrasive. But if there's one person in Berlin who can make your career, it's Kurt. You'll be famous by Christmas. You won't even need to try. Your only question should be: Do I want to do anything with my life while I'm still young enough to have a good time doing it, or do I want to read Greek in a wine bar?

When he'd finished drying the last glass, Owen shook his head and snorted.

—All right, let's have some fun.

Hal returned to Kurt and the young woman already seated in Kurt's lap. Kurt yelled over the music:

—You may not see us tonight. We won't be back early. But make yourself at home. You're a monster now.

Unaccustomed to the silence of the gods, Owen was left to follow whatever he had. In this case, a crudely drawn map. A day's drizzle gathered to a drop and fell from the awning onto the napkin in Owen's hand. Blue lanes drawn in felt pen began to swell and bleed into one another. Tethered clouds, which Kurt had drawn to indicate a forest, lay just ahead to the north. And beyond, in a park past the cross-field cemetery, was the cylinder with a star on top, the *Wasserturm*.

Owen folded the napkin-map along its frilled edges and placed it in his coat as a pocket square. As he checked out of the hostel, he asked if he could continue to use the beach cruiser, since it was the only bike big enough for his knees. That got a laugh from the manager.

And fair enough. It was better that he was walking into this new world, their world. He thought of Brancusi—or was it a character in Balzac?—walking hundreds of miles to Paris to begin his new life. Owen kicked past the gated cemetery and saw the entrance to the park.

The Volkspark Friedrichschain peeled around him. Maple and oak carpeted the empty winter fountain with layers of leaves in the lamplight, all waiting patiently for a *psoph* to flip them over and dry their undersides, a keel like Owen's that would wake the twigs and tangles. Fallen limbs. Thick mist swelling above the plaster fauns and fairy forms. Vapors condensing on goat-riding cherubim. A peeling park waiting for this night. And past the colonnade, past the keystone arches and knobby balustrade, the trees framed a vanishing point of the *Wasserturm*.

Now Hal's magnanimity made sense. How could anyone draw a map for a stranger to a monolith in the middle of a deserted, wild park without at least a chuckle? Owen circled the sandstone tower until he found the door.

Heavy enamel layers told the story of a war against graffiti. A deep red shellac was now overrun with silver Krylon and names like SKELO and ÜTER and TRAK written in white paint pen. The double-door junction was covered in what appeared to be the dried spittle of a fire extinguisher, but proved to be more paint. Several band stickers had been slapped on the flat panels of the door. Next to the doorknob, a stencil of Dr. Strangelove.

Hal and Kurt had both promised the door would be unlocked. It wasn't. Owen knew this was some elaborate prank and looked for a cameraman crouching in the bushes, waiting to spring out and yell "Gotcha." He listened, but heard nothing. He looked up each of the trees equally spaced around the tower, giving the impression that the tower had been planted at the center of everything.

He turned the knob counterclockwise with more conviction. It clicked, but wouldn't open. The wood had swollen into the frame. He slammed his shoulder into the weathered door.

A splinter flew from the doorframe into a puddle on the cement floor. Owen looked up: a continuous spiral ramp ran to the top floor, over forty feet above. He recognized skateboard scars on the metal rails and wheel marks on the white walls, several sandpaper decks glittering in the dark. The walls appeared to expand and contract with a labored breathing sound. Before, this type of warbling had arrived with peridot, crisp and expansive. But this expansion was muggy brown, damp. Where exposed, the tower walls whorled with the sepia and char of scalded butter in a pan. The air was thick and matted, like hair dipped in a bucket.

He called for Kurt. He called for Hal. And when his voice echoed back, he carried his bag up the spiral to his floor. Here the breathing was louder. A cantilevered yellow lamp sat on the cigarette-carpeted floor. Owen fumbled around the light's cage for a toggle. He jiggled the industrial plug into the wall, and the light grew hot. Overbright heat wheeled him around to find the source of the broken breathing: blue polyethylene tarp, duct-taped to the window frame, inflated into the room like a whale's lung and then exhaled back into the night.

Poplar planks balanced on blue sawhorses. He repositioned the light and read the writing on one of the sawhorses' two long beams: POLICE LINE — DO NOT CROSS. An NYPD sticker on the cross brace. He wondered how many hundred dollars Kurt had spent importing these from New York. Rolls of black iron plumbing pipe of varying diameter and mating flanges of all shapes and sizes rested icily on the cement floor, waiting like wind chimes. One massive cardboard box, which could have once housed a refrigerator or coffin, had the absent gravity of emptiness and brought a sense of expectation rather than refuse.

Walking from the plaster-dust prefabrication of his own room, Owen inhaled the dampness of the water tower. As he climbed higher, he placed the smell: hollowed-out pumpkin and candle-burned lid. He imagined how the water tower jack-o'-lanterned the park and kept the stroller pushers away.

The ramp twisted up another floor into a room that must be Hal's. Kurt blurred over Hal's profession, but he had made it clear that Hal was at least one tier below him in the art world. Their respective floors reinforced the hierarchy. The room was clearly a photography studio. There were more traces of work than habitation. Owen counted nine makeshift ashtrays, ten if you included the floor. Loose-leaf tobacco covered every surface. Cotton stuffing wisped out of the futon mattress on the floor.

A wall-sized print of Kurt smoking in this window lorded over the room. The picture must have been taken before the accident because Kurt's left leg was bracing him into the narrow window frame with a rock climber's mastery of tension. Kurt hadn't specified how long he had been without the use of his legs, but he certainly implied that he was handicapped rather than injured, and had been for some time—a long enough time for this photograph to haunt the room and make the window empty rather than merely vacant. Now four camera bodies and a dozen lenses sat gathering dust where Kurt had once perched.

Thumbtacked Polaroids of hundreds of models, all wearing white tank tops, jeans, and presumably high heels, tiled a giant corkboard. Owen wanted to say this was the western wall, but he'd been spun around the spiral too many times to claim a sense of direction. It was like processing a palindrome, forward and backward at once:

IN GIRUM IMUS NOCTE ET CONSUMIMUR IGNI. *We go into a spiral at night and are consumed by flames.*

He climbed the ramp to the third and final floor.

When the ramp leveled off, he was met by a scarred farmhouse table surrounded by a mishmash of twenty chairs, scattered at all angles as if a seated crowd had sprinted into the night. Past the dozens of half-finished wine bottles. Past the coffee cup ashtrays. Past dried-out lime wedges, empty bottles of stronger spirits, and fruit-flyed glasses. Past the residue of drugs, the residue of nights. Past it all was the wonder of what could be hidden if this much was left to be found.

On the opposite side of the room, a Bösendorfer upright stood against the curved wall, two of its corners badly chewed from repeated collisions with the brick. Instead of sheet music, Owen found $40 fashion magazines and a back issue of *Artforum* with Kurt Wagener in the sidebar. A trail of flannel shirts led to a blue plaid mattress and an oversize down comforter.

Owen thought of the pictures he'd just seen in Hal's black portfolio. He could only remember one: a shot from the deep recesses of an oak, captured with a fish-eye lens. The image teetered on the edge of parody, like most of the fish-eye photographs he'd seen. But it took him back to the veers and dives of suburban department stores. He remembered darting through the automatic doors and crawling into a circular rack of blazers or blouses. Not hiding from anyone, just hiding. Hardpan carpet and the acoustic tiles with the patterned dots. It took a while to realize "acoustic tiles" didn't mean a ceiling of speakers. Inscrutable as OBJECTS IN MIRROR ARE CLOSER THAN THEY APPEAR. A phrase he'd ponder for twenty minutes, inside the ring of clothes. Until his dad grabbed a handful of hangers, screeching the chrome ring with "Where have you been?"—which made no sense, because they both knew that inside a ring of coats was precisely where he had been for the past half hour.

And now you are too tall to hide.

And besides, there was no one here to hide from. The tower was empty. Only Owen and the blue tarp were breathing.

Owen dusted the floor and then curled up under the tufted piano bench for a nap. He read the small paragraph glued on the bench's underside explaining *Kunstfertigkeit*, the link between art and craftsmanship. The text looked a little warmer, a bit more red, than normal. One of his eyes saw the world with a slightly red tint, the other slightly blue. He used to toggle back and forth every few months to remind himself which eye had which bias. He thought he remembered the right eye being red, but he wasn't sure. He knew he hadn't written it down anywhere. Certain uncertainty. The ghost in the machine.

A sharp poke in his side. The Gods had been absent since his injury, so Owen had turned to churches. The church nearest his hostel was almost entirely godless. Inaudible reverberations of the deep house music played the night before echoed in the nave while Owen sat in a pew, sketching his thoughts. An inflection point was fast approaching when those crossing the narthex in search of Ecstasy would outpace all those who had come during dark times in search of ecstasy. After a few tourist-climbs to the bell tower, he began to show up early and wander, found stairs to the triforium, and sat on a stone bench opposite an installation of spackled abstract paintings. Just this morning he'd sat on one of those benches, flicking the side of an expired glowstick he'd picked up off the ground. That same glowstick was still in his left breast pocket, poking him in the ribs as he rolled around on the floor of the *Wasserturm*. He pulled out the husk of plastic, dead liquid ghosting around a single bubble, and set it on the bench over his head. Perhaps he wasn't so special. Perhaps the glowstick's bathwater grey was the color of everyone's religion: spent glow, with only the memory of enlightenment.

He cracked his neck and fell asleep.

Owen woke to a voice:

—Things change when you're in a museum's permanent collection.

Owen fumbled for his eye patch and rose to his feet, knocking the underside of the bench and upsetting whoever was sitting over his head.

Hal, Kurt, and a girl draped over Kurt's wheelchair laughed. Owen stood to full height and tucked in his shirt. Hal offered him a cigarette. He refused. The girl offered him red wine in a Solo cup. He accepted. She caught him up:

—Kurt was explaining that talent is bourgeois.

—No. Talent is a myth. I was explaining that no one makes it in art without a platform. You have to have a brand before you have skill. First presence, then an audience, then change your skill set if you're still not selling.

Hal brought over a bottle of Jack and a cup of hot coffee. Owen put the coffee between his feet and took a shallow slug from the bottle. His stomach pulled. Now juggling, he drank the wine and then took a cigarette at Hal's second offer.

It was the first smoke to ever pass the barrier of Owen's teeth. His forehead beaded with cold sweat. He knew his lung capacity to the mL and his VO_{2max} to three sig-figs, yet he smoked again. No one appeared to notice that he didn't know how to inhale. He turned away and tried the sharp double-inhale that he knew was required. He coughed violently. Hal patted his back.

—Captain America!

Owen's throat tightened. He undid another button of his shirt.

The one sitting on Kurt's lap noticed that this was a new experience for Owen. She was layered in washed leather. Hal wore dark layers of hooded sweatshirt, track jacket, leatherish jacket. Kurt wore flannel. Owen smoothed his white shirt and tucked it into the corduroy pants that were falling off his hips. He would need to punch a new hole in his belt.

He drank his coffee and spoke halting German:

—I have been traveling from California to Berlin. I am grateful to have found a house.

Kurt laughed.

—Your German is so formal. Stick to English. But yeah, unpack your bag when we get back. I know what you're thinking, Who goes out on a Friday? but the tourists should have cleared out by now.

—What is it, four a.m.?

—Almost six.

Owen looked at himself in a slept-in suit and everyone else in leather and plaid.

—Don't worry, you can get in anywhere we go, even in a suit and penny loafers.

Hal was still silent, looking at Owen through the viewfinder of a double-grip digital camera. He didn't take any pictures, just dialed the zoom lens in and out, inspecting Owen at different focal lengths, half-clicking the shutter until the camera confirmed focus with a beep. More voluble now that a camera mediated his view of the world, he asked:

—Is that eye patch for real? I mean, either way you look great.

—I was hopped up on painkillers all winter, so everything's a little foggy. But I'm thinking the eye patch is real.

Kurt laughed and clapped Owen's leg.

Hal asked if Owen had any more of the painkillers.

The girl on Kurt's lap stood and stabbed out her cigarette:

—You should come out. Stevie always brings an interesting crowd.

Owen looked at both Kurt and Hal. Kurt had the final word:

—Brigitte's right. But nothing interesting ever happens in a place with a door policy—well, unless Sven is working the door.

Owen had no idea who these people were, but tried to find an artistic response:

—I'm down for whatever.

—I like big fireworks first too, but you've got to work up to some of this shit. We'll go to a bar, then Platte to see Stevie. You'll like Stevie. She's smart. But you'll die if you go straight to Sven's place.

Owen said he would just be a minute.

He walked back down the spiral ramp to his room. He fished the mason jar of sand and oil from his bag and walked up to Hal's bathroom.

He turned the hot water tap and waited until the water steamed. He scooped a handful of sand from his jar, brought a cupped hand of water to his face, and kneaded his cheeks. His fascination with grit had started when an older teammate showed him the pregame trick of scraping his palms back and forth over the texturized gutter, or, if they were playing at a generic subur-ban pool, over the sandstone lip. His fresh skin gripped the ball better. While his competitors struggled to catch with their off hand or thrust the ball cross-face without losing control, Owen rose high with a lariat loop of tan arm and yellow ball, lassoing the entire game and launching it at the nylon net. From age six to twenty-one he scraped his palms clean and greeted the world with a fresh grip.

His coarse beard buried the grit. Until now he didn't know he could grow one. Chlorine or bromine, depending on which pool he was practicing in at the time, had kept his body delphine, his hair brittle and bleached. Before, he'd scarcely had eyebrows. Now a proper unibrow bridged eye and eye patch, outsight and insight. Since he'd left California, his hair had grown dark. *Monobrow.* More and more of his cheek was lost each day to the barbarian beard.

Brigitte opened the bathroom door. She shut it behind her and held his gaze for a split second. Owen saw her reflection at his side and watched her heft the eye patch hanging from the faucet. She leaned into his hand and whispered into his ear:

—Don't watch.

She took a diagonal step back and out of view. Owen turned to find her unzipping her black jeans slowly, teasing every tooth of the fly with little pops, like air ticked between tongue tip and palate. He pulled clean his eyelashes, put the eye patch back on, and clutched the counter.

She reached around him and turned on the tap, melting into his knuckles. Looping her arm in his, she dipped her fingertips in the warm water and smiled when she made eye contact in the mirror. She flicked her fingers once to dismiss the water beads.

He started to speak, but she interrupted on tipped toe with breath tingling the small hairs of his earlobe.

—You have great lips, but your beard will scratch me.

She ran her fingers over his cheek and then fastened her jeans and left.

Owen tugged on his chin and asked his reflection what the fuck that was. He looked up, breathed deeply, and ground a paste of grit between his two hands.

Owen rejoined the crowd. The first thing he saw was Brigitte. He knocked on the doorframe because he saw Kurt sniffing something off a plate. Owen figured out what he was walking into just as Kurt offered him a nearby set of keys.

—You said you guys never locked the door.

Everyone burst into laughter. Owen was confused until Hal dipped a key into a small baggie and offered Owen a channel full of cocaine.

He was surprised to see the real version of something that had been, until this point, a Hollywood prop. These people were so cavalier, carving lines with credit cards in a room anyone was welcome to stumble into. The only thing he knew about cocaine was that no one, save maybe drug lords, did it out in the open. Hal snorted the mound on the key's tip. Kurt passed the plate. Owen declined:

—I'm still on antibiotics for my eye.

—This'll make them work faster!

Kurt laughed and then pulled in with the jolt of a snake handler who'd just dodged a strike. When the bitterness registered on his face, he gritted his teeth and his smile dropped. He passed the plate to Brigitte. No keys for her; she nudged a bump into the recessed filter of her Parliament cigarette, snorted, then patted her nose as if she were putting the finishing touches on her makeup.

Out of the tower and into the Berlin night, Brigitte braided her arm in Owen's and pulled down with a steady pressure that lifted her ever so slightly from the ground. Hal pushed Kurt's wheelchair over worn grass and tried eagerly to fit his monologue into Kurt's monologue. Pulling even with Owen and Brigitte, he finally got out what he had been trying to say for minutes:

—I had a thought last night of all these people, or maybe one person, a critic, writing a monograph on me or whatever. But the quote was: "He did nothing in his twenties, everything in his thirties, and everyone in his forties." It's a good line, right?

Kurt looked like he might hit him.

—You cocksucker. Lorie Nussbaum wrote that about me in

the Capo Press monograph. The quote was, "He did nothing for a decade, everyone for a year, then changed art forever in mere minutes." I have the fucking article in my press kit.

Hal lit a cigarette.

—Sorry. That's right. I must have read that article a thousand times.

—Actually there is no article. But that's what I'm talking about. If your balls are big enough, then facts become fiction and fiction becomes fact. All that micro bullshit is for watchmakers and carpenters.

Owen thought of asking where they were going, but was afraid he would open himself up to a whole continental critique of American banality—"Where are we going?" being a species of the "What do you do?" genus. After a few minutes, Brigitte spoke:

—How do you know Kurt?

Kurt wheeled up quickly and answered:

—Owen and I are collaborating on a project.

This was the first time Owen had heard it announced.

—Are you going to make him famous?

—The critics are going to make him famous; I'm just bringing him to their attention. Did you invite any of your friends tonight? We could set him up with someone.

—What if I want him for myself?

Once Brigitte was a few steps ahead, ruffling Hal's hair, Owen asked Kurt which artists he admired.

—Admire? If you admire art, you're buying it. I make shit.

Owen pressed him for a reference.

—I don't know. There are people you rip off or whatever.

Owen decided to be provocative:

—I've seen photos of your work. Is everything you do art?

—Absolutely.

Now Hal turned around, surprised at hearing what sounded like a heartfelt answer. Kurt continued:

—Art is problem solving. And I've got lots of problems.

Hal laughed. Owen asked Kurt to clarify.

—Picture a guy. He has this great idea for a sculpture, but he can't sleep because of a problem: How do I make it look like this guy is *thinking* and not taking a shit? So he paces the planks of his atelier for a few weeks. He notes how his own muscles contract when he sits. He calls in models. He makes them squat. Asks a few to take a shit for contrast. They think he's depraved. He sculpts models, all at various angles of exertion. But in the end, he solves the fucking problem. And it's beautiful. And that man's name is fucking Rodin. There is no doubt that we are looking at a man *thinking*. What's art? That's art.

Hal suggested a new work:

—You should re-enact that story as a performance piece.

Brigitte asked if the story was true.

—Art is telling people what to think. If a work is open to other interpretations, it means you failed as an artist. There are always problems with how something can be seen. Artists end the discussion. Try getting hundreds of homeless people to wear tuxedos and remove the possibility that you're making a fashion statement or some Marxist bullshit economics thing. Try filling the Stedelijk with Ping-Pong balls and have critics recognize it's a comment on flotation and not a birthday party for five-year-olds.

Owen was a little lost:

—You filled what with Ping-Pong balls?

—The Stedelijk. It's a museum in Amsterdam. Twelve million bright orange Ping-Pong balls. I originally wanted to fill the Reichstag, to float off the Christo shroud, but I wasn't Reichstag-big until 2002. And besides, the piece fit with the whole boat concept of the renovation they were planning.

Brigitte had the final word:

—Genius.

Just past Mitte, they took an elevator to a bar. Until the *ping* of the top floor, Kurt told a story about convincing a hospital to collect newborns' breath in balloons. These balloons were then used by botanists to grow constellations of baby's breath, *Gypsophila*, from the baby's breath. Unfortunately all the flowers died within a week.

—And that's when I learned the first rule of being a professional artist: Always have something to sell.

Owen scanned the elevator to see if anyone else was grimacing. Brigitte and Hal were texting, and the other patrons looked cowed, already forming the story of the one night they hung out with Kurt Wagener.

The steel doors opened to a riot. The crowd, mostly models jumping up and down to electro and guys with pursed lips fist-pumping, cleared a path for Kurt and his entourage. They passed from the main room to the back bar with the pomp of Dalí in 1920s Paris. Those with their backs turned sloshed drinks and spun in flushes of anger before realizing it was Kurt Wagener who had ridden up their heels. Kurt gathered apologies as if they were roses tossed at a curtain call. Then, at the back bar, a group of suits erupted in cheers when they saw Kurt and Hal.

I've lost the crowd that would applaud my entrance, Owen thought.

Hal explained Kurt's celebrity among celebrities:

—Kurt's a member here . . . so to speak.

Hal jerked his head toward the bar. Owen didn't follow until the bartender stepped aside: above the bar was a large-format photograph of Kurt, naked in his wheelchair, leaning forward with a grin and spilling down the pleather seat on the brink of tumescence. Berlin was no Paris, Owen realized, and this was no longer the 1920s.

Hal spoke before Owen could react:

—It's the best portrait I've taken.

Brigitte explicated the significance Owen missed:

—Kurt explores the distinction between body and body part.

Hal explained further:

—It's called *Pedicabo*, which means "I'll fuck you" or something, in Greek.

Owen let Hal's translation stand; philology was the least of his concerns, now that he was looking at a full-frontal picture of his host. But the Latin came out anyway:

—*Pedicabo et irrumabo te?*

—Ha! You do know shit. You've got to meet Stevie. She's the one who named it. It's a brilliant name, right?

The bartender vouched:

—The owners want to change the name from 66 to the Pedicabo Bar.

—You took me to a bar with your nude, wall-sized portrait?

Again, everyone was watching Owen. He tried to find the Dionysian mood that always eluded him when he needed it most:

—That's the stupidest thing I've ever seen.

Kurt chose to take the remark as a compliment and shook Owen's hand.

The bartender poured shots of green Chartreuse for the group. Owen was starting to see himself from a great remove. It happened to him whenever he was in this sort of environment. Thankfully, his words and demeanor were someone else's—someone fun and revolting, Hephaestus in a Dionysus mask.

—Where am I?

Brigitte didn't appear to catch the question; she just leaned closer.

A young man with a wild Nietzschean mustache, bright red and flying from his lip like a barn on fire, stood at Owen's shoulder, waiting to be introduced.

—Jera, this is Owen.

Jera looked Owen in the eye and nodded once as if he were firmly shaking Owen's hand. Something in Jera invited Owen to widen his stance until their gaze was level.

—Did you order him from a catalog? Does he know what he is getting himself into?

Jera spoke to Hal in German, presuming Owen wouldn't understand. And Owen, for his part, opened his mouth a little wider, hoping Jera and Hal would assume he hadn't understood.

—Kurt wants to use him for something. But he keeps surprising us, so who the fuck knows what's going to happen!

Hal laughed. Jera didn't.

The music was its own punch line. The crunch and warble buried any hope of conversation. Jera shouted over the music:

—Have you ever heard of Jörg Immendorff? He's the guy at the end of the bar in the black shirt with the five o'clock shadow. He's the Gertrude Stein of the circle you've wandered into—of course, you have to imagine Gertrude Stein orchestrating cocaine-fueled orgies.

—That guy? You're talking about the one with the four-pronged cane?

—Why? People with canes can't have orgies? How about people in wheelchairs? Speaking of which, can we change rooms? I can take a lot, but that photograph fucking creeps me out. Kurt's never had a hard-on he didn't use.

Jera motioned to the bartender, and they were admitted to a private room of green leather couches and mercury-backed mirrors. They had traded Kurt's nude portrait for a wall of Helmut Newtons. There were no speakers back here, so they could actually hear each other.

—The police broke in on him last year with nine prostitutes and a Versace ashtray full of cocaine.

—They must have taken the ashtray along with the coke, because now he just snorts off plates.

—What?

—I mean, it's no big deal. It's not like Kurt's the first person I've seen do coke.

—I was talking about Immendorff.

—How many years do they give you in Germany for that kind of thing?

—We'll see. The trial is in a few months. He'll be fine, though. He's friends with Gerhard Schröder. I'm guessing the worst that happens is he loses his professorship, but that would be kind of cold at this point. He's not well.

—Did Kurt and Hal study with Immendorff?

—They were at Städelschule. I was at Leipzig. Kurt and these other guys live his lifestyle—seven days a week instead of Immendorff's two—but have none of the man's talent. There are so many young artists in Berlin willing to sacrifice everything for their art, but so few who are willing to learn how to see, much less draw. Somewhere along the way they forgot that it's easier to suffer for something than to fight for it.

—But you're here.

—This is research.

—That's convenient.

—I paint large wooden panels. I'm not crazy about comparison, but people say I paint in the same vein as Bruegel or Bosch. I see a bit of George Grosz, but the work's really its own thing. Here.

Jera undid the elastic strap of a sketchbook and opened to a ribboned page. Owen looked at finely hatched lines and minuscule dapples of shadow. It must have taken Jera a week just to get the gleam of the bottles.

—How do you make the lines so small?

Jera unpalmed a maroon drafting pen.

—It's a rapidograph.

Owen unscrewed the cap, revealing a needle-thin point.

—That drawing is amazing.

—It's just a study. But it's close, I'll give you that. Look at this.

Jera showed Owen a partially finished drawing of the interior of the *Wasserturm*. Owen recognized it at once:

—I just moved in there tonight.

Jera pursed his lips, pressure building as if he might detonate some plosive sound.

—How long have you been in Berlin?

—Just over a month.

—And Kurt took you on as a roommate in the *Wasserturm*?

—He wants to collaborate on a piece for Art Basel.

Jera lifted his eyebrows and screwed his head:

—That's great. I'm happy for you. Really.

Kurt and Brigitte returned from the bathroom, but were intercepted by Immendorff just as they entered the back room.

One of Brigitte's friends approached Owen. She introduced herself as Saskia with a succinctness that suggested that she didn't have a last name because she would never need one.

She appraised Owen as she would a statue. Smoke rolled out of her mouth in thick clouds. Words followed exhalation, cold, high, and cirrus thin:

—You should find new friends. Or go somewhere else.

He fell through the wisps.

—Why?

Saskia exhaled as a response.

—Seriously. Where should I go?

—New York, Paris, London. There are many places.

—But here I am.

—You don't belong here.

—What?

—You don't belong here.

Owen asked for a cigarette. Saskia offered her pack and then offered him her lipstick-stained cigarette to light it with. In his experience, women who wore lipstick that red touched his arm and laughed at anything, hoping another guy would notice.

—I've got work in New York on Friday, she said.

She let the syllables linger in a way that suggested she was considering bringing him as a diversion. She squinted.

—Are you from New York?

—California.

—Los Angeles?

—North of LA.

—Things are different here. Find a hole to hide in and watch your drinks.

And with that admonition Saskia evaporated. She remained glued to Brigitte's hip, but she was finished with Owen.

Jera was back at his sketch. Without looking up, he said:

—They're all trouble, but that one is lethal. Stay away, my friend.

—How do you know Kurt?

—We were in a group show at the Todd Zeale Gallery.

—Did you collaborate?

—With Kurt? No.

—Is he a good artist?

—He makes a lot of money. He's no Immendorff.

—Do you think he's any good?

—If Kurt had any discipline, he'd be a mediocre painter.

Kurt somehow managed to be everywhere at once. He rolled right into Owen's calf.

—I thought you usually described me as a force.

—But I never meant it as a compliment.

—Don't worry, Owen. He's frustrated because no one wants to buy Flemish reproductions from a dreadlocked white guy.

—I had dreadlocks for two years. I was eighteen.

—You should grow them again. You'd give critics something to write about.

—You know I do this for the work, not the press, not the volume.

—People buy loud.

—And you've got a whole team in some factory cranking it out.

—Is it my fault if I can do more in five seconds than you do in a year?

—What do you call the picture, *Pedicabo*? Really great stuff. I'd like to buy it.

—The bar owns it. Not me.

The private room crowd stopped talking and listened.

—Well, I don't know what to say. I have to have it.

—You can't afford it, Jera.

—A trade then.

Kurt registered his audience.

—Didn't I hear something about you having a show up?

—The opening was last month. You went to the afterparty.

Kurt didn't appear to hear.

—I'll trade it for whatever doesn't sell. If you sell out the show, I'll give you the picture for nothing. But I think we both know that's not going to happen.

—Two pieces are already gone.

—And it's been up three weeks. I know for a fact one went to your uncle. Is your gallery even in Berlin? Doesn't matter. Fine. Let's see, what am I getting? I'm going with some allegorical work. *Parable of the Blind*? *Ship of Fools*? Something I could buy at the airport that's taken you over a year.

Jera laughed, but didn't deny any of it.

—Fine. Sold. I haven't destroyed the film yet. I'll have Michael print another and send it over next week.

Jera looked at the picture behind the bar. His nostrils flared and his breathing stopped. Owen could see that Jera only wanted to buy the photograph to remove it from the world. Now there would be two of these pictures in existence rather than one. Owen couldn't hear what Jera was mumbling, but *hydra* would have been fitting.

—Have your gallerist call Michael when the show's down. Let's go out. This bar turned into a business meeting.

Owen recognized the heaviness and emptiness in Jera. He looked like a high-schooler watching the gravel kick from a prom limousine that had just left without him. Which confirmed that Owen had fallen in with the assholes.

It was a short walk to the next spot. This bar was louder, but not cacophonous; darker, but with the early electric glow of amber. Owen walked through a projector beam and was temporarily blinded. A standing crowd barely watching the Antonioni film on the wall turned to see whose silhouette was blocking the cliff scene. It took a minute for Owen to realize that they were motioning him to move.

He had read an apocryphal history of the eye patch in *Coping with Changes in Sight*, by Dr. Thomas Friedlan, MD: pirates wanted to keep one eye acclimated to the brightness of the deck and the other hidden until it was time for the darkness of the galley. Apparently there was nothing wrong with most pirates' vision. In fact, the eye patch gave them a distinct advantage.

The darkened crowd was lost to him. A woman in a black horsehide Perfecto jacket stood illuminated by the glow of her laptop screen. She looked stunning in laptop light. Which was something.

Hal was yelling in his ear:

—That's her. Stevie. She's a genius. She memorizes entire books.

Before Hal could expand upon his point, he was introducing Owen to the woman. She held headphones to one ear and had a cigarette behind the other. Hal shouted over the music.

—This is our American friend, Owen.

Stevie, in her deejay perch queuing up the next 1950s song and doing something with a turntable, stood just an inch above eye level.

She slid a knob to the right, hit a button, and dropped her headphones to look at Owen. He looked paralyzed by possibilities. Hal didn't have that problem and yelled up to her.

—We had to leave the Pedicabo because Kurt and Jera were having a pissing contest.

—Uh-huh. I finish in twenty minutes. Take these drink tickets.

She motioned to the bartender and pointed to Hal and Owen.

Hal asked if he could bring her something. Owen kicked himself for being slow.

Stevie held up her water bottle, took a swig, and put her headphones over one ear.

Right elbow raised like a tour guide, Hal led Owen to the bar. He was nodding eagerly to the beat, lighting up another cigarette. Owen ordered tequila and a can of beer. Hal had the same.

Owen cracked the tab and slurped. The cold foam buoyed him up.

—Is Jera's art any good?

—There's a whole school of German artists like that.

—Like what?

—Did he tell you about his diet? He only eats roots. Like beets, turmeric, carrots, radishes . . . he's obsessed with pigments and thinks if he eats roots it'll lead to some insight, because they're brighter. I don't know. "Colors so bright they buried them underground." That's what he called the only painting that ever got him any press.

—Was it beautiful?

Hal laughed at Owen.

—You're not embarrassed to use words like that? Whatever. I can't remember the last time I thought a painting was interesting. I can't remember the last time anyone important in art thought a painting was interesting.

They threw back their first drink and took the second glass to the back of the bar, where Brigitte, Saskia, and Kurt were waiting. Owen found himself more stimulated than he had been since his pregame speech. All was speedy, hollow, and unwell. He stopped nodding his head.

—Did you put something in my drink?

A crack of laughter started with Kurt and spread through the group. Overwhelmed, Owen laughed a confused laugh.

—Took long enough, said Kurt.

Hal stretched for profundity:

—If the entire drink is a drug, are you really putting something into a drink?

—It's not like it was false advertising, Kurt said. You knew those shots weren't going to make you sober. And if a drug works exceedingly well, why complain about that! Besides, you can't blame me. I have artistic immunity—it's like diplomatic immunity, but for people who don't own neckties.

Owen stood to leave. Brigitte and Saskia gripped his inner leg, fingers deep into his thigh, giving Kurt the chance to continue:

—Look. I didn't do anything. I ordered a drink. The bartender, who's not even my friend, took that order and improvised. He distills his own biodynamic serotonergic whatever.

Hal spoke solemnly:

—Psilocybin.

—Monsters drink monstrous things, Owen. Welcome to Berlin.

—I've been here for over a month, Owen mumbled.

—Well. Welcome to the real Berlin.

Owen looked content, and everyone laughed. They were laughing at laughing. Then laughing at Owen gallantly kissing Brigitte's hand and toppling into an armchair. He toasted:

—My dear fellow mandarins, I drink to our future holidays!

Brigitte asked why Americans have to toast with every drink.

Stevie had now finished her set and caught the tail end of that exchange.

—What's the fucked-up guy's name?

—Which fucked-up guy? Take your pick.

—The lost one.

—The guy watching the movie like he doesn't hear us is Owen.

Kurt's entourage rolled to the front-room bar in a wave of shouts and a shock of laughter. Owen remained behind, enraptured by the woman projected on-screen, wandering a rocky island in a caftan.

—Owen, are you okay?

Owen adjusted his eye patch and did the top button of his shirt, though he knew he was flushed. He saw her lips first. She kept them open, but expectant, not slack, her tongue tickling the roof of her mouth, waiting to speak in a language of els.

—Do you know where you are?

The corners of her mouth met at perfect angles. He didn't think he'd ever seen that before. He felt the corners of his own mouth. They dimpled.

—I'm working on a piece with Kurt.

She looked disappointed. He followed it with the question everyone else asked:

—How do you know him?

—I've played the *Wasserturm*.

She blinked quickly a few times then looked up. She might have been trying to blink away an eyelash, but Owen thought she was trying to blink away the recollection. She looked at Owen's forehead:

—You're sweating.

—I don't usually smoke.

The words weren't funny in themselves, but Owen pursed his mouth, on the verge of cracking up. He thought something objective—numbers, science—might help. He put two fingers to his pulse, counted twenty-five beats in fifteen seconds, and multiplied by four. One hundred bpm. Very high. Too high. Almost techno-music high.

Stevie touched his wrist, and everything opened. His toe resonated with his temple; charges delocalized to build a glistening bridge. He breathed with his arms, his neck. He couldn't speak. Stevie smiled.

—You look like someone dumped a glass of water on your head.

Owen wiped his brow with his cuff. He pointed at the aquiline nose on the screen. His father had called it her Nefertiti nose.

—That's my mother.

—Unless your mother is Monica Vitti, I believe you're mistaken. Let's get some air.

Stevie helped him up at the hand and elbow. Now that he was standing, mostly on his own, he saw that Stevie was at least a foot and a half shorter than him. They stumbled past the crowd. She spoke to the doorman:

—I'll vouch for him. He'll be fine.

—If he falls, Stevie, I can't let him back in.

Owen squinted and blustered:

—Not a problem.

Dawn had risen and run away. The sky was scalloped grey and drizzling down. They leaned against the cinder-block wall and smoked. The concrete snagged his corduroy coat like Velcro. Owen draped the coat over her leather jacket as a great cloak. When she laughed and thanked him, a gold ring shone in her blue eyes.

—What did you do before "collaborating" with Kurt?

—I was a student until a little while ago. I had an accident and stopped out.

—Stopped out?

—I left. I lost an eye, my eye, in a water polo game.

—It sounds so suspicious whenever something real comes from something trivial. Like people who fall in love at the disco.

He drifted at her mention of love.

—Did you do it on purpose?

She shocked him into sobriety.

—What?

—People mark themselves, destroy their bodies in every way possible, kill themselves . . . seems conceivable that someone would blind himself.

—I didn't do this on purpose.

She only smoked, didn't respond, prompting him to consider the matter further. When he began speaking, his voice sounded heavy and strange:

—Well, I don't know, maybe there's something to that. Most of the players on that level have this *qualia*, this x-factor, this ability to will a game-winning goal and perform best when the stakes are highest. I never had that. The only real thing I had going for me—other than size, but that only gets you so far—was the ability to intuit what was going to happen next, to feel what every player in the pool was about to do. So maybe I did know that the hole guard was going to swing for my head, and maybe I did turn right into his thumb at precisely the wrong time. Because, you know what, I always hated sports.

—But you didn't quit.

—Well, it was paying for college, for one.

—And for two?

—Being on a team is a great way to be alone.

She smiled. He smoothed his hair and repositioned the strap of his eye patch.

—Has having *that* changed how you see the world?

—I'm beginning to think it saved me from becoming an asshole.

—It didn't save you from asshole friends.

—They're your friends too.

—Does it feel like you made friends? Everyone here's on friendly terms, but Kurt isn't anyone's friend.

—You're right. Which means you need to save me from them. Let's get out of here.

Owen watched her lips roll the possibility of sharing coffee and breakfast with him. He saw a quiver at the side of her mouth and traced the tremor to her eye, where an eyelash comma held on to her skin in the tight morning gusts.

—Hold still.

It trembled with the wind, but remained perched on his finger.

—Can you hand me my passport from the left pocket?

She held the passport open to a blank visa page. Owen placed the eyelash in the center of a square and wrote beneath it: "4-30-4. In a goddamn disco."

Kurt, Hal, Saskia, and Brigitte, fueled by new and sweatier drugs, crashed through the heavy metal door and announced that everyone was off to Sven's party at an abandoned East German power plant.

—I'll walk him home. We need food.

Zero parts daunted in whatever drugs the artists were on. They blew through anyone not arrowed the same way and rolled east down the Spree. Owen and Stevie waved them away.

Owen would later think that Flaubert had it backward; there is always exactly one incorrect thing a person can say at any moment. These exactly wrong words are every bit as potent as *les mots justes*, but they are even more elusive. More of these mistakes, and life would cease to be livable—not from the paralysis of shame but from the force of necessity. Born as a blunder, one of these cosmic mistakes soon becomes a polestar that pulls a young man north rather than south, east and not west. In East Berlin, Owen's morning star was rising.

Oncoming legions of tourists, parents, and morning shoppers kicked away his memories of the Pedicabo as if they were a mess of dead balloons on the sidewalk. Owen needed to walk in a straight line and attract as few stares as possible. Stevie pulled his elbow to steer him past strollers.

—What are you seeing?

—The morning march of respectability.

—Then you're not hallucinating.

—All the lights look neon. Stoplights. They're all on the brink of exploding. It's like the light doesn't want to be bulbed in. And those little green pedestrian crossing signals are insane.

They had walked from the LED pedestrian figures of West Berlin to the homburg-hatted little green traffic men, *Ampelmännchen*, of East Berlin, which made him feel more at home. He focused subtleties of light and change and movement, but could barely put one foot in front of the other. A man curled in front of a cardboard sign pointed and, recognizing Owen's state, howled. Stevie pulled Owen into a café attached to a theater.

Owen creaked the vinyl seat, repositioning himself in the booth to hide his injury and offer Stevie the best profile he had left: lantern jaw clenched tighter than normal, strong forehead belted by a cheap elastic strap, his maternal nose blotched from a hard twenty-four hours. His pupil had swollen from the drugs and overtaken most of his iris, leaving Stevie to stare at the corona of an eclipsed blue sun.

The waiter knew her and asked her if she wanted the cold pasta. She did. And if she wanted a coffee. She did. And if this gentleman was bothering her. He wasn't. Yet.

When their food came, Stevie salted her pasta. Owen dashed the greenest olive oil he'd ever seen over his moons of mozzarella. Since her breakfast companion looked as if he was imitating Pollock, Stevie, with mock fascination, studied the trident-wielding cartoon on the salt canister's aqua label.

—This representation is *fascinating*! Look at this. What *genius*!

Owen paused, glanced up, then found the rarest of words, the exactly wrong thing to say:

—I don't think it's very accurate.

—Accurate? It's a cartoon of a god.

—I always figured Poseidon would look like me.

Stevie sniffed and cleared her face of shock with a hard blink. She smirked, genuinely amused and inviting Owen to dig a deeper hole.

Owen obliged:

—I mean, he should be wiry, like me, not muscle-bound and swollen—assuming he's embodied at all, and not a color field like the rest of them.

Owen felt the floodgates open. His cheeks flared with thin blood. He shared his world with no one, and what he was saying based on your growing prestige and not derived from a material product of said collaboration.

—. . .

—Should we have a drink to celebrate?

—. . .

—You're not the sort inherently against a good time, are you? I know you might feel out of sorts, but you're on vacation. And from what I gather, the girls of Berlin are certainly not ambivalent toward you.

—I need a drink.

—Perfect! I cellar wine here. Kurt told me you met at that wine bar, which suggests that you don't know the first thing.

—I don't know the first thing.

—Very well! A hymn sung to a savage is often more beautiful.

—Than what?

—Than a *concio ad clerum*.

—So I need to leave Berlin?

—Thank heavens! That's the sort of witless question one would expect from a young man who speaks in your register. Gluttony made my bass a tenor, for which I owe thanks to the gods of plenty. I needed the jowls to give my larynx a little how's-your-father. Where was I? Oh yes, should you leave Berlin? Let's put it this way: Kurt is rich and famous enough to afford me. You decide.

—*Pecuniae Obediunt Omnia*.

—They tell me you're a classics fellow. Not a poet—though I can see how someone these days might mistake ancient learning for madness. I studied pure math . . . because I liked the adjective!

—Now you're a lawyer?

—Pure is one thing. Rich is another. Now let's talk frankly: Where will you go when the show is finished? Because Kurt will have you forcibly removed after Basel.

the treadmill in no time. With a low-fat regime to boot. The only trouble is this group of brigands. How do you play Falstaff to the fallen? Who's corrupting whom? Here, hold this.

Altberg handed Owen a half-open packet. Owen peeled it back to reveal a small quantity of white powder.

—It's not what you think it is. Look closely. Did you ever see crystals that small?

Owen held the wax paper close to his eye to inspect. Altberg jerked open the heavy door. Wind ripped into the tower, blowing the powder in Owen's face. He wiped off the rain and the powder as the wind and storm soaked their shins.

—There's your air, Owen. Hardly air at all. Mostly water, I'd say.

Owen's lot had been cast. The Gods threw him into this profane world and were watching him tumble. Let Altberg steer him back up the spiral ramp.

—Now, do you feel you're compos mentis re these documents? Not to muddle the gin, but the sooner you sign, the sooner I can remove my lawyer hat and show off my balding pate! God, the word is nearly pornographic, isn't it? *Pate.*

Owen removed a pen from his pocket and signed the upheld pages at each highlighted tab.

—Well, you aren't going to become a rich man from this collaboration. But you may become famous. I want to draw your attention to the equity portion of the contract, which is very explicit in stating you will derive no immediate financial benefit from this collaboration. Now let's look at what you just signed. Good news first: the contract stipulates that you will absorb none of the costs and assume limited liability for the production of the aforementioned artworks. Now the bad news: you keep nothing. However, what is unsaid is often far greater than what is said, i.e., peripheral gains are yours to keep—provided the residuals are would never make sense to Stevie. He had hoped his words would illuminate like a full moon rippling Morse code over a choppy sea, beautiful if not discernible. Instead, everything slapped the surface of the morning like a missed dive.

Stevie sipped her coffee, then spoke:

—I'm trying to figure out which is more absurd: to say that you look like a god or to say that a god looks like you. At least with Kurt you get what you see. Sure, he's a megalomaniac, but megalomaniacs are nothing if not predictable.

Owen slowly skimmed the crema of his Americano, holding the little spoon upright and watching drips of liquid rust. He looked up.

—I'm as embarrassed about that as you are.

—Kristeva should write a book about you.

—Who's Kristeva?

—She's a theorist. I took a year off to save money and get some perspective—well, that was the thought at least—I'm going back to finish in the fall. I'm using Kristeva, although that phrase is problematic, in my thesis on communication within the symbolic order—I wanted to focus on Susanne Kappeler, but she's hardly a household name. It's the type of theory that Kurt and those guys use, not a problematic word in this context, to sell a few spray-painted words—doesn't really matter which ones—for half a million dollars, or a guitar string in a vitrine for one-point-two million.

—Philosophy sells art?

—People sell art. But all of the galleries hire someone like Brigitte to explain theory to collectors. And if explaining those cool steel trees Roxy Paine is making with the Deleuzian rhizome brings in a few more million, why not?

Owen laughed.

—You realize I didn't get any of those references.

She craned her neck to look at Owen's bad side.

—Just some badges of my intelligence. It looks like we're doing the same thing: hiding all the stuff the other person really wants to see.

Owen faced her. She bit her lower lip and took a second espresso from the waiter.

—Why are you with Kurt and those guys? They don't seem like your crowd.

—Because I could only be interested in sports?

—No. Because you don't even have a tattoo. Hal said you were an artist. But he didn't say what kind of art you do.

—Don't be so sure about the tattoo. And I'm working on a conceptual art piece at the moment.

Owen was no more conceptual artist than bullfighter. But after his earlier gaffe, his mind had entered a trance where any words could spill out. He knew he had added another tree ring, another regrettable phrase that would outline a year, another idiocy that would condense and define him. He saw himself in cross section:

AGE NINE. "I could start at tight end for half the teams in the NFL"—that one hazed him out of football;

AGE TEN. "I'm not saying I didn't get to second base with Ms. Bouchard"—masterful logic;

AGE ELEVEN. "The Gods say I'm going to win eight gold medals"—hubris and first shoulder injury;

AGE TWELVE. "She's blond, so she has a see-through vagina"—he clearly hadn't logged enough time on the Internet, something that would change for his generation in the next year.

AGE THIRTEEN. "I was already admitted to
Oxford"—why would he lie to a pen pal?

AGE FOURTEEN. "I'm an expert on jazz"—of course
Owen said that, because this was his first black friend;

AGE FIFTEEN. "Drugs don't work on me. I'm too
tall"—because she was very into the Beatles and
wanted him to smoke pot;

AGE SIXTEEN. "I've memorized every star in the
sky"—he knew Orion;

AGE SEVENTEEN. "Prowst";

AGE EIGHTEEN. "You should let me teach Homer"—
probably the first time the dean of liberal arts had
heard that from an underclassman;

AGE NINETEEN. "I've just learned how to have
tantric orgasms"—right before he quickly lost his
virginity;

AGE TWENTY. "I'm being actively recruited by
the CIA"—it was the post–9/11 world, she was
moderately impressed;

AGE TWENTY-ONE. "I always thought Poseidon
would look like me."

Tree rings were supposed to get farther apart as time passed.
His looked pretty closely bunched at the moment. Twenty-

one, and his first double ring: "I'm working on a conceptual art piece."

Lies, they were basically lies of one sort or another, but these particular lies cut channels in a mind, rivulets for all subsequent thoughts to run through, eroding as they grow wide and deep.

Stevie looked at Owen as if she were hunting for jewelry at a thrift shop, assured that if she found anything that looked like it had real value, upon further inspection it would prove to be fake. But that didn't lessen the fun.

—Do you want a drink?

Stevie waved him off and lit a cigarette.

—Do you remember the first time we met? Owen asked.

Stevie let the smoke curl up to the wings of her nose then sucked it down with a sharp breath. She decided to play along with Owen's game of mingling future and past, even though he was clearly edging off the hot seat. She launched the first volley:

—I had a pasta lunch, and you said ridiculous shit over coffee. You told me you were an artist right after you told me you were a god.

—A conceptual artist, Owen corrected.

—And then you described the big piece you just finished. What was it called?

—It was part of the Laminalism series.

—What was that again?

—You had just finished DJing and were explaining some philosopher to me. Who was it again?

—Nope. You don't get off that easy. You described the piece so well I could see it like it was here on the table. How did it go again?

—The art was your hair tangling in my beard. But I made up something to impress you.

—I'm going to the ladies'. Surprise me when I get back.

Owen drank half of his beer when she left, the other half when she returned. He began:

—So the piece was a sealed manila envelope. Inside was a transparency with these micron-thick etchings, sharp like a woodcut, that marked a day's memories. But you couldn't see them. You had to trust that the memory was in the envelope. As soon as you opened it, the work was forever altered. But if someone wanted to, they could open the envelope, put it on an overhead projector, overlay the memories onto a map of the city—Berlin, in this case—and see exactly where the memories were formed.

—How would someone know when it's in focus? The distance would matter.

—Well, I haven't actually made this, but I plan to.

—Let's talk about the other pieces in the series that you actually did make.

—I haven't made any yet.

—You have a name for an art movement before you've made any actual art?

—It's Laminalism.

—I think you're going to fit in here just fine.

—But I am going to make one. Several.

—When?

—How about now. This will be the first spot on the map. Let's go wander.

—I've got places to go.

—Lead the way.

Stevie stubbed out her cigarette, and they closed their tab.

■

Owen had walked past the brick walls of the cemetery hundreds of times but never entered the gates. The greens were glowing in the shade, trying to catch morning light dripping through
the canopy. Stevie watched him disappear with a few steps, then
followed and caught sight of Owen studying the moss of a gravestone, thin-rooted as a front tooth. Stevie ticked her incisors and
raised her eyebrows at the prospect of wandering a cemetery:

—Are you serious? Fine. Keats and Yeats are on your side.

—They were both buried in Berlin?

—No. It's from a song.

Stevie opened her mouth to call Owen a tourist and then
found herself laughing at his puppy enthusiasm.

—Why are we here again?

—The best way to remember something new is to peg it to
a fixed object in space. So we need to find a statue or crypt or
something we are never going to forget and then link the memory
to the place.

—Link what memory?

—That's up to you. We've created a place where you can put
anything.

—And then you draw it on the transparency?

—Exactly.

—But what do you draw?

—That's the art of memory.

They passed the Doric columns of the Pintsch family me-
morial, the Zeitler mausoleum, whose font and verbosity called
to mind a nineteenth-century German newspaper headline—
Selig sind die Todten, "Blessed Are the Dead"—and twin ev-
ergreens angling forward a gravestone. Any of these might have
been a suitable place for him to take her hand and bring it to his
lips, a few fine hairs rising as he met her eye with a look that
she might remember, but the lump in his throat was still there.

Stevie raced ahead and stopped in front of a sandaled goddess, obsidian and gold, embracing an urn. The pedestal read "EC and Sally Kleinsteuber." She was from London, younger, and born a Gunby. Stevie asked Owen his surname. She laughed at Burr.

—Well, then, you'd have to take mine. Owen Schneider would be trading up. How did Gunbys and Burrs ever come to be?

Owen didn't hear the last question. Like the silk seeds floating down from trees he couldn't name and twisting in the wind, his mind floated here and there from shade to shaft of light. He repeated Stevie's words back to himself, rewinding the words that gusted him apart and fixing the way she touched her lips before she spoke.

Her right hand was at her side, hanging heavy with fingers spaced unnaturally, as if she were forcing her hand to wait there instead of retreating to her rear pocket. Owen took her hand and raised it to his lips, meeting her eye with a look that could bear weight. She didn't smile until the instant his lips peeled from the hollow of her first two knuckles.

And then she laughed wildly. Stevie apparently had an entire quiver of disarming smiles and drew three different smiles in rapid succession.

—You look like you'll survive. I've got to get back. It's almost noon, and I work at seven.

He walked with her to the tram stop, holding her hand until her car arrived. She looked back just before the door closed, smiling with lips turned inward and shaking her head.

Owen's first stop was an art supply store for a rapidograph, micron pens, and a box of twenty overhead transparencies. Even though he had come up with the idea in the moment, Owen had a long history with overhead projectors. His father had brought home a machine built with the ergonomics of a Soviet tank. Burr's idea was to use the overhead to teach his eight-year-old son Plato's Allegory of the Cave that summer. Burr imagined this as a lecture series that would draw all the young people of the neighborhood, and maybe even a few adults. Needless to say, his vision for the summer of 1990 was misguided. But the projector stayed in the garage, and Owen spent hours every day drawing on the transparencies and making shadow puppets while his father organized notecards for an unwritten chapter on the liminal in Socrates.

Near the bigger water tower in Prenzlauer Berg, Owen found a library with a functioning overhead. A librarian took his passport as collateral and said he could use the conference room for the next ninety minutes. On the white concrete wall, Owen taped a tourist map of East Berlin spanning the corner of Mitte where they'd met to Stevie's tram stop in Friedrichshain. As soon as the projector was switched on, he knew that the orientation of an overhead didn't match what he wanted to do. He found a paper trimmer and dropped the blade, squaring the transparency. Glancing from transparency to map, he dotted twelve points to mark where he would draw in the memories he had from their morning.

When he had finished his micron etchings, using all six of the colors that came in the pack so that his drawings bloomed, he looked back on his work: jungle-green climbing out of the parks, geometrical abstractions, each a memory of her from a different vantage, drawn in cornflower blue and babbling from fountains, and each apricot lane they walked graffitied with little totems. He removed the map and examined them against a white wall. He knew at once how he would present the piece: a sealed envelope with the transparency inside would be sitting on a plain café table; beside it, an overhead projector would illuminate flat sheets of falling water. The map itself was not his creation and shouldn't be a material in the piece. He could work with vintage maps, the contour lines and colors of relief seemed to approximate memory. But they were too static. He needed something to fall. And the tokens of memory—always sealed in that envelope—would leap like dust motes in a sunbeam.

The only thing missing was the color of the world. Once the Gods' colors came back, he would have different sets of transparencies for different days. He could easily imagine the entire morning with Stevie in peridot or gamboge, but it hadn't been that way. It had been flat light. And, for now, the transparencies would have to be clear.

Owen thanked the librarian who had let him work in the reading room. Transparency in hand, now in a sealed manila envelope, he showed up at the bar where he had met Stevie. He was redirected to a nearby hotel and left the sealed envelope at the front desk, STEVIE SCHNEIDER written in all caps on stationery clipped to the envelope and the map.

He would have to clean the floor to have a place to lie down. Owen walked upstairs to see if Kurt had a vacuum. He stopped a few steps from the threshold of Kurt's floor when he heard laughing and morning yawns, though it was nearly four in the afternoon. Kurt spoke clearly:

—I like my body so much more when it is with your bodies. It is quite a new and beautiful thing.

E. E. Cummings.

Then more shufflings and puffings of the down comforter. The two girls purred at Kurt's genius.

Owen walked back to his room. The sunlit tarp created a heaving of stained glass on the walls and floor. He swept the floor with a stiff piece of cardboard. While plowing the powder and cigarettes to the wall, Owen uncovered the blue lines of painter's tape marking off the floor. He contorted the yellow frame of the light to get it out into the hall. He had cleared the room of everything but the materials—sawhorses held a few pine planks, a bale of cotton-candy insulation, slabs of drywall, and a table saw. A staple gun, drill, level, putty knife, some sort of eggbeater, and cords of all colors spilled from a milk crate.

Evidently Kurt wanted to build a partition. Owen arranged the wood on the ground and began the framing. Then he decided the hammering would annoy Kurt and the girls and that he'd be better off sleeping anyway.

As he was clearing a place, he remembered the poem: *i like my body when it is with your / body. It is so quite new a thing. / Muscles better and nerves more.* Fuck it. Let Kurt have it. Anyway, it's plagiarism by anticipation. The poem was always Kurt's. The story is incomplete without partial paralysis and could only be spoken, really spoken, from a wheelchair.

He heard someone behind him:

—What are you doing? Leave that shit alone.

—I thought you wanted me to build a wall.

—I've hired a contractor.

—To build what?

—I'm not sure what it's going to be yet. It'll be big, though.

—You guys just got back?

Kurt ignored the question.

—The girls were asking me how you did that to your eye.

—Playing.

—Playing what?

—Water polo.

Kurt lit a cigarette. Now it was Owen's turn:

—How'd you do that to your legs?

Kurt laughed for the first time.

—Saskia's gonna stay and help me with something. Can you walk Brigitte to the U-Bahn?

Owen agreed.

Kurt wheeled out of the entryway.

The sun was already lost behind the old oaks to the west. Owen wondered how the whole artist routine worked. Did they go to sleep now? Take more drugs?

He had imagined the crisp air and the walk would help. So far that hadn't proved true. The people whirred by before he could process their faces. They were drawn blank, like the background of a dream.

Brigitte was after-school-special coked to the gills and had been pointing out multinational corporations going up in East Berlin as an indictment of all things American. He tried to steer the conversation to art.

—So how did you meet Kurt?

—It was at his Too Loud concert. A friend told me that one of the most important young artists in Europe was giving a concert, and I was naive enough to expect that there would be music. So I showed up with a couple girls.

They waited to cross Danzigstrasse. Brigitte texted a friend, laughed, then asked what she had been saying.

—You were talking earlier about Kurt playing a concert without music.

Brigitte took a seat on a bench and lit a cigarette. She looked around and then at Owen, as if explaining art to him were a favor.

—If music becomes so loud that it ceases to communicate, then it can become sublime.

Owen massaged his temples.

—If we take music, and more generally art, to be a sign system, then we must admit there is an ideal volume to communicate the message. Volume may be subjective at a certain level—people's ears are variously damaged, people listen for different things, whatever—but there is also an undeniable level of objectivity. Typically, the only objective sound we confront is silence—the bright line of zero decibels. John Cage knew this, and his composition *4'33"* was the most significant performance in twentieth-century music. Until Kurt Wagener, the world only knew silence. In Kurt's international debut, he gave the world something it had never known: the opposite of silence.

—Noise?

—Kurt realized that if you turn things up loud enough, every listener will agree that the music is simply too loud to be comprehended. No one's eardrums can process anything over a hundred and fifty decibels. Play something that loud and there's no difference between one note and a thousand notes. Kurt played at two hundred decibels. At that volume it's not even considered sound, it's a shock wave.

—Let me get this straight. Kurt blew out a bunch of people's eardrums, and this was what made his career.

—No. Kurt cleared out the gallery. He played with earplugs under industrial-strength earphones while everyone watched on a projection of a closed-circuit video.

—So it was like an if-a-tree-falls-in-a-forest kind of thing.

—No. Kurt transcended a threshold volume where nothing is understandable in order to break the Lacanian reflex system with the Other. He raised historic questions: Where is the artist's agency in this performance? Should Kurt be playing this song to begin with, given the fact that he admittedly doesn't know how to play guitar?

—He has a Bösendorfer. He must play piano.

—You never studied art, did you?

—Do you like his painting?

—Painting? He's not a painter. He is a major young artist. I would have thought that even Americans would know him. I mean, you obviously read. He directed a video for Duran Duran. He's been on the cover of every culture magazine in the world. He is major.

—Do you work in art?

—I've been director at Timmons Projects for the last two years.

—And you show Kurt's work?

—I wish. I'm trying. You don't understand. He is major.

And with those words Brigitte entered the U-Bahn.

On his way back from the station, Owen found Kurt on the south side of Danzigstrasse, smoking either a hand-rolled cigarette or a joint.

Owen crossed the street.

Joint.

—Come with me. I need your help.

Owen thought of protesting that he hadn't slept in days. That he had just ingested his first psychoactive substance and was still shattered. But there was no way he would find sympathy in Kurt by complaining about something as banal as total exhaustion.

—You look run-down. Do you need something?

—I'll survive.

—Whatever. We have to swing by my old gallery real quick.

Kurt, now in his white undershirt, admired his triceps as he dipped the push rims of his chair from twelve o'clock to five o'clock. Owen followed him to the heart of Mitte. Suddenly Kurt stopped.

—Push me in. We're going to that black glass building on the left.

A brushed-steel sign jutted out from the black marble and glass facade, laser-etched: TODD ZEALE GALLERY.

Kurt flicked his cigarette to the street.

—Actually. When we walk in we should both be smoking.

Kurt lit two Parliaments and handed one up to Owen. Owen left it dangling from his lip, burning his nose and making his eye water.

Kurt hit the brakes, and Owen lurched forward.

—Just open the door. I'll do the rest.

Kurt spotted the security camera and bared his teeth.

He crashed through the door, hammering down on the tires and wrenching control from Owen's grip, headed straight for a white pedestal in the center of the gallery which held a brass head under acrylic glass. He slapped the heels of his palms at the rims of his wheels, going faster and faster until, just before impact, he shifted left and hooked the hand rim of the left wheel. Kurt and chair turned violently to the left, losing traction and skidding into the plinth with enough force to rock it back and unseat the sculpture from its stand. Both sculpture and pedestal teetered back toward Kurt, at which point he swiped the plinth to the ground.

The disembodied brass head fell nose-first onto the cement floor. The warbled clang meant damage.

—Oh dear God, what have you done?

The gallerist, Todd Zeale, came running at Kurt as if he were going to hug him and grieve rather than accost him. Kurt changed his vector and wheeled into the middle of some fluorescent orange yarn that had been knitted into a large net. The web entangled Kurt far more than he had intended. He ripped at the junctions, and the screws, blue plastic anchors and all, came unseated from the drywall. He held on to one knot, ringing it furiously back and forth like a madman at the clapper of the town bell. Kurt tore the yarn-art piece from three of its four moorings. One strand of the now frumpy piece clung to the spokes of Kurt's wheelchair and followed him through the room as he headed straight for a wall-size canvas of interlooping red and blue paint that looked like a close-up of chromatin.

—This is an interactive piece, right, Todd?

Todd walked briskly to Kurt's side, trying to reason with him:

—Why did you come here? If you wanted to destroy something, you should have gone to the satellite gallery in Charlottenburg. If you don't stop at once, I am going to seriously freak out.

Kurt couldn't quite reach high enough to tip the canvas from its attachments. He hopped in his chair to push as high as possible, but couldn't dismount the work. He tugged down three times until the wooden stretcher bars finally cracked and the painting caved in on itself. Kurt surveyed the piece, now crumpled on the floor like a car that had just collided with a telephone pole, and looked genuinely pleased.

—It's all insured, Kurt, but I'm still pressing charges. Oh you bet. And like it or not, I still have pull in Basel. I can get your booth moved to Siberia with one phone call.

—Get the fucking checkbook from the desk drawer and write my fucking check.

Todd seemed to be processing the whole scene as if a skunk had traipsed into the gallery: he needed Kurt to leave, but didn't want to get sprayed. Two tourists had been standing against the wall this entire time, stunned.

—It's been six months since the fucking show, Todd. I need to be paid for my work. I need money before you spend it all on Asian boys and have your assets frozen.

Now to the assistant, who had been smiling at the entire scene until that last comment:

—Oh. You didn't know that Todd touches twelve-year-olds?

—Fuck you.

Todd pleaded to Owen:

—Can you do anything about him?

For the first time he could remember, Owen had become a
spectator, a follower. Maybe it was the drugs. Maybe the lack of
sleep. He took control of the rubber grips on the back of Kurt's
chair. Kurt flailed wildly in his seat and turned around to grab
Owen by the balls. Owen doubled over, pushing down firmly on
the handles. The chair rocked back, nearly falling into Owen's
knees, but Kurt sprang forward and landed on the casters.

Todd swiped at the chair but missed and stumbled into Owen.

Kurt was now pushing against a white lacquered panel. He
opened the hidden cabinet, unplugged a USB connecting to
the video feed, and removed an aluminum laptop. He wedged
the laptop between his legs and then taunted Todd by wheeling
straight at him, then swerving and skidding away. Todd shrieked:

—That's enough!

—Pay your fucking bills and stop living like a Turk.

—I'm not giving you a cent.

—We'll call it even. You're probably going to have trouble
putting that net back together.

Owen left the gallery in a hurry. Kurt took time to make
small talk with the tourists:

—Don't see that every day. Isn't Berlin sooo exciting? Everyone is so creative, don't you think?

He autographed the older woman's purse with a Sharpie and
rolled after Owen. Todd and his assistant watched from the front
door as Kurt wheeled off. Halfway down the block he shouted
over his shoulder:

—Todd, you've been great. Can you get the tourists to sign
releases? Thanks! Love you! See you in Basel!

The sidewalks were too narrow for Kurt to wheel at Owen's
side. He nipped at his heels and then veered into the street and
yelled over parked cars for Owen to wait up.

Owen hit a red light and couldn't jaywalk through the swift

traffic. He glared at the red light as Kurt repeatedly nudged his calf. It was the carefree homburg-hatted traffic man telling them to stop, but Owen bit down so hard that he nearly cracked a molar. Kurt noticed a police car waiting at the light and gestured for the passenger to roll down his window. The officer in the passenger seat didn't know Kurt, but the driver did. He smiled and lifted his chin in greeting before accelerating off the line.

—See, artistic immunity.

—I'm leaving for St. Petersburg tomorrow. Thanks for everything.

—Bad choice. It will take you months to get a visa. Especially after Abu Ghraib. You really want to travel to sketchier places when your country is torturing people? Look. Don't worry about Todd. You don't have the full context. I'll patch things up tonight. And if I don't, Hal has the kind of pictures of him that can end an argument.

—It's not that.

—Just stay until our piece is finished.

—Holding up an art gallery wasn't what you meant by a collaboration?

—No. Speaking of which, we need to see my lawyer tomorrow.

—I don't think it matters what kind of pictures you have. You need to go to your lawyer's now.

—You're a twenty-one-year-old American. Can you trust me that maybe you don't know exactly how the Berlin art world works?

—No. I think I've got it. Be loud. Be good-looking. Break a bunch of shit.

—Art requires brutality because life is brutal. Thinking otherwise is fucking naive. You see paintings, I see bloodstains.

—You're right. I'm naive. So why collaborate with me?

—I have a booth at Art Basel next month, and I haven't sent anything yet. I was thinking we could bang something out. It's going to play with representation, and you know a lot about that shit, right? Look. You're smarter than I am. You're taller than I am—at least when I'm sitting down. But you're trying to make it in the single most competitive field in the world. You need all the help you can get. And I'm willing to help. Tell me what you want to do, and we will make it so. Seriously. After this project you'll be able to get a *solo* show at any gallery in the world. You may be the first artist ever who doesn't have to stand on the backs of all the morons in all his shitty little group shows just to get a solo show. You are a very lucky man. Now you've got to tell Daddy about your dreams.

—Will Stevie be in Basel?

—Sure.

Owen let that hope hang in the sky for a second, then continued:

—I'm working more on subtlety right now, keeping things hidden and sacred. Do you know about memory palaces?

Kurt lit another cigarette. Owen continued:

—It's how people memorized huge texts like the *Iliad* or the Bible. You find images in the story, find nooks in places around you, and then pin down those images to make a tight link, and every time you pass that store or park bench or whatever, you're able to remember the images from the text. Because our brains are amazing at remembering spaces. Take the water tower: I've only been there a few times, but I can remember the panels on the door, the doorframe, the knob, the strike plate, the threshold, the puddle on the floor, three skateboards in the corner, wheel marks on the wall, grind marks on the handrail . . . every place you've ever lived has thousands of these little nodes. To memorize something huge, you need to create a route, a trail. My idea is to present mental maps of Berlin, so that people can *see* memory—or at least, they could if they broke the seal of the envelope.

—You sound like you need sleep.

—We can integrate anything into the map. We can use photos, performances, whatever you want, but the map would be the scaffolding, the armature of the sculpture.

—Let's not talk details until after you've signed all the paperwork. I'd love to go into all this memory palace shit, but experience has taught me that you've got to sign all the paperwork before you start making art. And don't forget the first rule: There's got to be something to sell. Rule two: Don't make anything too dense. The world doesn't need any more fruity esoteric bullshit.

—So what's the full context for that scene in Todd Zeale's gallery?

—Why do you think I stole his laptop? Even my detractors wouldn't call me a petty criminal. I'm going to use the security camera footage for a video piece. I've been mapping out that whole fiasco for two years now.

—Why?

—Todd fucked me by giving away a piece for two thousand euros to a "significant collector" who happened to be his lover's brother, rather than taking an offer for fifty-five thousand pounds sterling from an actual major collector. Fuck that guy. Dealers are much easier to deal with than gallerists. There are fewer feelings.

Owen was beginning to see that for Kurt, everything and everyone was potentially exploitable as an art piece.

—I'm going to get a friend to postprocess that video with thermal imaging—which is why I wanted us both smoking when we walked in. It's going to be like if you took a Bill Viola piece and added the tension of a Mozart opera. The piece is going to be a convection—is that a word?—of rage and humiliation. You know what I should get though is one of those TVs that has red surrounding light so that the viewer's whole face is bright red. I want the whole room to be red. I don't think that's been represented: the shame you feel when a friend shows you bad art—and this video is going to be bad art in its own way. Of course it would be much easier to just sell the DVDs. It's really an economics question. And that's why you need a dealer.

Kurt kept talking, but Owen was in his own thoughts.

This is Kurt's community. And Kurt is going to do whatever the fuck he wants. I should tell my dad that I'm in Berlin studying under Ezra Pound.

Gold glints lit their backs as they returned to the water tower. Another event was under way. Scores of models, the aftermath of some sort of casting call, leaned over the spiral ledge to watch a band set up synthesizers and tune guitars. Kurt had to roll back and forth to clear the garden-hose-thick extension cord linking their amps to a gas generator jackhammering outside. The women smoked, drank, and tapped their phones, but they were clearly eyeing the band. Owen passed the group of girls as each one shook Kurt's hand and then leaned in to kiss his cheek.

Jera took Owen by surprise. He was sitting on the floor of Owen's room, slumped against the doorframe with one leg out, breathing deeply from his nose and humming as he sketched the curve of the central spiral. Owen waited patiently for Jera to say something, but he didn't register Owen's presence.

Hal spoke from the hallway:

—He's sketching the whole tower. You can take a nap in my room if you want.

—Does Kurt know he's here?

—It's complicated. Is it cool if Jera shares your room while he finishes up the drawings?

Owen, heavy-faced from two days without sleep, nodded with

exasperation. He trudged up the spiral ramp to Hal's room. His right foot twisted and he nearly rolled an ankle. To complete the short climb, he had to summon whatever enthusiasm remained at the prospect of artistic success. He collapsed on Hal's bare mattress. The bass player downstairs decided that he needed a little more volume. Owen wrapped his corduroy jacket over his head, but it didn't help. His legs spilled onto the parquet floor. He slid lower and lower until he was using the foot of the bed as a pillow. Just as he fell into his first deep sleep in forty-eight hours, Kurt wheeled into his foot.

—Hey! Stevie's here. Never thought I'd see that again.

Owen found his feet and picked tobacco flakes from the wells of his pants.

—Maybe you *should* take a nap. You look like shit.

Kurt threw Owen's duffel on the bed as an accusation.

—You went to Stanford?

—I think I still do, technically.

—What do you study? Psychology? No, wait . . . philosophy.

—History.

—As a European artist, if you want to do something, you just do it—you don't go to school.

—Jera said you went to Städelschule. That's an art college, right?

—I went for the connections. I probably could have gone to Yale, but I didn't want to waste four years of my life. Art's a young man's game. It doesn't make any sense to waste time.

—How late is tonight going to go?

—The concert is short, just a favor for some friends. They're touring for the new album and haven't played any of the songs live.

—I can't take a very long night.

—Clean up. We'll have a little fun. Then tomorrow it's all work.

Owen looked at the gnarled trees in twilight and tried to pull himself together. Stevie walked into his room.

Her voice had been echoing through his head, and at first he wasn't positive it was really her.

—Kurt looked you up. You played in the Olympics?

—I didn't get in the water until we were mathematically eliminated.

—You must have been, what, eighteen?

—They put a few young guys on the Sydney team to generate interest for Athens. This was supposed to be my year.

—You're talking about the Athens Olympics?

—I should have been training in Colorado Springs, but I decided to play out the season. Then this happened.

—You were that good?

—I was a body. I wouldn't have been on the national team if Wolf hadn't stumped for me.

—Wolf? Is that a person? Most of the time it seems like you're talking to yourself.

She started to leave.

—Wait.

—Too late. I'll see you downstairs.

Owen lunged and caught her arm just as she was spinning away. He curled her in close and she floated into his lips.

She clasped her hands around his neck as if she were swinging from a tree limb. She looked up. No one had ever looked at him like that.

Hal's camera flashed from the doorway, and everything fell. Stevie pulled Owen past Hal and down the spiral into the show.

A humid wall of guitar came from the Marshall stacks. Lazy hums condensed on the singer. And when his falsetto entered on the next song, Owen recognized this band's music from a computer commercial. These guys were not just famous, they were world-famous. This night would not end early, and if he let go of Stevie, it wouldn't end well.

—Do you want to go walk?

—I've got to wait for Jera.

—Why did Kurt invite him if they hate each other? And why did he come?

—It's more complex than that. First, it's not like Kurt sends out lace-fringed invitations to his parties. Second, there are many "artists" in Berlin, but the real artists are in a fairly tight circle. Jera comes here a few times a week for the series he's doing of contemporary spaces—he'd say "contemporary nightmares." Kurt probably has some angle. Jera doesn't care.

—The sketch he showed me at the bar was amazing.

—He's maybe the only person in Berlin still painting figuratively.

—Is that a good thing or a bad thing?

—I'd say both, but Brigitte is the art expert. Forget I said that. Stay here. I'm going to get us drinks.

Owen waited. He could see people staring at him and knew that everyone on his blind side was also watching. He put his hands in his pockets. Then put his hands at his side. Then crossed his arms.

Stevie came up from his right side and handed him a red Solo cup. Owen studied it.

—I feel like I'm at a frat party. Does Kurt import these cups from the US?

She gently nudged his hip so he opened toward her. Then she took his hand. Stevie pointed to the band, introducing a soaring falsetto.

The door was open the entire time, and half of Berlin was probably in earshot of the show, but only a few dozen more friends trickled in the door. For the last two songs, a trio of deliverymen in white pants waited in the doorway with bags of food. Hal slid from the lead singer to the men with food and led them upstairs. And then the entire night twisted up the spiral. Owen's head spun at the volume of introductions and short, snarky conversations. Was it the soap smell that brought him back, or was it the strands of her hair tangled in his beard as she leaned in again and asked him closely if he was all right?

But he pulled away and saw Kurt carve up a dozen lines on the top of the Bösendorfer. As soon as Stevie was out of sight, Brigitte bit his earlobe and placed a pill on his tongue. A deep punch in his bad shoulder and a bitter ring through his blood that canceled the sweet, the soap and tuberose, the sacred and sublime. Everything of value stretched and shrapneled, lapping the circular walls in lethal vorticity. In Berlin he was capable of anything. But only capable as a pawn: unsure of his file and clutched in someone's monstrous hand.

When Stevie saw him trail Kurt, she headed for the door. He called down after her, leaning over the ledge, which wasn't designed for someone with his higher center of gravity, and nearly fell four storeys to his death. Brigitte grabbed his waist and steadied him.

—Are you okay? You nearly fell.

Owen looked at her, not comprehending.

—And up the tired tower where every stone remembers the ground . . .

He had spoken this. And the tall woman—it wasn't Brigitte, it was someone new—laughed at him.

—A drunk poet, how original.

—I'm not a poet.

—Fine, a drunk artist? Every artist wants to fall to his death and live to tell the story.

—I'm not an artist.

—Why is your head wet?

Owen realized he was sweating.

Stevie had taken his hand. Now his hands were empty.

—You feel hot.

Owen found the large wooden table set for dinner and lit with dozens of candles in a pewter candelabrum. He slumped in a chair and sat down for his first meal in days. Hal was carving a giant turkey. Kurt had ordered a Norman Rockwell American feast and was pouring tequila.

—All bets are off tonight. Tomorrow Owen and I begin work on a new series for Basel. Those of you who don't know Owen should know that he is a major young artist from California. He played water polo in the Olympics. He doesn't speak any German and has asked that we confine our conversation to English.

—No. I don't. I don't belong here.

Hal barked out from behind his camera as he shot the scene:

—Everyone belongs here. Haight-Ashbury '67, Paris '68, Berlin '04 . . .

—Hal's right. This is the only city left, and we are making a difference. But tomorrow we can talk about work. Speaking of which, does anyone have math or science friends who can help me out? It's just one shot, but it needs a lot of chalk work. Math shit. Equations and shit.

Athene could stand this no more. With winged words she told Owen to close his teeth tight, because he was about to fall. Then the grey-eyed goddess, daughter of Zeus who bears the aegis for all travelers in strange lands, loosed Owen's knees and pulled him down by the ankle so that he collapsed right there at the table.

Owen awoke to fat fingers cupping his head.

—So this is the famous Owen!

—My lawyer, Altberg.

A ring was gathered around Owen, who was again near the Bösendorfer, this time with a pillow supporting his head and his legs elevated on the tufted, well-crafted bench.

—Are you okay? Hal asked.

—Apparently you had enough of dinner and felt entitled to a postprandial nap right at the table. Kurt called me immediately to make sure you were all right. Are you?

—I'm fine. Is Stevie here?

—She's long gone, I'm afraid. Kurt also asked me to bring over the contract, to save you the trip in your weakened state. Though I must say you look quite fit to me . . . no, no, don't stand. I'll drop down to your level.

And with those words the massive solicitor tentatively found a knee. And once that knee met the floor he couldn't stop the other from following. He braced himself with Owen's leg.

—Thank god I was never a medic!

The group laughed at the round man's topple and began to disperse.

—I need to go outside.

—In this! Have you not been outside today? Look at the weather, my friend. It is madness out there.

Owen now heard the lashes at the window.

—I just. I need some air.

Owen found his feet and stumbled.

—Hal, grab us some coffee. I'm going to walk our friend down for air. If we aren't back in twenty minutes, assume he's stolen my purse and made for Mexico. I don't entirely trust this fellow. He's a gentleman of the shade, and we are minions of his moon.

—Trencherman.

—That's right, Owen. But with a name like Oldcastle, what else would you have me quote, *Lear*? Luckily these people haven't met Falstaff, or they'd peg me as a pale imitation and have me on

—I know that.

—Tall men always like to pretend they know what's coming ahead, just as fat men feel they know the street and underground, but this is the first you've thought beyond today . . .

—I'm just trying to make it through the night.

—You must be vile to your body when it lets you down. There must be discipline in all things. My personal accounting of maladies: beer for a headache, whisky for knee pains, tobacco for dyspepsia, tequila for malaise, anise for vanity, port for the chills, wine for obesity . . . and general complaints.

Altberg had been turning the screwpull with his entire torso. He popped off the cork with a surety that came as no surprise, given that all he carried in his pockets was cash and a wine key.

—Let me educate you, my young and clueless friend. This is the noble syrah. The vines in a *lieu-dit*, sidewinding back and forth like this. The slopes are steep and the wine is savage. Earth, funk, bacon fat, and a violet soul. The dirtier the syrah the better. It is the only grape you need know.

Altberg felt Owen's forehead.

—My hands could be a shade cold, but you do feel like you've developed a slight fever since you signed that contract and are now in need of this wine's powers. I'm quite sure you are doing the right thing: deep drinks to drown the fever and counsel of a wise man to find the shore.

—You just said you fucked me on the contract.

—Of course! The contract you signed divested you of all intellectual property that derives from your time in Berlin. As far as agreements go, it's Rumpelstiltskinian at best: whatever gold you spin, or even think of spinning, is Kurt's. And if you try to pass it off as your own, you'd be lucky to get off with your first-born son.

—I assumed as much. But it's worth it.

—But why not spring the trap. That's why I like you. So, sure. I'm neither honest nor noble, but I don't claim to be.

—I'm very, very tired.

—Probably just jet lag.

—I've been here for two months.

—You may as well have a good time. One thing's certain: you're not going to fall asleep with any of those substances circling through your blood! Brigitte is looking at you. So is Saskia. Well, she may be looking at me. Here. Take an Adderall. It's your only hope of getting any clarity.

Owen took a pill from Altberg's swollen palm and gulped it down with a Côte-Rôtie. He looked at Brigitte.

Her image was right, but it was as if she didn't believe in it. She had the right arms, no wider at elbow than at wrist. She had the right chiseled lips. She had industry-prescribed proportions, but was only beautiful in the abstract. Her lack of belief kept her on edge. She took off her jacket, always watching over her shoulder. Her tan was not her tan. And her skin was not her skin.

She caught Owen looking and smiled.

He woke on a cold wooden floor. His first thought was that he deserved whatever would come. His first hope was that Stevie wouldn't see him. His second hope was that the gods wouldn't see him and that he could save himself. Hal's flash knocked him out again.

He woke shaking under heavy blankets. Kurt said he looked like Joseph Beuys and asked if they could find a coyote or maybe a dachshund. Something yappy.

Owen woke slumped on a wooden spool three feet tall and three feet in diameter. Three pieces of drywall, slathered in plaster and screwed together, were supporting a great deal of his weight. Owen blinked, his eyes gaining focus and his knees shaking to hold him up. When he found his feet, Hal withdrew his hands from under Owen's armpits. Kurt was speaking:

—Stay with us, Owen. This won't take more than a minute. Curl your toes over the spool—did you get that, Hal?

Owen barked drunken nonsense:

—Don't disturb my circle.

Owen shoved an assistant, losing his balance and collapsing with the Sheetrock on the cement floor. He rolled slowly back and forth until he was still. Hal and assistants began to recompose the scene, but were cut short by Kurt's yell:

—Don't touch anything! It's great as is. We'll see when he moves. Now that is actual art! Set that one aside. Call Danielle and tell her the first piece is ready for the show. That Sheetrock will look like the Shroud of Turin or a snow angel or an image of the crucifix when we get it out and install it. Perfect! Tell Danielle to pick it up today. We need the space.

Now in a chair with his wrists bound to the slats. He pulled his arm up, and the rope came undone. His face was heavy. His hair veiled him from the spotlights. Gravity was pulling forward rather than down. The chair's legs cut into the cement floor at an acute angle, rather than the right angle, meaning his seat was tipped forward and somehow bolted into place.

—Do you know about Custody of the Eyes? It sounds so much cooler than it is. It's basically, Don't look at hot chicks in church. So we're going to have some really beautiful women dancing around in casting thongs just on the other side of that painter's tape. You won't see any of this because of the angle of the chair and because your . . .

Facedown on the wooden floor. His shirt was off and his coat was draped over his shoulders. Floor wax caulked his fingernails. The scratches on the floor revealed an almost legible ideographic script. Owen couldn't place the language, but knew it had come from the depths of this fever. Rongorongo? Georgian?

Only my father's son would snap to consciousness and think of arcane scripts.

—I'm out of film.

—Use the thermal camera. Here, I'll do it.

Owen rolled over to find a yellow plastic housing inches from his stomach.

—Holy shit! He's got a massive fever. Hey, put your arm up next to his. Holy shit! That's awesome! He's like, pink and you're . . . Here, just come look at it. I'll put my arm up next to his.

—That is super cool! He's got to be over forty degrees. But isn't the video too . . . blocky?

—He's blocky. It'll work.

Kurt had at least a dozen assistants. They all seemed to be here.

Owen rolled over and scratched. His fingers flexed until his fingernails bent. Then his head collapsed.

Owen awoke to find he was no longer the center of the crowd's attention. A green chalkboard on casters presented an equation with multiple integrands, psis, and inverted deltas.

—It's called the Schrödinger equation, Owen. He was a German, you know.

Owen rolled away from Hal's camera. But he couldn't roll away from Kurt's booming voice:

—Why do you think Schrödinger and Goethe, the two greatest Germans maybe ever, both worked extensively on color? We're all artists here, Owen.

Owen grabbed a nearby towel and covered his eyes.

—That's why I, unlike Hal, never shoot in black and white. A genius thinks in color—just to make sense of the thousands of inputs in the world.

Kurt now turned his attention to a girl in a bathrobe.

—He's not going to bother you, is he? He is an Olympic gold medal winner, you know. For swimming. He and I are collaborating on a piece, but he's sleeping now. I've worked for three straight days to make this deadline.

She dropped the robe near Owen's feet. Kurt was actually quite tall now that he was unfolded from his wheelchair and standing. The woman was tall, and she was looking up at Kurt.

—Jesus, you're beautiful.

She laughed.

—I was picturing this with a lot of oil, but I think you look perfect just like this. Maybe we can work up a little sweat. Hal! Are you ready?

Hal finished loading his camera and left Owen.

—All right, Monique, lean over and pretend to write at the bottom of the chalkboard.

He woke and was bleeding. Or at least there was blood. The strap muscles in Owen's neck were about to snap. Blood heaved up his shoulders when he tensed, then hushed back down whenever he breathed through his nose. There was a shearing at his ribs—as if someone were carving a much smaller statue of him from the slab of his real body. His head was thrown back so far that he couldn't see the sculptor.

—It's a sponge. Just a sponge, not a Brillo pad. She needs to even out the oil.

Light grew. He mumbled:

—I'm studying at Wittenberg. I need to go to Wittenberg.

—What was that? You need to go to Wittenberg? Hal, stop everything. He needs to go to Wittenberg, wherever that is. You're not going to Wittenberg, my friend!

Owen's hands were now awake. They were bound behind him in a backward handshake. They found thick rope. Nautical rope. His jaw was hinged back, pushed up by some sort of implement wedged into his collarbone. His chest arched out from the strain. He was a Pez dispenser, a prop.

Each breath, an event.

Again, the scratching at his ribs. His wrist stretched the rope until it creaked.

A drop, Owen thought. *Mnemosyne, lend me a drop. For our waters are Lethe. And these days are endless.*

Water streamed over his cracked lips, and the light dilated until all became white.

—Look at the women clawing at your legs, Owen. I wish I were you sometimes. Just kidding! You're getting all this, right, Hal? It took my assistant all of yesterday to find the right size flange. Your jaw is fucking huge, man. I based it on something called a heretic's fork, which may or may not have been in Abu Ghraib. The blood's not yours. Stay with us, Owen. Hal, get closer. Fucking Falconetti close! Get a couple without Monique and Saskia.

Owen awoke on a corduroy pillow. Sweat dripped down his inner thigh.

—Grab his hand, Saskia. No. Lace his fingers. Yes. Now you have his attention. With the tip of your tongue. How long can you be attentive, Owen? Owen? Fuck. All right.

—Okay. Someone put his clothes on and take him to the hospital.

FOUR

"LAUD WE THE GODS . . ."

Mission University's Eastern Lawn had tried for decades to bury the Classics and Ancient History building. Grass swept into the walls like sand forming banks around a sunken ship. If the building was a ship, then its Corten steel exterior brought to mind a freighter, rusted out and dying above the surface, housing a vibrant reef below. This would make Professor Burr a polyp, a living extension of his coral home. His office was deep in the galley, with a single porthole. One large pane of chicken-wire glass peeked out onto the sloping lawn. On days when they had just mown, the professor could stand on a chair and crane up to see the fountain. But the emerald blades of St. Augustine grass sprigged to the top of the sill mere days after they were whirred down and mulched. While they stood, their edges were brightly parallel, the lined glow of barn planks moting out a summer dawn.

It had rained most of 2004, nearly every day since Owen left home in March. The newscasters were calling it an El Niño year.

Maintenance couldn't keep up with the summer rain and the grass had overtaken the window, casting half his desk in streams of white light, half in emerald. Even when they did mow, the maintenance crew now seemed content to let the grass keep its high-water mark above his windowsill.

Burr kept his oak desk bare, his computer jammed against the cement wall. Loose papers he exiled to the credenza behind him, accessible only with a creaky swivel of his rolling tanker chair. Today there were two itineraries on his desk: one brightly lit, the other cast in bottle green.

Burr hadn't heard a word from Owen since March. He had given Owen April to reply to his messages. Nothing. In May, Burr spent $4,000 on a campus security officer moonlighting as a PI—who, as he discovered in June, turned out to lack a passport. Burr then spent $49.78 on a drunken, maudlin heart-to-heart with a phone-in psychic named Amira. She said he needed to see the world through Owen's eyes. When he told her what happened, she said he would see his son, clear as day, if he went back to where Owen lost his eye. He drove to Stanford three times in June to interview players after practice. But none of this had produced a clue about where in Europe his son might be. Owen had been Athens-bound since puberty. The Sydney Olympics had been a surprise, a vacation. Athens was always his Olympics. Burr's best guess was that he would find him there. So both of the itineraries on his desk began in Athens.

The first itinerary had Burr presenting his research in lecture halls that amounted to little more than support groups—half of the twenty-odd listeners would be fellow travelers, tenured professors who wandered the world neither known nor valued by the hoi polloi. After graduation in June, he sent out some feelers and found a few auditoria in Athens where a modest audience would be willing to follow a *Hapax*-related PowerPoint on diaspirates and digammas. He had stretched his itinerary from three lectures to an optimistic six, a sad little triangle into a robust hexagon. Each vertex would afford him another vantage to look for Owen in Athens.

The second itinerary, cast in a green light by the blinds of overgrown grass, had him speaking as a social theorist. This extracurricular adventure was still a secret from the university, but had intensified since Owen went away. It couldn't remain a secret for long. Burr was already making compromises, canceling lectures to meet publication deadlines, showing little concern if his mustache blended into a beard for a few days. Major articles were in press. His fellow contributors wore leather jackets, not elbow-patched blazers. This proposal, this radical course, had no more planning than a message in a bottle; he would surrender to the gyres with the hope that someday soon Owen would unstopper the bottle and find his message. Or, less metaphorically, that his son would finally think that his father was worth getting to know.

If Daedalus couldn't find the dancing path to freedom, what chance did Burr have of leaving the labyrinth of his own devising? Since Caroline, he'd stumbled through his lair, bringing every text, every thought, into the pit of liminality, hoping that something would light the way out. Recovery from what most of his colleagues were calling an addiction rather than a theory had proved particularly difficult, as his original project was designed to *un*cover meaning, to reveal, to unveil. After being outed in tenure review, Burr had to find a cabinet for his curios. His oak desk became the secret tomb of his liminality project. He jotted each insight on its own index card and locked it away in his upper drawer. He read some of them and thought he must have been drunk to write that. He read others and remembered being drunk writing that. On the whole, looking at this early work was the only thing that approximated what he felt when he looked at his son: pure bafflement that *he* had produced *this*. The later work meandered and was different in kind from what he'd produced when Caroline was still around, but whenever he poked around the desk, he found some of the fireflies still glowing in their jars. The morning after Owen left, Burr began rehabilitating his system and hammering in the floorboards of his future stage.

For the ambitious professors of Mission University, it had been like Armstrong walking on the moon when Chomsky sold out the amphitheater and packed a spillover auditorium with students hooting at a projected video feed. Public intellectuals were nothing new, Chomsky himself was far from new, but the recent outpouring of interest in theory was astounding. People wore these men's faces on T-shirts! Burr couldn't help but imagine how he would look in stencil. He had been too young before. He might have even been ahead of his time. Now there was a cult of the difficult, a generation of Web designers who read late Heidegger for sport in their local coffee shops.

The formula for the new public intellectual seemed simple enough: (1) develop a critical lens and then hold it up to whatever young people are interested in; (2) say something outlandish, seemingly at random; (3) through sophistry arrive at the radical conclusion you blurted out at the argument's outset. He had nearly done as much in his four years teaching Plato as an associate professor.

Of course it was hubris to think he could become a public thinker. And it was a stretch to think that Owen would be any more likely to respond if Burr transformed thusly. But it was all he had left.

It had been eight months since Burr first dipped his toes into the water of critical theory. Thus far his biggest following was in the LGBT community, where his article "We Are All Third Gender" (*QT Quarterly* 42, 2004) had earned the merit badge of a pink triangle sticker affixed to the glass panel of his office door. He now kept late hours, but never met his one confirmed fan. He liked to think a second fan slapped on the next bumper sticker, a yellow equal sign against a blue-background, but of course there was no way of knowing for sure.

Once the second sticker graced his door, he began finding more excuses for summoning faculty to his corner of the building. Occasionally a colleague would ask what the yellow equal sign meant. Burr's reply was always cryptic, chiefly because he wasn't completely certain: "What do you think it means? I can tell you definitively, I'm not interested in math." When they asked about the pink triangle, his response was equally pithy: "One can be straight, but never narrow." When he walked through the quad after sending off an article, he liked to imagine every nod of the head was aimed at him to say, "We have read you, Joe. And you have read us."

One morning tragedy struck. A member of the janitorial staff had taken it upon himself to remove both stickers from the inset glass of door 24B. In that one move, Burr had gone from defender of equality to bigoted brontosaur.

He raced to the bookstore and was able to find a replacement triangle, but not an equal sign. The triangle was the exact same size, but he couldn't remember if his fan had pointed it up or down. He was almost positive it pointed up, but the alternative formed an afterimage that made him waver. Up. It pointed up. He found conflicting arguments online, but in searching he stumbled upon a picture of his missing yellow equal sign. Burr wanted to hug the Internet. His printer traced the text, loudly, from left to right. Cyan would have to do. And not a day after he taped the printout to his door, someone had written "Ha!" in ballpoint pen.

More stickers followed. Half of them proved to be the names of punk bands. For the first time in his career, he felt a part of the university. Still, no one was wearing his face on a T-shirt.

All of this appeared to be a secret from the classics community. Or perhaps it was just impolite to mention an open secret. Nevertheless, not one of these new enthusiasts had purchased a copy of *Hapax*—he had the two-figure royalty checks to prove it.

Since Owen's disappearance, the professor had penned a liminal interpretation of profit and loss for *Modern Socialism* and posted an alternative interpretation of Lacan in the *New Left Review*—which S_____ Ž_____ himself had almost praised in a letter to the editor:

> Burr precisely inverts two of the three classical laws of thought. He annihilates both Aristotle's Law of Non-Contradiction and Law of the Excluded Middle. So far so good. He has read his Freud and sees the link between *superego*, here the Law of Non-Contradiction that seeks to suppress libidinal desires, and *id*, as the excluded middle child who longs to break free of his older sister's fascist constraints and free himself for one moment of *jouissance*. Burr fails radically, however, to account for the ontology of logic. No thanks, says Burr. I won't submit myself to analysis. It is precisely here, in Burr's denial of the *ego*, that the reader is most aroused. The implications of his work on Agamben are profound, but his handling of Hegel is infantile at best—and probably would be much worse were it longer. If we ignore a few systematic idiocies, we are left with a deeply insightful analysis. He is one of the few imbeciles to whom we should listen closely.

What business did Burr have appearing in print railing against the excesses of global capitalism? None. His stomach rumbled just thinking about his lack of qualification. But railing against capitalism was apparently a sine qua non for contemporary critical discourse, and pointing out the liminal in Marx and Lenin was certainly not as taxing as trying to fact-check 3,500 words and hieroglyphs in twenty dead languages for which there is only one record in all of history. *Fucking* Hapax.

These extracurricular articles started to generate a buzz in Europe. Now when he entered his name into Google, every link was to a leftist cabal. He didn't think he had broken any laws, but given the company he kept online, he wasn't sure. His in-box was cluttered with hundreds of speaking opportunities from student groups all over Europe.

Compiling a scholarly itinerary worthy of presenting to President Gaskin had taken two months of back-and-forth with universities and generated dozens of auto-reply e-mails that whomever he was trying to contact was on vacation until September.

Compiling an itinerary qua theorist had taken all of three hours. The crucial first step was getting to Athens.

"Athens" was a poor filter for Burr's in-box, but he could think of no alternative. He entered the term and narrowed it down to a few hundred messages. He began with a recent e-mail from a Greek activist group. He opened it with caution, sure that he had animated some god-awful virus that would result in the collapse of the entire Mission University computer network. After finding that the electronic infrastructure appeared to be intact, he had replied that he was considering the invitation to talk and included a link to Ž_____'s response in the *New Left Review*.

Burr had his response from the Greek activists within the hour. He would be opening for the theorist whose ideas had spawned a billion-dollar film franchise: Jean Baudrillard. Once he confirmed, they would begin printing the posters. Needless to say, he had never seen his name on a poster.

᾽ΙΩΣΗΦΟΣ BAPP

He *tsk-tsk*ed his imagination at once for reverting to Classical when the sign would be Modern. Nevertheless.

They offered him 500-point font and an opportunity to mingle with an icon. No airline ticket, but still. He added a few provisional speaking engagements to his itinerary—he would send off the e-mails later, on the off chance Owen wasn't in Athens—Prague, Budapest, Paris, Barcelona, London, and Tokyo.

Professor Burr unlaced his Alden boots and buffed them with the elbow of his corduroy coat. After relacing the boots, he smoothed his wavy hair, realizing he might have done that in the wrong order again. When he looked soberly at the two proposals, he realized the *Hapax* talks were blanks; they would never garner real attention. Only a bold talk would bring out Owen. He stuffed the dissident proposal into a manila folder and transferred the prudent course to the credenza.

This talk would be a flare fired into the night, which would surely cause Owen to seek him out or at least reply to any one of the weekly e-mails Burr had sent.

His heels clacked down the still-empty sandstone arches. He was a tenured professor; his heels should clack. Sure, Mission University was a few tiers from the top, but Gaskin was here too, and he always seemed pleased with himself. Burr removed his coat and switched the folder to his left hand, trying to stem the torrent of perspiration at the thought of his meeting. He was never sure if he was going to be meeting Gerry, his friend and former colleague, or Gerard, his employer. Whichever one he found in the office, there were going to be handshakes. President Gaskin had a politician's grip, which was hell on Burr's right hand, poorly healed from punching a wall in the fall of '82 and connecting with a wooden stud. There are two ways to hold anything: with an open hand or with a closed fist. He had no business making fists, it was Iliadic; he held things with open, Odyssean hands. The orthopedist, a George Hamilton doppelganger, had laughed at him, even though he was affiliated with the university and had to have heard about Caroline. "These hurt *them*," he said, pointing to Burr's first two knuckles. "And these"—he pointed to the knuckles of Burr's ring finger and pinkie—"these hurt *you*. Don't hit any more walls, no matter what they say to provoke you."

The door opened too quickly, and he stumbled into the president's office. After she recovered from the brief shock, the administrative aide offered him coffee and ducked in to see the president.

—He's on a call, but he said to show you in.

President Gaskin made a scene of trying to disengage from the phone as Professor Burr stood before a wingback chair. The bookshelf behind the president was the perfect resting place for *Hapax*. None of these books looked like they had ever been cracked. He could sneak fifty copies in here, and no one would be the wiser. A framed picture of President Gaskin and Clint Eastwood rested on top of a mahogany humidor so that it would have to be moved when Gaskin was entertaining a dignitary: "Do you like Cubans? Here, hold this." On the ledge near Burr was a photograph of Bill Murray leaning heavily into a fairway wood and edging away from Gaskin's embrace.

The goldfish had been here during his father-in-law's administration. Ten years ago, he and Caroline's father would have been drinking rotgut whisky in silence and chain-smoking over the pedestal ashtray between the two chairs. Now the metal tray had been removed and the goldfish bowl fitted to the top of the pedestal. This goldfish bowl, certainly not the actual fish inside, was the third provision that Bill made before driving off that cliff. He wanted his grandson to be safe and had given Burr a job, a home, and a fish. There was some odd poetry to those three nouns that Burr could never get to the heart of. He thought about the words as the goldfish swam in and out of the sunken wreck on the gravel bottom. Plastic seaweed waved with an unseen current.

—Joe, how's Owen holding up? It's got to be tough on the kid to watch the team in Athens.

The president breathed through his teeth and shook his head as he settled in the opposite chair. He crushed Burr's hand and then threw himself into the wing of the wingback.

—I think he's doing what he wants to be doing.

—Bullshit. What kid doesn't want a gold medal? Like Knute Rockne said, "The next best thing to playing and winning is playing and losing." Don't give me the speech about how the Olympics would be a distraction. It's a crock of shit, and you know it. But I do applaud your efforts to get him back on his horse. Maybe it's different at Stanford, but only twenty percent of our kids who take a semester off end up with a diploma. He's working hard to finish a triple major this fall, I'm sure. Or what, you've got him doing a coterm?

—I don't have that much pull with him, I'm afraid. I had to call the registrar to find out what he studies.

—I see. I see.

Gaskin scratched at the burgundy leather with a fingernail, legs still crossed at the knee.

—So what are we talking about?

Professor Burr sat on the edge of his chair with an elbow patch on each thigh. After a few false starts he managed to spit something out:

—You see . . .

He stammered, he sputtered, he froze—none of which upset Gaskin's crossed-leg recline. Burr could see the safety of his tenure rolled up with the rugs and carried out the front door by a team of movers. No, this was too great a chance to take with a twenty-five-year career.

—I'd like to take a few weeks to speak at a conference on the use and abuse of the schwa in Proto-Indo-European languages.

—Impossible. Next.

Burr clapped his hands together and gritted his teeth. He wanted to be looking out the window with gravitas, but he couldn't take his eyes from the picture of Bill Murray.

The president leaned forward to give his next question a conspiratorial air:

—Is there anything else we need to discuss? What's in the folder?

—I've taken a few liberties with my position at Mission University that will most likely be brought to your attention before long.

—Sounds serious. Are you cooking drugs or selling off ancient pottery? Neither? Then why the long face, my friend? Listen, I won't say this on the record, but as a tenured professor you're allowed to be in any sort of consensual relationship with an adult so long as no one gets his or her feelings hurt. When feelings get hurt, these kind of things inevitably go public, and then I am *forced* to do something. You know that I don't like being forced to do anything. Listen. Because what I'm going to tell you now, I tell you as a friend. There's only one rule: Keep whoever you're seeing *very* happy. Congratulations, by the way. It's been a while. Why don't the two of you swing by for dinner? It will put your mind at ease as well as . . . hers?

—It's nothing like that. I have compromised my standing in the classics community by seeking a more popular audience.

—Go on.

—I have this . . . growing following on these Internet message boards. Some of them espouse anarchy, nearly all of them are anticapitalist. Do you remember what happened when Noam Chomsky spoke three years ago? I'm no Chomsky, but I do get the sense that my extracurricular writing has outpaced my scholarship. I never planned for this to happen. But these things snowball.

Gaskin laughed.

—Tell me, Joe, what percentage of these invitations do you suppose make it directly to your personal e-mail account? How many thousands of petitions addressed to you do you think my office received in the past year? Can't guess? Neither can I. But I can tell you I got a professor in CS to fix my e-mail account so that every message with your name in it goes straight to my spam folder. And I still didn't think this was serious enough to have you sweating. You really imagined this was a secret?

—I suppose I thought you would have said something if you knew.

—What's there to say? Hell, there's a copy of the *New Left Review* article in here somewhere. That little shit from the Federalist Society brought it over and demanded your tenure be revoked. I'll tell you what I told him: there's nothing wrong with being popular. To be honest, Joe, I'm glad a professor finally got the memo. The trustees are berating me to get you guys on talk shows or CNN or something. Here's a phrase that will keep you up at night: post-tenure review. It's coming. I'm fighting for you guys, but it's coming. Look, Joe, my default assumption is that everyone here is a goddamn Marxist; that's the only explanation I've got as to why none of you realize that Mission is a business. If you ever figure that out, god help us all, I'll make you dean of faculty.

—Well, I don't know the first thing about business, so you're going to have to find another reason to promote me. I've tried speculation, which ended . . . poorly. I've tried pure scholarship, but you've already highlighted the limits of that approach. Maybe provocation is the way to get a bigger paycheck. Just this morning I received an invitation to speak with Jean Baudrillard in Athens.

—Fantastic! But all kidding aside, there's no way we can re-negotiate your salary this year. The endowment hasn't recovered from its Pets.com position.

—Pets? No. Gerard, what I'm saying is that I can't keep turning down these speaking engagements. These are huge audiences, thousands. Here, have a look at this.

He took the itinerary from the folder and placed it on the president's desk.

—Art galleries in London? A stadium in Spain? This is great news, my friend. You're definitely not going to have a problem getting this sabbatical past the provost's office. You represent a clear value to the university. These stadium talks may well be the most significant academic development of the fall semester. The alumni magazine hasn't gone to press yet; we should be able to get you on next month's cover. Or should we wait? Either way, you have my full support for sabbatical leave.

—Well, there's more to it than that. As you may remember, I took leave three years ago to finish my book.

The president looked at the shelf behind him and then looked over the other shoulder. Neither finding the book, nor recalling so much as the title, he responded:

—Fine piece of scholarship. Testament to the university. People will be reading that book for the next hundred years. But forget all that, Joe. Our course catalogue for fall is already printed, but we need to get you in the Philosophy Department as soon as possible.

—I'm a classicist, Gerard. This isn't some hobby I can just drop. I've built my life around my work, and if that work is not appreciated, then I can—

—Jesus, Joe. Slow down. No one is suggesting you abandon your career. I'm just saying you need to augment it. Like it or not, classics is dead.

—That's neither fair nor funny.

—The storm's coming, Joe. Whether you like it or not. You have what, twenty-five seniors majoring in classics? There are three times as many Portuguese majors. Portuguese, Joe. Granted, they all figured out early on that there hasn't been a grade lower than a B in that department in a decade. But, hey, I applaud that sort of initiative. They found a way to become the third biggest language department at the university. Keep the customer satisfied, *ibid*. Find a way to attract more students, or your department will be absorbed by History in the next four years.

—Technically this new work is theory, not philosophy.

President Gaskin looked close to throwing the paperweight he had been gripping through the bay windows overlooking the quad. Then he saw that Burr wasn't being his usual pedantic self; he was smiling.

—Look at you. Hmph. Mission University may be yours in a few years' time. But while it's still mine, let's have a glass of the 18-year. Neat's fine?

—Please.

—You'll have to accept half pay unless you want me to start a war with the provost.

—I'm sorry, but I can't. Owen forfeited his scholarship in light of his recent injury. He's two quarters shy of his diploma, and it's too late to apply for loans.

—How about we make up the difference by paying you to lodge visiting scholars, of which I'm sure there will be none? Classes start next Wednesday—can you find a replacement?

—Already done.

The president looked at the itinerary again.

—Jesus! You're speaking in Athens in four days.

—Nothing has been confirmed yet.

—Should I know who this Baudrillard guy is?

—Oh yes. He's a very big deal.

—Do you have anything to promote other than yourself and the university?

—No.

—This could be big, Joe. I'll authorize the leave under the auspices of serving as a university liaison to the Olympics. We have a young man on the kayak team, and it's not entirely far-fetched to think that you and Owen would be well suited to the role of ambassadors. I assume Owen is going with you. You'll barely get there for the closing ceremony, but I'm sure I can make something up. It would be a great help if you could get back here before midterms—or at least Thanksgiving.

—I'll see what I can do.

President Gaskin refilled Burr's drink and handed him a picture frame so that he could grab a cigar to chew on.

Before he'd had time to finish his drink, Burr was shooed out of the office because of a pressing call from the athletics director. Mission University, he learned, was in the running for a top basketball prospect.

At first Burr was relieved to be dismissed from the principal's office. Then he grew indignant, refusing to accept that he was less important to the university's future than a sixteen-year-old phenom. Burr clacked his heels as loud as they could clack down the sandstone archway from the president's office to the humanities library.

Gaskin would never have pressed him on it, but he hadn't the foggiest what Baudrillard had written. Had he actually written anything, or was he just a figurehead? After the computer terminal confirmed that, yes, he had published a dozen books in the three years it took Burr to write *Hapax*, Burr grabbed the stub of a wooden pencil and wrote Baudrillard's name on the Author line of several call slips.

The librarian returned with *Simulacrum and Simulation* crowning a two-foot stack of hardcovers. Burr could feel eyes on him. Turning, he found one of his most talented students of the past few years, who had, regrettably, veered toward Sanskrit and chosen a different adviser. The student wasn't hiding his inspection of the titles. Burr coughed.

—Have to reread some of these French thinkers to stay in shape, you know.

—I know what you mean. You have to constantly refresh to keep Badiou distinct from Bourdieu, Bataille from Baudrillard from Barthes from Blanchot. To be fair, it seems like Baudrillard confuses himself with Bataille, and Blanchot. But Bataille exudes a primality, "a communion with the spirit of language" as you once said in lecture, that makes me think he read his Greek.

Burr was drowning. At first he was thrilled to think of himself in that tangle of B's. But there was a name in there that he hadn't heard since grad school. He began to sweat. The poor lighting of the atrium hid his discomfort. The student stood by silently, waiting to record whatever Burr said. He had to say something.

—To be sure. The Gauls' historical role has been to remind the Germanic hordes of one thing: the lyre is every bit as primitive as the drum.

—Peace is just as primal as violence?

—I couldn't have said it better myself.

Face saved, he noted that it was quite late and walked briskly to the door. With a student like that, you have to keep conversation as pithy as possible.

The US water polo match began in an hour, and it just so happened he was desperately in need of a drink. He drove home and then walked to his local.

The Tilted Wig had screened every minute of the Olympics. The Wig wasn't a bar with TV screens at the everglowing ready. It was a thick-lacquered place for conversation whose owner cared enough to hang his collection of maritime lanterns and light them every night. During the day, the head of your pint could be cobalt blue, cranberry red, or topaz, depending on which glaze of the stained glass window the sun was shining through.

In the month leading up to the Games, Burr had reiterated to Sonny, the bartender/proprietor, that they would need a television these last weeks of August. It was like a doctor telling a patient that he needs to start smoking; the message was jarring enough to get Sonny's attention. Sonny ran his bar on a cash-only basis and used a brass till, even though he had to thump the side every time he wanted it to open. He'd rather burn down the bar than mount a flat-screen TV, but a projector seemed innocuous enough. Sonny's big summer project had been mounting a projector to the ceiling and then camouflaging the box and wires with metallic paint.

On August 13, 2004, Sonny and Burr clinked pint glasses to a parade of Olympians waving mini flags and summer hats on the back wall of the Wig. Burr squinted and pointed to the projection as the US delegation marched toward the dartboards, but never convinced himself that it was Owen in the infield, watching fireworks bloom behind the Olympic flame.

Since the opening ceremony, Burr had held vigil every afternoon. He sat close to the wall-projected image, hoping to catch sight of Owen in the crowd or in street clothes at the end of the bench. He explained to Sonny that although the commentary was grating, the announcers were likely to mention Owen's absence and possibly reveal a helpful tidbit as to his whereabouts. Sonny agreed to shout down his midday patrons, but only during water polo games.

The audio was on when Burr walked through the door.

Sonny began pouring a pint.

—Hear anything today?

—Had a baby shower in here for lunch. They didn't seem to mind looking closely at a screen of young guys in Speedos. I offered them a round if they found Owen. No luck.

Burr watched his first Guinness settle.

—Could I trouble you for a shot of Bloody Mary mix?

Sonny knew that order was coming. Rather than shake his head, he just pretended to forget and made Burr order it every time.

—In the highly unlikely event that a man named Gerard Gaskin ever makes it in here, I'd appreciate it if you would keep Owen's uncertain whereabouts under your hat. I kind of implied that he was back at Stanford.

—Gaskin comes here on Tuesdays. He'd say it's on account of the Uilleann pipe players, but he's not Irish and they've usually packed up by the time he arrives. Could have something to do with the Greek girls ordering Cosmopolitans.

—Bill Dennison banned them from campus.

—Greeks or Cosmos?

—He sent an editorial to the *Times* titled "Barbarians in the Gates." Then he revoked charters. When he discovered that he couldn't actually do that, he banned school parties in bars.

—I remember. Those were lean years. Nearly put me out of business.

—Might have had more to do with the state of your restroom.

—Actually it was mostly your bar tab.

That landed harder than Sonny had intended. The year after

Caroline, Burr had indeed run up a grisly bar tab, one beer and one whisky at a time, that they had to work out. Burr motioned to the sports and grabbed his two glasses.

His standard snug was a mahogany-stained booth at the back of the bar, where he drank his Guinness and sipped his Bloody Mary mix from a double shot glass. Caroline's only gripes had been about his sodium intake and his drinking. Thankfully she wasn't around to see the hypertensive man he had become. In youth, when his metabolism was too high to get hangovers, he drank cheap red wine and port. His head hurt just thinking about all those empty bottles and full ashtrays.

They came here in the days before the Wig was a stop on the bachelorette party circuit. Back then it was peanuts on the floor and everyone shocked that a young blonde touched by the gods themselves would be in this of all places and with him of all men. He was always stunned too, but pretended not to be. These days he took care even to unwrap her memory, as if his hands might slip and change her eyes from green to brown, as if she might fly straight from his chest and dissolve into impossibility.

—What is that?! he yelled at the screen.

After ten years of watching this sport he still had no idea what constituted a minor foul versus an exclusion. Regardless, it was a good excuse to yell. More significant for him was the term *exclusion*, which called to mind his liminal critique of the law of the excluded middle—a critique even he was tired of resurrecting. But this was precisely the sort of content that his lay audience would require: the fundamental laws of rationality are wrong—or at least this one is. He went back to the bar for another pint. And a shot. And a pint.

—Sonny, if I'm standing in a doorway, am I in the room or out of the room?

—If you're standing in the doorway, I'd say you're in the way.

—There's something to that. It is a way. A process. A noun of verbs. I would be standing in a Process that people mistake for a Thing. And you know the secret? Everything is a process. That beer is not a thing, even though it appears on my tab as an item. It's a service.

—Preaching to the choir. I've poured enough Guinness to know it's a process.

Sonny paused. Then looked Burr square in the eye.

—Joe, you're talking like someone who's about to make a sharp turn.

—Just got the okay from Gaskin to take off on a European lecture tour. He thinks it's going to be big. I'm just hoping it will be big enough to show up on Owen's radar.

—Settling up before you emigrate?

The professor walked quickly to the screen, thinking he'd caught sight of Owen on the far end of the bench. The young man wasn't wearing a robe—none of them were—which meant he'd need to pack for warmer weather than the paper had led him to believe. He was convinced that the athlete sitting in the corner of the frame was Owen—or at least had the exact same physique. He stood, squinted, walked in a few steps, before realizing that this player had a rounder face. And he wasn't wearing an eye patch.

At that point he began moderating his drinking a bit. The commentator became very animated at the word *brutality*. Burr gave in to the tenor of his afternoon and began repeating the word with his Sean Connery accent:

—Brutality.

No one was around to laugh or give him a strange look.

Some of this commentator's language was quite colorful. And they'd taken care to place him with a good straight man.

—Now you just said Wigo bunnied the goalie. What do you mean, "bunny"?

—You'll see it on the replay here. Wolf with a great step-out gets out of the water to his suit and rips it right over the goalie's head. Between the bunny ears.

He had never heard Owen talk like that, and thought the announcer was exaggerating the argot for effect. The one thing that the players did yell incessantly was "Slough slough slough," perhaps the most disagreeable word one can hear shouted a thousand times in an afternoon.

Burr closed his eyes and hoped the announcer would know to explain Owen's absence from the squad, perhaps by way of explaining their loss, and perhaps cue a crowd shot of his son. But no mention was made of Owen. They cut to field hockey, and he stood to leave.

Sonny extended a hand.

—Good luck in Athens. Just stay away from the homemade raki, and you'll be fine.

Burr walked past a group of students waiting in line to see a rapper perform in the main auditorium. Could he compete with a rapper for these students' attention? He would see in Athens, before a crowd of thousands. One of whom might be his son.

He made it the mile from bar to home without incident, grabbed a few Baudrillard books from his trunk, and collapsed on the leather chair in the study.

Burr selected Cannonball Adderley from his rotating tray of CDs. He tried to make sense of Baudrillard. Either he was really drunk or this text was really opaque. Perhaps both. He put some gas on the fire and opened a bottle of 4 Puttonyos Tokaji he had been saving for a special occasion. The floral aromatics of the sweet wine clashed with the well-worn pages. He detected a hint of graphite. These ideas had been digested. The pages had been touched, absorbed. He wanted this fate for *Hapax*. He wanted the highlighters, stretched spines from photocopying, ink notes in margin—even though this was a library book. The self-pity in the air would have been overpowering were there not also a bracing note of excitement. Renown by association was renown no less. Sweet thoughts of being heard by a large crowd, lemon thoughts of connection, leapt from the heavily underlined and dog-eared pages. He was happy for Baudrillard, not jealous of these well-cared-for, which is to say lived-in, books. As the bottle began to vanish, he teetered on the edge of maudlin. Luckily his terror at what might happen on that Athens stage kept him from drowning in his cups. But it didn't keep him from falling asleep in his chair.

Burr woke up to the sunlight—a problem, given that his flight was at 8:00 a.m. He threw a few handfuls of clothes into a canvas duffel, folded a half dozen suits and shirts into a hanging bag, and stuffed the Mission University copies of *Simulacrum and Simulation* and *America* into his laptop case.

On his way out the door he remembered his passport. He grabbed the first hundred pages, Aare-Atuamatariri, of the unfinished French translation of *Hapax*, and threw it in the passenger seat with his duffel. He slammed the car into reverse without looking back and would have destroyed a garage door had he not previously had it removed for the very theory he was on his way to promote.

The professor spent the flight trying to imagine himself as a provocative man. Provocateur. One who provokes. Invoke, evoke, revoke . . . Do provocative men trace etymology? Not likely. He squinted at the flight attendant, trying to look both dangerous and mysterious.

—Are you okay, sir?

This wasn't going to work. But it didn't have to. He was really just banking on the posters being printed and his name attached to the event. He didn't need to deliver the actual speech for Owen to get the message.

This would be his first lay audience. Whatever they might or might not know, he was certain that they would boo him off the stage if he came across as condescending. This made his whole "You have been lied to your whole lives" strategy a bit suspect. He had his first line ready: "The twentieth century was ruled by the Subliminal. This century will be devoted to the Liminal." He juggled emphasis: "The *twentieth* . . . The twentieth *century* . . ." It would really be best to avoid beginning a provocative speech with a passive sentence construction. He drank. He slept.

Rosy-fingered dawn appeared at the horizon just before he landed. She reached up and slid her palm under the belly of the plane, then closed her fingers in a gentle cascade. The windows grew warm in her clutch until they blended into the tarmac. Passengers applauded the landing.

A young man with long brown hair was waiting for Burr in his hotel lobby. He'd had to check the name several times because the university always put him up in the Grande Bretagne or the King George; this was far rougher than either.

—Joe? George Skandos. Good to meet you.

Joe? He had never been one for titles or yessirs or even respect insofar as it extended beyond common decency and practical considerations. But dammit, they had invited him, and this young man wasn't even thirty.

—I don't go by Joe, actually.

The young man looked as if he had just been slapped.

—Professor Burr, I apologize for not being at the airport . . . I wasn't there for Jean either. I'm afraid there has been a logistical emergency.

Upon further examination, "Joe" somehow sounded provocative when this young man said it.

—It's fine. Really. And you can call me Joe if you prefer. Joe or Professor B.

147

—Fine, Joe . . . Right now we don't have a stage. The mayor caved to American pressure and deemed our event an unacceptable security risk during the Games.

—Where does that leave us?

—In limbo. As of now, we are scrambling to find an alternative venue, but I'm afraid it is going to be far from the city center.

—Couldn't we just speak in the streets?

—Jean said the same thing. For him every bureaucratic pitfall is an opportunity to return to the glory days of Paris '68, so I expected that from him. But I am a bit surprised to hear you advocate "taking it to the streets."

—It's far from ideal, but I would like to speak before the Olympics crowd has cleared out.

—You won't have to worry about crowd size. There are sure to be well over five thousand students who show up to hear— well, let's be honest, they're really going to be waiting to hear Jean, but in a decade they may look back at the event and remember it as the night they heard you speak. This is something like your international debut? But no. There's no chance that the mayor is going to let people listen to leftist taunts in a city square when he has already deemed too threatening a university auditorium in Zografou.

This was the first time Burr had been called a leftist. It was exciting, but it seemed like they had the wrong man. This was also the first time he had heard an estimate of the audience size. For a crowd of five thousand, he was willing to be a leftist, socialist, Maoist, whatever. That size crowd, during the middle of the Olympics, serving up whatever blend of dissent Baudrillard had concocted, would surely get Owen's attention. He could only miss it if he were living in a cave.

—You won't have to worry about crowd size—provided the talk even happens. This doesn't look good. We're no strangers to improvisation, but we've never met this much international pressure. This is the best I have in the way of an itinerary . . . as you can imagine, everything is subject to change.

The professor was handed a gaggle of acronyms, typos, acronyms that looked like typos, and a full schedule of crossed-out speaking engagements and time slots listed TBA. Conspicuously absent was any engagement with the Olympic crowd. He had expected to find hologrammed tickets and an all-access pass in the inner pocket of a binder. In comparison, the sheet of paper seemed a little flimsy.

—I need to mention an elephant in the room, and I hope you don't take offense, but the word *Olympics* doesn't appear once on this sheet. I'm not sure if you are aware, but I am officially here as a liaison.

—Perhaps my English is not so good. You understand you are speaking at a conference against state hegemony, and it would be glaringly hypocritical for us to be involved with something as postcolonial as the Olympics? Oh. I see. You were joking.

—Not really, no.

—You want to make time to go watch sports?

—I'm no fanatic, but I would like to see the spectacle.

George seemed to be looking over Burr's head. Burr leaned up to catch his gaze and then felt a hand clap on his shoulder.

—Sounds like a splendid idea!

Professor Burr turned around to find a man in khaki pants, a crisp white shirt, and a blue linen coat. His strong jaw, bushy eyebrows, and aviator-rim glasses reminded Burr of Tommy Lee Jones. He leapt forward to take Burr's hand.

—Jean Baudrillard. Pleasure to meet you, Professor Burr.

His manner was as firm as his grip. A patient grin. He was presumably happy to hear Burr stammer in French rather than immediately taking their conversation to English.

—Go unpack, and I'll arrange the details with George. Is there anything in particular you'd like to see?

—The US water polo team plays tonight. I need to go for personal reasons.

Baudrillard looked genuinely puzzled.

—I'll see what I can do.

—Oh, I almost forgot. I brought you a copy of my latest book. The unbound pages are from an incomplete French translation I'm having some grad students help me with. I'm hoping to win an endorsement from L'Académie française.

Baudrillard recognized *Hapax* immediately for what it was. He read an entry, his finger marking his place, then held the book in front of him as if he had been given something as obsolete as a Laserdisc player, thinking, no doubt, of how he was going to fit this new ten-pound contraption into his luggage or in the small rubber trash can in his room.

He smiled.

The dusty air of Athens looked as if it might catch fire. Chalk-white buildings, like the cirrus clouds wisping the bright sky, drifted together or drifted apart; it was an architecture subject to plate tectonics. Some buildings leaned in as if bowed in prayer. In a century, their upper floors would touch foreheads with the building opposite. Others fell back, increasingly estranged from their neighbors. Athens ever-bright. Brightness unavoidable, because in this city Burr always looked up.

In his earlier life, Burr had traveled here for dozens of conferences. Those trips adhered to a well-established formula: (1) a walk through his host's building, culminating in coffee and baklava in a conference room; (2) dinner at a taverna with a three-hour decline in the quality of wine and the originality of thought—the espresso course being most similar to the recitation of a Works Cited; (3) the conference itself; and finally; (4) an apology from a drunk dinner guest, which was really an overture to blurb said dinner guest's forthcoming book. Athens had given him some of his sharpest memories, but it had never given him a chance to roam.

This was Olympics Athens, where a vast current of tourists in soccer jerseys from all nations and hats of all outlandishness swept past Burr and Baudrillard whichever direction they walked. Rare was the unadorned neck. Every tourist over thirty wore a camera necklace or a lanyard holding prized tickets to an event. Like a blackjack player counting cards, Burr kept a running total of lanyards versus cameras. Lanyards were winning by 31 when he turned to his companion.

Baudrillard was certainly not a lanyard man. He did carry a camera with him, and he carried it like a billy club. The photography books had been an unexpected surprise in the two-foot stack of books that the Mission University librarian hauled to the desk. Burr was surprised that Baudrillard took pictures, and he was surprised at the pictures themselves. Every picture looked silent. As they walked, Burr heard the shutter snap and the gear wind and click at the ready. He wondered if any of these shots from the Athens din would have that same quiet.

The crowd thinned. No one trampled their shadows. Baudrillard's shadow overlapped Burr's own on the honeycomb street tiles, a darker intersection drawn on the stone. He thought the pooled shadows before the two of them would make a good photo and thought, perhaps, a fan might be taking it right now. As vain as it was to admit it, he saw the image reprinted in an intellectual biography: "Baudrillard and companion" in the first edition; "Baudrillard and Joseph Burr" in the second edition; "Baudrillard and Burr" thereafter.

—I love all of the face paint, Baudrillard said.

—Very Celtic.

—I suppose they have stencils for this sort of thing.

—I think most of these flags, at least the ones that kids wear in the USA, are stickers.

They stopped and watched the crowd.

—That reversal is telling: it is a movement from land, in the form of pigments, applied to *visage*, to *Visage* applied to land. It's lazy.

—The difference between an athlete and a fan. I've never been either, but my son is the former. Or rather, he used to be. And in my experience, athletes neither apply symbols nor wish to become symbols. Olympians have a unique view of subjectivity; they are almost unconscious when they are performing. I'd say they're vacant—in a non-pejorative sense.

—I would never presume emptiness is a bad thing. Emptiness and sight are closely linked. You can only see when it is empty.

—*Vide* and *videre*. You're right, of course. You can only use a chalkboard when it is wiped clean. Historically, however, I believe it's a false etymology.

—Then you would say it is both true and false.

Burr was shocked, literally speechless, that Baudrillard was alluding to liminality.

—Isn't that what you say? Everything is both true and false? Or am I reading you wrong?

—No . . . that's right. Absolutely right.

—The one question I had, and pardon me if this comes across as an attack, is, "How is what you're saying any different than the Buddhist notion of Bardo?"

Burr flushed and became defensive.

—As far as I know, Bardo represents the intervening time between death and reincarnation.

—That's just one Bardo. There are six.

—To be sure. But the very act of dividing requires fixed points. *I* am never born—birth is something my mind doesn't have access to—nor do *I* ever die. *I* am everything in between those two points, but for me, as a subject, the points necessarily do not exist. But it's not just people. I am saying that *everything* is Bardo; everything is betwixt and between. There are no real identities, only relational identities.

—And how far do you take this?

—All the way. As far as I'm concerned, Aristotle's three laws of thought are only a useful approximation and should be torn down.

—Ah. I get it. That's why you were so insistent that we see this game against Serbia and Montenegro, a plural singular. You wanted me to make the connection myself.

—That was a coincidence. We're here for my son, Owen.

—You said he was an athlete. In water polo?

—Yes.

—Will he be here today?

—That's my hope.

—Your hope. I suppose I don't need to ask why you lost touch. There's only ever one reason.

Burr faced Baudrillard and waited for the full explanation.

—Men in our profession don't have less-stubborn children. Ever. You said before that he *was* an athlete. Is he now a trainer or a coach?

—He's only twenty-two years old. He had a horrible injury in November. The plan had always been for him to anchor the US team in Athens in 2004, then Beijing in 2008, then give up water polo entirely and focus on his real life. He surprised everyone by making the Sydney roster at just eighteen. But this was supposed to be his year.

Baudrillard looked at Burr critically, wondering how an

Olympic physique could have emerged from this slightly pearish form.

—His bags were more or less packed for the training facility in Colorado Springs when in his final collegiate game, in a horrible instance of brutality, an opposing player punctured his eye, rupturing it instantly. He had surgery and then basically disappeared.

—How basically?

—Totally. No one has heard from him in six months. I asked everyone at his school. I even hired a consultant to tell me how to proceed. This is the only place we could guess that he would be.

—Then I suppose we have to find tickets. Let me handle it— scalpers are my people.

Burr didn't want to get arrested on the eve of his talk, but he could easily picture Gaskin's pleased reaction to the page-five story: NOTED INTELLECTUALS ARRESTED IN TICKET SCALPING SCANDAL.

Baudrillard took the lead:

—I can't see anyone but cops. The Metro is always a safe bet for contraband. Scalpers. You have to take your hat off to whoever neutered a term for state-sponsored genocide.

Burr hesitated, then finally asked a question:

—So you're a Marxist?

—Recovering post-Marxist, maybe. I went to rehab in the early eighties. You're never fully recovered. But the last thing I want to do today is talk theory. We'll save all that for tomorrow.

Burr understood the playful reproach, but had no idea how Baudrillard sounded so much more authoritative just by putting a *post* in front of something. The problem with Burr's background in classics was that he always used *pre* and rarely *post*.

He repeated the observation to Baudrillard.

—My goal is always to be ahead. Working-class origins kept me from ever having academic ambitions. Keep your university;

to me it's just a factory. All I want is to be ahead until I die. Actually, to be so far ahead that I have to say, "*Putain*, I forgot to die!"

They swam against the current of painted-belly tourists. Plastic whistles of neon pink blasted over the calm conductor calls of the departing train. After they'd made it halfway down the stairs, the crowd began to drive them back to the light. Baudrillard knifed his shoulder forward and Burr followed. They trod over feet until they were past the crowd.

Only two types of people remained in the station after the surge had passed: young people in concentric rings, heads resting on thighs, feet touching feet, and thumbs either holding open paperbacks or rolling up Zig-Zag papers; or mid-thirties men in Hugo Boss jackets with fanny packs worn low and facing front like nylon codpieces.

Burr made eye contact with one of the scalpers, which was enough for the man to briskly walk over.

—Two for water polo, please.

Both Baudrillard and the scalper laughed at Burr's succinctness.

—Track and field, yes. Got tickets to everything. Empty stadiums. You name it. Hundred-meter-hurdle final ticket will cost you a hundred bucks apiece, face price is two hundred. Basketball is three fifty for the pair . . .

Baudrillard took over the negotiations.

—Can you help us with water polo or not? The game is in an hour. USA–Serbia.

The scalper asked another young man with a fanny pack, who, after texting a friend, shook his head.

They returned to the afternoon glare, empty hands shading their eyes. Burr was puzzled at how the scalpers could make a profit selling tickets below face value.

—Are we sure those tickets aren't fake?

—The scalpers get most of their inventory from no-shows in

tourist groups. Which is a fantastic idea, actually. Let's cut out the middleman, as they say.

Baudrillard led them to a nearby parking lot with monstrous tour buses of silver, blue, and white. A flamingo-pink bus passed two sky-blue buses, a sideways sunset as it slowly rolled to the curb. Baudrillard waited by the door, offering a hand when the tour operator alighted. As the passengers stretched and snapped pictures, Baudrillard glanced through a schedule on the operator's clipboard. He returned, shaking his head.

—Danes. Unless you think your son has a newfound interest in handball, I suggest we look elsewhere.

Before he could finish, Burr was at the steps of a green and red bus apologizing for his Italian.

Baudrillard smiled from the sidelines, tamping his hand-rolled cigarette on his left wrist.

Burr held up two oversize tickets, their silver holograms a green flash in the sun.

Any man wearing a shirt was overdressed. Baudrillard, who was sitting on his jacket and had now rolled up his sleeves, looked more the part than Burr in his linen suit. The game was still fifteen minutes from starting, but the crowd was already chanting. The Slavs seemed disappointed that the American fans wouldn't engage in friendly banter. Instead, the former Yugoslavians contented themselves with heckling the citizens of other Balkan nations who hadn't been able to get a better ticket than the USA game.

—Did you sit us on this side because you think I'll root against America?

—No, that's all the guy had. And this way I can see the whole US contingent and look for a parent who could help me find my lost son.

The phrase *my lost son* hung in the air.

—Excuse me. I see a guy I know. I'm going to ask him if he's seen or heard anything.

Burr apologized to the dozen fans he filed past, circled around to the USA stands, and climbed to the top rails, attentive as a concession vendor. On his descent, he found one father, himself an Olympian. He was confused by Burr's gesture, which looked like he was asking the man to roll down the window. The father finally stood, commanding a wave of interceding fans to stand, and walked to the aisle without taking his eyes from the US squad firing balls into goalposts and passing back and forth with a dizzying pace.

Screeching bagpipes accompanied some sort of rap music on the PA. To talk over the music, which was exhorting the fans to jump around, was nearly impossible. Burr motioned for the father to lean down and yelled in the man's ear:

—Have you seen Owen?

Now the father appeared to recognize Burr. His tight jaw loosened and he clapped Burr on the arm.

—How's he doing? Is he here?

—Well . . . yes. Somewhere. I just lost him. Have you seen him around?

—Afraid not. Wish him my best. It was a real loss to the team . . .

The second chorus began quickly after the first. This time fans were actually jumping. Burr nodded like a bobblehead doll, and the Olympian father smiled and rejoined his family.

Burr walked back to Baudrillard, defeated. Baudrillard, loath to talk theory off the clock, tried to lift the mood.

—Who was that guy? Is he competing?

—He could be.

—We're in the belly of the beast. I never feel comfortable at these things. The experience is so fascist. We are so far removed from the field of play that the athletes are no more than their fascia.

It took Burr a moment, but he processed the comment and became animated; a real theorist was engaging him as an equal.

—There's an important performative difference with water polo: you and I cannot, nor could we ever, compete in even a rudimentary fashion.

Baudrillard smiled.

—I swim quite well.

—With all due respect, I doubt you could tread water while a hundred-kilo man tries to drown you. I know I can't do it. I have enough trouble just floating.

—You're proving the hyperreality of ritualized combat. Most sports begin as a mutation from something that once existed. Unlike football, a sport that historians argue is a simulation of kicking the decapitated head of a Danish prince through town, this sport is a simulacrum. Grown men swimming around and throwing a ball into a net is symbolic of nothing. It lacks a referent. Water polo is perfect. I can't imagine a sport with less of a link to reality.

—Athletes represent nations.

—You're assuming nations exist, which is clearly wrongheaded when watching Serbia and Montenegro. Did your son ever seem to represent anything?

—He didn't appear to think much about it. His movements seemed compelled.

—Narcissus was compelled.

—Narcissus was impelled. The desire came from within.

Burr still said things like this involuntarily. He kicked himself for it. He kept making mistakes. Now that he was inside the Olympic venue, he realized how wrongheaded he'd been to bring them here in the first place: if Owen had any attachment to the team, or competition more broadly, then he would find it impossible to look on as a spectator. Even Burr felt the tension to do something, to compete. Baudrillard, however, looked bored to tears.

—We can leave if you like.

—Absolutely not. Friendship would be so much simpler if people understood that criticism, for me, is rarely a condemnation.

The teams finished their warm-ups and then huddled around their coaches. The American coach, in a polo shirt, clapped and exuded calm. The Serbian coach, in safari khaki, kept one finger pointed at the pool and hammered down his arm until every player knew that nothing short of total dominance would be tolerated.

Seven men on two sides lined on their respective goal lines. They drove their legs in eggbeater kicks, waiting for the referee's inhale, not his actual whistle, to crash toward the midline, led by a sprinter bearing down on his opposite number.

Each of these sprinters could have been swimming in the fifty-meter final with a slightly different training regimen and a radically different attitude toward violence. At this level, the best swimmer on each team is very close to the limit of human performance. As a result, the race for that yellow Mikasa ball floating in the middle of the pool is always tied for the first thirteen meters. It's the final two meters that dictate who wins the tip-off. The winner is he who swims harder at the charging player—imagine running toward a brick wall and accelerating right before impact.

Burr, who knew what was coming, was mesmerized by the obliviousness of that yellow Mikasa ball, caught in the middle of two arrowing forces: >•<

The water rose slightly over the sprinters' caps and fell off in a great trough behind the advancing V. Both sides met in-phase and swelled a meter over the pool's edge. The USA sprinter timed his last stroke perfectly and tipped the ball back to his side, simultaneously turning his back to the Serb and crashing into him.

The crowd roared, not for the players, not for the result, but for the sheer spectacle of colliding waves. Baudrillard applauded.

—Beautiful.

Burr thought of responding with a line from Book 20 of the *Iliad*, the crash of conflict as Achilles reenters the fray, but bit his tongue and clapped. His companion had in one word absolved him of decades of shame at feeling the beauty of sport.

—That's going to be tough to top, Baudrillard continued. It's like beginning a symphony with a crescendo. Like . . .

—Like . . .

—I'm glad neither of us knows the first thing about classical music! I've always had an allergy to high culture.

The Serbian hole defender kneaded the points of both elbows into the trapezius of the USA hole man. He kept both hands palm open and faced the ref, showing that he wasn't fouling even though the American was thrashing about. A wet entry pass came from the wing. The Serb leapt for the ball and was whistled for a foul. After a kick-out pass the fight resumed.

—Total disregard for the whistle, apparently.

—I've watched this dozens of times, and I can't tell you a thing about the fouls.

—They can't touch the bottom?

—It's ten feet deep.

—They're like centaurs. The boundary of the water creates a doubling of distance between spectator and athlete. It is a skin that we cannot . . .

Burr couldn't keep his eyes off the bench. He tried to compare the grown versions of these players to the teenage versions he had seen on the junior national team. Come to think of it, that was the last game he had seen. The only player who might recognize him was Wolf Wigo, who was always at the center of the action in the pool. Burr was startled by the roar that swept over his section at a Serbian goal. The head coach gritted his teeth, looked at the clock, then looked at the stands.

—If I look too closely there—

Baudrillard pointed to the spot just before the goal.

—I get vertigo.

—It's called the hole.

—Fitting as a locus of disappearance.

It certainly was for Owen, Burr thought.

The first quarter ended, giving them a moment to talk.

—I suppose we can't smoke in here until a Serb lights the first road flare.

—You're thinking of soccer.

—These guys certainly look capable of swinging road flares. The only reason they're not is because it's a day game.

—It's one of the biggest sports in the Balkans. A lot of these young men will go on to play professional water polo in Greece, Serbia, Hungary, Italy . . . a future that for some reason I always feared for Owen.

—Do they play much water polo in America?

—Only in California.

—Because of the climate, I suspect. But it's also consistent with the role of appearance and disappearance. California is a state that wants to do both. Like Eastern European countries where the sport has also taken a hold, yes? Plunge and resurface.

The second quarter provided a few stoppages for them to talk about what was happening above the water *contra* what was happening below. Neither was remotely interested in pursuing a psychoanalytic interpretation, so they dropped it and enjoyed the rest of the half.

The teams filed into the locker rooms, and the PA music began. Baudrillard spoke:

—You and I are very similar, you know. I admire the fact that you don't try to reconcile antagonism. Why pay attention to the resolution of conflict? Inconsistency reveals everything.

—Yes, but are you so sure consistency even exists? I view it as an illusion. In reality, everything is inconsistent—which is of course a paradox that makes perfect sense.

Baudrillard pulled a mini bottle of Campari from the side pocket of his coat.

—I thought like you when I was twenty.

The comment could have been taken as malicious, but Baudrillard's tone was whimsical. And he said it while offering Burr a second mini bottle: sambuca.

He continued:

—All of the pataphysicians were interested in paradox, but paradox as a disruptive force rather than a unifying one. I'm more positive than that.

—Can you give me some sense of what the crowd will be like tomorrow?

—A lot depends on you. You have two choices when confronting an audience: fascinate or seduce. I would argue that these two are opposites. Fascinating speakers group the audience into one bundle. The bundle is flammable, but it is not in itself disruptive. A speaker who seduces, however, isolates each audience member and whispers in her ear. It is impossible to seduce a room. You can, however, seduce a man or woman. Disruption. And, depending on who you are whispering to, potentially very explosive. Even though I am a Frenchman through and through, I am not seductive. I am fascinating.

—So long as you're not boring or repulsive, which, as an American in Europe, is my constant fear.

—Yes. I am focusing on the positives here.

—I thought you were in the business of being radical.

—I've seen enough fire. To answer your question more specifically, the kind of young people who will be there tomorrow night—see, there I go again, grouping them together!—this audience will be ready for seduction. The question remains, are you a fascinator or a seducer? You are going to have to choose.

—I've never been either.

—Then they'll make you one or the other.

The teams emerged from the locker rooms in bathrobes with their caps already knotted. Wolf Wigo led the American team with an even pace, eyes straight ahead. In team-issued slide-on sandals they shuffled to the pool's edge. Looking closely, Burr could see the latent shouts, the microsecond of fast-twitch in each stride, the tightly bottled-up wide-eyed action that was about to spill into the pool.

The second-half sprint went to Serbia and Montenegro. Their lead was moving from formidable to insurmountable. The crowd quieted. Baudrillard cleared his throat.

—There's a lot to learn from this sport, actually. The greatest seducers are magicians of course. Do you think Claudia Schiffer was a fluke? No, my friend, that's the rule. Don Juan is nothing compared to Copperfield. On the other hand, our greatest fascinators are fascists. The former hides cause and effect, the latter's power hinges on an elaborate narrative of causation: Jews stole your country, the ruling class is corrupting politics. As soon as the narrative falters, the regime fails. A magician loses his seductive power when we see how the cogs are connected. Much like why everyone is still watching this game, even though the pretense of it being a winnable contest has passed.

—And this sport is magic because we have no idea what's happening beneath the surface?

—That's better than what I was thinking: it's magic because I have no idea what the rules are! The experience is not unlike feudal serfdom. The respective phatic capacities of fascinators and seducers are noteworthy: fascists talk as much as possible; magicians only talk when they have to. All I hear is whistles and shouts. But the officials do appear to whistle at fouls underwater, what they don't see.

—I've never understood that either. Owen explained it to me in terms of probability: it's most likely that someone who sinks was pushed down; we cannot say for certain, but we are comfortable blowing the whistle and saying a foul was most likely committed.

—The role of officials itself is fascinating.

—Quantum officiating. The judges are always liminal.

—Magic.

The clock expired. A Serbian field player rose high from the water and launched the ball into the stands. Baudrillard had the last word of the match:

—An entire sport founded on the possibility of levitation.

Reluctantly, they entered the postmatch scrum. Shoulder to shoulder with the victorious Serbian/Montenegrans, they squeezed through the dark concourse, were temporarily blinded by the late afternoon glare, then weaved into the Metro.

On a westbound train to their hotel, two young Americans drank blue drinks from foot-long funnel glasses. Burr smiled.

—These young men would be fascinating? Certainly not seductive.

—We, as non-blue-drink-drinkers, are the smaller bundle on this Metro, my friend. We can be fascinating to them, which I don't think is true in the present case, but they cannot be fascinating to us. What is your talk on tomorrow night?

—The genealogy of shame and guilt. I also hope to explain my conception of liminality.

—I've read a bit of your early academic work.

—I would have brought more copies of *Hapax* for your colleagues. I understand the European distribution has faced several setbacks.

—Thank you. No, I mean the first essays you published. They were really out there. That mumbo-jumbo about world harmony is almost indistinguishable from the writing on those hemp soap labels you have out there.

—My only excuse is love.

Baudrillard laughed.

—Then all is forgiven.

—I keep forgetting that tomorrow night may not even happen. Do you know anything about the venue, or lack thereof?

—These things have a way of working themselves out.

They returned to the hotel to find the organizer, George, sitting with a man whose long, thin hair nearly reached the shoulders of his suit. Baudrillard raised his eyes at the newcomer but spoke to George:

—It looks like the calls to supporters worked.

George introduced them to Petros Spadzos, socialist mayoral candidate in the forthcoming election, then waxed revolutionary:

—Those calls weren't to supporters. They were to our opponents. The mayor was smart, at first, and managed to shut us down without making it news. I needed to threaten them into making a public statement. Once it was officially declared that our protest was being muzzled, the people realized that this was another example of their government caving to American pres-

sure rather than having the balls to show a free and democratic
Greece to the world.

—When my office got the call, I initially thought it was
worth a press statement, not a rally. Then Konstantinos singles
you out on the nightly news as the type of insurrectionists that
could destroy the Olympic spirit and wreck our tourist industry
for decades.

George laughed.

—I told him the one thing we wouldn't stand for was being
swept under the rug. He said if we wanted to be his scapegoat, so
be it. He lived up to his word. Konstantinos declared his animos-
ity as publicly as possible. We must respect that.

Burr, a little drunk from the sambuca and the sun, called Konstantinos a fascist.

—He gave you a lever for the young vote, Baudrillard added.

—He gave me a reason to meet you two.

—If you can find us a stage, it'll be Berlusconi, Bush, and your
incumbent rival versus us—and you'll have the people's vote.

—The stage isn't a problem.

Baudrillard had seen this before.

—The stage is always a problem.

—I'm president of the Hellenic festival committee. I can get
you the Herod Atticus.

This meant nothing to Baudrillard. But it meant everything
to Burr.

—The Odeon of Herodes Atticus is a stone amphitheater on
the southern slope of the Acropolis. Herod built it to commemorate his wife . . .

Burr drifted for a second then continued.

—We heard Shostakovich under Mravinsky's baton in 1982.
My . . . wife was in her second trimester. Mravinsky. His great
arms flapped like an eagle. Each player in his orchestra was ter-

rified, absolutely terrified, of that beak turning in his direction. Mravinsky on the proskenion of the Herodes Atticus, the same stage that we . . .

Burr opened his eyes to a perplexed group. George's head was in his hands.

—You're going to have to watch those tangents, Professor Burr.

Spadzos was content enough, ready to get on with his day.

—We needed something to class up this campaign. How perfect will that be? Konstantinos and his fascist friends silence you guys because you're too revolutionary. How weak, I ask you, is an administration that fears a middle-aged professor? Nothing personal.

—It's fine.

—Most of the people will be there to see Baudrillard. And he's more radical and attracts a more radical crowd than you suppose. Are you sure about this?

—Learn to take yes for an answer, George. I just came by to make sure you guys weren't wearing leather pants.

Baudrillard took a step forward.

—We are working class. We leave the leather pants to the politicians.

Spadzos chose to laugh at the remark.

—George, you get your guys to the show on time. I'll take care of the rest. Are you going to have trouble filling the theater? That would be bad for press. I can plant some campaign volunteers in the crowd.

—Your volunteers might already be there as fans. It won't be a problem. I texted my team to start printing the posters fifteen minutes ago. They'll be up all over the city in hours, and our graphics guy is amazing. Meanwhile, I'm making the rounds at cafés tonight. How do you want to work the box office?

—Tickets will be free, but it's better for press, and tax purposes, if we have a definitive head count. Let them print out tickets online or get them at the performance . . .

The conversation continued past the word *performance*, but Burr didn't hear it. Commencements, lectures, symposia, readings— not quite as many of those as he would have liked—talks, these were all familiar species in his world. He couldn't recall ever giving a performance. Save for seventh-grade viola, which went so well that there was no eighth-grade viola.

—Good day, gentlemen. Professor Burr, get some rest. You look tired. These summer days can be draining.

Baudrillard took this as an excuse to walk the stairs with Burr.

—What was all that shit about Mravinsky? You said you didn't know about high culture.

—I don't know anything about the actual music. The conductor simply looked amazing up there. It's one of the most indelible images I've ever seen. A real magician: tuxedo, white tie, wand.

—You were seduced.

—I was worried my wife was! I was still so spellbound when we returned that I lectured about the eagle of Zeus, *Aetos Dios*, for the entire week.

—That reminds me. Two things: One, you're not a teacher anymore. These are not your students, and there are no more lectures. Two, and this is far more important, it's not liminality, it's Liminalism. There are some really smart people who have been talking about this for a while now. You need to stand on their shoulders and tell us what living with your mind feels like. Give us radical theory, not a book report.

Burr shook Baudrillard's hand.

—Out of curiosity, what are you going to be speaking on?

—I'm going to be denouncing Liminalism.

Baudrillard winked and said good night.

Burr cleared his head with a shower and then began outlining his performance. What does a performer wear? He tried every combination of shirt and pant. Nothing worked. Thank god he didn't have time to act on his instincts, or he would have looked like rhinestone Elvis.

—Let's define performance, he said to himself, as a public event intended to draw an emotional response. No, that excludes an artist painting in his studio.

Burr studied the etymology online and then looked for e-mail confirmation of his next performance in Madrid. The organizers had yet to respond.

He was then arrested by the following message, subject heading "URGENT: Owen Burr":

Dear Mr. Burr:

Please call Dr. Galetto's office at (831) XXX-XXXX as soon as possible. The doctor wants to discuss an UPDATE on the status of your son.

Several attempts have been made to contact both you and your son for a follow-up to globe rupture and subsequent operations on December 3, 2003, and February 28, 2004. URGENT information has arisen that is vital to your son's successful recovery.

The doctor has instructed the answering service to forward your call should you be unable to contact us during our normal business hours of 8:00 a.m.–3:00 p.m.

Yours sincerely,

Jenna Baker, Office Manager
Galetto Globe, Strabismus and Orbit Surgical Center of
California, LLC

42 Cypress Way

Carmel by the Sea, CA

(831) XXX-XXXX

He called the doctor at once and was patched through to a cell phone.

—Professor Burr?

—Doctor.

—Thank you again for the book. I look forward to reading it when I get some spare time. Listen, some serious news reached my desk after the holiday.

Burr wasn't sure which holiday the surgeon could be referring to. Independence Day? Ramadan? Burr put all his effort into not shouting: "Where is he?"

—What sort of news?

—Well, it seems that an intern at the . . . Charité Campus Mitte . . . not sure why they have a French name if it's a Berlin hospital. Anyway, a John Doe, Max Mustermann as they call them there, presented on May fifteenth, at two a.m., with acute meningitis. Etiology was assumed to be from postoperative complications following implantation of a hydroxyapatite globe. As we discussed in December, an integrated implant, like the HA, has a very low risk of infection and gives Owen the best motility and ultimately the best prosthetic motility. Which is my first question: Why hasn't he scheduled the follow-up appointments for the prosthesis?

—He said with a patch, people would look away rather than stare. But you're absolutely right. Where . . .

—That makes no sense to me. Even if you have a patch, get a prosthetic. All of this is completely insured. It's not even an option in my book. He needs to complete the process or he's at greater risk for socket shrinkage.

—Exactly. The contact information that your office has for—

—That's not even why I'm calling. A German charity hospital was presented with this young male, just over two meters tall, but *only eighty kilos.* Less than one hundred and seventy-five pounds. Acute bacterial meningitis and attendant confusion, memory loss, phonophobia, no petechial rash, but otherwise a classic presentation.

—And you think this Max Mustermann was my son?

—Now here's where this gets interesting. The patient fully recovers. On the afternoon of Tuesday, June eighth, the rounding interns come by, and our man has vanished, which was bad timing for Mr. Mustermann, since the attending physician that day was a well-respected neurologist who would have asked some difficult questions about how bacteria made it to the meningeal space in the first place. I mean maybe there's some attendant inflammation from the implant, but for that infection to progress there has to be severe neglect along with drugs for the pain.

—The patient was gone before they could find out what happened?

—Vanished. But not without a trace. Toxicology was negative. But one of the interns noted high levels of scopolamine. Ever heard of the drug?

Burr reached for a mechanical pencil.

—How's it spelled?

—Like it sounds. Sco-po-la-mine. Has two legal uses: scopolamine patches are used for motion sickness; scope solutions are used in ophthalmic surgery. The drug's not first-line for postoperative trauma, but the drops are very common. It is totally natural to suppose that anyone looking at his blood screen would make the link between scopolamine and enucleation. The timing is a little off, but not enough to raise a red flag. However, I want to be perfectly clear about this, I never use scopolamine.

—Why?

—One, atropine is more effective. And two, scopolamine, though unscheduled, has a severe criminal subtext. I don't keep so much as a sample in my office.

Burr underlined the name on his notepad.

—Scopolamine was first used during the Cold War as a "truth serum."

—Does it work?

—It's a nasty drug. Colombian drug lords swear by it.

—How does all of this affect my son? Are you saying he was in Colombia? Couldn't he have gotten some prescription drops from another doctor?

—The levels in his chart are orders of magnitude higher than what you would see with prescription dosages. This is why our clever intern contacted me in the first place.

—How did he know?

—*She* noticed the tattoo of the rings on the proximal aspect of the patient's left biceps and figured it wouldn't be too hard to find a six-foot-eight Olympian who had recently undergone enucleation of the left eye. The hydroxylapatite implant confirmed

it—most of the integrated implants out there are Medpor or alu-
mina. Their Max Mustermann was without a doubt your son. As
for the scopolamine, that didn't come from my clinic or any other
semi-reputable clinic. So far as I can tell, there are two possibilities: either your son met with a very bad physician, in which case
he's in some danger, or he met with some very bad people, which
means he's in a great deal of danger.

—So what happens next?

—We have to get Owen out of Germany and back into my
office. He could be hallucinating from scopolamine toxicity, un-
cured meningitis, or complications from surgery—although, as I
said at the time, the procedure couldn't have gone better.

—That's in the book you recommended—phantom eye syn-
drome?

—Yes. It occurs in about thirty percent of patients. The charity hospital report describes Owen as severely hallucinating. Even
if his physical health is fine, his mental health is at best an open
question. You've got to find him. The clock is ticking. The longer
he waits to schedule a follow-up, the harder it is going to be for us
to ever get a prosthesis.

—Thank you, doctor. I'll get to work.

Burr cradled the phone.

A heap of clothes took Burr's place on the bed. He slept on
the floor for the first time in a decade. He rolled back and forth,
scratching his temple on the carpet when he thought of his speech,
opening his eyes and staring at the ceiling when he thought of
Owen in Berlin.

He thought of how he could get there immediately. Though
he had spent a great deal of time on the continent, European cities
still seemed tightly bunched. He was shocked to find out that the
train to Berlin took forty-five hours and had at least three lay-

overs. His calculations had it taking him at least twenty-six hours by car. Whereas if he took the direct flight after the speech, he could get there in three hours. He tried to tell himself that this was the math. These were numbers. You can't argue with numbers, even if they support an ulterior motive. It would have to be a flight. And at that point, he might as well deliver the speech.

Sleeping on the floor had done his back some good, but his head was knotted up. He trudged downstairs to the tail end of breakfast.

After filling a small plate with what remained of the scrambled eggs, he surveyed the room: two empty tables or a free seat opposite Baudrillard.

Baudrillard was still looking down at his paper when Burr pulled out the chair, but he smiled.

—You look well rested.

—I heard some news about Owen last night. They found him. Or at least I know where he was three months ago. It's a start.

—Great.

—He came in as a John Doe at a hospital in Berlin. An intern took the time to track him down. This was all in May, but the hospital just got hold of Owen's surgeon this week. It seems as if Owen might have been drugged. He was admitted with advanced bacterial meningitis. There's a direct flight to Berlin this afternoon. And I'm sorry, but I'm going to have to cancel tonight's speech.

—Of course.

—I'm sure it's inauspicious to cancel one's debut, but my son comes first.

—Of course.

—You understand?

—Of course.

—Of course he was in Berlin three months ago, and he left the hospital unofficially headed for god knows where, but I still have to see if I can find him.

—Bien sur.

—It could be argued that I would greatly improve my odds of finding him if I put up a flare so that he would know how to find me.

—That was my thought. Sort of. He's been gone six months in total, you say? And he could very easily find you if he wanted to, just by logging on to his e-mail. Or by picking up the phone. That technology has been around for a while. You can't lose contact anymore. You shouldn't presume otherwise.

—There's also a direct flight tonight that gets in a few hours later. Right after my speech. Either way, I'm afraid I'm going to miss yours.

—There's no great loss there. You probably don't want to hear what I have to say about Liminalism anyway. I wasn't kidding about that. Not that I think it isn't the perfect thing for you to be preaching as a nonacademic philosopher.

—Why do you say, "perfect thing for me"?

—Why Liminalism, Joe? Because you were meant to sail, not anchor. I am old enough now to look around and see mainly waste. But I am still young enough to see potential. There's a reason you're here. You wouldn't have been any more likely to find him by going to Berlin a day earlier—even weeks earlier; it's already been three months since he was in that hospital. You also won't be any more likely to find him by staying and firing a flare, as you say. It is impossible to find someone who doesn't want to be found. And it is impossible to lead a search party when you're staring at your shoes. You need to change your relationship, which is almost impossible to do. You know that. Which is why you want to stay.

—That's what kept me up last night. I want to stay and speak.

And there's no way I could get there faster. It's just . . . I feel like I should be praying or something.

—You should go breathe. Seriously. Go upstairs and take ten deep breaths.

Burr excused himself because there was nothing left to say. He hung the Do Not Disturb sign on his door then fell onto the rayon comforter and stared at the lazy ceiling fan. He slept, then watched *Scarface* on the TV. He had never seen the film, but could see how the hyperbole would polarize a crowd.

He opened his computer and chose his seat assignment for his evening flight to Berlin.

Burr settled on an old black polo shirt, no logo, and khaki pants. He looked different in the mirror, less innocent. He was surprised to find a tan on his cheeks. He lathered up for a shave, paused, and washed it off. He grabbed his windbreaker and turned out the light.

Tanned, stubbled, revolutionary, Professor Burr walked the stairs from his third floor room to the hotel lobby. George was waiting.

—I'm ready to go when you are, Professor.

—Let's have a drink until everyone else is ready.

—I'm afraid you are everyone else. Jean is wrapping up a speaking engagement at the University of Athens and will not be accompanying us to the Odeon.

—Oh.

—But let's have a drink. It will help with the nerves. Beer?

—Whisky. For a number of reasons.

They doubled their drink order and then left for the venue. As George lifted the seat of the coupe and crammed into the backseat with two of his friends, he added:

—Jean told us to be sure to record tonight—that your speech was going to be historic. No pressure!

The whisky wasn't helping with the nerves. His stomach had already been hot and jumped up. Now it was picking fights. He felt less present and more flushed. He tried to recollect himself, reconsidering his assumption that presence was a good thing. Perhaps this occasion demanded that he be absent. Like Owen.

Burr had logged thousands of hours of public speech and laughed at the idea that people could fear a speech more than a snake—let alone death. But tonight he was terrified. And he was terrified that he was thinking in clichés.

It was the paucity of imagery that made him nervous. He was slated for an hour-long performance and was going on cold. There was no PowerPoint to fall back on. Perhaps he could open up the last quarter hour to the crowd. Q and A.

The driver smoked. Burr wished he could find relief in that act, in any act.

They drove past a wall-size poster advertising tonight's speech. His name was every bit as big as he had imagined, but nearly every letter was different from what he had anticipated:

Τζόζεφ Μπερ

Modern Greek, a mystery every time. The text was red, the background black. Baudrillard's name, unlike Burr's, required no transliteration. First and last name were on different lines, so big was their font. Someone had graffitied an

into the three A's of JEAN BAUDRILLARD. Graffiti in itself made Burr nervous. Anarchy on the page was one thing, safe and contained; the larger-than-life billboard, however, made distressingly clear that this concept was far more potent, far more alive. This was a higher-stakes game than he had imagined. The proof was emblazoned in Krylon, dripping down in red through the white letters of his name.

Once he caught sight of the Odeon, he began to breathe more regularly and his hands stopped shaking. The harmony of form was why he'd first studied classics, something that made a scintilla of fucking sense in this world: you want to get people together for a speech, a play, a dance? Carve out a beautiful stone ampitheater on a brightly lit hill looking out to the sea. Seems pretty simple. And an elegant way to live. You couldn't see the Aegean any-more, because of the smog, but the symmetry of these classical shapes was still arresting. The sweeping curves, the mating lines, the balanced mass; this was the resonant push, the enthusiastic kick on the downswing of his life that brought him higher than a determined universe could have predicted he would ever rise.

Tracks of hot floodlights cut through the descending skies. The car curved away from the theater to find parking. Losing sight of the Odeon hurt nearly as much as being torn from a dream of Caroline. Usually, if she came in a dream he would sleep in, ignoring whatever morning responsibilities were nudging his subconscious. Occasionally, however, he would have to leave the dream and hate himself afterward for not surrendering to any glimpse of her thrown to him in the quaking light of aether. Turning away from the floodlit Odeon was that same swerve into the light of morning.

Caroline came back to him.

She didn't want to leave yet. She never wanted to leave. She was everywhere, but she'd always be here. After Mravinsky, she floated away down the slope, bobbing and sweeping away as if she'd been caught in an overflowing river. He trailed after her, skating down the slope of the Acropolis. She waited in a patch of coreopsis. And that was their last foreign kiss.

Burr put his head in his hands.

—Relax. We're only parking.

They unpacked from the hatchback and fell into the rank-and-file of general and soldier. Burr led. Burr was the general. A performer, but in absentia, watching himself backstage nodding to all of the young people who came up to ask him questions and offer him water, espresso, juice.

Burr parted the curtain and looked out on a crowd of thousands of long-haired or shaved heads.

—Can you get them to turn down the blue lights? It's a bit intense, and I'm not sure I'll be able to read my notes.

The audiovisual technician had no idea what he was talking about, but said she would try. George Spirados had left his side and was introducing him to the crowd.

—I present to you professor of classics at Mission University, Joseph Burr.

Burr made it to the rostrum before he had time to process what he was doing. He shook George's hand and thanked him earnestly. George tried to free his grip, but Burr held on. Eventually George had to use two hands to free himself. By this time, the once enthusiastic applause had died.

The mic creaked as Burr adjusted the segmented neck. He cleared his throat and heard that correction horribly amplified before a vast and eager public. He swallowed.

—I know what you're thinking. Mission University? But don't worry, I'm not a Mormon.

He waited for laughter, which leaked from the crowd in drops rather than crashing in the torrent he had hoped for. It sounded more as if a couple of people were suppressing sneezes. Surveying the audience, he was reminded of the Catalogue of Ships in the *Iliad*: the Darfur fleet with captains in all directions, Anti G-8ers, Anti NATO, Anti NATO Expansion, Pro Chiapas, Puppet Head Bush, Puppet Head Berlusconi, Man Dressed as Tree, Zapatistas, Gandhian Socialist Farmers League of India, Argentinian Teachers Union, Kuna of Ecuador, Peoples Global Action, Association of Sri Lankan Fisherfolk, Anti-Rwandan Genocide, No Off-shore Drillers, No Iraq Bombers, No Afghan Bombers, No Sudan Bombers, No Chechnyan Bombers, Pink Flag Flyers, Rainbow Flyers, Hemp Flag Flyers, Kosovo Flag Flyers, Palestinian Flag Flyers, Disco Dancers, signs for Free Tibet, Fair Trade, Less God, More Sex . . .

—Let me amend that. I'm not a Mormon, but like a good missionary, I'm going to begin by questioning the natives: What is the difference between shame and guilt?

Shit. He'd forgotten his intro about the Century of the Liminal. And here he was opening himself up to a well-grounded postcolonialist critique. And he'd said "missionary," which made him sound like a pervert. *Shit. Shit. Shit.*

—I look around and see a lot of signs. We'll return to those later.

Shit. It was getting quiet. The blue gels over the floodlights made the crowd appear to gather in a giant wave, those seated near the stage sucking back to that inflection point somewhere just above his head. Soon they would all crash down.

—It's always seemed wrongheaded to me to try to teach Greek to the Greeks. But that is precisely what I'm here tonight to attempt. However, I am going to attempt to do so through the peculiar idiom of *Scarface*.

A few people in the audience cheered.

—I want to begin with a scene of decadence . . . I suppose I need to narrow it down. Drug lord Tony Montana, smoking a cigar at the conclusion of a sumptuous feast, addresses his best friend and wife, two necessarily distinct people for our hero, mind you. "Her womb is so polluted, mang."

In the history of bad impressions and embarrassing things older people do to relate to the younger generation, that "mang" was easily top ten.

> Probably shouldn't have attempted that impression. Tony's sentiment is no doubt familiar to you as miasmatic theory. *Miasma* is universally translated as *pollution*. Tony, however, is tapping into a different definition.
>
> Pollution, for Tony, is an all-pervading mood. We can see this mood when he speaks. Pacino is a fine actor, but we are not concerned with his ability to deliver dialogue, we are interested in the dialogue's ability to inhabit him. This is not Pacino speaking. We are listening to an ancient man.
>
> Tony relates to the world in a way that can only be described as Heideggerian *Stimmung*; he swims in the mood of Lust, Capital, Drugs, Power, Violence. Everything in this world is polluted. Not his world of cocaine, mind you, but his wife's world of quaaludes. Tony cannot have intercourse with the stultifying quaalude world. After realizing his checklist of Money, Power, Women, he sees the contamination, the pollution, of this world as all-pervasive and damned. Continuing to navigate this world is not stepping in a pile of shit. It is swimming in a sewer.
>
> What is the difference between shame and guilt? Look one word up in a thesaurus, and you'll find the other. I hate thesauri. Every word is a world. There are no synonyms. Shame opposes guilt. Shame is a self-directed standard. It is the bar that we raise in our soul; fail to clear

it, and we suffer. Guilt, however, is externalized. There is no guilt without the Other. The last man—who unfortunately may inherit his kingdom quite soon if our current policies are not radically reversed—the last man cannot feel guilt, because there is no one left to infringe upon.

A fallacy persists that guilt is a feeling resulting from our actions, shame from our thoughts. Bullshit. This dichotomy serves to keep the fiction of shame alive. Shame is dead.

Shame vanished around 450 BC with the death of Heraclitus, and has yet to return. But I'm not here to argue against our guilt-based, hyperlitigious, slip-and-fallen society. Nor am I here to bemoan the shamelessness of Paris Hilton. I know. Cheap joke. This administration? [*Cheers.*]

Postmodernity is so lost from this center that we think only of the negation of the negation. We think only within the guilt paradigm of capitalism—not the shame paradigm of anarchism, where every woman is her own queen. Why does capitalism side with guilt? There is profit in the enterprise. Period.

That's getting closer to the point, but it's not the point. The point is that capitalism is a structural economy of negation. So inured are we to the system that we've forgotten the obverse of shame. Glory. The word is embarrassing for us to even say. Glory? Is this guy going to show me his war medals next? We feel shame at voicing the opposite of shame. I am using the word *glory* in the sense of *timay*, public esteem. As you know, the ancient poets say that *timay* is stored in the *thumos*. The *thumos* was here. [*Burr pounds his chest right at the xiphoid process. Winces.*] Today we have no repository of *timay*, but that makes no difference because there is nothing left to store. The obverse of shame is glory, the obverse of guilt, innocence. Tell me, how is a society whose greatest goal is innocence capable of anything?

Raise your hand if you want to be remembered for innocence. See? By framing innocence as our highest aspiration, global capitalism, which is to say, the modern world, has made us not only forget but forgettable.

Right there [*points to the Olympic complex*] is the only locus of glory permitted by capitalism. Athletic glory is a Kay Fabian, however, an achievement meaningful only after we suspend disbelief. We allow athletes glory, but realize we are in a symbolic order where putting a ball through a hoop has significance.

Capitalism is a bad penny that keeps showing up. The two sides of this penny: guilt and innocence. Unfortunately progressivism operates under the false consciousness that we can use this coin to acquire things of worth. This isn't economics, it's alchemy.

The coin of the realm must be scrapped. Their pennies must be traded for gold.

István Mészáros's contemporary reading of Marx reminds us that as soon as you introduce capital, you introduce capitalism. So perhaps we should dispense at once with my metaphor of coins. Here I would follow the Slovenian Socrates and say that in order to collapse a system you must issue an impossible demand, using the logic of the system against itself. This would be step one: demand an accounting of shame. Reject innocence as an ideal.

This brings me to the signs. The naming of the ships from Book 2 of *The Iliad* comes to mind. The parallel is not trivial. Why the myriad of protestors? Because there is no locus of power to protest against. We are all protesting against global capitalism, but that's like protesting against the air. There is no "against." As soon as we think of against, we are trapped in a binary, us/ them, which is exactly what allows the beneficiaries of capitalism to rest easy on their huge pillows. Every protest sign is accusatory. No news there. The act of protest itself is accusatory. We will not stop environmental devastation by finding someone guilty. Instead, we must instill the ethic of shame and stop blushing when we say glory.

Back to Tony. The man clearly has no comprehension of guilt. In this way he is ancient. Tony's story is the story of a flipped coin spinning in the air: shame, glory, shame, glory, shame . . . He has a different coin than the other people of his world. This is enough to make him unstoppable.

I want more Tonys.

Here Burr removed a euro coin from his pocket and flicked it in the air. Rather than spin, it knuckled in the air like a Frisbee and fell off the front of the stage into the orchestra pit. He coughed.

The more significant aspect of Tony qua spinning coin is not the fact that one side is shame, the other glory. The most significant fact is that the coin is spinning. And he has utter disregard for whichever side will end up on top.

We are always at a crossroads. All ways.

Tony inhabits a liminal space, poised between the poles of shame and glory. There are no other lights for

Tony. Just these two. The word *twilight* comes from *dwei*, two, and *light* . . . light. Tony is a twilight dweller. You should all be twilight dwellers.

Any revolutionary is a twilight dweller poised between the government that was and the government that will be.

I'll caution you before we go any further: Liminalism is a dangerous theory. Heard this one: "You're either with us or against us"? Critique Guantanamo, fail to deploy troops to Iraq, run photos of Abu Ghraib, and you're a terrorist. Democracy rests on people both with and against. But make no mistake, the war on terror is a war on the liminal.

Jean-François Lyotard, really the only author you need to read on the postmodern condition—other than Jean Baudrillard [*applause*]—Lyotard posits that postmodernity is a Möbius strip. The metaphor is apt in pointing to the impossibility of ever being outside our hypercapitalist despotic world. The only escape is to embrace the contradiction and conflate inside and outside.

Before Tony exits stage right, he graces us with his terrific "Say good night to the bad guy" monologue. His last line is the one I want to focus on: "Me, I always tell the truth, even when I lie." No one in the restaurant laughs, which suggests an underlying truth to what should be a punch line. A liminal being, like Tony, inhabits the mood of paradox. The Left must conquer its fear of opposition, its preprogrammed bias in favor of logical exclusion.

What do I mean? Guilt requires exclusion rather than inclusion. I cannot be guilty vis-à-vis someone who is included in "me." Exclusion is a fallacy. Exclusion was created by that line of humanity who would go on to found country clubs.

But wait, it gets worse. Our very notions of logic require exclusivity. Fundamental to mathematics, science, reason itself, are two notions: the law of noncontradiction and the law of the excluded middle. These laws prohibit us from ever understanding paradox, infinity, the Möbius strip, and Liminalism.

Liminalism is my claim that every person should reject the binary and inhabit the twilit space. We must believe in new gods, even though they don't exist. This is the aforementioned step two. After guilt and innocence have been exchanged for shame and glory, we have to spin that coin. It's not going to be easy.

Why must we fight? Because our digital age is not just wrong, it is exactly wrong. Our entire world is becoming a string of 1s and 0s. There are no fractions, no irrational numbers, in coding. This is a serious problem. Math is going to have to be scrapped. I hear some cheers on that one. Math: start over! It's more serious than just allowing our math to comprehend contradiction. Our math needs to be built from contradiction. This is the hard work that your generation will have to do. Rather than accommodating answers that are both true and false, our math must be rebuilt on the premise that everything is both true and false. Except for the curious fact that the previous statement is both true and false.

Did I lose you in the paradox? No? Your silence just means you are in the *Stimmung*? Good. This is where we really live. One vast threshold, neither in nor out of the room.

I am describing a space. Tonight, here in the theater,

the Odeon, are we inside or outside? Some might look up at the stars, see the lights of the news crews around the Olympic center, smell the lean air from a hot day, and tell themselves we are *in* the *outside*. Others might see the enclosure itself as a ring of inclusion. They might think we are all sitting in mutual admiration at our progressive—yet nuanced—liberal view of the modern age and therefore an inside community.

Both are wrong. The Odeon is a Möbius strip.

These problems aren't a remainder that we must ferret out of an otherwise well-functioning system. The remainder is the system.

Rather than wander a thousand plateaus, we should return to the cave. Everything liminal must be inhabited, and every habitation must be liminal. The twentieth century was ruled by the subliminal. This century will be devoted to the liminal. So what is liminal?

The present is an intersection of the past and the future. Sex is an intersection of two people. Riot, protest, conflict, these are all liminal intersections. We must always riot. We must always rebel. Heraclitus reminds us: "From discord comes the only harmony." This is the playful spirit of liminal action that you must exhibit if you ever wish to break the oppressive dialectic before you. The dancing protestors have it right. "To be in agreement is to disagree." That's not me; that's Heraclitus.

We must not treat contradiction as a fly in the ointment. It is not the exception; it is the rule.

There is a reason Heraclitus thought the entire world was fire. What is fire? Fire is not a thing. It's a process. Fire is the process of combustion. Fire is the arrow in an equation, it is the *yields* on the way from this to that. Be the arrow. Be fire. Burn everything to the ground.

Otherwise you're just going to be disappointed that you weren't able to go from A to B. You must become that arrow. Activism must be defined by action.

If we take truth in politics to be justice and falsity to be injustice, then we must reformulate our disappointment. Everyone here tonight is, I'm guessing, adamant about the ubiquity of injustice. I'm here to tell you to give it up. There is no justice. Political life is true and false, just and unjust. In order to live a meaningful political life, surrender the hope of justice. The best this hypermodern world offers is bovine innocence. Instead I ask you to revolt. I ask you to turn away from the hegemonic order and claim a glorious alternative. True freedom. Violent freedom. The freedom of twilight . . .

Just as the crowd had finally started to nod, to laugh at the right places, to whoop, Burr caught sight of a young man in black slowly making his way down the center aisle. At first Burr thought the young man was carrying a lighter. The flame flickered on the faces of the crowd. Burr waited for others to raise their own lighters, in some sort of Eric Clapton concert moment, but it didn't happen. He noticed that this was a new twilight. The intersection of the electrical and the analog. Modern man's floodlights and ancient man's torch.

Then it became clear that the flame was too large to be a lighter. This was an actual torch. As the young man reached eye level, still about thirty rows up, he broke into a trot. Burr watched silently as the torch came closer and closer.

The young man was running now, sure that if he didn't move fast, someone was going to tackle him from behind.

The crowd watched expectantly, still not sure that this wasn't a scripted spectacle. There were no whistles. No walkie-talkies. No one at the entrance yelling *Stop!*

The young man leapt to the stage and stood, panting, at Burr's side. He was far more nervous than Burr, which made Burr far more nervous in turn.

A liquor bottle, burning slow blue from its cotton wick, passed from the young man to Burr. Flashes from here and there in the crowd. A young woman saw the bottle and yelled *Whoa!*

The young man wiped his sweating brow, saying *Go ahead* with a series of quick nods.

Burr leaned far back from the bottle. He leaned in and blew out the wick, which lit back up at once like a trick birthday candle. Now the flame was higher and running faster toward the fuel. The crowd began to recede. A flash of fire, green glass trembling about to explode.

Burr straightened his inquisitive cocked head, looked once more to the crowd, and lobbed the bottle toward the three-storey backdrop of the theater. It flew end over end, whistling and chopping the night air with each turn. Burr prayed it would pass straight through one of the arched windows, any one of the windows.

Glass shattered against the marble wall of the ancient facade. The gasoline spit a fireball toward the crowd. A wave of hot air swept past Burr's face. The crowd gasped. Horrified, Burr looked to one wing of the stage for support and found no one. He looked to the other side and found Baudrillard closing in on the podium like Diomedes, possessed by a will to challenge whatever he would find, be it god or man. He walked with a familiar firm stride. Owen's stride. Long-legged, commanding total attention, with each footfall came purpose. He made his way to the rostrum, blue flames backlighting his wispy white hair.

189

Silence. The crowd watched the spitting blue fire in total absorption.

Baudrillard pressed the cleft of his chin into the microphone. With an arm around Burr, he addressed the stunned crowd.

—My remarks tonight will be brief: *Go!*

The crowd was still in shock. Baudrillard shooed them with both hands:

—*Vite! Vite! Vite!*

The young torchbearer, still at Burr and Baudrillard's side, jumped up and down and shouted to the crowd. Baudrillard took him firmly by the triceps:

—That was not your decision to make. Run!

The crowd glommed in the walkway of the top row like thick-flowing lava. Every second someone burbled up over the stone wall, popping over the rail and landing on the gravel of the southern slope of the Acropolis, headed for the Parthenon itself. Here the crowd met a cordon of visor-helmeted police, billy clubs in one hand, clear plastic shields in another, and heavily padded men who loaded their blunderbusses with tear gas canisters.

The police began thumping their shields with their black clubs.

Burr was on the side of the sackers. Burr was on the side of the Vandals. He was, for the first time, on the other side of the shield. Each beat of the fifty-police-shield drum brought more terror, more dread.

He had turned his audience into protestors, and now they were in danger of becoming protestors who violently clashed with police, which few of them had signed up for. These were grad students, mainly, who wanted to support a riot in the article-writing third wave, not the armed conflict front line. Half of them looked like they'd come here on dates. They began to withdraw down the slope.

But someone had called in the ringers. Outside the stadium, busloads of shin-guarded, gas-mask-wearing protestors carrying rocks instead of signs jeered at anyone who retreated and vowed that they would overtake the Parthenon, which had been taken over by NBC.

Baudrillard and Burr were watching all of this from the wings of the Odeon. Baudrillard watched the arc of the first shot from the crowd. Though the jagged white chunk of limestone was flying uphill, it had the damned inevitability of a flowerpot dropped from a high-rise window. Baudrillard clenched his teeth. The white rock thumped off a plastic police shield. It was the first answer to the billy-club drumming. The Acropolis was silent. He grabbed Burr's shoulder.

—We need to get you out of here at once.

—We're going to have to hike down. I know the way.

Looking back over his shoulder, Burr saw the police advancing down the hill, driving the crowd back toward the Odeon and away from the media tents, one of which was now smoking.

Baudrillard followed Burr through the main facade. Every available floodlight had been turned on, but they still had to pick their steps carefully down the slope of the Acropolis in the shadows of gnarled olive trees and over thorny clumps of acanthus. Though spines crept up his pant leg with each step, Burr slalomed from clump to clump to avoid sliding down the gravel slope.

They rested against a cypress tree. Baudrillard cleaned his glasses and gestured to the Parthenon. The familiar ecru columns against Athens' clear black sky, the night Parthenon of millions of postcards, was smogged red and orange from tear gas meeting fire. Coughs and screams carried all the way down the rocky outcrop.

—I've seen more than my share of riled-up crowds, and I've heard speeches far more inflammatory than yours that didn't end in this.

Burr was too stunned to speak. He had set fire to the Acropolis. He thought about Owen.

—They're not going to let me on my flight.

—It might not be a problem. You won't come into the story until morning. The first wave of media is always effect with no cause. It creates mystery. It enhances viewership. Tonight will be the spectacle. It should be a few days before they put you on the no-fly list. But we should hurry.

They found a trail on Filopappou Hill and eventually connected with a major road, where Baudrillard flagged down a taxi. Burr gave the directions to their hotel. Baudrillard corrected him and said they had to go to the airport.

—Do you have your passport with you?

—At all times. But we have time for me to get my laptop. The clothes I don't need, but I need my laptop. Getting to the airport now doesn't make the plane leave any sooner.

—Something smells wrong about this. You may be in trouble. I may be in trouble.

The driver began eyeing them in the rearview mirror.

—Those protestors outside the Odeon. They weren't sent by George.

—Who's George?

—George Spiros, who is so fond of calling us by our first names. No. George didn't send them. That was strictly political. I'm just trying to think of how Spadzos or someone higher up would benefit from a riot. One thing's certain, the staid Professor Burr is no more.

—What happened to my two or three days before the story broke?

—That's theory, not practice. So far as I can tell, this is a game of fish. We are the small fish. Spiros is a small fish. Spadzos is the big fish who used us to attract attention to the incumbent mayor's hyperconservativism, but there is some bigger fish, some bartender-of-Molotov-cocktails fish, who wanted Spadzos to look as if he would destroy the city, the economy.

—Why?

—For attention. For a story. It may have been the president showing he could quell dissent. Here that's the number-one qualification for the job. To be honest, I don't care. Whoever is behind those shields is going to look like a hero, and he has no reason to help us.

Burr looked out the window. Then he looked out the rear window.

—Is this going to follow me around forever?

—So much for that Nobel. There are consequences to all of this. It's no Bastille, but it's enough to get branded a terrorist, given everything. And like any revolutionary, terrorist, or visionary, you'll have to live with being a metonym. Let's hope that the protests end tonight. I'm guessing that the deck is rigged for that to happen. If not, maybe we can lecture together in Guantanamo.

—I'm deeply, deeply sorry if I've damaged your career. You've been a more luminous guide than I could have ever hoped for.

—Athens is on you, Joe Burr. I'm just a footnote. If you're ever in Paris, look me up here.

Baudrillard wrote an address in a notebook and tore out the page.

—Are you going straight to Paris?

—Absolutely.

—I'd love to write you an inscription in *Hapax*, but I just realized you must have left it in the hotel.

—Honestly, I was always going to leave it in the hotel. And you must too.

Burr's hand hovered for an instant. He patted Jean on the knee three times, exited at the *Interflug* ticket counter, and said:

—Thank you. Athens is finally real.

FIVE

HIDE THE STARS, HIDE THE MOON, SOMETHING TERRIBLE IS GOING TO HAPPEN

—Can you read that top letter for me?

Owen blinked several times and focused on the E of the eye chart, sharpening the serifs. Then he fumbled a hand to his eye patch, but found a gauze bandage instead. The bed was broken and small. IV taped to the fold of his arm, saline bag on a rack. He looked around to a roomful of whitecoats, all with pens waiting for his reply.

Now the woman asked him in German he only half compre-hended:

—Können Sie mir den _____ auf der Tafel vorlesen?

He was in Berlin. He remembered Berlin. But his throat caught at the déjà vu. These were the tests that followed his in-jury, before the enucleation, testing the eye that only caught light:

Close your right eye, please. Can you read any of the letters? Even the top one? Which way is my hand moving? How about now? Tell me when the penlight is on. How about now? Is it on or off now?

Then they asked him in French that ended in garbles:

—Pouvez vous lire la première lettre _____?

He was totally fucked if his right eye was damaged. He turned away from the chart to catch the window blinds trembling with the summer breeze. Beyond the window, flagstone wedges that reminded him of buildings in the Quad. But he was far from California, or they wouldn't waste time with other languages— maybe Spanish. He looked at the acoustic ceiling tiles and froze the scattered ants in place. He counted.

—What's your name?

He could see just fine from his right eye.

Now another doctor leaned in.

—Where are you staying? Where are you from?

He ran his thumb over the chrome bed rail and said nothing. Eventually they left and let him sleep.

He woke to nurses smoothing him like a crumpled piece of paper, certain that if they ironed him out, they would find something legible amid the folds and creases.

He refused to answer the questions in German, English, or any of the other languages they tried, partly because he was unsure of his footing, partly for fear of being hit with a six-figure bill. He smiled slightly when the hospital interpreter tried sign language, appreciating the exhaustiveness of their effort.

In fact, Owen had learned enough German in his time in Berlin to know it was no good that he kept hearing the word *sterben*. *An einer Überdosis sterben,* "overdose death," a poetic pairing of words that kept him occupied for an otherwise uneventful day;

vor Entkräftung sterben, to die of exhaustion. He nodded ever so slightly at the prognosis, which an Eastern European intern duly noted: *Er wird leider sterben,* "I'm afraid he'll die"; and the coup de grace, *Er hatte sterben können,* "He could have already died."

During the night, he overheard their diagnosis: "Idiopathic aphasia resulting from acute bacterial meningitis." It wasn't that his German was prodigious, it was that all the words were cognates. The only two he wasn't quite sure of, *idiopathic aphasia,* spiraled down in his head, hypnotizing him.

On his first day of full consciousness, after the cabal of rounding physicians passed, an intern explained in English that his new placeholder name, Max Mustermann, meant "specimen," and that the attending physician would continue to encourage everyone to treat him as such until he helped them out with his name and history.

He remembered the flashes, the lights, sweat, women, shaking pain. And he suddenly liked being Mustermann. At least he'd found a name for himself. Better than retrieving his vandalized name and soiled image. Thinking again of Kurt's staged shots, which were probably headed to Basel right now, Owen shook. Even the wallet-size school photos they had to take in middle school were a nightmare. Tilting his head not like this, like this, enduring the photographer's smoke-stained fingers lifting his chin, waiting for the flash and refusing to smile with his teeth. It was a horror show every year. But that was now nothing. The thought of Kurt explicitly manipulating his image to shock and someone else mounting that picture on a gallery wall right now, as he lay here in a hospital bed, made Owen's hands quake.

Brief distinct memories of his exploitation rolled against each other like marbles in a pouch, each glass sphere abrading its neighbors with a grind and a gnash. He bristled at the sound.

The fat marble in the pouch had an inset photo of Owen standing on an immense wooden spool, toes curled over the wooden lip, only the balls of his feet keeping him from falling forward. He saw his hands before him, bound in rope with novice knots that he should have been able to untie. Then plastic ties that sliced his wrists when he resisted.

The doctors had noticed the bruising when Owen was admitted, but stabilizing him took precedence over criminal speculation. Once he was stabilized and still nonresponsive, a neurologist intervened. He knocked out the bowl of his calabash pipe and decided to start with the bruises on the patient's wrists:

—Those ligature marks are from police-issued restraints. Notice the depth of bruising over the capitate bone and the distal spread of the contusion. Other restraining devices will cause scaphoid fracture before you see that. Irene, notify the police. We've got a fugitive.

Check, please. Tonight would have to be the last night of his stay. The greater part of him wanted surrender, a room full of MDs and cops all jotting down his story and shaking sympathetic heads. But a small part of him knew that he was going to do something horrible. And it was easier to do that with anonymity. The police wouldn't be satisfied with Owen qua Mustermann for very long, which meant he needed them as far away as possible. He hoped the appointed informant, Irene, was the Eastern European intern who had come by after rounds to see if there was any improvement. As for the handcuffs, Owen didn't remember any. But the doctor was persuasive.

Owen could clearly remember his hands to his side with stereo wire strung around his finger, or was that the pulse monitor that had been on his index finger for the past week? He saw Hal shifting the spotlight from his dry and cracking lips to the tattoo on his left arm. Stripped bare, and without the heat of those lights

197

on his core, he had started to freeze and spasm. Someone was working the surface of his bare hip with a fingernail, a sponge, a Brillo pad—most of the time his head was pried upward, and he couldn't see. Hal trying to make everyone laugh with exaggerated photographer patois: "Give it to me! Give it to me! Yes! Yes! Bring it! Yes!" It worked.

Everyone laughed.

Owen scraped his teeth over his tongue, a new tic born from days of having the fibers of a burlap sack stuck in his mouth. He still heard Kurt's whispers, constant and haunting. They were an ever-present wheeze: a pinched balloon slowly leaking poison deep inside his ear. How did Kurt hiss directly into his ear from a wheelchair? He saw Kurt hovering, stomping around the water tower, and grabbing the other models by the shoulders, blocking each scene with the exaggerated impatience of a director who's trying to impress his lead. Then sitting in his wheelchair as if it were a director's chair and ordering Hal to get the shot.

The past week of clinical enumerations of trauma added nothing to Owen's sense of injury. Words, even Latin words, could neither harm him nor heal him. For Owen, having Kurt's anodized metal I-bar wedged between his chin and his sternum was violation enough without adding the anatomical spells *mylohyoideus* and *sternocleidomastoid*. There are infinite ways to be unwell. He had experienced enough unwellness to know that was true. He was far more interested in finding the one way, the lighted way, to be well.

The insult to his body would heal. But the insult of something so banal, derivative, and plain fucking wrong as taking images of tortured people—Kurt and Hal were looking at photos on a laptop: wire, burlap sacks, stress positions, they had to be referencing Abu Ghraib—restaging a prison in your multimillion-dollar water tower loft, and thinking you're brilliant because you have an American prisoner this time, all of that was impossible to bear, something he would never be rid of. And not just any American, fucking him American. And the high pretension with which this Mickey Mouse bullshit was justified under the banner of Art. To almost die for fucking shock art? Are you serious?

What would he die for? Owen had never heard that the job of religion was to prepare him for death, so he'd never placed that onus on his Gods. Carmine, peridot, gamboge, ultramarine: Ares, Hermes, Apollo, and Athene. They were busy enough without his problems. All he had was *being* as a soap bubble: an iridescent wonder, holding so much but for such a short time, always one plink from nothingness, one plink from surrendering volume to the sky.

Just because he'd found a metaphor didn't mean he was comfortable with the idea.

At eight, pocket full of quarters, I wander away from a birthday party in an arcade. In the rush to choose a game, I land on something not particularly violent, not the newer games that other kids' parents write congressmen about. It's just a paperboy trying to deliver his papers—papers that are apparently so subversive that nonsubscribers throw cats at his bike and roll tires into his path. A pixelated ghetto blaster knocks my paperboy to the ground, which this algorithm deems a fatal blow.

I've lost a life.

The notion that I have three of them means that no one understands. My chest burns. I looked at a friend's screen just as a fighter jet explodes. To my right, a firebomb cracks on the red hair of a lance-waving knight, causing his animated peach skin to recede and reveal a rib cage as empty of life as a cow skull bleached by the desert sun.

An angel rises from the heap and then vanishes in a puff of smoke.

A panic, a hunger, a stab, something tearing at the contents of my chest, or as Dad calls it, the phrenes. *I try to shunt the loss of volume.*

The stab doubles me over and sweeps me out of the room and then out the front door of the pizza parlor arcade.

I wander for hours in a daze. A friend's mom finds me walking up a hill nearly a mile away—and this is the American suburbs, where the only pedestrians are vagrants, hobos as Dad calls them. The story gets around. And I officially become weird. The word hovers around every all-star team, every victory.

So what's one more thunderclap to a boy raised in a lightning field?

Owen kicked off the ankle socks the hospital had given him. Water polo had taught his toes prehensility. His toes needed to grasp. And nothing was more comforting for him than grasping an Achilles between his big toe and second toe, pulling just above a heel and pedaling down.

Owen stood barefoot on the floor. He stepped from the scrubs and put on his corduroy suit over a black tee. His passport and wallet were missing. Not in his suit. Not under the bed. Not here.

The bracelet on his wrist read "Max Mustermann." He hooked it from under his sleeve and pulled until the plastic stretched and finally snapped. When the bracelet gave, his left arm flung wildly and rang the chrome bed rail. He dampened the cold buzzing metal. Stepping into his shoes, he braved the tiled hallway.

Owen had become a man of shifting sands, emptying every grain into one leg until he had enough ballast to swing his other leg forward and repeat the process. Above the waist, he was as thin and empty as an expired hourglass, and just as easy to shatter.

Though these steps were labored, they were firmly directed. Pivot to pivot, he bore down on Kurt's *Wasserturm*. With a few dozen steps, his attention shifted to his head, bandaged yet again, as if some international agreement had been reached that Owen Burr must always stay under wraps. All he wanted was to be the invisible man beneath the gauze. Free to laugh, free to disappear.

His temples throbbed and swelled until he was nothing more than the sum of his pains, an effigy of chicken wire and plaster, a tiki-bar version of an Easter Island *moai*. And just as those ancient monoliths trudged from mountain to shore, one corner at a time, so Owen sloshed his way from the height of the hospital to the depths of Berlin.

He walked through the automated glass doors of his second hospital in six months. His legs held him loosely; once-taut braids were now wet rope.

This time, he could have used a wheelchair escort, and maybe even someone waiting to deliver him home. The early summer wind ripped through Owen's shirt and blew out the vents of his corduroy coat.

North and east, north and east, he pegged along until he was winding around the ring of Torstrasse. His steps were now a crumbling shuffle, leaving behind a trail of sand. He patted his pockets again and found no wallet, no passport. Were his pockets not empty, he would have stopped at one of the cafés, had a coffee, regrouped, and devised a plan more elaborate than breaking into the water tower and throwing Kurt through the blue-tarped window. But he had no plan, no money, no identification, no things.

As if he were ascending a broken escalator, no stride took him as far as it should. The dissonance of intention and movement nested in his head. Looking to his feet didn't help. His steps were fixed when they should be moving. He clomped. The once mellifluous was now a clatter. Each step hit the ground like a stack of plates.

Collapsed clubgoers sprawled on the rough lawns of the Volks-park Freidrichshain. The conscious in any circle tracked Owen as he staggered through the park. He watched skaters hold video cameras inches from the ground, ironing the asphalt to document kickflips and ollies. In the thousands of times he had walked by a group of skaters, he had never seen a trick landed. Ever. Because they were always trying something new. Perhaps their absurdly low ratio of success to failure was not exceptional at all. Perhaps the skateboard, one of the most primitive inventions imaginable, a plank with wheels that somehow eluded Leonardo and took civilization thousands of years to invent, was measuring a universal constant. Perhaps we were meant to fail thousands of times, in public, for every achievement. This was learning laid bare. He remembered the wheel-scraped walls of the tower, which was now in view, and wondered which, if any, of these park kids was Kurt's lookout.

He scrutinized the hollows of each tree. A big camera would be hard to disguise, but one of those small snake cameras, curled vipers, would be impossible to spot on a tree branch. It would have to have wires, right? And there were no wires. The door had been repainted firehouse red. No need to check the lock. Nothing could be less relevant. He looked around him one final time, twisted his left foot as if extinguishing a cigarette, then let the tension of a month of being kept in a cage uncoil from his hip to his heel.

Four sounds as he kicked down the door: one, the explosion of the hinge drowning the sound of heel meeting wood; two, the quick skid of the door's base against the ground; three, the drawn-out *timber* as the door confirmed the hypothesis of gravity; and four, the gunshot of a sixty-pound door hitting the concrete ground.

No one was around, and no one came running, but he was certain people on the other side of the trees had heard him stave in the door. The door was rocking on top of something and wasn't quite flush to the ground. Loud electro played from the wall-mounted speakers, but he knew that didn't guarantee occupancy.

Emboldened by the door at his feet, he roared to the heights:
—Kurt!

He wanted to add, "You're coming down here or you're coming down here without the ramp!" But instead he listened.

Owen stomped up the central spiral to the top of the tower, shouting for Kurt as he walked. No one responded. There was no one to push against, so Owen gripped hard against his own lapels and led himself to the table of the top floor. The table was scrubbed of everything he remembered.

In the place of drug residue, nearly empty liquor bottles, takeout, and napkin sketches offered up to the world with the surety of cocaine genius, Owen found an airline ticket for Basel with red carbon triplicate. Underneath, a note from Altberg.

May 28ᵗʰ, 2004

Dearest Owen,

As you may have surmised by now, this motley crew is deeply indebted to you for the vision you brought to this project. You are more than a male model to us. We would be delighted if you would join us for the premiere of Kurt Wagener's latest artwork at Art 35 Basel. The opening reception is Wednesday, June 16ᵗʰ.

Enclosed you will find an airline voucher. You can redeem this coupon at the Lufthansa ticket counter of either Tempelhof or Tegel Airport. If you are unable to connect all the way to Basel, fly to Zurich, and we will compensate you for the rail expense. We leave accommodation to your own discretion. Should you choose to lodge in Basel, I will say that you should book at once and look far afield, for the hotels fill up fast.

You will also find (1) the executed contracts for your work

in the photo shoots of May 3rd through May 15th, 2004; (2)
payment of €500 for the aforementioned photo shoot; (3) the
fully executed Non-Disclosure Agreement covering the months
of April and May of 2004.

    Everyone is unanimous in expressing what a pleasure it was
to collaborate with you.

    Come join your fellow Gentlemen of the Shade, Minions of
the moon.

    Yours truly,

    Robert Altberg, Esq.

Screams bottled in his head. He checked the dates again. Almost two weeks they had him on the floor. Probably every floor.
Which meant thousands of pictures, not the dozen he could remember. Pictures until they were bored.

A signed agreement in duplicate relinquishing all rights to
Kurt Wagener to use Owen's image for any project intended as a
work of art. None of the documents included his last name, just
Owen, which gave him hope that the pictures could be removed
from the world. They either wanted to keep him anonymous or
hadn't taken the trouble to investigate. Stevie must have been the
one who looked him up online. He looked at his shaky signature and clutched his head. Beside the two copies of the agreement were a cashier's check for €500, a hundred-Swiss-franc note
paper-clipped to the paycheck, and a brochure from the Basel
Tourist Council. He took the money, left the rest untouched.

He felt watched.

Owen found a camera. It was sunk into the wall, directly in
front of the table, and recording everything. He snuck around the
side of the field of view, grabbing a Joseph Beuys monograph and
a ballpoint pen on the way.

He thumbed open the pen, letting the cap fall to the floor, and scratched the roller ball along the masonry until it sank into the spyhole. He stood with his back against the wall, camera just beside his right hip, blue PaperMate pinched between his fingers with ballpoint against the glass sphere. He slammed the thick book in his left hand directly into the tail of the pen. The glass didn't shatter like he had hoped, but the pen had driven the camera from the spyhole. He repositioned the pen, then hammered it into the hole with the same slap he would have used to kill an insect. The hole now appeared to be no more than a blue screw anchor.

Owen found two more cameras and drove two more Paper-Mates into the wall. Downstairs, he entered the room that had been his for a few ill-fated weeks. It too had been swept clean. The black-iron plumbing pipe was gone, and the cotton candy insulation had been stripped from the unfinished walls. The woven plastic tarp remained, but in the still afternoon it was silent. At this time of year, at this hour of day, the tarp imitated stained glass, filtering the room in cerulean blue that gave Owen pause.

On the ground floor, he walked over the broken door, see-sawed on whatever it had landed on. Glass rolled on the concrete and popped under his step. He lifted the door, uncovering his duffel bag. He unzipped it to find his clothes neatly folded, sand and oil on his black rollneck sweater, wallet, passport, and oil-soaked copy of the *Odyssey* with a note from Stevie peeking out the top. She wrote that she was worried for him when she went back to the tower and only found his bag. She was waiting for him in Basel. She then said she had no idea what he and Kurt were doing, which quickly digressed to a discussion of the role of the outsider in Andrzej Wajda's film *Ashes and Diamonds*, James Dean, and the music of Jacques Dutronc. She ended with the following: "If the Sun and Moon should doubt, / They'd immediately go out."

Owen kept the note because her handwriting sang and the trace of tuberose bloomed into his head like the first steeps of a dark red tea. The note smelled like the back of her neck, and in the moment he caught himself sculpting the air in eddies, whorling a fingerprint of the moment, despite the olive oil soaking his bag and the hollow pumpkin air.

He dumped the shattered glass and sand from his bag. Oil dripped from the white plastic teeth of the zipper and hit the floor in droplets. The combination of sand, shattered glass, and oil looked a little too intentional on the cement floor; the shitty little pattern looked like something Kurt might fob off as art. Owen kicked the sand and glass to different ends of the water tower. But this scattering vaguely resembled a mandala, so he kicked the sand and glass farther, to the edge of the brick. Stubbing his toe as he kicked glass into brick, he realized that he looked totally insane. But insanity is the only rational response when trapped in the profanity of someone else's world.

He sat on a park bench overlooking the tower to make sure Kurt hadn't been watching the whole scene from around the corner. He bent his credit card back and forth until he could tear it in two. His bank account was an empty crypt. His earlier attempt to withdraw 300 euros had been rebuffed by the ATM, 200 got a polite chuckle. He successfully bargained for 100, but was denied 40, then denied 20—unbearably frustrating, given that he'd definitely had the money before the international transaction fees. In three months of travel he had spent the entirety of his assets in this world. He folded the card back and forth until he tore it in two. He threw half in the trash can and put the other half in the ticket pocket of his corduroy jacket.

Everything that he left in Berlin would be left for good. He tried to see the latent potential of his situation: Berlin could be a time capsule, a burying ground for everything he wanted to be

206

rid of; crisis as chrysalis. The idea fell apart as a cliché of transformation; he had clearly lost color and his former strength, he was no butterfly, couldn't fool anyone there. The chrysalis thing worked, however, when he thought of this moment as an inevitability. Flight, no matter how it seems at the time, is never voluntary. Owen had no more control of his path than a dapplethroated nightingale in a hawk's talons. He recalled Hal's tarot card tattoo of two men falling from a tower. The final thought of anyone falling: I can fly.

Rather than redeem the airline voucher Altberg had left in his name, Owen would take the ICE train to Basel. He walked the length of Berlin, bag strap crossing his chest, to the ticket window of the Berlin Zoologischer Garten. He paid for his ticket in cash—from here on out it had to be cash to avoid transaction records.

He found a window seat in the rear of a car, at the rear of the train. He thought about the reality of what might happen, what his hands might do.

He remembered when injustice was a B+ on an essay. What he'd said to Stevie was fundamentally true: the injury had saved him from being an asshole, and the insult had taught him that there are people like Kurt out there to give you real problems if you're too trivial, people who will make your values an exposed nerve that you have to keep out of the wind.

The train ticked through the Black Forest, and Owen thought of how he would explain what had happened, and what was coming, to his California friends. It wasn't that he was acting, per se, it was that he was refusing to have limits placed upon his action. His hands told him that there could be no restraint on the violence. These were smaller arms, half their creatine-swollen diameter and twitching with atrophy. Frequently the muscle would fire from a single node in his arm. Right now his right biceps was involuntarily contracting. He watched with detachment, imagining nanonauts in his bloodstream docking on these twitching fiber shores and excavating the trapped resources of all those tofu-steak and black bean taco lunches. Though his arms were shaky, his grip was tighter than ever, and that was something like harmony.

When he was still an athlete, he had lacked all trace of competition, *agon* or *zelos*. He was never a competitor in the sense of being against anyone. To the extent that he cared about the relative performance of each individual adversary, Owen was one of the few who wanted his opponent at his absolute best. Not so he could defeat a more worthy rival—that would have amounted to vanity. His view was religious. Rather than being ruled by Eris, the daughter of Night, Owen was driven by *arete*, the mandate to always be his best. When he dove into a pool, he dove into an *aristeia*. He was too empty while performing to worry about competition. He extended the same courtesy to his opponents that he extended to everyone else in his life: the need to see potential realized.

Since Owen's injury in the game against Cal, he had become a competitor, fighting against the world rather than surrendering to it. Too conscious, Owen now rode through a colorless world, free of conviction. In this pale godless world anything could happen.

With nothing but competition driving Owen to Basel, he arrived in agony.

Smooth and ink-trailing as the sweep of a broad-nib pen, the Rhine cuts Basel in two. The northeastern half of the city had been transformed to fairground, people walking the riverbank who spend most of their lives being driven. Owen wandered into the southwestern half of the city: gated châteaus interspersed with block housing.

After learning from three hotels that the last room in the city had been booked a month prior, Owen wandered to the university and managed to secure a futon in an apartment of computer programmers for eighty Swiss francs a night.

In the big multinational bookstore, Owen sifted through the magazines and newspapers, looking for the pictures. In big block letters on the cover of *Vice* magazine, KURT WAGENER. Kurt wore a tank commander's helmet, visor up, and a camouflage flak vest with iron-on patches of Disney characters. He was pointing at the sky, calling his shot.

Owen brought the magazine to the Zum Schmale Wurf near the Rhine quayside and read the interview over a lager.

Kurt Wagener has defined what it means to be a twenty-first-century artist. Exploding onto the scene in January of 2001 with his show 1.1.1.1 and bringing with him the now-legendary group of artists at the Todd Zeale Gallery, Wagener has pushed art further in the past four years than anyone could have foreseen. Critics have been racing to catch up with him, refining the new critical lexicon of post-op modernism. He is quite simply the most exciting young artist in the world today.

VICE: Can you begin, Kurt, by telling us what post-op modernism means to you?

Kurt Wagener: Sure. I came up with the term when this *New York Times* writer was interviewing me for my first solo show in Chelsea. This was before the assault, you know, but I was already thinking of the artist as a surgeon. It was all about the role of the transformed body—either as a picture that you fuck with or as a tattoo or something. And about, like, getting beyond the signifier and signified operation. The pieces are post-operation.

VICE: I saw someone yesterday with a T-shirt that read Poop Mod . . .

KW: No. Just no. Next question.

VICE: Can you describe to our readers the assault you alluded to?

KW: So yeah. We were partying at this fashion thing, and I kind of go outside with this girl and then get separated from everybody. These three guys come around the side of the car and say something about her. I couldn't let that happen. I knock out the first guy, but the other two get me down on the ground and stomp on my neck.

VICE: The assailants were Arab, correct?

KW: Yeah. Maybe Turkish.

VICE: How do you feel about the wave of anti-immigrant attacks that followed?

KW: I was surprised. It was a few months after Bush invaded Iraq, but I was surprised about how big the response was. Because, I mean, I'm famous in the art world, or whatever, but that's like being the king of Liechtenstein. In the larger world, you know, you need to be a movie star or Michael Jordan or something to make an impact. I get one week a year of being really famous: Art Basel.

VICE: You're being modest.

KW: Can I get that in print? No, seriously. I had a solo show, not a group show, at Red Rhombus in London and then couldn't get into Kate Moss's party across the road. Basel is the only place where people ask me to pose with them for pictures—I never do, but at least they ask.

VICE: Do you think honesty is important to your work?

KW: Absolutely. I would say it's the only aspect of my work. Kurt Cobain was huge for me. He shot himself when I was fourteen and going through a bunch of shit. I read his suicide note over and over again. I memorized it for theater class. Flunked. But Kurt was really the greatest genius of his generation. That letter is probably the most significant literary work of the twentieth century. His message was simple. I mean, read the fucking letter. You'll never read anything more honest. He said, Look, sometimes I mail it in. And I feel awful about it. I'd rather put a shotgun in my mouth than sell you something fake. That's the sort of honesty I'm after in my work. There are fucking strikethroughs, and it's messy. Everything that we used to call craft, artists are now realizing is dishonesty. Sure there are better painters out there, but if I ever feel like there's a more honest artist, then I'm going to suck the fucking slug from a Glock like it was an oyster.

VICE: What about violence?

KW: Violence can never be a metaphor. Neither can sex. Which is why my work is concerned chiefly with sex and violence. Sexual violence. As far as it being my message, just walk around any art fair and count how many people are ripping me off. And it's like whatever. On the one hand, the more bad work that's out there, the more valuable the great work is. On the other hand, don't plagiarize, fuckers!

VICE: Your work has been up at Art Basel before, but this year you're actually attending?

KW: I'm with a new dealer. Part of the reason I went with Pfaff Galleries was their booth space. Floor one. And with enough square footage for all three of the large-scale installations I'm planning.

VICE: Can you describe them? Would that be okay with the mysterious Myron Pfaff?

KW: The greatest thing about my life is that I can do whatever the fuck I want. Right when you walk in, there's an installation on your left and an installation on your right. On the left is a giant terrarium with a glass front. It's going to be big, like five meters high, ten meters long, and two meters deep. Inside, a dozen models naked except for high heels. I decided to outfit each of the girls with a Polaroid 340 camera and an endless supply of flashbulbs and film. My idea is that the models will take photos of whoever watches them. Those flashbulbs are fucking crazy. I did some preliminary testing and these magnesium bulbs are fucking crazy bright and they sound like a gun when they go off. [Makes an explosion sound: "Boom Boom Crack."] To get the bulbs to explode, you have to put your fingerprints on them. And that's the artist's touch. They've got to have some kind of oil on the surface and be touched to explode. It's pretty sexual. Those bulbs are my favorite part of the show. I've told Myron to line up buyers for any of the bulbs that make it through the week. I can't think of a more pure artistic work.

VICE: So your idea is to have a bunch of naked fashion models, whose legs alone are probably insured for a million euros, parading around in a tank with hot glass shards flying everywhere?

KW: Well, we aren't going to be getting top-tier models! They're not really that much fun anyway. These girls are happy to do it and should be making some serious cash from the Polaroids. The money from those sales is all theirs. Once the photo develops, the girls will hang it from the front of the tank so that visitors will only see the black film-back. I think a lot of people will pay just to make sure no one else sees their leering. The entire front of the tank should be tiled with these little Polaroid pictures by Saturday morning. It will be a peep show in reverse. But the focus will be on their feet, eventually. And here there's some real tension because as the thousands of flashbulbs explode, there's gonna be a lot of fucking glass on that floor. Every step is going to be an event.

VICE: What's this work called?

KW: *Exposure.*

VICE: What was the vision behind the other two installations?

KW: Vision? That's a very romantic view of art. In practice, art is more like a threesome, beautiful only in the abstract. In reality, it's a little awkward. Drug fueled. Somebody inevitably gets a little bored. If my work has a goal, it's to defy boredom. As far as the pieces here at Basel, one is an exact reconstruction of the bar room of the *Wasserturm*, my place in Berlin. It's going to serve as a fully stocked open bar for the course of Art Basel. Free drinks. No tricks. The other work is an installation of four photographs. The source images are the photos released in late April from Abu Ghraib. I recreated each image, added a few touches, but the big thing was how I inverted the subject. Rather than a poor Iraqi cabdriver, I captured Captain America himself.

VICE: What do you mean, you captured Captain America? [Mr. Wagener's legal counsel clarified that Halfred Baumberger "captured" images with a medium-format camera.]

The story contained three full-page pictures: one of Owen hooded and standing on a wooden spool with electrodes coiling from under his hands to a car battery; one of Kurt's refabricated dining room from the *Wasserturm* with the table full of liquor and disposable cups, cups as ashtrays, everything that wasn't at the tower yesterday.

Hives broke out under Owen's collar, turtlenecking up to his jaw. He turned to a full-page picture of Kurt in profile, interviewed by a young woman, presumably the author. A lanyard on the table reflected bright light. Beside it, 2004's neon-green Art Basel catalogue. He tore the picture from the magazine. Comparing all the city guides, he gathered that the only game in town was the Hotel Trois Rois.

He imagined Kurt on a balcony overlooking the Rhine,

pinching the filter of his Marlboro Red and smoking each drag as if he were being photographed in black and white, summoning the ennui of French New Wave, but really contemplating the limitations of his newest cell phone. Owen imagined him chucking it in the river and then rolling back inside.

Owen, now with a map of Russia rashed around his throat, walked the carpeted stairs and was stopped short of the revolving door.

—Are you staying with us, sir?

The doorman's tone made it clear this was a rhetorical question.

—I'm meeting a friend at the bar.

—I'm afraid the bar is closed for a private event.

—Then I guess I'll just meet him in the lobby.

This was about as long as a conversation with a doorman can last before someone touches an arm or makes a threat. Owen walked by. The doorman gave a tight smile.

Owen paced the lobby, looking for the patinated wall in the photo. Instead, he found nothing but ecru and dim lighting. He asked a bellhop if the room in the photo was in this hotel. The bellhop shook his head just before the manager approached.

—May I help you, sir?

—Just on my way out. I had the wrong hotel.

Owen walked into every hotel in the *Wallpaper* City Guide* to Basel and had much the same experience. After striking out at the last of their recommended hotels, he realized he was at a dead end. Which in the adult world, as he was learning, typically meant a trip to the bar. He found a spot on the promenade north of the Rhine.

—Bourbon and a beer, please.

—Any preference?

—Whatever's cheapest.

The bartender joined him for the whisky. She raised her glass and met his eye.

—Are you in town for the show?

Owen could see this conversation replayed to a ring of cops.

—I'm here for a few days and then I'm off to Thailand.

She raised her eyebrows to say okay, then continued reading her book.

Owen unfolded the photo of Kurt in the hotel lobby and smoothed it on the bar. He read the last page of the interview:

KW: This American Olympian comes up to me at a neighborhood bar and goes on and on about how much my work means to him and how he would love to collaborate on something. This kind of thing happens all the time, but usually the guy is a loser and looking to get a boost in his career. And why would I do that? But this guy looked the part. He was really fucking tall and had an eye patch. The day before, that picture from Abu Ghraib of the dude standing on the box hit the media and my first question at that point was, "Why isn't this art?" So I pitched the idea of re-creating it, but with the American as the model, and he thought it was brilliant, so he said yes.

VICE: And what are these pieces called?

KW: The bar piece is called *The Impossibility of Getting Anything But Plastered in the Shadow of a Dozen Naked Models.*

VICE: That name seems—

KW: I'm just fucking with you. It's really just a bar. It's not really art at all. But this way it's a tax write-off, you know. The title is *Bar* (2004).

VICE: I'm reminded of Duchamp's Hat Rack, starting life as a functional hat rack near the entrance, but every day creeping an inch closer to the center of the gallery. After something like eight days, with the hat rack now 1.5 meters closer to the center of the room, people stopped hanging their coats and hats on it and started regarding Hat Rack as a readymade sculpture. Duchamp had, in effect, provided a quantified answer to the question, What is Art? Is this your project with *Bar*?

KW: Really. It's just a bar and you get to look at lots of titties.

VICE: What is the other piece called, the Abu Ghraib photos?

KW: It's titled *Spooky Action at a Distance*.

The bartender pulled her hair back and, noticing Owen scratching at his neck, made conversation:
—You know that guy?
Owen's eye turned a little whiter. His automatic response was to say he collaborated with him. He was furious at what had happened, furious at what he had just read, and yet his stupid brain still betrayed him and wanted to entangle itself with Kurt. He bit down on his cheek.
The bartender refilled his whisky.
—You do know him. He hangs out here during the fair. I haven't seen him this year, but he'll be here at some point.

—Can you tell me where this photo was taken? I thought the hotel was in Basel, but I've been in a half dozen lobbies and can't find this room.

She held the flimsy page to a late afternoon beam of light.

—That's not a real hotel. It's an art collector's house. She's the widow of some pharmaceutical titan. The only things she cares about are art and friends. They have unbelievable parties there. Crazy parties. During Art Basel it's called the Guesthouse.

—Is it in the city center?

—It's a ten-minute walk. Does he owe you money?

—That's the only thing he doesn't owe me.

—Kurt's not much of a human being, but at least he knows it—which may be why he tips so well.

Owen set all the cash in his pocket onto the counter.

—How do I find this guesthouse?

—You don't need to tip me for that.

She pinched a twenty-franc note from the mound of bills yawning out their crumples.

—The widow's named Lady Percy. Her place is in Saint Alban. Walk along the Rhine, pass the Mittlere bridge, then turn on the Wettstein bridge. You take the first street on your left, St. Alban-Vorstadt. Take St. Alban-Vorstadt until it hits a crossroads. From there you can either continue on St. Alban's if you want to go to the front gate or take a left on Muhlenberg if you want to go unannounced. If you take the Muhlenberg route, it's the mansion on the hill with the spire. You're going to have to climb a wall or knock on a big iron gate. If you take the St. Alban route, it's just past Malzgasse. You won't miss it.

Owen wrote the directions in the back of his father's *Odyssey*, thanked her, and shouldered his bag.

—When you find Kurt, tell him Clara said hi.

Owen chose the frontal approach. A solid panel of iron on rails protected the Guesthouse from street traffic.

He held the button down and challenged the security camera.

Someone was sprinting down the street from the east and calling his name. He turned around to find Hal running with his arms waving, as if he were trying to stop someone from boarding the wrong train. His goatee had grown so long and scraggled that Owen hardly recognized him.

—Whoa whoa whoa, man. What are you doing here? It's great to see you.

Hal caught up, then took two steps back. He lowered his chin and began lightly scratching his temple, shielding his face with his forearm and elbow, clenching his teeth and ready to take a punch.

—I owe you an apology for everything that happened in Berlin. I want you to know I had no part in any of that. Kurt threatened to evict me. I feel horrible about the pictures. I want to help you get even.

—Is he in there?

—No. There were technical problems with one of his pieces, and he had to go to the pavilion to fix it. He was planning on streaming video of the empty table in Berlin, now the feed from Berlin is snow; he wanted to have a few TVs showing the real table over the replica table. I'm assuming you found Altberg's note?

—But Kurt is staying here?

—He met some girl. Some girls actually. They may be partying tonight if he can get the work finished. But listen, he's an asshole.

Owen looked through him. Hal continued:

—Kurt thinks that because he pays me well, he can take all the credit for my work. It keeps getting worse. This morning a reporter from *Der Spiegel* asked him about my role. What did he say? "Hal's a graphic designer. Sometimes he takes a picture or two." Kurt's seriously hampering my sales. I'm getting no credit for Basel.

—Be careful, Hal. As soon as I give you an ounce of credit for the photos strung up on the other side of that river, you and I are going for a swim and we're going to find out who can hold his breath longer.

—Point taken. I had nothing whatsoever to do with those images. You remember me yelling at him to stop, right? He's out of control.

Hal fanned his goatee, then continued:

—I'd have a hard time seeing him pose for any of the Art Basel press stuff if he had, say, a broken nose or a black eye or a knocked-out tooth. I think he would just disappear to a resort for a few months, like some plastic surgery refugee.

—Leaving the press with no alternative but you.

—That's not my fault. The public needs to hear from its artists to sustain these prices.

—When does he get back?

—This is the wrong place to confront him. The house comes with its own security personnel, and they have pictures of you.

—Everybody does. Thanks for that. Give me an alternative.

—That's what I've been thinking about. Art Basel doesn't officially start until Thursday. There's nothing happening tonight. Monday and Tuesday are the select VIP preview, Wednesday is the normal VIP preview. Right now, anyone with any money is in Zurich or Berlin making deals. Most of the good work is already sold. Tomorrow night is when the collectors come to see what they bought and hear about their prescience. Kurt knows the routine. He brought our dining table to Basel so everyone would be hanging out at the Pfaff booth tomorrow. Everything is in place for it to be packed tomorrow night. He won't be expecting you to be there. It's perfect. Tomorrow night is when you have to confront him.

—Hal, I don't give a shit if he's expecting me. I'm not the kind of guy who sneaks up.

—Fine. But if you can keep calm until Tuesday night, the payoff will be worth it. It's going to be the biggest night of his career by far. He might stick around for the official opening, but chances are that come Thursday he'll be stepping onto someone's yacht in Antibes or Croatia.

—Stepping?

—You know what I mean. Don't be a dick.

—No one stays for the actual fair?

—The crowd stays. The tastemakers will be headed for Venice on Thursday or chasing after the collectors who flew their private planes to the coast on Tuesday. There's a party here at Lady Percy's tonight. After tomorrow night, it's more about the parties than the art. But right now, it's all about art. Every billionaire is looking to walk away with the names of five new artists who are going to change the world.

—Can you get me in tonight?

—You're not listening. Kurt is not going to be there until tomorrow night. That's when you need to go, when all his collectors are there.

—And you can get me in tomorrow?

—Absolutely. Brigitte will put you on the Timmons gallery list as one of their artists. And hey, look on the bright side, you've gone from no one to official international artist.

Owen put both palms to his brow, trying to undo the world.

—We could go through Pfaff, but then Kurt would know you're coming.

—Fine. It'll be tomorrow. Take care of it.

Owen left Hal standing outside the iron gate of the Guest-house.

—So I'll tell Brigitte tomorrow night, then? Hal shouted.

Owen was already off Mühlenberg Strasse and headed for the river. The idea that Hal could get him into anything but trouble was laughable. But he had met someone else in Berlin who could give him a slight advantage.

Once more, Owen walked through the lobby of the Hotel Trois Rois to the back bar. He needed a strong drink before confronting someone who may or may not have pending legal action against him. But he couldn't afford any of the hotel's strong drinks. So he found a seat and drank an Amstel. A 500-watt light bounced off a Mylar umbrella. Kurt hadn't diffused anything for Owen. Straight heat and glare.

One young man, apparently some art-world oracle, was delivering his assessment of the run-up to Art Basel to a mic-wagging interviewer from CNNMoney. Half of the crowd pretended not to be listening, but they weren't fooling anyone. The room clearly belonged to the one who drew the light.

—Did you see anything noteworthy?

—I saw Dave Cohen looking at a Richter like he was going to buy.

—I thought he only bought Impressionists.

—That's why it was interesting.

—What's his net worth?

—Two-point-four billion.

—And who's his buyer?

—He buys himself. That's the secret to being a major collector. It's not how much money you have, it's your taste.

—John McEnroe.

—Exactly. John McEnroe.

Owen only knew of one John McEnroe and wondered if this was some sort of code.

—I'm hearing that some of the galleries have already sold out. So tell us, who's selling?

—Gagosian, but his booth is mostly Kiefer, so that was a foregone conclusion. The big surprise so far is Jacques Lacroix's work at Lawrence Timmons's space—those pieces are really out there. It reminds me of Yves Klein's imagined paintings more than anything else. Lawrence was kind enough to show me slides of the pieces last month. The first two were the types of performative reconstruction we've come to expect from Lacroix; the third work in the catalogue was "*Titled*, 2002, $285,000." It was the only work that didn't have a slide. I asked Lawrence if the work wasn't finished yet, or what.

—What did he say?

—Well, he scowls at me and says, completely deadpan, "The listing is the piece."

—Fabulous! I'm sure it will go in the next few days.

—And maybe it should. Yves Klein has never been more relevant.

—Is there anything else you're interested in?

—Biggest question mark of the fair is what's going on over at Pfaff Galleries.

—Kurt Wagener's new work.

—It's a mess. Apparently there was a technical problem with a video installation piece. The rest is kind of all over the place. There's a scratched-up piece of wood that looks so much like a Keith Haring that it must be a tribute. There's a performance piece, yawn, of models behind acrylic glass taking pictures of the people who walk by. I hate to say it, but Kurt Wagener is making painting seem relevant again—just as an alternative to this fiasco. There's a full bar. There's a smashed-up piece of drywall, huge cardboard box, and a triptych of Abu Ghraib torture photography called *Spooky Action at a Distance.*

—Torture photography? That took all of a month.

Owen shot from his chair before his waiter arrived for round two. At the front desk he asked for Todd Zeale. The desk manager looked annoyed that someone as disheveled as Owen could name one of his guests. He took his time dialing Zeale's room and then passed the phone to Owen.

—This is Todd. And who exactly are you?

—I'm the tall guy with the eye patch who stood by while Kurt destroyed your gallery. Sorry about that.

—Oh, the naughty Olympian. Well, what do you want?

—I want to offer Kurt a choice.

—I have fifteen minutes or so. Pass the phone back to the nice man at reception. They'll show you up.

Todd Zeale was wearing a brown chenille robe that made him look like a plush toy. The white towel coiled like a turban pulled tight his shining forehead. Unwrapped presents took up half the floor space. A three-wicked lavender candle the size of a flower-pot burned on the table at Todd's side.

—Please. Do take a seat.

—I'm fine standing.

Owen parted the curtains to be sure no one was waiting outside on the veranda.

—All of the suites were sold out years ago, but I've always thought an average room in a great hotel is far better than a great room in an average hotel, wouldn't you agree? But it must be bizarre walking around with your head raking the ceilings. Should we go downstairs? Do you feel trapped?

—By the time I was fifteen, I realized the world was built too small.

—Talk to me in twenty years. The world only seems small when you imagine you have all the time in the world. But we don't, hence these little microcosms.

—Like Basel.

—Precisely. Now what was this about offering Kurt a choice? You do realize that in this world you're still a commoner, someone who is offered a choice, but never gets to present one.

—I need to get into the preview tonight.

—And why should I help you with that?

—Because you are the only person I can think of who wants to harm Kurt as much as I do.

—Stick around. Few people in this town haven't been fucked or fucked over by Kurt in the past four years. As you pointed out, I'm one of them. As far as wishing him harm, you're alone there. I'm heavily invested in Kurt's success. I have several of his works in my private collection, and the gallery was built on the back of Kurt Wagener. So no, I have very little interest in destroying the career of the biggest artist I've represented. Nor do I wish him more suffering than he's already endured.

—After what he did to your gallery?

—Did you ask him which gallery is representing that video art piece? No?

—The same gallery he tore apart.

—Precisely. I haven't found a buyer yet, but once he proves his price point at Basel, I can get it sold for $5 million. He is the King Midas of the moment. Even in the act of destruction, he creates. I think that piece, which I'm urging him to title *Midas*, is his most significant work to date. The loop is closed: Kurt destroys the gallery that stood behind him his entire career, and in that moment of destruction he creates a monumental work—represented by the very gallery he just razed. He proves the institutional theory of art with an elegance that would make Duchamp smile. Art is whatever you find in a gallery. The gallery is whatever you find in art.

—I'd be a lot more amenable to this kind of talk if I had a VIP pass in my hand.

—There is no "pass," my dear. There is no badge you can wear around your neck, no ticket to be collected, no secret handshake I can teach you. I'm sorry. I'd love to help.

—I'm sure you would.

—There's a bottle of Scotch in the armoire. I'm going to smoke this. You're welcome to join.

Owen left Todd Zeale rolling a joint on a mirrored drink tray.

—Suit yourself. I'll be telling Kurt about our chat.

The lock hit the strike plate and slapped shut. He walked down the green carpet stairs to the street.

On the other side of the revolving doors, Basel exploded with early summer: violet heather and the last of the cherry blossoms. He followed the hook of the swift-running Rhine until he reached the copse of alder trees shading the Guesthouse.

A footworn path through wild hazel shrubs and smooth-barked poplar ran from the cars parked along the riverbank to the mossy stone wall guarding the house. From the safety of trees, in the luxury of dappled sun, Owen looked for guards and listened for a clue to what was on the other side of the wall. The rusted iron door, cut deep into the thick stone wall, belonged at an industrial facility, not a residence. The wall itself was built to brace against eighteenth-century floods. The top of the wall was almost fifty feet above the water table. Owen struggled to imagine how a river could rise that high. The wall's present function was clearly to keep people out. Curiously, the buttresses were on his side, forming stone ramps he might scramble up. But the ramps stopped far short of the wall's lip. The ramps would leave him stranded and exposed. He would have to scale it.

If Owen adhered to anything as inflated as a philosophy of conflict, his underlying precept was: get as close as possible to the most dangerous thing in any environment. Constrain options through proximity. Get close or get hit. Right now, the most dangerous object was the security camera. His plan was to sprint straight for it. If he was standing beneath it, they'd only see the top of his head. They might know he was there, but they couldn't inspect him. And there was some comfort in that.

The wind shuffled the alders. A red catkin fell in his tangled hair. He bit his fingernails so they wouldn't catch on the stone and tried to talk himself out of what he was about to do. He listened to more laughter and clinking glasses. The murmur could be music or it could be a trick of the river, throwing its voice into the walls of the Guesthouse and then casting the entire backyard in a rustle.

As the wind rattled the trees more forcefully, Owen dashed for the stone wall. He stood directly below the security globe. Now he could hear the sound of silver against porcelain, the meeting of glasses against side plates. Scores of people were waiting on the other side of that wall. A ring of red LEDs lit up around the globe, bright enough to overpower the setting sun and light the hackled hair of his arms.

With wings stretched wide, he snagged two handholds and kicked his left instep into the wall. Pushing hard off his left leg, he swung and found a foothold for his right. With one kick, he leapt and caught the camera's anchor. The ring of red lights started blinking. In seconds someone would be through the iron door. Owen's hips were flush against the stone; his lace-up moccasins smeared across the face of the wall. To make it over the ledge, he swung from the security camera, sacrificed his grips, and punched up to catch the overhang. He dangled there for a breath and then pommeled around so his back was against the wall. He looked north to the river and took another deep breath. In one fluid motion he vaulted backward, somersaulting over and once again facing the wall.

He skidded down the face and dropped onto the lawn. He dusted the grit from his arms and shirt, expecting that when he turned around he would find a group of outraged socialites. He would have to say something dramatic.

He stood tall, and the murmur flowed on. Two dozen tea candles danced on a waiter's cocktail tray. Tablecloths billowed and shawls cascaded over elegant necks. White cocktail dresses, white linen suits, white-rimmed sunglasses, and the whites of a hundred eyes all turned to face Owen. Most of the guests looked slightly perturbed, vaguely amused at the gate-crasher, as if a raccoon had dropped from a tree. But they were thoroughly assured someone would soon take care of the situation. The waiter smirked, but continued placing white candles on white tables for white people.

Altberg, in a white panama hat, came tumbling down the hill in grass-crushing heaves. Green blades cowered before him, and he was at Owen's feet in a bounding instant, never spilling a bubble of his champagne.

—He shows up to the white party in a black T-shirt. You have to love Americans. Rebelling against whatever we've got, ladies and gentlemen, the famous Olympian-turned-artist, Owen . . .

Owen scanned the crowd. Half the expressions were flat—presumably the half with money. The most amphibian of toadies smiled politely. The more savvy looked to their hostess, the stately Lady Percy, to determine whether they should feign action or even gallantry. Lady Percy motioned to security.

Watching all this play out and reckoning the inevitable loss of face that would come if the man he'd just announced were accosted, Altberg ushered Owen to Lady Percy's table.

Altberg pulled Owen through the sculpture garden. Owen scraped his hip on a rusted iron wedge jutting from the grass hill like an oversize canoe. He passed a recumbent woman, ten feet long and white marble, lustrous with long-wave reds that had made it through the setting sky to graze her knees and glow her arms.

Then Owen's gaze was pulled to the two most startling people he had ever seen: matching shaved heads, matching white embroidered jackets over matching white embroidered dresses and ropes and ropes of pearls. They raised their eyebrows, stretching a canvas of matching multihued multilayered eyeshadow painted with the exact blue, green, pink, yellow, and orange of a flame about to drown in a pool of melted wax. The couple leaned in and craned their necks. Their movements uncannily, nearly telepathically synchronized.

Owen turned away to find a pair of children on bronze orbs that cut into the grass like snail shells. At the top of the slope one table glowed with a solitary sunbeam, possibly the last direct light in all of Switzerland. That this table should happen to be Lady Percy's was no coincidence. Two security guards, wearing white polo shirts awkwardly collared around their tree-trunk necks and tight in the biceps, leaned in at her side. Neither guard visibly wore a gun, but neither appeared to need a device to inflict lethal harm.

Conversation still clinked and tittered, but everyone was watching what could very well turn into a violent scene. Lady Percy's gloved hand was staying the guards for now, but the overbound men snarled as Owen and Altberg approached.

—My lady, may I present one of the most exciting young artists in the world today. We discovered him only recently in Berlin. He is Myron Pfaff's newest talent. I assure you, when I mentioned he might be dropping in, I had no idea I was speaking so literally.

—Owen, was it? What led you to our little fête in Basel?

Rumor had it that Grace Kelly shadowed Lady Percy to prepare for her role in *The Swan*. Listening to Lady Percy speak was listening to the template of European aristocracy. She left Owen awed. He managed to stutter something out:

—The kindness of strangers.

—I assume you are talking about Robert? If I saw a glimmer of kindness from someone matching his description, I'd know he was an impostor. Robert only helps himself. And like a spoilt child, he helps himself to whatever he wants.

—My only virtue, Lady Percy.

—Robert lured you to Basel with the promise of fortune and fame?

—Something like that, ma'am.

—And you believed in your talent enough to play along?

—I automatically trust passionate people.

—How quaint! I'm assuming you are American?

—Yes.

—Oh, don't say it like you're ashamed of being a member of art's ruling class. Do you think Jasper Johns blushes when someone asks him if he's American? I can tell you from first-hand experience, he does not. Your generation has no sense of self-promotion. But you have our attention; now tell us what's valuable in your work.

Altberg interrupted Owen by pulling back on his arm.

—His work is very athletic. One would even say primal. Very raw. Very physical.

—Why does everyone feel compelled to use the word *very* when explaining art? Some of us have learned to make do with moderation. Others of us . . .

She gestured with an open hand to Altberg's midsection. The backyard tittered.

—Let the boy speak for himself, Robert. I saw those pictures in the catalogue. He's certainly striking, but I can't decide whether he's the artist or the art.

—I'm neither, ma'am.

—The esteemed Robert Altberg disagrees—though for him disagreement lies somewhere between a hobby and a profession.

Lady Percy's subdued volume meant the public castigation had ended. With the hope of droll anecdotes removed, the guests resumed their murmur.

—He means that he isn't showing this year, but he will be in attendance Wednesday night. This is completely *entre nous*, but a certain artist from Berlin owes him more than an acknowledgment and a handshake.

—Wednesday we'll be away. And that won't do. I look forward to seeing you at the preview tonight. I'll leave a pass for you at Will Call.

Lady Percy lowered her voice to Owen:

—Now if you'll excuse us, you really can't stay here wearing that, dear. And I can't very well have every handsome young artist in Basel flinging himself over my wall.

—Of course not. Thank you for not throwing me back over.

Altberg ushered Owen from the hostess's table to the bar on the deck. Its elevated position over the party did much to deflect stares. A waiter offered a champagne tray. Owen thought the knife in the bartender's hand looked tempting, but took the champagne flute instead. Altberg slurped, as if whistling backward:

—*Blanc de blancs.* Lady Percy really never misses a detail. The mid-palate almonds and that unforgettable carnal pear suggests . . . Ruinart?

The waiter smiled and lifted the champagne bottle by the punt: Ruinart.

—I'll stop while I'm ahead. My vintage charts are ajumble. This autumn will need to be devoted to intensive study, cramming as it were for holiday exams.

The bartender revealed it to be a '73.

—I'd like to say I would have guessed that. Ruinart was the very first house to produce champagne, yet curiously . . .

Owen grabbed Altberg's wrist.

—He's in there.

Altberg ripped free from the grip as if he were being accosted by a vagabond. Then he looked around to make sure no one but the staff saw. He spoke in a low voice:

—Kurt won't be back until Wednesday. Two of the models backed out, supposedly from the flu, so he took the night train to Paris to find replacements. Meanwhile, Kurt's eight assistants have been working in overlapping ten-hour shifts for the past week to build everything Kurt had envisioned. They've been spilling beer and putting out cigarettes on the table so that every detail of the *Bar* piece is right. Their work was made more challenging because someone, let's not mention any names, destroyed the video feed from Berlin.

—Oops.

—That's a million-dollar oops that demands at the very least a pantomime of contrition.

—Or?

—Or I get to play lawyer instead of oenophile.

Owen opened his hand with a gesture that both apologized and said never mind.

—He needs you at the opening on Wednesday, Thursday at the latest, for the press. Before you object, note that you are contractually obligated to a month of promotional talks. We're just asking for one day. There's a pass in your name at Will Call that gets you into the Wednesday preview—I seriously doubt, by the way, that even Lady Percy can get you in tonight. I wouldn't even bother. Rest up. Those marathon interviews are brutal. I'd sleep today and tomorrow. These people matter, and you must appear to them as untarnished, or at least artistically tarnished. Otherwise you're a nobody, and the work isn't art, it's exploitation.

—See, here I'm at a loss. If I tell everyone those pictures were exploitative, then I give Kurt's work an element of truth. If I play along, then he is trivializing something horrible. So I'm sorry if being here and being ragged made the work true, but I couldn't care less about fucking up your sales.

—You're not listening. We want you here. The stronger you become as an artist, the more those photos sell for. I have sizable equity in *Spooky Action*. Right now, there is no one in the world more invested in your career than me. In fact, you popping in like this saves me the trouble of sending my courier.

Before the sweep of Altberg's fat paw Owen spotted her through the sliding glass door.

Stevie was reading Auden in a chambray shirt and cut jean shorts. White flip-flops, dangling over the arms of a wingback chair, were the only concession she'd made to Lady Percy's rules of attire.

Owen looked behind him. Late afternoon light had made the whites glow.

His neck hair bristled at someone's breath. He had left Altberg talking *cuvées* to a Russian oligarch. Someone else must have followed Owen inside. Someone was behind him. A very gentle hand touched his elbow. He turned around to find the shorn-headed, heavily made-up couple from outside. They were both smiling ear to ear, ready to talk to Owen and Stevie before they could talk to each other.

—I'm Eva.

—And I'm Adele.

Stevie had already met them and tried to explain:

—They're from the future. From Berlin in the future.

—Our spaceship landed there. We are Futuring.

—Futuring, her partner echoed.

Owen had never been so lost.

—Futuring?

—Futuring.

—Futuring.

Stevie broke the awkward silence.

—In the future it just so happens that people are really, really nice. Who would have guessed, right?

Neither Eva nor Adele stopped smiling. Adele, the shorter of the two, seemed more comfortable with English. She sounded like Owen's first-grade teacher:

—There is strong emotion in this room, which is good. It is the most important thing to feel something. Feelings are yours alone. No one else will ever have them.

They both stared at Owen, again seeming to communicate something without language or even movement. A theremin should be playing, he thought.

Eva couldn't help but add one more.

—Futuring.

Stevie was now standing. She led Owen to the kitchen, marking her place and then dropping Auden's poor wrinkled mug in her beach bag.

—Let's get out of here; those two were the only ones I liked. And I think you weirded them out.

Stevie pulled the door shut behind them. A half dozen cars were parked on the cobble drive between the front door and the security gate: the four black SUVs were hired. He could easily see Lady

Percy driving the green roadster. The sinuous red exotic, the type of car with letters and numbers that are supposed to mean something—G4, X9, M7A, V10—always left Owen feeling like he'd wandered into a game of Battleship. This red car, mere inches from scraping the ground, had to be Altberg's, regardless of the demands his weight would put on the suspension. Owen stopped.

—Don't tell me that's Altberg's.

—Oh, you mean Veronica?

The slick black sidewalls of the tires made him wish he had a pocketknife.

—You're shitting me. He named his car?

—I had to hear about it on the drive down. Some Italian woman he saw once.

—And you rode down here with him because . . .

—I saw your bag just sitting by the door and I knew something was up. I called every hospital and police station in Berlin asking if they picked up Owen Burr. No one knew anything, so I came here. Altberg was my only ride.

—This just keeps getting better.

—I saw the ticket and read the letter. I came here to stop them. And maybe stop you from doing something stupid.

Stevie pushed a button, sliding the iron gate to the side.

The Guesthouse's motion-activated security lights ticked on when they crossed the threshold, halogen arresting the incandescence of Basel's streetlamps. They walked past St. Alban's church, made a left toward the paper mill, and then met the river. She took his hand.

—You've just got to focus on something else. Right now, that's getting as far away from Kurt as you can. You can't do anything about the pictures hanging up in the booth. We all have a gallery of mistakes.

—Gallery of mistakes? They drugged me, at least twice, and

took a bunch of pictures like it was no big deal, like I was some guy who passed out at a frat party. I almost died. You ride down here with Altberg to make sure I'm in Basel, and now I can't stay? What am I missing here? My foot's in a trap, and you're telling me to run. I'm sorry, but no.

—I'm trying to get you out. Just go. We'll go to Paris and stay at L'Hotel, which I've always wanted to do, and have lots of cheap wine in cafés.

Owen squinted into the vanishing sun. He saw a thought flash over her. She was nervous for the first time that she might have actually done something wrong.

—I came back to the tower twice. The first time you were with those girls.

—I don't know what you think you saw, but I was literally about to die from meningitis.

—Whatever it is Kurt's angling for, you need to keep a safe distance. Just point to a map. The tickets are on me. I'm thinking Prague or Paris.

—Those pictures come down today. And if Kurt tries to do something, I'm going to kick him in the teeth.

—Get a court order.

—How long would that take? A month?

—You're right. They're already in the catalogue. But if you make a scene about it, you'll just draw more attention to them. And that's what they want. We need to cut our losses and run.

Owen considered what she was saying.

—Have you heard of the Mann Gulch fire?

—You're not setting Art Basel on fire.

—That's not what I'm suggesting.

—I'm talking about real things, like getting on a train in the next hour. When we're on the train you can tell me all about fires, hurricanes, whatever.

—Let me explain Mann Gulch. It's the best story I know, and it just so happens to be the key to this whole situation.

Stevie took his hand, her fingertips exploring the soft pads of his fingers and the calluses ridging the tops of his palms. She opened her eyes and told him to go ahead.

—Mann Gulch is this place in Montana where a huge wildfire broke out in 1949. Fifteen firemen, smokejumpers, parachuted in farther down the gulch and carried out the foreman's plan of attack. The terrain up there makes everything seem historic, like Thermopylae: mountains sliced by a river into a V-shaped valley, a perfect channel for fire. So these particular smokejumpers parachute into a raging wildfire and decide their best bet is to steer the fire into the Missouri River.

—I thought we were in Montana.

—We are. It's a big river. So they're trying to steer the fire back toward the Missouri, but it sucks up the cool air over the rushing water, gets a shove from the wind coming down the eastern ridge, and leaps over the little stream they were using as a firebreak. When the fire jumped the gulch, they were cut off in an ever-narrowing ring, a C that was quickly becoming an O. There was nothing left to do but sprint up the ridge. Two problems: the Gulch ridge is very steep; and fire spreads even faster uphill.

—What does this have to do with anything?

—I'm getting to that. The foreman, a man named Dodge, ironically enough . . .

—Why is his name ironic?

—You'll see. Dodge, fire singeing his eyebrows, had a moment of genius: fire needs fuel to burn—no fuel, no fire. In this case, the fuel was dried-out late summer cheatgrass. So Dodge gets on his hands and knees and starts *lighting* all the grass around him, he lights a fire then stomps it out, lights another fire, stomps it out, until he has a totally burned-out little circle. He's yelling at everyone to join him in this charred ring, but his men either can't hear him or think he has totally lost it. They run right by him, charging up the ridge with a hundred-foot wall of fire at their backs. Only two of those fifteen survived. Meanwhile, Dodge lies flat on his back in the center of his scorched circle, rolling back and forth because the wildfire is blazing in his face and the smoldering soil is cooking his back. But the flames danced over him and left his little circle untouched, skipping over his scratch of earth as the fire overtook the entire gulch. He was fine. Everything else burned. They teach firefighters to do that now. It's called an escape fire.

—So Kurt and Hal are the smokejumpers who ran?

—No. They're the wildfire. And now that I'm surrounded by the flames, I've got to light a little fire, step forward rather than run away; otherwise this is going to burn me up.

—The problem with your analogy is that we aren't surrounded. Name a city on a rail line and we've got two tickets and a snack car feast, my treat.

—This has to happen. I am going to burn all of that fuel, and Kurt should know to stand back.

—Sounds a lot like your plan to move in with Kurt in the first place. That worked out well, right?

Stevie shook her head and looked at the river.

He watched the hollow above her lip for a twitch that might turn into a smile. No smile. It was hard to tell if she was even breathing. Her lips looked stuck, as if it would hurt to part them. When he spoke, she looked away. He reached a finger for her hand.

—Do you ever have days where your vision shifts?

Without context it sounded like a horrible pickup line. She started walking away.

—That came out wrong. Let's take as a starting point that people see colors differently at different points in their lives.

—Let's take as a starting point, "I'm just kidding. I don't want to get thrown in prison. We're on the next train out of here."

—No, listen. People see things differently at different times. Nothing groundbreaking there. Maybe you have one year where you appreciate yellow more than usual. Or whatever. So that's our starting point. What I'm talking about is maybe two steps from that. I'm talking about when every color you perceive is shifted. A couple of days will be slightly red or light-green or yellow or blue, like someone is holding a gel over the sun.

—I'm not sure I agree with any of that. And I'm not sure what you're saying. Is this a metaphor?

—No.

—Can we at least pretend it's a metaphor, because otherwise you're completely crazy, which really is a shame. To be fair, I'm only interested in guys who are at least seventy percent crazy. I'm willing to go as high as ninety-two percent crazy if the guy has tapered obliques and original opinions. But I can't go full crazy. So. It's a metaphor, right?

—It's a subtle thing, but it was always there. Apparently I'm cured now. So I may not even meet your threshold seventy percent. The color shift happened every day growing up. Now everything is just . . . normal.

—Oh, yeah, normal like this.

—Everything used to have a . . . mood. The world was tinted a particular color, as if I were looking through a colored film, a laminate. There would be this green flash, then an afterimage of gem-like green that lasted for days. I'd wake up in the morning, see that the wood beams on the ceiling looked sapling green, and know my day was going to be different. It wasn't just a sensory thing. It's like the inside of my head was lit with a strange light; my intuition, my thinking, it would get shifted. When I was little, before I knew enough to think I was crazy, the world was a sacred place.

—What did your parents say?

—My dad's a classics professor. He teaches Greek. I grew up thinking that Hermes and Athene and Ares and Apollo were real things—and I made colors into Gods. And I had to know what I was seeing. Other kids skated to the beach. I biked to Home Depot to see if they had any new paint cards.

—The colors never changed, when you grew up or moved or whatever?

—We lived at Mission my entire life. The colors a year ago were the exact same ones I saw when I was five. I used to never talk about this stuff because I thought talking about it was a form of betrayal, and it would go away. But it's been gone for a while now. The names are pretty obscure—I don't know if you've come across these words. Peridot, which is a light green gem—it's the only gemstone found on comets. That was the one I named Hermes. Which ended up fitting when I learned later about the comet connection—a lot of these things I'm going to say just ended up fitting, there's no real way to explain it. The next color was gamboge, Apollo. Gamboge is this Buddhist-monk-robe orange. I thought the gamboge days were this deep mystical thing, but it was pretty much like being drunk. I don't even know the difference now. There was no *me* on those days—to the point where essay grades were a lottery, like I was handed back some random student's paper. I took a failing grade sophomore year when a professor accused me of plagiarism—I couldn't defend the paper because I had no fucking clue what I had written. Carmine is blood red. That's Ares. It's the part of me I'm not going to try apologizing for. My eyes turn completely white, apparently. Ultramarine is this crushed mineral blue that goes with Athene. I went entire months seeing white as a light blue. Ultramarine has been the dominant mood of my life—which makes it tough to say that those days are different. Without that blue, I have no claim on perspective. I used to know how to see with topsight and know how things are linked. It's like I used to be a mason with all these secrets, and now I'm just a brick.

—You stopped seeing these colors when you had your accident?

—Can we just say "lost my eye"? "Had an accident" makes me sound like a little kid. Not a guy who lost an eye. From his head.

—What you're saying makes no sense. It's the blind people who hallucinate colors and shapes and little creatures—I'm not kidding. Don't laugh. My grandmother went through it with macular degeneration. What you're saying is the exact opposite. It doesn't make sense why you would stop seeing these colors after you lost your eye. I also don't get why you're upset about it.

—I'm not upset.

—So you're talking about starting a fight at an art fair so you can, what, try to see the world again with some cool afterglow effects? Why don't you just take drugs like a normal person?

Another idea like a slap to the cheek. She could be right. He could be picking a fight to bring back the Gods.

—I've never told anyone about this, except maybe a couple therapists when I was ten. I know I sound certifiable, but the colors had nothing to do with my injury. And I want you to know these things early on.

—Why tell me?

—I spent a lot of time envisioning the one person I could tell this to.

—And?

—And she was a redhead, but it looks like I'm going to have to make do.

Stevie jerked down on his hand, making his bad shoulder pop. She pulled down on the same arm with her other hand, climbed him, arms raised and hands outstretched on his collarbones. He bent like a bough in the wind.

For a second, their breathing braided. She pulled back.

—Remember that one time you told me you were crazy and saw gods as colors?

Owen picked up the ball even though Eva & Adele had made this dabbling in time travel seem far less original.

—That's not how I remember it. It was a warm spring evening . . .

—I'm pretty sure it was summer, because Art Basel was on.

—That's right. We were in Basel. Midsummer.

—June.

—And I didn't say I was crazy. I said you would think I was crazy when I told you what I believed in, how I saw the world.

—What did I say after that whole color thing?

—You said preliminary results were ninety-four percent crazy, but that you were going to have to run some rigorous tests to confirm.

—I had to say something to keep you from kissing me. I was still convinced you were using me to get to Brigitte.

—Who? Oh, she was that girl you hung around who had the mustache, but no one told her?

—No, she was the girl you were with when I met you.

—I think you may be remembering that wrong. The kiss, I mean.

Stevie stopped in front of him. A rising moon bounced off the struts of the last bridge in Basel. She craned up to meet his lips and then fell back on her heels, leaving Owen with the open mouth and closed eyes of someone given fully to sleep. She smiled and looked down. With her head cradled in his hands, he kissed her again. She immediately picked up the conversation and dragged Owen along the riverbank.

—You were, what, twenty-four at the time?

—Twenty-one.

—You were twenty-one and . . .

—And I had just dropped out of college and was still trying to make it as an artist.

—That's right. That was in Basel, just before we left for L'Hotel in Paris.

—You're remembering that wrong. L'Hotel was in 2007. When I had some money. I'm talking about 2004, when I was making good on a promise.

—That's right. You made a transparency of it for that laminalism thing you were into. The first one was in Berlin, and you felt it was too limited, so you mapped the next memory on all of Eastern Europe. First we went to Prague, then Budapest, and we stayed in Croatia until we found that villa in Trieste with the enormous ceilings.

—No. I'm pretty sure that was the night I ended Kurt Wagener's career.

That broke the spell.

—Good solution, humiliate yourself some more. You should be more worried about your default machismo than having some photos hung up.

—That's how I deal with things.

—Here's how I deal with things. I don't let people I care about get themselves in trouble. Whatever happened, happened. Let's enjoy a few days together, because what you're talking about is going to get you arrested, and even if it doesn't, totally fucking sucks.

—Those pictures are going to hang in my head if I don't do something about it. I'm not willing to see those images every day. If I can get them out, I may be worth your attention.

Owen thought there was truth there and hoped she wasn't going to laugh at him.

She didn't laugh. But she did walk away.

Owen collected his bag and told the computer scientists that he wouldn't be staying the night after all. They gave back a twenty and kept the rest of his money.

Behind their building, a stream burbled over rocks and raked cement, eventually hitting the Rhine. He rambled in the dark through the tufts of grass and sat down on a riverside slope, closing his eyes to visualize the map of the fair's floorplan.

The hall had only one entrance and exit, but emergency doors opened to what looked like a Hollywood back lot. The best way to get to Pfaff Galleries, Kurt's booth, was to pass through Anisha Desai's installation of children talking inside a pitch-black room, *Projection* (2004). Passing through this ink-black corridor, the viewer would face Kurt's exploding flashbulbs and naked models strutting behind Plexiglas.

All Owen had discovered about *Projection* was that it would be dark, and viewers were asked to watch their step. It was easy to imagine Kurt cannibalizing Anisha Desai's piece, explaining it away in the context of his own work. He had probably given a few dozen interviews in the past week, telling anyone who cared about how he'd requested a redesign of the layout so that a viewer would emerge from total darkness into flashbulbs, into the disorienting glare of his work, *Exposure* (2004), like a prisoner who suddenly has the hood ripped off his head and is forced to stare into interrogation lights.

To Kurt's credit, it did appear that he was holding Art Basel hostage. Anyone who wanted to see Red Rhombus and the bulk of Hall 2.0 had to pass through Kurt's booth. Until the flashbulbs ran out, everyone who mattered in the art world would be treated as a suspected terrorist.

Owen had seen Kurt enter enough rooms to know that he

never stopped anywhere near an entrance. He always rolled to a back corner, which is where Owen would surely find him, surrounded by a triptych of life-size torture photographs.

Beyond the description Owen had read of cracking flashes and the replica lighting of the *Wasserturm* barroom, he had little idea what to expect in the way of art. He had no recollection of the Sheetrock sculpture or Keith Haring tribute that the art critic had mentioned. The work hanging could be anything, but it had to become nothing by the end of the night.

He estimated it would take less than a minute to walk from Kurt's booth to the main exit. He imagined a big box store five minutes to closing. He could lose anyone trailing him in Desai's pitch-black installation. No time for speeches. This was going to have to be fast and decisive and final.

With a sharp white eye he cut through the night and headed straight for the fair. Over the bridge, exhibition hall now in sight, he put on his coat and tried to look like someone who wasn't about to do something horrible.

Surprisingly, hundreds of guests were filing in the main entrance when he arrived. Lady Percy had made it sound like an extension of her dinner party, and to be fair, half the people shuffling past security were wearing clothes that used to be white, should have been white, but now appeared rose quartz in the tamped light of sunset.

The crowd at Guest Services waiting for their access cards seemed puzzled by his appearance. The knots were Windsor. The shoulders padded. He was soiled corduroy and moccasins, and these people noticed shoes and cuffs. Whenever the collectors looked in his direction, their conversations stopped. Even after giving him the benefit of the doubt of being a major young artist, they were visibly annoyed to be waiting in any line, let alone a line with people like Owen in it. The stares and edged silences came straight out of Fellini. This crowd would be at Kurt's booth. The main hall closed in an hour, but no one crowded. They reminded him of opera patrons after the first xylophone tolled them to their seats.

■

—I see a lava waterfall, cooling into black glass.
—I see a turquoise butterfly, shimmering with gasoline wings.
—It's like looking under a microscope. Little floaty things.
—I see an anglerfish snapping at her prey.
—Ooh. I'm seeing something now. A glowing jellyfish.
—It looks like a plastic bag.
—I see a lion's mane.
—Are you guys really seeing things, or are you making it all up?
—I see a trumpet, but it's a trumpet in the dark.

Owen stood in the middle of a room that was nothing-black, total darkness except for the phosphorescent blue bracelet on each viewer's wrist and a glowing strip along the floor. Children spoke from seven or eight different speakers positioned throughout the room, relating what they saw in the blackness and spinning the viewers around to follow the conversation.

Rose had swollen to red. In the heavy dark of Anisha Desai's installation, red fringed the blackness unexpectedly, like ink type lit by the summer sun. With open eyes, the red was uniform, dark, and not quite familiar. With closed eyes, he hovered over red waterfalls, red accelerating to white in the impact zone. The hue was too hot to be carmine and glowed brighter the closer he looked.

A minute tranced. Like standing over a pit of embers.

He gathered himself near the exit, clutching the hem of the thick velvet curtain that separated Kurt's show. He stood high and flexed his broad back, muscles winging out then holding him together. He didn't know this color. Most of his vision was smeared red, as if someone were pressing a finger over his closed eyelid. He smelled cigarettes, heard laughter and shouts of exclamation, and gritted until his molars nearly cracked. Arms strong and ready to tear.

Three loud exhales and then he threw open the curtain, wheeling into Kurt's booth.

The artists seated at the replica barroom table, clad in lumberjack plaid to a man, erupted in a series of hoots at Owen striding from Desai's black curtain to Kurt's strobe and glare.

The women behind the glass dropped their Polaroids and momentarily watched. One of them shouted out, "He's here!" Owen turned to see a six-foot model on a three-foot platform wearing nothing but red high heels and a double coat of baby oil.

Bang!

A flashbulb exploded in his face. Then white.

The afterimage settled, a thousand reds falling to the ground like raining ash. An ultramarine rose from the deposition. Blue shook red away like an unbelted robe. Athene stepping from the husks and lifting a blue film over the expectant scene. Owen stood in a misting blue light, everything lifted and saturated by a light he thought had passed.

Owen's flash-eyed stumbles backed him into a blue sawhorse reading POLICE LINE—DO NOT CROSS. He focused on the props and photos from the staged torture in Berlin.

Hal leapt from the crowd of artists drinking at the makeshift bar and jammed the shutter of his digital camera, bursting at four frames per second and bouncing flash into the walls. One hand held the battery grip, the other finned the crowd clear. Then there were too many people for Hal to get a clear line of sight and he dropped to the floor and shot up through a collector's legs.

A white pedestal, similar to the one in Todd Zeale's gallery, held a slat of parquet flooring under an acrylic dome. Back in Berlin, Owen had scraped a deathbed message on that narrow piece of wood in some fever-dream language. He had carved the runes from pure pain, and now it was not only public but on the auction block.

His reaction was instant.

Cross-armed, Owen grabbed the flutes of the plinth and shouldered it like a club. He carried it around looking for a target. The wooden slat, with characters in some fever message etched on top, fluttered in the air and then fell like chopsticks. He swung the pedestal at the Sheetrock partition separating Kurt's booth from the annex.

At the sound of a real collision, of something shattering in real time rather than art time, the crowd silenced. His heavy movements made it seem as if he was underwater, but everyone else was frozen. In this slower time, he knew this performance had been staged. He knew that he was meant to emulate Kurt at the Todd Zeale Gallery. They wanted him here to destroy everything and trusted that they could sell it as art. But interpreting the situation changed nothing. Some things are either faced or fatal. This all must come down.

Owen's extraneous thoughts sucked back like water and the sand itself, all poised to detonate on the shore. The group at the bar was either standing on the table or on the stools to get a better view. The models were now clumped into one corner of their glass enclosure, craning their necks and pushing up on one another's shoulders to see what would happen next. Two of the girls exited through the invisible door in the wall, racing around the perimeter to make it back for the climax.

Halogen spotlights were intended to cast an air of mystery over a dented-in cardboard refrigerator box. Owen thought Kurt might be inside, waiting to spring out like a jack-in-the-box. He kicked the box to the ground then stomped a corner. No Kurt.

Owen then saw his shadow imprinted on a Sheetrock panel. He didn't remember making that imprint, but no one else could have left a six-eight trace. Kurt had spotlit the image and hung it upside down, so that it dominated the room like an anti-crucifix.

Owen took two steps and then jumped and gripped hard on either end. He swung with the piece, temporarily suspended by the framing wire, then jerked down, dropping his weight and snapping the suspension cables that held it aloft. He landed squarely on two feet and brought the panel down with him, cracking it in two over his knees. He threw the two halves to the side and turned around.

Kurt clapped. He sat in his wheelchair, twenty feet away, crowned by life-size gelatin-silver prints of Owen being wrenched: Owen naked with his arms to the side, electrodes wiring his fingers to a car battery; Owen flat on the ground, carving out the very splint of wood on display and wearing a nylon braided leash that ran from his red neck to Brigitte's hand; and to complete the triptych, a full frontal shot of him on the spool with Saskia and Brigitte in wet clothes licking his leg, clawing his ribs, and offering him to the camera with cupped hands.

Hal circled around Kurt and Owen like a boxer working a heavy bag. The only noise was his shutter slicing in a continuous whirr. The two escaped models came sliding up in bathrobes. They nestled in next to Eva & Adele, who for the first time weren't smiling. The models running through the halls of Basel had corralled half of the fair's attendees. Billionaires with light-up LED bar coasters, Hal's idea, continued to file in. The ring was closing. Altberg stood next to Zeale, calculating the cumulative net worth of the hemisphere. The white party was here, now washed ultramarine and shoaling together like glittering fish. Louise Bourgeois was the eye, whispering which way to move and what Lady Percy and her followers should be looking for in the performance.

The last echo of Kurt's clap died in the rafters. Hal released the shutter and checked the exposure value on his camera. For a moment, there was total silence.

Kurt cracked his neck—two quick pops on the right side, three slow cracks on the left—locked the brakes of the wheelchair, and slapped a palm on each armrest. Hoisting himself like a gymnast on a pommel horse, he swung open his legs and then clapped them together in front of him as he leapt to the ground. He stuck the landing, rose to full height, and pumped his fists to the sky. He looked around, expecting a roomful of applause, but satisfied with shock, awe, and silence.

With three long strides Kurt closed half the distance between himself and Owen. Those first steps were quick and decisive, Kurt still trusting that he was the biggest presence in Europe. But once he reached Owen's shadow, he slowed, eventually to a stop.

The ring of spectators clamped shut. Each movement, however slight, annealed the three rows of tailored jackets, five-figure pantsuits, bathrobes, and all variety of uniform. The crowd, now malleable, expanded with Owen's inhale, contracted in a tight flex with his exhale. All filtered blue and the crowd breathing through gritted teeth, wheezing like the blue jets of a flame. Though they were all prepared for violence, no one expected the suddenness and finality of the show.

—I stand for art. While the world stands idly by. The role of—

Owen's white eye and fast approach truncated Kurt's monologue. Kurt kept his arms to his side, squinted with every muscle of his face, and clenched his teeth in anticipation of Owen's looping right fist. Hal, inches away, focused on Kurt's jaw, shutter whirring to capture the punch.

Owen swung wide of Kurt's ear then jerked him forward by the base of the neck. Kurt mouthed the air once, like a goldfish, in the quarter second it took Owen to hook the frayed cuff of his own left sleeve with two fingers of his right hand, locking the choke. Owen sliced his left forearm in front of Kurt's trachea. Kurt could breathe well enough to sneer and spit out a few expletives, thinking he would be fine.

But this was a blood choke. Kurt's victory of breath was meaningless. Like a gaping fish on a deck, he needed circulation, not air.

Owen compressed both carotid arteries and twisted his right wrist until Kurt went from flushed to thundercloud blue. The stitching on Owen's left sleeve held. He hanged Kurt high, pinning him against the wall, jolted him up and then slammed him into the photo of Owen on the floor with a dog collar around his neck. Mere inches separated Owen's ulnae. Kurt's neck in between.

Kurt's combat boots skidded the floor in two parallel lines running from the wheelchair to Owen's shins. He wound up and kicked at Owen's knee, groin, but it didn't matter. He tapped Owen on the back and then began hammering down on Owen's spine. The beats came muted and rhythmic like the patter of fingertips over covered ears.

Owen found Stevie in the background of the photo. Blurred from profile to turning away, caught in doorlight, retreating in disgust. Owen saw white.

After two kicks landed and did nothing, Kurt lost the focus of his struggle. He looked to Altberg, who was smiling. He looked to Hal, who was still taking pictures.

Owen leaned into the choke. Ear to ear with Kurt, Owen ground his own forehead into the picture on the wall, looking at the reflection of the crowd behind him as the glossy print fireworked with the flashes. Owen sliced his left arm even farther across Kurt's throat. Five seconds and Kurt would pass out, ten seconds and he might be dead. But Owen was in pure space, stomping down time whenever it bubbled up under his feet. Unable to count the seconds, he had no way of knowing how long the choke was on and the flow of blood to Kurt's brain blocked.

Kurt's kicking stopped. Owen had been holding him up, pinning his weight into the wall, so there was no telling when exactly Kurt went limp. Owen dropped the body. Head, shoulders, arms, and hips all landed in the same heap and simultaneously struck the left armrest of the wheelchair, which flipped over as if it had been hit by a tossed trash bag of half-filled bottles and cans.

Altberg pawed at the wheelchair, making a halfhearted attempt to lift it from Kurt's body but clearly waiting for someone else to step up and do the actual work. Hal waved him out of the frame and kept shooting until the memory card was full. He fumbled the reload and missed the shot of Owen parting the crowd of toreadors and sprinting away.

For the first time in Owen's life, he found the part of a curtain. The Desai installation was empty and he strode into the main gallery. He sprinted past million-dollar art without anyone so much as telling him to slow down. Ahead, he saw guards in blue berets adjusting the volume knobs of their walkie-talkies. He would have to outrun information.

Which was impossible. Two police with guns were at the main door. He ran straight toward them. Four palms told him to stop. When he was closer, the one on his right told him to stop running. Owen slowed to a fast walk. One guard put his hand on a Taser. The other stepped forward and grabbed Owen's lapel.

Owen picked up a marble head and threw it into the air, forcing them to catch it and release him or let the artwork crack on the ground.

Owen knew the rule for fighting more than one person: Throw your first punch at the guy you haven't been looking at. It wasn't quite a punch; Owen planted his right foot and shoved the larger cop on his blind side. The officer took the brunt of Owen's assault without so much as a stagger, his chest a springboard that sent Owen careening toward the door. The officer he had been looking at caught the falling head.

Into the night. Owen circled behind a crowd of tourists and waited for a whistle or a gunshot. A carousel crowd circling around him, heads tilted back and laughing theatrically. Half the faces lit with cell phones. A parking lot attendant in a navy wind-breaker yelled. Just before the fair, Owen had stashed his bag on top of a hexagonal kiosk. He was now at the kiosk, jumping up and swiping for his bag's handle. He caught it and ran away before the report echoed throughout Basel.

The Rhine pulled him downhill. The mass of tourists and art elite clogged in front of a stopped tram.

Then someone grabbed his left hand.

He sank.

The eddies, the electric, and her voice. He sank further.

—Easy. This is your little burned-out ring. Just stay calm.

The tram darted away, and the crowd vectored out like an asterisk. Stevie pulled him into the largest current.

—I killed Kurt.

—What?

—I killed Kurt.

She pulled him away from the tourists, who may not have all spo-ken English but could all comprehend *killed*. They veered to the Wett-stein bridge to the left bank of the Rhine. The bridge was at least a quarter mile. If police came in either direction, he'd have to jump.

—You're fine. They staged it. He's done that before. At first it was like someone shattered an aquarium. People spilled out the main entrance, flopping all around, gasping and lost. I thought you set the place on fire until security started shouting for a doc-tor. But they were being filmed too.

—What?

—Look, I think Kurt planned all of this, but we've still got to run. I thought we could take a kayak a quarter mile downstream to the French border and get a friend to meet us. Then I had a better idea.

—You don't understand. He's dead. No more.

—Breathe. There are about fifty cops around here, and after the few alarmists finished screaming, all of the radios said to ignore the distress call, that it was all part of the show. As far as the cops are concerned, it's all dismissible as art.

—He's dead.

—I can guarantee that Kurt would never actually become a martyr; he would only pretend. I'm sure the whole thing was staged.

—He wanted me to punch him. Hal was taking pictures. Kurt can walk. The whole wheelchair thing was a game.

—I'm not waiting around until you start making sense. We need to get you out of Basel. So. Breathe. And take this.

Stevie handed Owen a yellow carbon with some numbers scrawled in boxes and a lackadaisical signature at the bottom.

—What's this?

—This is how you avoid life in prison. We're going on a cruise.

Owen squinted at the typed header of the carbon: VALHALLA RIVER CRUISES. He still didn't quite understand.

—We're sailing the Rhine from Basel to Amsterdam. Six days. Nothing but mouth-breathers—people that police ignore. These are the people you want to be with right now.

—I can't pay for this.

—We're booked. You're holding the receipt. I booked us a cabin. The money is spent.

Owen drifted for several blocks. People were definitely pointing. Stevie had said she bought us *a* room. Plural *us*, singular *a*.

The tremor in his hands had stopped. One excitement had canceled the other. Her scent cleared everything. And what was it? Soap? Dove soap? It was as if every other thought, every other association he had ever made, was grime he needed to wash away. This one smell was the thumbed water hose that revealed the purer, paler goose-bumped self that he had forgotten.

Owen jumped when a car's headlights swept the wall before them. He shook himself into a panic and realized people must be watching.

—Keep talking to me. You'll look less suspicious. We are just walking and talking about art. Actually, fuck art. Let's talk about music. Keep talking. Our boat is just there, under that bridge. It leaves in an hour.

—You told me the police radios were reporting that nothing happened.

—I might have made that up to calm you down. They were definitely saying something. You know, numbers, crackles, ventriloquist-mouth stuff. Whatever they said, there were about fifty police cars headed straight for Messe Basel with their sirens blaring, about five minutes before we met. You didn't hear that?

—I never hear anything when I'm walking.

She took his palm in both of hers.

—It'll look much less suspicious if you kiss me and tell me I'm a genius.

Owen kissed her.

—You're still shaking. It's fine. There weren't fifty cops.

—Then why did you say that?

—There were probably forty, forty-five tops? Let's hang back, then slink on board. Can you slink?

—I'll try.

Stevie and Owen were now behind a foam of elderly tourists

flowing through the bottleneck of the gangway plank and onto the Christmas-light-lit Valhalla River Cruise ship *Saga*.

The *Saga* was a double-decker ship—they used the word *ship* but it was built for rivers, not oceans; specifically, the *Saga* was built to navigate Europe's two great rivers: the beautiful blue Danube and the majestic muddy Rhine. *Barge* would be a more accurate term for the *Saga*. If Interpol was after Owen, agents would be combing the barges—but only barges that admitted to being barges. Stevie was betting the agents would avert their eyes from a barge in drag.

Officially, everyone on this trip was booked from Zurich to Amsterdam. Buses had brought the flight-weary passengers from Zurich this afternoon. Most were ready to float—even if the ship wasn't yet moving. The naturally bold, and those emboldened by the dictates of the itinerary, spent the day tromping from one riverside souvenir shop to another in search of the Platonic cuckoo clock and a good deal on a Swiss-made watch.

Stevie and Owen sat on the quay until the last of the senescent trudged up the plank. An east wind blew the welcoming reception from starboard, where the gangway met the quay and where they were now walking. The diffusion of the welcoming ceremony, coupled with the fact that everyone else on board had begun this tour yesterday with a bus from Zurich to Basel, gave Owen the chance to sneak on board with none of the passengers noticing and only two crew members, both of whom Stevie had already met, smiling nervously.

Spotlights from hot halogen bulbs bounced off the receptionist's whitened teeth and twinkled off the brushed aluminum appurtenances and walnut veneer of the welcome desk. The receptionist explained to Owen and Stevie that their cabin was on the lower deck. He looked once at Owen, winced at Owen's eye, and directed the rest of his comments to her.

—First, welcome aboard. My colleague told me you were a last-minute addition to our registry.

Owen would later discover that his insinuating tone was because of the particulars of the arrangement Stevie had brokered. Because Stevie paid in cash, the stewards were able to keep the trip off the books and add the money to the tip share. The handwritten receipt, of which she had the original and Owen the carbon, was the only record of their presence.

—I'll keep this brief. Our welcoming reception is in thirty minutes. You may want to skip that. We set sail any minute now. You'll find all of the particulars of life on board in your welcome packet. You're in cabin 154. Here's your card. I'm afraid that in your case, I can only issue one. So don't lose it. Due to the nature of our arrangement, you will not be able to charge dining purchases to the room. Please don't forget that. It would cause problems for us all if we have to involve the hospitality manager. And if there's nothing else, enjoy yourselves. Many couples return year after year to get away.

Stevie said it before Owen could, as they were slinking downstairs to their cabin:

—So we're a couple now.

Stevie slid in the key, waited for the green light, and turned the handle.

Owen could respect that Valhalla Cruise Lines didn't disguise the deck plan: standard rooms on the lower deck with porthole windows; junior suites on the middle deck with bigger but inoperable windows; luxury suites on the upper deck with French windows. Stevie and Owen were standard, *Mustervolk*, who would see the grandeur of the Rhine Valley through an acrylic porthole. *Porthole* brought to mind far worse connotations than *window*, which was why Stevie, in appropriate cruise-pamphlet jargon, renamed it their Window to the Rhine. "Oh, look at the spray on our Window to the Rhine." "I wish we could open our Window to the Rhine." "Someone carved his initials on our Window to the Rhine."

The room was lit amethyst. At first he thought it was more cruise kitsch. Then he thought the color was in his head and ignored it, trying to keep things normalish.

—It's not too late for me to hitchhike. That'd keep you safe.

Owen had to crouch to walk into the room. He put his bag down and sat on the bed. Stevie sat beside him and took his hand.

—Safe? If they were really after you, we wouldn't be here right now.

—You heard them say everything was okay on the police radio?

—Not really. The guy I saw answer was smirking when he spoke into his epaulet. They did send an ambulance to the pavilion. But I saw the police, and they were treating the scene like a movie set.

There was a second of silence. Then Owen asked the question a bolder man might have blown past:

—Then why did you stay here?

—In spite of all your flaws, you're clearly in love with the impossible. And I'm stupid enough to think there's something redeemable in that.

—It's more like I never learned how to give up a belief.

He hooked her belt loop and pulled her toward him. She smiled and unpeeled his finger with both hands.

—I didn't mean that as a line. I'm serious.

Owen tried to look serious. So did she.

—They probably put us in the stern to be as far from the staff as possible. I think the staff rooms are all on our level. But this works, right? I think this room is exactly your height. Stand up.

As Owen posted both arms to get up, Stevie straddled his waist and grabbed the front of his shirt.

She curled up to find his top lip and miss his beard. She lingered for minutes. As the ship left port, someone above lit a chain of Black Cats, two dozen snaps loosing the nightbirds. Champagne corks popped into the river, and a chorus of the cruise diaspora alighted upon the lingua franca of *Bon voyage!* Stevie pushed Owen's chest until he fell on his back. She looked down at him, his hands now laced behind his neck, biceps long plateaus.

—I swear to God that really just happened.

He laughed.

—You really are going to need to shave that. Like now.

Owen unglossed his lips with the back of his hand, then stood.

She tossed a pair of scissors on the bed.

—You might need these for your beard.

—I don't have a razor.

—Thought of that.

She tossed him silk-foam shaving cream and a pink Bic Lady, which with its single blade posed a challenge.

The bathroom was comically undersized. The shower was a quarter circle wedged into the corner, with a plastic door that slid in a poorly sealed arc. The shower nozzle was dead even with his sternum. He pointed the nozzle as high as it would go and slid the door open so that his ass was hanging in the wind and water spraying the floor.

This was how Stevie found her man.

She laughed.

Owen stood too quickly and raked his back on the curtain track at the top of the door.

—*Ooph.* You've got to stop hurting yourself. I'm going up for food.

—Thanks.

Owen toweled off and wiped the steam from the mirror. Hunchbacked to fit in the frame, he cut wet clumps of beard into the sink. A few patches remained, burling his cheek with rosettes. His ears popped when he pulled his chin, revealing previously inaudible whispers and rolled guitars from the clock radio in the other room. Eardrums scarred by a lifetime in cold water meant his hearing was mostly garbage. These little pops of clarity were always a welcome surprise. He shaved in a goatee. He wrung out the water and combed it with his fingers.

Wind rushed from the closing door and cooled his cheek. Stevie was back. She turned him around.

—Getting there. But I still can't see your lips. And that's the part I want.

—Had to see how that looked. Not good.

—I'll leave you to it.

Owen's hair had almost grown to his shoulders in the past eight months. He took a handful in one hand, scissors in the other. Then thought of Jim Morrison: "Some of my worst decisions have been haircuts." He trimmed and shaved the bottom half of the goatee, keeping a Mark Spitz mustache. He looked like a '70s surfer. Had a kind of *Morning of the Earth* look that he should have tried in college.

—You missed a spot.

—I'm putting my top lip on notice. I'll probably shave it tomorrow.

—I never realized you were so vain.

—Everyone's vain in front of a mirror.

—Why wear an eye patch, then?

—I don't know. What do you want from me? It's just shitty. My only options are shitty or creepy. I used to think, "It's just a face. What's the big deal? It's just a face, not a person."

—I still think that. Do whatever you want. Except, please, shave that goddamn mustache.

—It's cruise wear.

—Ugh. You're worried about an artificial eye making you creepy? I'm checking the ledger and it looks like . . . yep, you owe me negative one mustache.

Owen relented. He scraped away the last trace of the past six months. Clean-faced, chest pink and mottled from hot water, towel still around his waist, Owen turned back into the room to find Stevie propped up on a fluffed pillow, one leg outside the covers gleaming in the soft light of the bedside lamp, one leg underneath, tracing small circles with her toes.

A waltzing brush up to her hip, then slow and more fitting as the web of his hand pushed the pulse down to her knee, then a broken chord, one finger at a time up her inner leg in a glowing trace. Beneath the rayon comforter, a brightness, the infant-tender orange of a hand over a flashlight, the living colors that only a body can produce. His fingers combed the electric, just above her skin.

—Your hands have finally stopped trembling.

Which was one way of looking at a world where every tremble is orchestrated, a dual cascade with someone else who was a flat steel bar before, a single tine dampened, but now, now mated like a tuning fork, resonates and rises up to sing.

Owen rolled into the bright light on Stevie's side of the bed. This wasn't early morning light. This was smothering midsummer afternoon light. He sat straight up and found Stevie drinking coffee in the lone upholstered armchair. She was back in her chambray shirt, smiling through the coffee steam.

A new feeling rose up Owen's chest to the base of his throat. It was the first time he could remember finding more of himself, rather than less, like kicking aside some weathered old planks and uncovering an abandoned well. He smiled awake.

Then he panicked.

—Promise me you didn't check the papers.

—Good morning to you too.

—I can't see the news. You can't see the news. Okay?

—Looking at it won't change anything. It never hurts to have more information.

—What would we possibly gain from that?

—It would help to know what's coming.

—Maybe I don't want to know what's coming.

Stevie looked at him. She needed him to acknowledge that she was trying to help. He dug a finger under the elastic band and rubbed his forehead. His lower lip shook.

—What do you want me to say?

—How about, "Wow, you look even better in the morning, and what's that? Coffee. You got me one too? You're so sweet. I should really have a cup before I start yelling. Last night was amazing, and now I'm here with you on the Rhine and I'm just going to enjoy it and be happy."

Owen raised his hands and gripped the air like it was a plank of wood.

—WORLD-FAMOUS ARTIST ATTACKED BY MONSTER, COWARD FLEES!

—WILD APE DESTROYS ART FAIR, FLEES WITH BEAUTY!

—COWARD FLEES WITH BEAUTY WHO PROMISES TO STAY AWAY FROM NEWS REPORTS.

Stevie sat by him on the bed. She took his hand.

—Mine sounds more believable.

—Still. Do me a favor, no news. This way, if anything happens, you might have plausible deniability. How plausible will probably depend on how good your lawyer is.

—I don't have a lawyer anymore. You may have killed his biggest client, remember?

Neither one could speak. After a minute of looking at each other, Stevie continued her thought:

—Which means you can't go back to Berlin.

—I think it means *we* can't go back to Berlin.

Stevie flipped her lighter over her fingers. She looked at the freckles and fingernail scars on his shoulder and wondered if he knew everything this meant.

She caught herself biting her lip and looked away. He put his arm around her when she needed to be kissed.

—I don't drop things. I hold things. Good and bad.

—You don't even remember how we met.

—We met when we got away from the bar with the others. We met over coffee. I said ridiculous things—

—No. You were tripping over yourself, stumbled, and caught yourself with my legs. Right here. With electric hands. Then you looked at me. And there was something impossible in the way you looked at me, and it was all going to spin away if I didn't look back the same way. But I did, and *that's* what you should hold on to.

He kissed her just before the moment slipped away.

After they surfaced, she looked at him and guessed what he was thinking.

—No. I didn't look at the news.

The *Saga* was scheduled to dock in Strasbourg at 14:45. Back-thrust roiled the water at that exact minute. The air in the cabin suddenly felt spent. Stevie rolled from one shoulder to another, put one leg on top of the sheet, then ballooned into him and deflated, like a jellyfish fighting an eddy. She threw off the sheet.

—Do you think they pipe in chemicals when we're docked to get people to leave the ship and follow the itinerary?

—What?

—You aren't antsy?

Through their window, Owen saw the white plaster walls of half-timbered houses, writing a story along the Rhine in runic beams. Stevie emptied her bag on the dresser. She looked as if she'd found a specific item missing.

—We need provisions.

—I'll go. You stay here.

—That's stupid. The only people you need to avoid are the tourists on this ship, and they're all going to be at their most observant just after we dock.

—What do we need that we don't have here?

—Music, for one. I've only got the CD in my Discman and a pair of headphones.

—Deejay loose in a record store. How could I say no to that?

Stevie thought about it. Her curiosity to see what he'd choose was too great to ignore.

They dressed and then waited for the last of the cruisers to cross the plank. They walked the quay beside coral, ochre, and sea-green houses, all with timber braces tessellating MXY in house-length ruled lines. Down cobbled streets, curved wooden roofs overlapped, giving the impression of oncoming gulls.

She spotted a small record store near the Place du Corbeau. She stopped and turned Owen's chin.

—The music isn't really what we need. What we need is harder to explain.

—What's the problem?

—Right now it's too easy.

—Something's easy?

—It's easy to think you're falling for someone when you know he's going to be gone in a few days. There are no real consequences, no consequences for us, since you're never going back to Berlin.

—For me, it's the other way, at least in theory. Why open yourself to someone you're never going to see again?

—Because the rest of your life will go back to normal right

after that. The ephemerality never registers. It's a dream without clocks.

Stevie began laying out her plan as they walked into the record shop.

—All right. Here's how the deal works. We have seven days left on the ship. We need to get six albums. Today we listen to whatever is in the Discman. I think it's Iron and Wine, but it might be Bonnie Prince Billy. Don't get either of those.

Owen felt the shop owner's stare. He gripped a handful of CDs next to the BEATLES tab.

—I don't like the way she's looking at us. These'll work. Let's go.

—Put some thought into this. You choose three. I'll choose three. I haven't even finished with the rules. Every morning we choose the record for the day. After that day you promise to never listen to any song on that album again. Ever. If one of these songs comes on in a restaurant or a bar, you have to head directly for the exit. So you obviously don't want to choose *Abbey Road* or the White Album or Dylan, because after this trip you'd never hear it again.

—After the day we designate for the album, we can never listen to it again. Got it.

—It's not like, "Oh, we played *Blood on the Tracks* on a Tuesday, so I can only hear those songs on Tuesdays." Or, "There's nobody here. I can listen to it just once." You can never listen to those songs again.

—The albums we chose are dead to me. Got it.

—One more rule: No compilations, sound tracks, or greatest hits. And neither one of the Portishead records.

He turned to the headiest section he knew: jazz. His father's jazz collection had been a dusty *Britannica* looming over the household with iron-clad authority. The very word *jazz* made Owen feel a little stupid, so he adopted the music of the older players on the junior national team. That music was of little help now. Bad Religion, Minor Threat, Social Distortion, NOFX, Das EFX—these are not the bands that win a heart. He needed the very best of his own taste, even if it meant he would never hear his favorite songs again, and a healthy dose of other people's music, even if it meant that Stevie would be getting a skewed portrait—but what's the future for, if not to make people okay with who we really are?

He turned back to rock.

He drifted into the M's and paged through plastic cards, wondering if there was any chance he could pull off a Modest Mouse record. He'd only heard it twice, but liked the songs. Stevie spoke without facing him:

—If you even think about Bob Marley, the trip's off.

Stevie had a CD behind her back and leaned her shoulder into Owen's side to inspect. He tilted a CD forward with his finger.

—Ooh. Modern Lovers. Very good call.

A new band to Owen.

—But, see, this one is live. They only wrote one album—which says something. I was going to go for early Roxy Music, but the store only has the greatest hits. You're not following, are you?

Owen snapped to.

—What do you have?

—This one is really going to hurt. Poor Lou.

The shop owner muted the phone's mouthpiece as if she were about to yell. Instead she listened. Stevie, focused on her own offering, ignored his protest.

—No. I can do it.

Stevie bit her knuckles and shook her head. She bowed and extended a hand.

—For you.

Owen looked down at a white-faced and heavily eye-shadowed man holding a guitar. Stevie squeezed his arm, looking down at the album as if it were totally apart from them:

—Fucking *Transformer*. The rest aren't going to hurt that much. It's easily top-ten ever. And I'm giving it up for an American.

Owen laughed.

—All right. One in the bag. What do you have?

Owen looked for Van Morrison. His mother had all the records in her collection. The nineteen records on the bottom shelf of a cabinet were the only traces of her in the Burrs' music library. Her records were real vinyl records. There were only nineteen of them, but they had an immense gravity that drew him to the corner of the den whenever he woke up in the middle of the night. His dad said *Astral Weeks* was her favorite. A wealth of fine scratches supported the claim. Owen played the records all the time, but he never heard the music in the same way that Stevie probably heard music. He watched the stylus trace the grooves and thought he could see his mom doing the same thing over candlelight, barefoot in a caftan.

—How is there no Van Morrison?

—They must have misfiled him. Check in the Vs.

Owen found an entire rack of Van Morrison albums, but also saw the TOM WAITS tab. He returned in two steps.

—*Closing Time*.

—No commentary? Why did you ditch Van Morrison?

—This is my favorite album. We have a week for commentary. Let's go. We can make do with just these two.

—Not the rules!

A new customer took an interest in Stevie's shout. Owen spun around to the jazz section. He grabbed something he had seen in his father's study.

—And this one.

—Charles Mingus, *Cumbia & Jazz Fusion*?

—It's really good. Mingus is Mingus. And this is Mingus at his finest.

Those were his father's words.

—Okay. That's fine. I just didn't peg you for a jazz guy. More hip-hop. Or Green Day. The best I was hoping for was Pixies, and you go and drop an obscure Mingus record. Bizarre.

—You'll like it.

—As long as it hurts. This game only works if you're giving something up. Okay. Two for you. *Transformer* for me . . . and . . . *Tago Mago*.

—I haven't even heard of most of the bands you're talking about.

—Can's German. That record is hugely important. I think you'll like it.

—No. It's fine. Choose the last two. We've got to run.

—No. Can wasn't right. Do you know Sigur Rós?

Owen shrugged.

Stevie walked to the S section, grabbed a white album with closed parentheses on the cover ( ), then quickly added something else to the bottom of the stack.

—I made my last pick. Unfortunately it's another one that hurts to give up. You?

Owen was inspired by a song he'd heard belted out on acoustic guitar a few times in college when nights rubbed up against sunrise.

—We're going to Amsterdam? I've got to go with Jacques Brel. Do any of these albums have the song "Amsterdam"?

—It kicks off *Olympia '64*. Are you sure? Fine. I'll meet you outside. I've got to get speakers and batteries.

Owen handed her a crumpled red note.

A patron was looking at Owen inquisitively, but it was more

of a vague stare than an I-can't-quite-place-you stare. The shop owner still looked suspicious. Stevie said something about a funeral in French, which made the woman laugh. The shop owner began to wrap their albums. Owen slunk away to the crinkling applause of tissue paper.

He nodded to the lone smoker in the courtyard. The guy turned to the street as if Owen were asking for money. Owen looked up to the sun, glare cut by the bright green leaves. He watched a caterpillar on the trunk lean back and scribble the air until Stevie returned.

—What was your last choice?

Stevie caped away the bag and hid it behind her back.

—At the checkout counter I realized I should have gone with a Plastic Bertrand record. *"Ca Plan Pour Moi"* has kind of become my calling card as a deejay. I'm so sick of hearing that song that drowning it would have been a pleasure.

He thought she was testing him with idle chatter, or maybe training him to relax. It wasn't working.

—You were wrong about one thing, though. There is no chance that I just return to my normal life after we get to Amsterdam. I heard a siren while you were inside. We've got to get back to the boat. I can't believe we stopped for this.

She cemented her heels until he apologized and acknowledged that they needed their own stakes, not someone else's. He apologized.

—Just keep talking to me and don't look forward. You should have realized by now that you'd be fine.

—Why's that?

—Are you kidding? I'm in a sundress. Nobody's going to be looking at you.

On the banks of the Rhine, thousands of tourists sat on the steps or rocked in and out of shadows with arms behind their backs. With Stevie on his right and no peripheral vision to see what was coming behind him, any one of the young men in sneakers could signal friends, spring up, and seize him. Owen spoke out of the side of his mouth.

—What should we talk about?

—Music.

—I can't talk about music. I don't know anything about music. Who's Lou Reed?

—Now that may be a deal breaker. How could you not know Lou Reed? Velvet Underground?

—Crickets.

Stevie laughed and pulled him down a bit.

—So I guess there's no point in me keeping my third choice a secret. But I'm going to anyway. By the way, I edited one of your selections.

—You did what?

—*Olympia '64* is a live album, so I replaced it. I hope you don't mind.

Owen shrugged.

—And Jacques Brel. I mean, the only reason you chose him was because of the name of that song. I thought of another great album with a song about Amsterdam.

—What is it?

—*Aeroplane Over the Sea*. You'll like it. I'm not sure if you knew it, but Jacques Brel is Belgian, not French, and I'm kind of on a Belgian purge right now.

—If you were on a purge, shouldn't we listen to nothing but Jacques Brel? Why Belgium anyway? That's so random.

—My ex is a Belgian cyclist. Nice guy, but he loved his calf muscles a little too much.

Owen smiled.

—Seriously. He wears cargo shorts in winter.

Stevie found an accent:

—*You must respect the sacred calves.*

Owen laughed.

—That's good. You look less conspicuous when you smile.

—What's your favorite song?

—I thought we were past that. Actually, no. It's not that banal of a question because I had no real answer to it until just now. When we were in the store my first instinct was: go for Björk. To educate you, to lead you out of the dark non-Björk world. I'm judging from your silence that you don't know Björk? Sugarcubes?

—I know. Awesome Icelandic singer. Childlike wonder. Wore a swan.

—But you don't know her actual music. And I thought, He should know Björk if he is really going to know me. Then I thought, that's the wrong impulse for a gift. You don't give a gift to shape someone into the person you want him to be. You give a gift because it's something you couldn't bear to be without, but it's even more unthinkable for the other person to be without it.

—Now I'm thinking I didn't put enough thought into my choices.

—There were only two. *Closing Time* is your favorite record, right? You weren't making that up . . .

—No. So why didn't you choose Björk?

—Even if I could have gotten over never hearing those songs again, I would *never* listen to them for the last time on these chintzy portable speakers.

She opened the bag and held up the plastic package. It was the sort of package that was going to be hell to open without a knife. He started to peek at the mystery sixth album. Stevie reached in and handed him a pair of knock-off Wayfarers. She couldn't have known, but imitation Ray-Bans were the only ones that stretched wide enough to fit his head. He slid off his eye patch and wore the glasses.

They clacked the slats of the aluminum plank. They had returned before any of the other cruisers and snuck back into cabin 154 without attracting attention from anyone but the concierge, who had been arched back over the metal handrail, tanning.

She leaned across Owen and rifled through the bag for the speaker pack and rechargeable batteries. After she handed him the package, he crimped his fingers in the hanger hooks and tore it open. The speakers jumped from the plastic and hit the bedside dresser.

—*Ooph*. That's one way to save music. None of those guys wants to become a ghost. I'm sorry Lou, I'm sorry Tom, but Owen and I are going to do this.

Stevie connected the speakers to their three-pronged adapter and plugged the unit into the power strip above the narrow desk. The speakers lit green. She connected the output cable to her Discman. She popped open the top and then snapped it shut.

—Iron and Wine.

They listened to the disc accelerate, talk to the player in some sort of digital garbling, and then stop. The Discman screen read:

$$11\ 39{:}26$$

Stevie hit the play button, and the CD skidded to life. With the first finger picks she kissed him again. She climbed up him, mated their breath, then covered him in a tent of her soap-scented hair. He pulled her hips into his and traced an axis down her body with the pools of her hollows.

They opened a bottle of wine and listened to the album again.

—This is beautiful. I don't want to give it up.

—Sorry. That's life.

—You're fucking killing me with this game.

—Everything fades. You're going to have to stop listening to this album one day. Why not today? Why pretend like you can hear it forever? It seems comforting at first, but is painful in the end. Really *hear* it now. You can always think about this record and think about tonight. You can think about me. About trying to wear a mustache. These are beautiful things, fragile and flawed.

They kissed.

—Why not just admit that we can't listen to these records forever, but let's listen to them while we can because they make life more bearable?

—Bearable? You don't really care for music, do ya?

—Clearly not enough.

—You're missing the point.

—No. I see the point. I just don't know how you cope with loss if you're thinking about it constantly.

—I tell myself we're all in the same boat. And I let some things drown. You can't experience anything without peeling off the illusion of permanence. Everything ends in nothing.

—Everything ends in nothing? Are you high?

—That's in a critical letter from Heidegger to Sartre. But it's also Ricky Martin's latest single: *"Y Todo Queda En Nada."* That's the trouble with theory. One second you're in league with philosopher kings, the next you're in nightclubs with pop stars.

He woke at three in the afternoon. The ship didn't appear to be moving. He checked in the bathroom for Stevie. Gone. No note.

He opened the leather-bound information packet and read that they would be docking in Mannheim from 11:00 to 17:00 for an afternoon of exploration.

He read about the city he couldn't explore—the city he

couldn't even see from their starboard Window to the Rhine. The speakers had been unplugged from the Discman and now sat idle on the desk, already in a knot. He found the Iron and Wine jewel case on the desk. He might find a way to play the CD before she got back. It wouldn't be breaking the rules if she wasn't here. The days didn't start until he saw her.

He opened the case and found a note:

Cheating bastard!!

He put the note in his back pocket even though he could imagine her finding it and thinking he was weird to have kept it. He opened the liner notes. A thought that wouldn't have occurred to him before Basel: one of them should keep each empty CD case. The actual CD probably needed to be destroyed. Or donated. Stevie was apparently seeing to that. But the empty case was something they should always have.

He was still reading the liner notes when she returned. She set her beach bag on the desk.

—You missed a beautiful day. And you slept through about five listens of the best album you've never heard.

She took the Discman from her purse, undid the headphones, connected the speakers, and swapped out the double As.

—I brought you food. And here's how I'm thinking this works. It's amazing outside. Sorry, but it is. I'm headed to the sundeck so you can listen to *Transformer* over lunch.

Owen stretched, laced fingers over his head touching the ceiling.

—I got a suit in town. Can you turn around?

The braver, fuller version of Owen would have grabbed her. But today's Owen looked at the wall and heard Stevie step from her sandals, unfasten and then slide her shorts down her smooth legs, and snap the elastic.

She was smoothing the white ribbons over her hip when he turned around. She backed into him and put white nylon straps in his thick fingers.

—Can you tie the top?

He pulled her toward his lap. She took two steps forward and tied her own suit.

—You have to listen to the record first.

She pushed play on the Discman. The first word was *vicious*, which Owen thought she might have planned.

—Okay. I'm gone.

Owen spun down the volume wheel until the song was no louder than the ship's motor. He brought the Discman and speakers into the bathroom and showered.

He toweled off and dressed to the first verse of what turned out to be the last song, and took Stevie's hand as she entered at the last line, "It's a lonely Saturday night." It was Thursday. They were in Mannheim. He had almost given up the idea that he was being hunted. Or if he was, they were giving him a dramatic head start.

—Well, what do you think?

She was wearing a robe, but he saw nothing but how she wore the bikini. The Discman's default setting was repeat; "Vicious" started again.

—The first half is better than the second half.

—But the whole thing is Lou Reed. You can't just take the good parts.

—The one song was in *Trainspotting*.

—You've seen *Trainspotting* but haven't heard *Transformer*? That's unbelievably sad! "Perfect Day" is probably the genesis of this whole game. The only thing that's not perfect about the song is that you can listen to it over and over again. More than any other song, this one is conscious of the impermanence of perfection and the perfection in impermanence. The song is perfect, it's our listening to it whenever we want that makes it imperfect. This is our chance to fix that.

—So this is how perfect things end.

Owen hit track repeat. "Perfect Day" started again. Stevie pulled a bottle of wine from her bag and walked toward Owen. Her stomach was warm. The sunblush on her cheeks made her eyes seem impossibly blue, a milky opalescent blue with the same promise a drowning man sees when his foot is pinned in the reef and he looks up to the bright sky.

They woke to the twining piano and violin of the song's last minute. Stevie stretched.

—My perfect day has about four more hours of sleep.

She only ever slept in a T-shirt. Starched white sheets breezed over her legs. She spooned back into Owen, settling into him, caught between eros and sleep.

Owen whispered:

—I think we'll be in Koblenz soon. And then Cologne tomorrow.

Stevie freed *Transformer* from its one-track repeat. They had to have listened to the song a hundred times by now and should have been ready for something else. The jangling guitar and faster tempo of the next song was like when credits roll to music that both rips you from the dream world of a film and contradicts everything that you've just watched. Even though they had the rest of the night to listen to the album, "Perfect Day" was gone. Stevie realized it.

—I shouldn't have chosen this.

They listened to the album again. She turned over to find Owen dead asleep. She put a fresh set of batteries in the Discman and mourned until she drifted away.

She woke and rolled to her feet. *Transformer* had expired in the night. She ejected the disc before getting dressed. Her hair was in damp knots from sleeping with a towel around her head after a late-night shower. After getting dressed, she walked up to the observation deck.

She had envisioned flinging the disc into the muddy Rhine, but couldn't overcome her aversion to littering and put it in the trash slot instead. The rest were going to be easier than that. Today was Owen's choice. If he had any sense, he would pull the Band-Aid, as she had done, and play his favorite album first. Jazz? Who was he trying to impress?

Her. He was trying to impress her. More than Hendryk of the Sacred Calves, more than Tom the American footballer who said he was in Berlin for the semester but was gone by Tuesday, more than Johan the drunk and hilarious, more than Erik of conglomerate money, Owen was trying to impress her with the things he didn't have rather than the things he did have. He acted as if he had nothing to offer her but his awkward striving, his falling over himself to get her a glass of water.

She did the right thing to play *Transformer* first. And he should play Tom Waits today. Otherwise, they would grieve the whole time over what would eventually be lost. Is there a difference between grief and mourning? Grief is more sobbing. More destructive. Mourning is welling tears. And that will come after.

Stevie watched the castles tick past. The ship left Mannheim sometime before they awoke. They were now traveling through a scooped-out valley with ruins or vineyards on every hillside. Stevie imagined herself against the walls of one of the castles looking at the white ship, Owen buried somewhere in the galley, sliding past.

The woman at the concession table asked if she was okay.

Stevie found Owen sprawled diagonally across the bed, face-down on top of the sheets with the thin synthetic pillow in his arms. He unaccountably still had a tan, and with the towel around his waist, he looked like an Egyptian hieroglyph. She scooped his legs over and gently set them down so she had room. His ankles and feet hung in the air. He grumbled.

The comforter was in a heap on the floor, still tucked into the mattress. She gently pulled it over his feet, only to find that it now came to her hip. She combed his hair behind his right ear and kissed his big cheekbone. Even before Basel, she had a sense that more than anything else he wanted to be small and forgotten, miniaturized and tucked away in her pocket.

He pressed his forehead into the bed and coughed.

—Today you get to choose the record. You're going to go with Tom Waits, right?

—Hrrffrrgrr.

—Okay. Say something if you don't want me to choose Tom Waits.

He sniffed.

—Okay. I'm going to play it now.

She took *Closing Time* from the bundle of tissue paper, ticked her fingernail over a corner until it caught, and then peeled off the clingy cellophane and put the disc on the spool of her Disc-man. The album was new to Stevie. She checked the track names and didn't recognize any of them as Tom Waits singles. The 1973 copyright took her by surprise. He must have been about their age when he wrote this.

The CD spun to life on its own and waited for her to push

play. But Owen had to be the one to push the button. When she said his name he only coughed in reply. She unplugged the Discman from the speakers and brought it to the bed.

—Okay, I can't be the one to push the actual button. You need to do it.

She took his right hand in hers. It was dead heavy, huge and lifeless. She turned it over to look at his palm.

He grumbled at the slight strain and pawed the mattress until he found the black plastic box.

She guided his index finger to the button and rolled it as if she were taking his fingerprint. Leaning from the foot of the bed, she set the player on the desk and connected the speakers.

The first song was vaguely familiar. It sounded like a coffee commercial. She hit pause and went upstairs for a cup, came back and found Owen still sleeping. She hit play again on the record and sipped her coffee from the corner chair, near their Window to the Rhine. She finished a long poem in Auden and slunk into bed.

He was hiding his injury in the pillow. She swam a hand under his neck and pulled him in as tightly as she could. This was their third run through the album, these were quiet minutes before the nap that always followed sandwiches in the now familiar triangular cardboard boxes. The afternoon light reflected off the river in violet brown. Owen sat by her side with his arm around her waist. She ran her thumb over the knot in his wrist.

—This is a nighttime record.

—Well. It's called *Closing Time*. There's even a song called "Midnight Lullaby" that ends with . . . a lullaby.

—Maybe we should wait until the sun goes down.

—You can't see the moon out our Window to the Rhine? Look. It's a giant full moon. A grapefruit moon. That's so strange. It was just the middle of the afternoon and now it's pitch-black—

except for that big full moon—I'm thinking we just go with it and don't ask any questions.

This was the type of game she would usually play. But she just looked at him. He asked if everything was all right.

—You can't even go on the observation deck.

—Probably not. But I wouldn't want to anyway, would I? You make it sound like it's all white wine spritzers and old people in tanning oil.

—I didn't want to tempt you. It's actually models playing shuffleboard.

He laughed.

—You think I want that?

—Substitute "reading Greek" for shuffleboards.

—We dock in Cologne at sunset. I'll go into town with you. It'll do us some good.

—Cologne's huge. That's just stupid.

—You seem to bring that out in me.

They spent the next hour in bed tracing subtly different routes along each other's bodies. She was still radiating yesterday's sun. The observation deck had been mostly women tanning their arms. She had donned her shorts and chambray shirt as soon as she was out of the cabin and in the hallway, but even in that outfit she attracted more attention than she wanted. Rather than cover up, she'd undone her top and fallen asleep on her stomach reading. This was a childishly defiant sunburn, so she couldn't wince now if Owen rubbed her shoulders too hard, but she did let him know the soft touches were more welcome.

The past day did have a violet tint. Amethyst. He would say Demeter or something, and she didn't want to talk about mythology. She worried that Owen's strange way of seeing the world was becoming her own.

—You stay here with your record. I'm going to go explore Cologne.

—I can understand if you need some time by yourself. But let me be the one to go. I'll go.

—Take a nap. I'll be back in an hour.

She kissed him good-bye and went straight for the Hyatt Regency. In the lobby bar she ordered a half bottle of Veuve. The bartender hit on her twice, which annoyed her enough to keep her in the present.

She boarded the *Saga* with the other tourists to find Owen reading volume two of the *Odyssey*.

—I thought you were gone.

—Not yet.

—Wait. After a good twelve years of trying, I finally finished volume one. I want you to have it.

She looked at the book, sure that it would stay with her forever, but unsure how she could ever replicate the desperation with which Owen cradled it.

—No books. Just records. Besides, I'm only up through like twenty-year-old Auden.

—No, I want you to have it. It's from me and my dad. He'd understand. In fact, he'd insist. It's his book. Half of his life is in there . . . well, a quarter, the other quarter is in volume two—you know what I mean.

—Are you sure? Shouldn't the two books stay together?

—Actually not at all. His whole thing is called liminality, the space between.

—Like laminalism.

—I don't think either one of us wants to get into that.

—Well. Thank you. And thank your father for me when you eventually get back to California. Now let's listen to this record. I'm curious to hear anyone's all-time favorite album, let alone yours.

Stevie sat on the edge of the bed, facing the speakers. Owen sat by her side with his arm around her waist. Her skin was orchid in the late afternoon light, light blue veins visible under the glowing. She ran her thumb over the mounts of his palm. Thick clouds rolled in. They smelled the storm through the glass, or they imagined they did.

Owen had listened to the album five times through already. He knew what was coming: right now they were purring to "I Hope I Don't Fall in Love with You," but two songs from now "Old Shoes" was going to play, and there was no hope of that going over well. He tried to distract her by running his fingers through her hair, cupping the tops of her ears with his palm, and feathering the base of her neck.

The first verse rolled by without Stevie seeming to hear. He tried praising her beauty in German to distract her from the song's words.

She pushed him back hard, clawing his chest.

—"I can see by your eyes, it's time now to go? So I'll leave you to cry in the rain?"

—I think he's—

—"Though I held in my hand the key to all joy, honey my heart was not born to be tamed?"

—That's not what I'm saying at all. Bad Tom. That's so sophomoric, 'I'm a free spirit. I'm a wild horse that can't be tamed.' Uh-uh. Nope. That's not what I'm saying at all.

—You're ruining the record. Not to mention totally killing the mood.

—I'll be quiet now.

They listened to the next songs. When "Rosie" finished, Stevie spoke:

—I understand the distinction between a speaker and an author. I've spent plenty of time in the performativity literature. But I can't help but want more . . . loyalty. He follows a heartwrencher about one girl, Martha, with a song about a completely different girl, Rosie. And if this came out in 1973 he must have been about our age, so it's not like he's looking back on a lifetime of heartbreak.

—There you're wrong. Losing someone at any age can easily mean a lifetime of heartbreak.

—You still didn't tell me why you chose it—and I'm hoping here for a specific answer, not something vague about the stars and the moon.

—There are about five thousand CDs in my house. All jazz. All my dad's except the dozen or so I listen to when the team has to take a bus to SoCal or Arizona. I listen to Bad Religion, Social Distortion . . .

—Love Social Distortion.

—Well, I didn't think you would. Anyway. I have a few dozen CDs, another dozen mix CDs, but the albums I listen to the most are the nineteen vinyl records that my mom left me.

Stevie had guessed.

—Her favorite album was *Astral Weeks*. I was going to give that to you, but felt like it wasn't mine to give. She had *Closing Time*. I'm not sure that she listened to it much. It stuck out because the rest of her music is fairly . . . astral. For a long time I thought it was left there for me. Maybe that this was a window to the men on her side, her father, her grandfather, people I would never know. Now it's clear that she bought this record for us.

—I'm going to get us some wine. This is a red wine record. I'll be back.

—I'm not going anywhere. By the way, you're Martha. And I'm trying hard to avoid a life where I have to make that phone call.

Owen listened to the album another time through. It seemed right to give it to her, and to give her his favorite song. He was going to have to destroy two records: the one playing in the Discman and his mom's vinyl copy at home—assuming he ever made it home. He listened to "Martha" on repeat until Stevie came back, at least ten listens later.

She filled their water glasses. Owen gulped the glass down and then filled another.

—I hope you don't do this game with other guys.

—This isn't a thing. This is between us.

Anytime she said "us" he was ready to tell her that he loved her.

—I know the circumstances were a little rough. But have you had a good time on the boat so far?

Anything remotely positive, and his response was, I love you.

—It's been okay.

Owen dropped. He could see his jaw dropping with the inevitability of a spoon's handle tracing the inner rim of a bowl and then falling into the soup. He had nothing. He couldn't leave. He took a few steps and looked out their Window to the Rhine.

—If this is okay, I'd love to see what matters.

—You matter. But I matter too. And I'm not about to give up my life for an American who's about to . . . about to what? Have you thought out anything, other than not going back to Berlin, ever?

—You heard something when you were on deck.

—The only thing I ever hear is footsteps. And I hear them all the time now. I start to sweat every time I hear boots on the stairs. I don't know how you stay down here all day.

—Boots mean people. And if those people open the door, it means this is over. And fine. I can deal with this being everything it is. I can deal with it being over. People I can deal with. It's the papers that make me sweat.

—Yeah. You're a real people person.

He had enough presence to laugh at himself. And enough sense to lie to himself and believe that everything was going to work out.

Stevie tracked down the concierge and got him into the cabin after they had docked in Dusseldorf and the last tourist had disembarked. Mingus took him aback. He looked at the offending speakers until Stevie hit stop on the Discman.

—Owen, this is Paul. He thinks he might be able to help.

—That depends on what you need. First off, will you state officially that you are part of no police organization, no governmental organization, and that you are not entrapping me in any kind of illegal activity?

—I'm not a cop. She's not a cop. And as far as we know, nothing about this is illegal. This is just a hypothetical conversation.

Owen's tone was too aggressive. Paul was already taking slow steps to the door.

—What Owen means to say is, for purely research purposes, what would happen, hypothetically, if there was a person who needed to disappear somewhere between here and Amsterdam?

—Clarify what you mean by *disappear*, or this conversation is over.

Owen spoke.

—I need to disappear because of something in Basel.

—I'm going to need two hundred euros to even continue listening to this.

Stevie peeled out four hundred euro notes.

—So, let me get this straight: hypothetically, someone needs to be unfound.

—Permanently unfound.

—Permanently unfound? That's a very difficult proposition.

I want to help with your research, but I'm afraid no one can be permanently unfound.

—What's the best you've got?

—What Owen means to say is, hypothetically, what's the best solution you can come up with for a not-real-world plan for getting a person away from the authorities—let's just say any authorities?

—Well, we're headed north, which is the dead wrong direction. This hypothetical person would want to go to an expat community in North Africa or even Ukraine. The farther north we go, the worse things get for this hypothetical person.

He now turned to Owen.

—This hypothetical person is on this ship, or one very similar to it?

—Let's assume this hypothetical person is in this very room.

—Let's not. Look, you've got nothing but B plans, my friend. The next best bet to going south is going very far north. Our next port is Nijmegen. Several container ships leave Rotterdam for Iceland every day. Shipping has become much more automated since these container ships were built, which means there's not much crew and bunks are usually available for the right price. If this hypothetical person had the right amount of money, someone like me could hypothetically broker passage on said container ship tomorrow, day after tomorrow at the latest, and in a few months the person would wake up in port in Iceland.

—How much money would this take?

—Someone like me could get it done for three thousand euro. Cash.

Owen looked at Stevie. He had no more than a hundred and twenty in his jacket pocket.

—Thank you for your consultation. You're quite sure of that figure?

—Quite.

—Less the four hundred I already gave you.

Paul sized them up, then shook Stevie's hand.

Owen grabbed the bottle and poured wine into a third water glass.

—Thank you. But I can't drink red wine. Stains the teeth. My predecessor was not as careful. Know that. I am extremely careful. When I come down here tomorrow at 13:00, after we've docked in Nijmegen, I'll need both of your passport numbers. If there are no other hypothetical matters to attend to, I need to return to the foredeck.

Stevie stood and opened the door.

—Thank you, Paul. It's the little things that make a Valhalla Cruise.

Owen shook his hand.

—Your hypothetical fugitive thanks you for your advice. We'll see if it's practical.

Paul buttoned his coat and softly closed the door behind him.

Owen looked to Stevie.

—Well?

—Well. He didn't say anything about the music. And I guess we have to get through three albums now.

Stevie unbundled the plastic bag stuffed in the nightstand and fanned the remaining albums on the bedspread.

—I'm going to the ATM. Maybe even ATMs. I have the second half of next year's tuition left. I'm assuming you don't have anything?

—I have a few hundred.

—How few?

Owen counted out 110 euros.

—You're in charge of the music. I'm going to get you to Iceland.

SIX

PERFECT BROKEN THINGS

The producers had chosen Burr's favorite of Mission University's three emblems. This was the diploma seal: maize and lapis lazuli, an open book because that was the custom, SAPERE AUDE on an unfurled scroll with stars at either end. And a torch behind the book. God help him if the producers chose to use the scholar's torch as a segue to scenes of Athens on fire. Sawing violins would be bad. Plucked violins would be bad. Drums would be worse. Punk guitar would mean he was putting his head in the stocks.

On the monitor, the seal dissolved into stills of protestors lobbing rocks at police. The journalist spoke in what Burr imagined was a neutral to sympathetic tone—her tone was certainly more lilting than most of the German he had heard. Inquisitive piano, imitation Philip Glass, underscored her rhetorical questions.

The lack of computer-animated graphics and the host's measured tone brought some comfort to Burr.

With nothing but two-month-old facts and figures from the

four hospitals that had helped Owen recover from his meningitis and a stack of printed-out Netscape search results of Owen in cardinal red, Owen at the Sydney Olympics, the random noise of Abu Ghraib photographs, Burr had placed pay-phone calls to every major news outlet in Germany. Left, right, populist, it made no difference. All he needed was an audience.

The producers of *Zeitgeist* were the first to take him seriously. He wasn't even sure which network this show was on, but he was told it wasn't cable. He had no idea how they would handle him or his story. It was worth a lashing from a conservative pundit as long as Owen, or someone who knew anything about Owen, was watching the show.

On the monitor, Burr watched the anchorwoman pace from one stage of the studio to another. She would soon be interviewing him "via satellite," even though they were two walls and two hundred feet from one another—for his protection or theirs? When they walked him through the studio, he noticed that there was not a single chair, which meant this was probably how they handled live guests. Makeup mopped his head and grips swung lights to play with the shadows. The audio engineers tested the earpiece that would translate the host's German to his barbarian ears. They dialed in the sensitivity of his lapel mic. He had been waiting at the studio for three hours and couldn't decide why only now, five minutes before he was due on air, they'd decided to mic him up and camouflage his haggardness with sprays and dabs. Perhaps they wanted him to appear as if he were in a hurry. On the run, as it were. Perhaps these lights are just too hot to stand for more than twenty minutes. He was sweating through his shirt.

The screen now showed a photo of him at the Herod Atticus with both arms aloft, as if inciting the crowd to rise. He looked like a televangelist, possessed and sweating.

Makeup dabbed him off one more time. He checked his

pocket for the high school photo of Owen he usually kept in his wallet. He ran his thumb over the matte print and then put it away like a rosary. The host would be interviewing him in German, but an intern would translate his feed to English. The video of Athens ended with him throwing the bottle. He was clearly throwing it away from the crowd, but the angle suggested he was throwing it at the Herod Atticus. How could they not include the crowd? At the same time, no one could deny that the man in the photo, clearly not the real him, looked quite capable—capable of anything. Did that mean that the real him was incapable or that he had become this capable, dangerous man? He hated both alternatives.

She now talked to a floating screen of his head, suspended at eye level between a pillar and a red curtain that matched her dress. She was looking at her notepad. The monitor cut to a shot of him, blinking.

—Professor Burr, welcome.

—Welcome. Thank you. Thank you for having me on.

—Thank you for joining us.

The LED lights behind him cycled from blue to red. The background was a smear of light on an aluminum screen, like a very drunk man walking through rainy night traffic. The handful of television appearances he'd previously made had been staged with either a solid black background or wingback chairs. *Zeitgeist*'s drunken-stagger backdrop, however, made this seem like news, made him seem like a man who could make news.

—Professor Burr, we've read today's papers. What's your account of what happened last night in Athens? What level of responsibility do you believe you had in the riots?

Okay. So this wasn't news per se, more editorial. That probably meant they would let him talk. The producer had said it was a fifteen-minute segment.

—First, let me contextualize the problem. My son . . . I have a picture here. Can we get a close-up of this?

No one answered him. The young man next to the young man with headphones began slicing the air with both hands. He put the photo in front of his face so that they couldn't crop it out. The cameraman obliged and zoomed in on the photo. He could hear the cannon-size lens recalibrating and wondered how those digital whirs could be inaudible to a viewer. When he saw the photo on the monitor, he counted to three and then put it back in his pocket.

—My son would have been competing in Athens in water polo. Which was the context for that particular venue. There was no premeditated attempt to speak out against the Olympics. As a classicist I have my qualms about the particularities of the resurrection of the ancient games, but these are far more picayune than a systematic critique. I hope that any viewer who has information about the whereabouts of my son will make every effort to contact me at Joseph-dot-Burr-at-Mission-University, one word, dot-e-d-u.

The translator was speaking rapidly in his right ear. He wasn't sure if his e-mail address had gotten through; it didn't appear in the subtitles on the screen. He put his finger to the earpiece, prompting another round of waving and flapping from the assistant.

—You say this was not premeditated, yet you flew to Athens and delivered a speech advocating a violent response to state hegemony. We have obtained video of the talk. Please, if you would watch and then comment.

The man lecturing at the Herod Atticus seemed far younger than the version of himself he'd seen in the mirror that morning. What's more, this Burr was yelling:

"What is fire? Fire is not a thing. It's a process. Fire is the process of combustion. Fire is the arrow in an equation, it is the *yields* on the way from this to that. Be the arrow. Be fire. Burn everything to the ground."

—I'm not sure that came through. It's joseph-dot-burr, two Rs, at Mission University, one word, dot e-d-u. I'm not sure that capitalization matters with these things, but try all lowercase.

—Can you answer the question, please?

—I hope your viewers realize this is grossly out of context. I was speaking about liminality—Liminalism rather. Which is my belief that we must reject object permanence and adopt a more relational definition of consciousness.

The host's silence invited him to continue.

—The Mission University seal that you showed at the beginning of the broadcast bears Kant's Enlightenment principle, *Sapere aude*, "Dare to know." *Aufklärung* as *Ausgang*. Kant's idea is that Enlightenment is a departure from the familiar, from home.

He wavered, suddenly thinking of the more excusable alternative that Owen ran away to seek enlightenment—not in a hippie sort of way, but in a rigorous way. The host was still looking at the disembodied TV screen Burr.

—The idea is Enlightenment as an exit from received wisdom. For Kant, exit from intellectual tyranny was the only goal. What I believe he missed, and this is crucial, is that overconcern with the exit misses the entire point of the Process. We have called for a change, as if change is a thing that we can possess. Again, I'm advocating that we reject *things* and focus on the *relations* between things. At the heart of the Olympics is the perfect metaphor: intersecting rings—an image that the founder of the Games lifted from Carl Jung, by the way; but more importantly, the intersecting Olympic rings are tattooed on the inner left arm of my son, Owen Burr. When I first saw it, I was horrified, but now—

—Professor. You're avoiding the question. Psychology and intellectualism aside, you admit to wanting to tear down the Olympic Games. How does capitalism play into this? Do you consider yourself an anarchist, socialist, or terrorist?

—No. None of these. Terrorist? Heavens, no! My only concern with capitalism is its inherent bias toward idolatry, because you can sell idols. Far more money is spent advertising *things* than advertising services. The very notion of advertising a service summons lascivious connotations. Liminalism is politically neutral. Liminalism merely suggests that objects take a backseat to relationships.

—No one would consider throwing Molotov cocktails at the walls of the Parthenon to be a mere suggestion, Professor. No one would consider riots that left dozens wounded, millions inconvenienced, and storefront windows shattered to be a mere suggestion.

This was the sound of the other shoe dropping. *Zeitgeist* was clearly a liberal show for a progressive audience, or they wouldn't have let him talk for so long, but even they were castigating him. She was accusing him of being a terrorist.

—A young man in black put a flaming bomb in my hands. I tried to blow it out, but it relit like a trick birthday candle—I'm not sure if that reference is going to translate, but nonetheless. At that point I had three choices: one, let the ordnance explode in my face; two, throw it *into* the audience and take cover; three, throw it *away from* the audience. I chose option three. I'm not sure how familiar your viewers are with the Odeon of Herodes Atticus—can we pull up that image again?—but there are empty windows in the *skene*. I'm not the athlete my son is—again, if you have any information on Owen Burr, that's joseph.burr@missionuniversity.edu. I have no experience with these things. The Molotov cocktail hit the *skene* of the Odeon, hundreds of yards from the actual Parthenon, mind you, because I was trying

to save people. Lastly, the injunction to see beyond binary relations is hardly the kind of thing that provokes a citywide riot. I
urge an inquest into why riot police were assembled at the Parthenon *before* the demonstrators marched.

—Is that the line of defense you expect to take with the US
State Department?

It finally struck him that what he had done, he had done as a
person, not as a persona. His life really had changed. There was
no mask to remove. This was his face, cartoonish as it might be.

—I wasn't aware that I needed to defend myself to the US
State Department.

—So you remain unapologetic about the havoc you created
in Greece?

—I just want to find my son. Again, if anyone has any information about the whereabouts . . .

They cut away from him mid-sentence. Without a mic there
was little point in him sitting there. He started to get up, but the
assistant asked him to please sit down. He stood up anyway and
handed back the earpiece. They untangled the cords from his
chest. Burr spoke to the head of production, who was now there
to escort him out of the studio:

—Well, that went well.

Burr's plan now was to wait in front of an anonymous computer
for the messages to come in. He entered his first cybercafé and sat
before a monstrous black computer with an aggressively sloped
keyboard. The boy next to him was playing a shoot-'em-up game
and chatting to a friend on his headset. He didn't appear to recognize Burr from the news, but one couldn't be too sure. Burr
casually read an article about Athens in the *Times*, but then read
about the Olympics results.

Before the interview, Burr's in-box had held a smattering

of e-mails expressing puzzlement and hate mail from the more conservative members of the classical community. Following the *Zeitgeist* interview, he discovered negative response bias. All he appeared to have done was invite people to wish horrible things for his son or spitefully bait him with disinformation. Every one of these malicious messages, subject heading CRUCIAL INFORMATION ABOUT OWEN BURR'S WHEREABOUTS, brought fifteen seconds of hope. Then minutes of humiliation until he opened the next message. Hundreds of people hated him enough to write, meaning many people must have seen the program.

Only one of these messages appeared genuine. The young woman, or person using a young woman's e-mail account, mentioned that Owen always carried a Loeb *Odyssey*. Her words were "little green book." She claimed to know where Owen was and recommended that, before they met, he should research Kurt Wagener's artwork at Art 35 Basel.

He searched.

Good God! He hoped this was all photoshopped.

The first page of image results showed Owen choking this poor young man. This young man in a wheelchair? There must be some mistake. It must be photoshopped.

The second page of results had a few new images. Owen was in some dungeon with a potato sack over his head and wires running from his fingers. These were clearly restaging that despicable prison torture. Every picture he saw was a grotesque trophy shot where Owen was the lifeless flesh held up in service of someone else's vanity. And then it clicked that the "someone else" was Kurt Wagener himself, which brought a heretofore unknown level of cognitive dissonance. Vigilantism was far too barbaric, but, but dammit! The photographs were smut. They were undeniably cruel, and Owen's response had been cruel—he learned that Owen had choked the artist unconscious and left him paralyzed in the process. Burr's immediate thought was that no one had the right to do this to another human, and if Owen didn't finish the job, he'd hunt this Kurt down and finish the job himself. His second thought was that this was far more humiliating than he could bear: the photos were humiliating, their exhibition even more humiliating, and Owen's response, his own response, was humiliating in a way that he simply lacked the language to describe. And lying in wait on the other side of this incomprehensibility was the additional humiliation that the artist had treated the whole spectacle as some kind of joke, as some kind of trap, and had planned on Owen coming to Basel to confront him.

Burr wasn't alone in lacking the wherewithal to process this event. The art community seemed equally divided about whether this was genius or psychopathy. Basel had drawn a line in the sand. Younger critics eagerly hopped over to the side of violence. Some argued that Kurt should not be prosecuted because he was making art, whereas Owen was nothing but a criminal. Others claimed that Kurt should be prosecuted for kidnapping because his performance was kitsch, and Owen should be pardoned because he transformed kitsch into art. One reviewer called Owen an important artist. Burr felt ill.

The art market had voted with the biggest sale for a contemporary photograph on record. Over a million dollars paid for torture and Owen's violent response to torture. What barbaric world was he living in, where these events were not only valued but glorified? What barbaric world would allow the original event to happen? This was not the world he would have built for his son.

She shouldn't have told him about Basel. It would have been better had she just mentioned the Loeb. He wasn't capable of these things. He was a man who belonged in an office with comprehensive health insurance. He was a man whose chief provocation was to unveil the soul of ancient words.

He was. But the man they showed on *Zeitgeist*, thumping his hand on the side of the rostrum, wide-eyed with powerful hands—the Burr who would turn Athens into a signal fire—that man would relish confronting her. That man was capable of walking from this wreckage. That man was capable of finding his son.

That man was also clever enough to think that this might be an ambush, and suggested meeting this young woman, Brigitte, in a public place. She offered the name of a wine bar in East Berlin that Owen had supposedly frequented.

They had some tempting scheme for selling wine, but he needed to be ice-vein sober. Coffee mug before him, Burr let the steam moisten his eyelids. He warmed his hands and wondered where Owen would have sat. Burr had chosen a seat at the farmhouse table because most of the upholstered furniture looked flea-infested. It didn't seem to bother all of the students who drank here. They all frowned and slunk away, opting for any disintegrating couch in a far-flung corner. He had apparently come on some sort of knitting day. Several acrylic needles clacked against the tables as the front door opened and closed. A wash of whispers followed the tall blondish redhead approaching his table.

She was aggressively attractive and surely on magazine covers or television. Everything about her beauty—her height, her angular face, accentuated by what had to be professional makeup—confused him, embarrassed him. It was as if the valet had mistaken his Volvo for a red sports car. How many engineers did it take to send a woman like this into the world? Dozens?

—Brigitte Hessen. I'm the one who wrote to you yesterday evening. Director of Timmons Projects. Intimate friend of your son's. Your son Owen. Professor Burr?

—What do you have for me? The hospital only had records to the second of June. Is Owen still in Berlin?

—It's a pleasure to meet you.

—Skip it.

Brigitte mumbled into her exhaled smoke. He didn't catch what she said. Either German or Dutch. He caught "Americans." She turned to face him.

—My lawyer has advised me that there are certain things I'm at liberty to say and certain things I, unfortunately, cannot say.

—Let me start over. Nice to meet you. Nice to meet you. Where's my son?

Brigitte smoked.

— Is there anything at all you can do to help me find my son, Owen Burr?

—Naturally. Anything I can do to help, Professor. I have long been a fan of your work. It seems like many, many years since I read your first article, but you are still so young. And then a friend saw you on *Zeitgeist*.

Burr wanted to accept the flattery, but he knew that no one in the world, excepting perhaps those within the LGBT community, had had an opinion of him before the past few months. And Brigitte didn't strike him as the pink triangle kind.

—I can't think of which one was more of a disaster, Athens or the news last night.

—I was shocked to see how rudely that journalist was talking to you. In a way it proves Kurt's work at Basel. If art and politics weren't so distinct, they would have put the two Burrs together— even if Kurt and Altberg did everything to keep your son anonymous and allegorical.

—The whole thing is a disaster.

—Naturally. It is hard to put oneself into media for the first time. It is swimming in the shark's water. You realize there are bigger powers than you who will come and snap you up.

She clapped the hand that wasn't holding the cigarette to indicate a shark bite.

—Hmmph.

—Trust me, there's no one in Berlin who can help you more.

—Is this where you met Owen?

—We met at a bar, not this bar, though he was at this bar that night. I could tell at once that he wasn't an average American tourist.

—Of course not. He's a 6'8" Olympic athlete!

—Naturally. What I mean is, he didn't seem interested in the usual things. He seemed kind.

—He *is* kind.

—Maybe he was kind. Now he's world-famous for the great unkindness he showed my fiancé, Kurt Wagener.

—There must be some misunderstanding here. Those pictures. That's not Owen.

—Perhaps you should look at these.

Brigitte thumped ten pounds of glossy art magazines onto the table. The top cover showed Owen, still wearing an eye patch, using his jacket sleeve to choke a young man, Kurt, while hundreds looked on in horror. The heading blared: THE RESURREC-TION OF KURT WAGENER. The printed pictures looked more permanent than the digital ones he'd paged through in the cybercafé.

—I've seen this.

Brigitte just looked at him and lit a cigarette, blowing her first drag over the pages.

Burr fanned out the five magazines. The images were all the same, but taken from different angles, with a varying number of people between the photographer and the violent tableau. The headlines were also much the same: KURT WAGENER, ALL IN; KURT WAGENER, THE REBIRTH OF RELEVANCE; THE IMPOSSIBILITY OF DEATH IN THE MIND OF KURT WAGENER; THE NEW ART.

When the word *art* gives you a sinking feeling, what's left for you in the real world?

—Owen is not a violent person by nature.

—We'll leave that an open question. What did you learn about Art Basel, Professor?

—It's a sort of Armory Show?

—It is the most significant event in the art world. Each June the world meets in Basel to determine which galleries and which artists are relevant. Art Basel 2004 will forever be remembered as the beginning of twenty-first-century art.

—Impossible for me to care less about art right now. Where's my fucking son?

—Your son thinks he is a fugitive. There's only one person who knows where he might be.

—Wait. What do you mean, "thinks he is a fugitive"? He was pardoned? Is it official? How does it work here—they decided to not press charges? Do you understand me?

—I understand you perfectly well. I can tell you that it is my understanding that no one at this time is pressing charges against Owen, provided he has no intention to press civil or criminal charges, and I can connect you with the one person who could tell you where Owen is hiding, but you have to keep your voice down.

—Then please tell me why I'm talking to you and not this other person?

—Professor, due to the delicate legal matters of your son's assault on my fiancé, there are several releases my lawyer needs you to sign before I can give you my friend's contact information.

—Just hand me the papers.

Both father and son had an alarming habit of signing anything put in front of them. After Brigitte left, Burr read the release of responsibility he'd signed as Owen's next of kin. He looked at the shaky signature on the release Owen had signed and made it through half of the clauses on the contract before dialing the number that Brigitte had scrawled on a napkin.

The Pergamon Altar, after a decade of extensive renovation, had reopened to the public in June. A pilgrimage to the friezes of gods battling giants, the Gigantomachy, was a must on the summer itinerary of every grad student in classics. This made the Pergamon Museum the one place in Berlin Burr should assiduously avoid, for fear of running into hyperaware twenty-six-year-olds, who might even be with senior faculty, his former friends, now eager to string him up for his newfound barbarism.

You chose a life in ruins, he thought.

He stood waiting for Stevie by the eastern frieze under the relief of Hekate. The Pergamon goddess had three human heads rather than the more commonly depicted animal heads of dog, horse, and snake. He couldn't see the statue at all with these ridiculous sunglasses. At least sun was pouring in through the skylight so they didn't look doubly ridiculous.

Who was this girl, young woman, who'd run off with Owen? A disc jockey? Burr was now a Voice for the Left, but he still couldn't wrap his head around Owen having meaningful conversations with a disc jockey. She must have had some role in making his son think he was a fugitive. Why Berlin? He couldn't have chosen Edinburgh or Dublin? If Burr was the fugitive from justice the media made him out to be, this could be the last city he ever saw before being extradited to a maximum-security prison. How serious was Jean when he said "See you in Guantanamo"?

His gaze drifted from pinions to sandals and hems. Someone was at his side. She looked at Hekate and spoke:

—I have a hard time imagining all of these painted. Is that true, or is it just something they tell you in school?

—Are you Stephanie Schneider?

—Call me Stevie.

301

—Call me whatever. And unfortunately these shapes were once in Technicolor, but it wasn't as bad as what you'll find in art books. Shall we sit?

Burr led her to the highest step of the Pergamon Altar. A crowd of American tourists mingled behind them in the Telephos frieze. Burr, trying to seem as nonrevolutionary as possible, continued his exposition on ancient color.

—Of course these statues had to be seen from a great distance, so I'm afraid they were quite garish. It is dreadful to imagine all of these were in pigment—earth pigments, mind you, but pigments nonetheless. I vastly prefer the blanched forms; it's easier to see them emerging from the marble, which seems to me to be a central point.

Burr stretched out his legs and lightly nudged the man in front of him. The man stood up. Burr apologized. The man moved down several steps.

—Just because the colors are bright doesn't mean they have to be garishly painted. Maybe the statues wore a light mist of carmine or peridot.

Burr squinted.

—Owen talked to you about his therapy? I have more difficulty seeing him mention this sober than drugged.

—I wasn't talking about therapy. I was talking about Owen's way of seeing things.

Burr unfurled the rolled-up art magazine that had kept his hands occupied.

—What do you know about all of this?

Stevie looked at the cover photo of Owen strangling Kurt.

—He thought he'd killed him.

—Who thought who had killed whom?

—Owen. Owen was sure he'd killed Kurt. He didn't know he was walking into a trap. He thought he killed him.

—No. He paralyzed the man by cracking his vertebra on a wheelchair. Which. Well . . .

—Yes, but it was a trap.

—Where were you in all this? Were you in Basel? In June? Where is Owen now?

—Owen's in Iceland. At least, when I left him, that's where he was headed. He seemed headed there for good. He was sure he killed Kurt. I seriously doubt he knows Kurt is alive. I only found out in Amsterdam.

To Professor Burr, Amsterdam meant drugs.

—Was he involved in anything sordid? How do you know he went to Iceland?

—Everything about Kurt and Altberg is sordid. They exhausted him, drugged him at least twice, and took lurid photos to bait Owen to go to Basel. Kurt's idea was that Owen would crash Art Basel, make a scene, and maybe punch him in front of the crowd. Kurt was always trying to sell the performance.

—But he didn't punch him. He choked him.

—Going into Basel, Kurt didn't consider what happens if someone won't tolerate being used.

—Kidnapped is more like it. Who is this Altberg?

—Kurt's lawyer.

—Will you testify against them?

—I have no loyalty to Kurt or Altberg. I saw the state Owen was in when he signed those waivers. Of course I'll testify against them, but my testimony would be thrown out.

—These waivers? You're saying these were coerced? There has to be someone else who will testify to that. Why would your testimony be thrown out? Because of drugs?

—What? No. Because I gave up my savings to find Owen and make sure he got out of Basel.

Burr's eyes widened. She continued.

—I tried to get him out earlier.

—To where exactly?

—Anywhere, just away.

—You seem nice enough, but the only reason you're here is because of your connections to this . . .

Burr was nearly apoplectic, but tried to bottle up his voice in the echoing hall.

—This corps of shadows doing horrible things in that broken tower. You expect me to believe you've been looking out for Owen's best interest this entire time?

Stevie took a deep breath and looked at Burr.

—I love your son. You can doubt anything about me, but don't doubt that.

It was as if Stevie had just attached a torso to the fragments of his son that remained vivid in Burr's head. He remembered every detail of his son's face, his arms and kicking legs, but the extremities had been free floating, unanchored until now. Burr looked at the frieze. He loved it here because of the incompleteness of the gods—missing limbs, missing bodies, creating a space for imagination, a space for him to make things beautiful and whole. Hearing Stevie say that, he realized he had made the same mistake with his son: imagining him perfect instead of seeing the broken thing he was. The last remnant of Burr's stern expression dropped. She leaned toward him.

—All the other money I had went to getting him out of Basel and on a ship to Iceland.

—You put him on a ship bound for Iceland? Was that the only stop?

—I'm not sure. It was headed for Iceland, then Greenland, and then New York. Our concierge on the river cruise out of Basel arranged for Owen to stow away on a container ship from Rotterdam.

—Where was this? Surely he was apprehended.

—My bigger concern is that he would hurt himself.

—Why would he hurt himself?

—He was sure that he'd murdered someone and would never be able to escape those pictures. By the fourth day of the trip, he was really not well. That's when we arranged for his passage to, shit, Star-hvar-something. It's a port on the east coast. I have it written down.

Stevie fished through her bag and pulled the note from a CD case. Burr copied the name onto his notepad. While she was digging through her purse, he caught sight of a manila envelope addressed to her in Owen's hand. Burr tried not to compare it with the Post-it note Owen had left for him. Stevie noticed him looking.

—This is the first artwork he made in Berlin. It's designed to only be opened once.

—What is it?

—Memories on a transparency. Memories of the day we met.

She handed it to Burr. He handed it back.

—It's safer with you.

Someone walked upstairs with a copy of the *International Herald Tribune* under her arm. Burr strained to see, but didn't take off his sunglasses.

—Is that the reason for the sunglasses? Don't get me wrong, they suit you. Very James Coburn. But I think you're fine. Everyone here is a tourist.

—I suppose I'm fortunate that your friend caught the broadcast.

—She's not a friend. And she saw the clip online. It made the rounds over e-mail. There's a gif of you doubling over when the interviewer says that the State Department is after you.

Burr wasn't sure what a gif was. It sounded like pornography.

—Good lord.

Burr took off his sunglasses.

—So you know everything about Athens?

—I know you spoke with Baudrillard. What's he like?

—Before we get into that, I'm going to have to see about Iceland. Will you accompany me outside? And can I borrow your phone?

Stevie led the way out the front doors, down the steps, and around the corner.

They sat on the granite ledge in the warm sun. Burr wrote down the details for the first flight to Reykjavik. He chose to keep his name off the manifest as long as possible. They said the ticket counter would be open until 19:00. His flight to Reykjavik was 19:30. There was a good chance it would be the last flight he ever took.

—Have time for lunch? I haven't eaten in days.

—I know a place.

Stevie led them to a restaurant in Kreuzberg.

Two avenues to the Spree cut a wedge out of northeast Kreuzberg. A thick iron door with a porthole marked the apex of the triangular island. First Stevie, then Burr, passed through the dark entry. Burr crept down the three steps with the breathless attention to balance of someone entering the prow of a rowboat.

They took a seat at the first table. Burr traced its hammered tin corners. Edison bulbs and oil lamps lit the room. A triangular copper bar, a teardrop island within the island block, dominated the ground floor. The café was very dark, which was good. Burr had the impression of a dining car, derailed in the 1920s, left in a field to patinate for a decade, then crammed into this wedge just in time to shelter people during the air raids.

—Very bohemian. Do artists come here?

—Some.

—Does Kurt Wagener come here?

—This part of Kreuzberg is mostly Turkish. Even before Basel, there were whispers around the neighborhood that Kurt had fabricated his assault and injury. You won't see Kurt here. He wouldn't last ten minutes.

—How long did he pretend to be in a wheelchair?

—Over a year. But now all these pictures are popping up online of Kurt running on beaches in the Antilles with Brigitte. So apparently there were a few months where he took a vacation from his disability.

—That's awful. And now he really is confined to a wheelchair? Horrible.

Stevie gestured to the waiter that they needed more time. She took Burr's hand.

—Is it? Yes. I guess. I mean it's awful.

—It's awful.

—If Owen came back here, he might face charges of aggravated assault. I know that Altberg is close to a prosecutor. And I imagine that the ordinary court wants to overlook the entire Basel show. There's a kidnapping charge awaiting both Altberg and Kurt if they push for aggravated assault, so I'm thinking the charges may be dropped.

—You've looked into this. Do you study law?

—No. I don't actually know what I'm talking about. I'm a semester away from a degree in philosophy.

—*Ooph*. Philosophy? Then you really don't know what you're talking about.

—I want to get a doctorate in phenomenology.

—Know that I'm unofficially retired as an academic, so I can admit that I never had the foggiest idea what that word meant. I mean, I know the names and the terms, but—

—Already qualifying your remark. You'll be back on a university campus before spring term.

—I made my choice in Athens.

—Still. It's a good life you're giving up.

—You didn't have to miss lectures to meet me, did you?

—No. I'm working gigs again.

They ordered lunch and started a bottle of white wine. Burr surprised them both by finishing his glass before Stevie took a sip from hers.

—I don't know the full story, but from what I've read, the machinations worked.

He felt like a fool as soon as he said it.

—What worked?

—Kurt's plan. The fake show to get Owen to confront him, the pictures of the actual conflict.

—He's in a wheelchair. I am positive he never took the show that seriously. Maybe he was trying to do a Chris Burden thing. But he definitely didn't plan on any injury being permanent.

—Of course.

—It certainly didn't work for Hal, the photographer. Kurt used one of the pictures from the confrontation, deleted the rest, sold it for a million dollars, and cut out Hal completely. The bigger insult was that Kurt called all of those Abu Ghraib pictures kitsch and said he never intended them to be art, just bait to get Owen to Basel.

—Hal planned to make money from them?

—Lots. Kurt had promised him that he would get fifty percent of the sales. Then Kurt gives away the high-res files on the internet and says it's not art.

—Was he trying to be honorable?

—I keep forgetting you've never met Kurt. He just wanted to drive up the price for his sculpture of fighting Owen—which some Hollywood prop makers designed based on the video and photos from Basel.

—I didn't read about it.

—It's called *The Settlement*. The word is, it sold to an American collector for $12 million. Think of a hastily thrown together Maurizio Cattelan.

—To be sure.

—A few weeks ago Hal was talking to the same host on *Zeitgeist* about how Kurt was always planning to sell the torture photos, which is probably true, in the event that Owen didn't turn up in Basel and confront him.

—So he was going to make millions from torturing Owen either way. That's great. Do you want my advice? Get as far away from Berlin as you can, and find a way to finish your degree.

—Okay. I'll just transfer to Oxford next semester. No problem.

—How's your academic standing?

She tilted her head and smiled. Her expressions were so curious. Whenever she said anything provocative, she lifted her eyebrows and jutted out her lower lip until her face resembled a wooden mask.

She rose to go to the ladies'. Burr asked for her phone so that he could confirm that his flight was on schedule.

Burr did the math: it was 5:00 p.m. in Berlin, 8:00 a.m. in California. There was a decent chance Gaskin was up. But there was little chance he was in the office, and that was the only number Burr knew by heart. He would have to hope Clarissa was there. She picked up on the second ring.

—Clarissa! Thank heavens! I don't expect Gerry is in, but I need to speak with him at once. This is Joe. Burr. Joe Burr. I expect Gerry is very cross with me.

—He called in twice yesterday asking for an update, Professor Burr, for the first time in I can't remember when. He's out golfing this morning, but he said to patch you through whenever you called. Let me transfer you.

He'd never felt so important to be on hold. Gerry picked up at once.

—Of course you call the moment our group is about to tee off.

—I'm so sorry.

Burr was sweating.

—Spyglass is tough enough without this horseshit. First hole: six-hundred-yard par five. Straight into the teeth of the wind.

Gaskin let Burr stammer for a second, and then continued.

—Boy, am I glad I can hang back in the cart shed while those assholes lose three balls a man. Are you okay, Joe? What happened? All I'm getting is the news feed from CNN. You've been gone less than a week, and you start an international incident? Are you okay?

—I'll be fine. But I need a favor.

—This sounds like a nineteenth-hole conversation. It's eight a.m. here. Where are you?

—Berlin.

—I'm afraid I'm a little out of my depth here. Garreth, Olivia, and Taylor are calling for your head. I had to get out of the office to buy us both some time. What the hell happened?

—Things got out of hand. The whole speech was a setup. But listen, Owen is in trouble. I need to put one of his friends up in our house.

—Joe, I want to help, but you can't put the university in the position of harboring fugitives. My lawyer says I shouldn't even be talking to you. He says my phone is probably tapped.

—She's not a fugitive. She's a student. And she helped extricate Owen from a great deal of trouble. Is the house free?

—The house isn't the issue. You need to worry about your

safety, not your assets. Do you have a good lawyer? A criminal lawyer? My guy may know someone.

—The house is the issue. Can you help me or not?

—I'll do what I can. I think it's free at the moment. There was a couple from Amherst who was going to stay there for Thanksgiving. I can probably bump them. Who is this person?

—Her name is Stephanie . . .

Burr realized that if the phone was tapped, he shouldn't say.

—She's a phenomenology student. Once she's there, you need to get her a meeting with Jim or Chuck or someone in Philosophy or Semiotics.

—One step at a time. When is she coming?

—I'm not sure. You're going to need to get her a ticket and make sure this happens.

He heard the static of coastal wind, or Gaskin exhaling heavily.

—Gerry, are you still there?

—I am. Can you connect me to this Stephanie over e-mail?

—I'm afraid I can't use e-mail anymore. But I'll pass on your address. She should be in California soon. If I had my druthers, she'd be on a flight tonight.

—Say "Caroline" if you are in trouble.

—I'm not going to say her name. But this woman . . . well, I hope she'll be good to Owen. I want to get this right before I go. And Gerry, thank you for this. She'll know where to find me.

—This sounds final. I'm going to do my best to retire you, but I've got to be honest, right now it looks like you're going to be fired.

—Do what you can. And leave anything in Owen's name. Whatever happens, thank you. I'm in your debt.

—We'll call it even, Joe. Be safe. Wait, where are you going from Berlin?

—I'm going to find my son.

Burr clapped the flip phone together with a finality that confirmed this chapter of his life was over. He didn't feel relief. He felt off balance.

Burr paid for lunch with the cash he had withdrawn at the Athens airport. He had left his checking account a cenotaph, an empty tomb whose remains he was now transferring to the winds. Before this, he had never carried more than a few hundred dollars at any one time. This wad of euros could stop a bullet and made him feel more than a touch criminal. To complete the picture all he needed was a thick rubber band, the ones they used at Trader Joe's to bundle the broccoli.

Stevie had seen him end the call and knew he wasn't listening to an automated flight schedule.

—What was that, then?

—It's not Oxford, but it's home.

He wrote out Gaskin's e-mail and his home address.

—The house should be in good shape. But you'll need to get a garage door.

Neither of Berlin's two airports is the best place in the world to be if you're worried about being accosted by a nebulous international police force. The security guards could have been wearing feathered Alpine hats and Burr would still shrink from their bulk and tone. Going on *Zeitgeist* wasn't just ballsy, it was crazy. The only clever thing he had done was buy a ticket to Chile along with his ticket to Iceland, in hopes that both destinations would be presumed false or, at worst, that he would divide the chase.

Or at least he'd thought it was clever. Though he was relieved to be thumbing the magnetic strip of a boarding pass, and further relieved that there were no strange security markings, like asterisks or "SSSS" in a corner, he realized there was a real difference between a plane ticket and a boarding pass. Chile meant nothing. His name would make the manifest for Iceland.

He handed the boarding pass to security.

—You are going back to America from Iceland, yes?

—Yes. I just have an uncertain return date.

—How long have you been in Germany?

—Just passing through.

—It says on your ticket you checked no luggage. Where are your things?

Burr was still wearing the black polo shirt from Athens. The collar, once pressed tightly to his neck, now belled out and curled up at the edges. The hem of his pants was marked with Acropolis rubble. The brambles clinging to his shoelaces made him thankful that European security had yet to adopt the indignity of making passengers remove their shoes.

Security asked him to remove his shoes.

He pricked his index finger and thumb removing the nettles. The guards patted him down repeatedly. Two different guards traced his body with wands. He had a stuffed wallet and a wad of cash in the security bin, a leather portfolio with hospital records, waivers, and contemporary art magazines, and the distressed wardrobe of someone on the tail end of a peyote trip. But he was good enough to fly.

He tried not to celebrate the return of his passport. He immediately pinched the smile into a sober countenance that he hoped matched his photograph in the passport without also matching his photograph in the news.

As the gate agent of Iceland Air called his boarding group, he told himself that this was the last private hurdle he would have to overcome. This was the last time he would be a vulnerable individual rather than a part of a collective. Once he was on the plane, they would have to stop the entire plane, as a group, if they wanted to single him out as a person.

He buckled his safety belt as soon as he found his seat. He tightened the strap and nodded to the passengers on either side. Both were moon-faced and remote. He assumed they were Icelanders. On the taxi ride from Kreuzberg to the airport he had resolved that if anyone asked, he spoke no English, had no idea what they were talking about. He decided he would play it Polish.

The plane lifted from the tarmac, lifted from the trapping lines of land and into clean air. Never had he listened to the pilot's channel on the plane radio before tonight. He overheard chatter in Icelandic about numbers, and most importantly, he didn't hear the name Joseph Burr. This would be a drinking flight.

He took each of the three cans of beer the steward offered on the four-hour flight from Berlin to Reykjavik. The passengers on either side were asleep. He felt guilty at each crack of the beer tab, but thought his accounts were even because he didn't get up for the restroom and didn't recline his chair.

Burr had always wanted to see the auroras. He would be willing to rot in an Iceland prison as long as he had a window to see the aurora borealis a few times a year. He leaned forward and peeked around the passenger with the window seat. No auroras.

It was nearly 22:00, according to the clock on the flight chart, but the sun was defiantly high. Would the sun set by September? And then how long before the aurora borealis became visible? Wispy green magnet wind. It was magnets, right? How different the pantheon would be if those northern lights hit Mediterranean climes.

Burr focused on the map. Part of him knew that it wasn't how these onboard locators worked, but the other part expected to see the yellow dot of Owen's hair wandering through the mountains. That was a place to start. Owen knew enough to avoid the metropolitan areas. Burr counted six major urban areas, all with a bay and endless winding mountain ranges.

The captain announced that they were making their final descent. His final descent. The newspaper the stewardesses dealt out upon boarding had stories about the Icelanders competing in Athens, but nothing about Burr's riot. He scanned the paper a third time to make sure there was no mention of the Acropolis on fire.

The A300 canted into the runway as if it were dodging an attack. Despite the pilot's warning that the air was turbulent, everyone was surprised at how unsteady the plane was and applauded the double-skid contact of tire on land. Burr looked for police on the tarmac and found none.

His first thought, looking at the pockmarked moonscape near Keflavik, was that someone could become lost to the world with two steps and a will to crouch.

SEVEN

THE TUNING OF THE SKY

The autumn ice came late to the eastern coast of Greenland in 2003. By November the sound had frozen solid, bridging the wild horn of the south with the robin's-egg-blue, barn-red, and ochre homes scattered along the rocky settlement of Ittoqqortoormiit.

By December an elastic skin of ice reached out hundreds of miles into the sea, rolling with every wave. Seals either broke through the glaze or hauled out on the rolling ice sheet to dig lairs in the hummocks, rising and falling when the larger waves passed.

The bears' only advantages were on the ice. For their five terrestrial months they were scavengers, picking at the bones of a washed-up whale or, more often, pawing the remnants of fledgling birds and other trash. When the ice came, however, they became predators. They ranged hundreds of miles from their dens on the east coast of Greenland in search of the blubber-rich ringed seals that would sustain them for the coming year.

By spring of 2004 the thinning ice sheet, stretched by wind

and currents and waves, began to crack. By April, fissures sheared the platform in two and separated the bears from the fast-receding shore. They could swim across the channels, they could even swim hundreds of miles to land, but they needed to stay on the drifting floes to snare the last meal until the sea ice froze again. Most of the ranging males were able to kill enough and store enough fat. A few were not and remained on the pack ice deep into the summer of 2004.

The blue and green anvil ice, sculpted by deformations of pressure and melting and freezing, remained closer to the shelf and proved a poorer stage for hunting than the pancake ice. One young male bear hunted from a thin ice raft throughout the bright summer night, remaining hunched with his muzzle inches above the arctic water long past the sweep south on the East Island current, all the while trading fat for desperate lunges and dives for the swifter seal pups and beluga whales. Then his raft met the warmer Irminger Current in the middle of the Denmark Strait.

As the pack ice melted, the bear's ribs became a greater portion of the bear. When balance on the flooded raft became impractical, the bear swam past the fractal coast of Iceland's Westfjords until he was caught by the downward water mass that would bring him four hundred miles from his native habitat and ten miles from the Sigurðsson homestead.

Based on the description Paul the concierge had given him on their ride from Nijmegen to the Rotterdam shipping yard, Owen assumed he would be sleeping in an actual shipping container and not in a private berth.

Everything was bolted to the ceiling, floor, or walls. A black-iron rod secured the Holophane light to the ceiling, flutes on the clear shade bending light to form a white asterisk on the flat red ceiling, rays widening to the corners like a Japanese war flag. Four hex bolts anchored each foot of his trundle bed, built for shorter times, into the floor of his hold. The flip-down chrome sink, his thin mattress, and his pillow were the only objects that he could move.

Owen read volume 2 on the squeaking bed and was quite sure he would never be Odysseus, the man of many turns. Faced with a Penelope, he'd chosen to run away instead of fighting to get home. He was also coming to terms with the reality that he would never be a poet—a consolation version of Artist he had been kicking around for the past week. The same inclination that had driven him to this cloister of the world was crippling him. It was a nasty paradox: he had developed an aesthetic that drew him to significant art, but that same sensibility made him realize he could never do anything remotely significant. He would have to float on the periphery of those doing truly great things. He would float. He would disappear. Stevie offered harbor, and he had chosen drift. And now he was floating farther from her every day, with no plan for making himself good, let alone good enough for her.

Unlike the river barge, every inch of this was sea-primed brine-battling ship. Owen's great hope was to stow away, to be left alone in a box, to sleep the entirety of his eight-week passage to Iceland. Instead, the sun was up twenty-plus hours per day. He played chess over Wu-Tang records with Isaak, the first mate, and picked up a smoking habit.

The team was in Athens now. They had a good shot at a medal. He wondered if he was still officially on the roster, and then he laughed at himself. That was a sport, and this was a life—albeit an extremely fucked-up one. But sure, who doesn't want a medal?

On Sunday, August 29, 2004, after a week of river cruising, a week in port at Rotterdam, two months of skips at Cuxhaven, Germany, Aarhus, Denmark, Varberg, Sweden, and the Faroe Islands, Owen finally made landfall in Iceland and breathed the free blue air. The only lines were horizontal, stretching the sky until it whitened like bent plastic or pulled taffy. Isaak closed his eyes, threw back his head, and took a deep breath.

—It's like having a third lung, right?

—It's almost prehistorically clean.

—They're about to fuck the whole thing up with smelters.

Isaak pointed to a mountain fifty miles away. Owen didn't process the words. He was too astonished that in this country he could see to the horizon.

The port security in Reyðarfjörður was as informal as Isaak had promised. Owen walked the aluminum track while Isaak described the previous customs officer.

—A real asshole. First time I came here he took me to his portable office, made me strip down so he could photograph all my tattoos. Said they were worried about a gang problem. And then, as if that's not humiliating enough, he does these third-grade sketches of every single one of my tats. Why? "Because you're black, and they might not show up that well against your skin." Fucking asshole. They transferred him, or who knows. New man's all right.

The clipboard-holding guy had been in earshot the entire time, but pretended not to hear Isaak's grievance. They shook hands heartily.

—Hey, Tómas, good to see you again. We're gonna stretch our legs and bend our elbows. Want to join? New guy here needs to get a stamp.

Tómas declined to shake Owen's hand.

—What's in the bag?

—Few clothes.

—You have money? You're not going to be begging on the streets a week from now?

—My father's arranging for my return ticket.

The officer pointed at Owen's bag.

—You're American? Headed back to America from here?

—Aye.

—Aye?

—Yes sir. I'll just be here for a few days, then to Reykjavik, then back to California.

—How old are you?

Owen realized he had missed a birthday.

—Twenty-two.

—Let me see your passport.

Owen handed him the edge-worn broken thing.

The officer grabbed a stamp from a holster, thumbed the dial, and asked Owen to turn around. Owen reluctantly spun, thinking he might have mistaken a stamp for a Taser, and slowly brought both hands back, just past his hips. He was envisioning how he and Isaak would respond when he felt a punch in his shoulder and heard the smack of the stamp wheel spinning.

—Have fun, Hollywood. Watch out for this guy.

—I'll keep my eye on him.

Tómas found the bad joke inordinately funny.

Isaak knew a plank-floored bar that became a country-western dance hall after dark. Owen bought the first round as thanks and the second round as "No really, thanks." They shared strong beer and watched the closing ceremony of the Olympics.

—About five minutes' walk in any direction, and nobody's ever going to see you again—if that's what you want. Stay in the north. The north is warmer than the south.

—Why?

—Gulf Stream. You can get all your camping shit in Egilssta-dir. It's twenty miles up that road.

—How big is it?

—It's the biggest city in the eastern half of the country, and there are only like two thousand people. Every Icelander would fit in that Olympic stadium. And once you packed them in, everybody with a seat would live in Reykjavik.

—Been there?

—It's like you'd picture the capital of Greenland or something. It's amazing, but feels small, which you'll need when winter hits. I'm telling you. If you want to get lost forever, just walk. The whole country's like an upside-down bowl. The people who aren't in Reykjavik are in Akureyri. The rest, all twenty thousand of them, speckle the lip of the bowl with these little farms and only want to be left the fuck alone.

Isaak saw Owen smile and positioned his chair away from the fireworks and dancing on the television feed.

—What exactly did you do?

—I murdered a guy.

—Only one?

—I'm serious.

—The fuck you did. I'm 5th Ward, motherfucker!

He showed Owen his forearm tattoo of a 5 with "T-H" spelled out in twisted blunts. He explained it was a Houston thing.

—I've heard that line before, and you can bet your ass none of the guys who said it were J.Crew–wearing motherfuckers. You fucking up is a D in History or some shit. Get serious, man.

—I should have been up there.

Owen showed his tattoo.

—Instead this happened. And I murdered a handicapped artist at an art fair in Basel.

—Oh, you're *that* Owen.

Owen couldn't tell if Isaak was kidding.

Isaak slapped him in the arm, spilling Owen's glass of beer on the wooden floor.

—Fucking History. I hated that shit. And look at me now: international maritime engineer.

They let History be the final word on Owen's plight. They traded sports stories, played one last game of chess, and parted the best of friends.

Security met Burr as soon as the plane landed. He had taken hundreds of international flights and never disembarked to a security screen. The X-ray machine couldn't have been brought here specifically for him. Two automated doors stood between him and the freedom of the baggage claim. Six men in hats, all communicating through lapel radios, earpieces, and walkie-talkies, looked directly at him. He had carried on nothing but a leather portfolio and put it in a grey plastic bin that passed from the brushed metal rods to the conveyer belt. He waited in line for his turn to walk through the metal detector. He beeped. A guard pantomimed for him to remove his belt and pass through again. He passed.

He joined the very short line of non-EU passport holders. When his turn came, the guard asked him why he was in Iceland. He panicked and explained that he was a visiting professor lecturing with John Hollander on scansion of rune poems vis-à-vis Ionic meter. The officer didn't seem to care. He told him to get some sleep.

Burr assumed customs would be a formality, given that he had no possessions he could possibly declare. He pressed the Immigration button with brio and was stunned to see that rather than a green light, his hand had created a dreadful red X.

A guard stepped from the one-way-mirrored booth and led him to an office very clearly on the wrong side of freedom. The man waiting in the office didn't shift in his scoop-backed upholstered chair. The escorting guard had seized Burr's passport and now handed it to his supervisor. The tired, massive man was looking at the screen of his off-white monitor, which was nothing but bad. Before making eye contact, he spoke.

—Your itinerary and return ticket, please.

—Well, you see, I'm not sure how long I'm going to be in Iceland, exactly. There are several contingencies that have not yet . . .

Now the supervisor made eye contact.

—What is the purpose of your visit?

—I'm lecturing, or rather I hope to lecture, with John Hollander.

—Who?

—Professor John Hollander of Yale. I'm Professor Joseph Burr, of Mission University.

—And I'm Professor Admiral Haldor Grimsson. What's in the folder?

—Just documents.

—May I see? And do you object to a witness?

He spoke into his intercom in Icelandic. A new guard, with the thickest neck Burr had ever seen, entered the room, gasping the blinds to a tremble and then slamming the door behind him so they jumped in panic and settled misaligned.

Burr opened the portfolio. The yellow legal pad on the verso had a numbered list of shamefully opportunistic projects:

1. The Liminalist Cookbook

2. The Science of Liminalism: We are all Gauge Bosons (look up what those actually are)

3. Liminalism and Seinfeld

The recto held his crossed-out itinerary for Athens, his fantasy itinerary for talks in Madrid, London, Dubai, Tokyo, and

Kyoto, a single-sided twenty-page printout of an entry on Jean Baudrillard, several torn-out reviews of Art 35 Basel with fierce highlighting and numerous exclamations in the margins, and the *Vice* magazine cover story on Kurt Wagener.

—Are you an artist?

—No. I'm a professor of classics.

—Are you a troublemaker?

—I came here to hike.

—You don't look like you're in shape for hiking.

—I'm hiking to get in shape.

—Where's all your equipment?

—I hoped to buy it here.

—Why?

—I figured it would be more suited to the climate.

—Where are you going to hike? The Westfjords?

—I'm really trying to arrange my lecture with the university first, then worry about the hiking.

Burr had no idea what "the university" was called, but he figured there had to be one university more prestigious than the others.

—Where are you staying?

—I haven't made a reservation yet. This entire trip was on the spur of the moment.

The thick-neck guard now addressed him.

—We don't see many Americans arrive without a hotel, without a plan, and without luggage.

Three decades of teaching had taught Burr that the greatest weapon in an uncertain conversation was an awkward silence. He made the silence his.

The two guards spoke in Icelandic.

—Enjoy your stay in Iceland. I hope your lecture is a success.

Burr took his passport from the desk and angled past the guard.

The automated doors opened onto the yellow and green signs of car rental companies. He needed a car, but both rental companies required a credit card. He wasn't going to chance tripping any invisible wires. At least not here.

Looking out the window of his taxi into Reykjavik, Burr was sure that the land had been lifted and they were now so close to the edge of the firmament that instead of appearing curved, the dome of the sky was one blue line.

Ólafur Sigurðsson kept a thousand sheep on his home pasture twenty kilometers from Hofsos. His wife's father had managed the farmstead, like his father before him.

Ólafur met Stina at art college in Akureyri. He studied painting. She studied poetry. At twenty-one they married and moved back to the farmstead. At twenty-four Stina gave birth to their only child, a rosy-cheeked girl called Ástríður. At twenty-seven, Stina left to study poetry in New York City. She said it would be three years abroad. Nearly a decade had passed, and she had yet to return.

Ólafur thinned the flock from four thousand to one thousand sheep. His desperate prices drew the ire of every landowner in the district. The council meeting of October 2000 was the last time he'd spoken to a neighbor. His former flock had been left to roam the interior during summer months. He kept his new, smaller flock in the field and the paddock, with the cliffs to the sea acting as his western fence. The flock was too large to name individual sheep, which was the world he wanted for his daughter, but small enough to keep on his land. He missed the horseback rambling of the summer months, when he would bring every lime-green-eared sheep back to his fold. There was no way to wrangle sheep on horseback with a kid. He had tried the first year and he had tried to mow himself, to keep others from his land, but the first year was a year of death and snarls and shivering that he hoped never to repeat.

Shearing a thousand sheep was barely manageable for two hard workers and a dog. Like most farmers in his country, he preferred to keep things there, barely manageable. Ástríður rang the bell from the water's edge on the southeastern corner of the pasture. Ólafur yelled and stomped in first-step stammers from the northeastern edge. Together they led the flock into the first holding pen, itself as big as most fields. Then Ástríður, in her favorite part of every June day, clanged her bell for an hour until every sheep passed through the narrow chute to the second, smaller pen. Ástríður latched the gate and left Ólafur in the middle of a fearful stubborn mass of wool. She straddled through a wooden crook and grabbed the electric shears attached to the wall with two cream-colored extension cords.

Ólafur held the horns of the recalcitrant sheep, twisting the neck until it became docile, while Ástríður clipped the knotted hair with her scissors and sheared away the first coat of wool. He straddled the neck of the sheep, dropping his weight and bringing it to the ground if it stirred enough to unsettle the metal blades or buzzing clippers in his daughter's hands. Together, they could shear the entire flock in June and recover from the sixteen-hour days while the industrial mowers from Dalvík packaged the grass in white polyurethane marshmallows of hay.

By August, after the big mow, his home pasture was dotted with the bright white hay bales that Ástríður, in her bright blue windbreaker, could almost roll. This was the month they could return to the Sagas of Icelanders and read about the brave men seven storeys tall.

An outdoor supply store is a horrible place to be with no money. In Egilsstadir Outfitters, Owen browsed through tents and bags and packs and shells, all with waterproof laminates. He could add. The gear he needed cost more than a used car. Enter the used car salesman:

—What kind of a hike are you planning?

—A thru-hike.

—Dettifoss to Myvatn? It should be nice this week. But the midges are out. You'll need a bug net.

—Can you show me Dettifoss on a map?

—Oh. So you don't know what you're doing.

—This isn't going to be a traditional hike.

—Look. Just write down your name, phone number, and your parents' contact information. It'll save everyone from Search and Rescue a lot of time.

—I need the gear to make it until at least the first of winter.

—Oh. You mean two weeks from now. What do you have?

—Nothing. These clothes and a couple shirts and a sweater.

—What's your budget?

Owen pulled out the crisp thousand-krónur notes he had been given in exchange for his wadded euros. They seemed so powerful until he put them up against prices. The salesman tilted his head and laughed.

—You have a credit card, I'm assuming.

—No.

—Hired gear will cost you more than that. And without a credit card, I can't rent you anything.

—I'm in your hands. That's what I have. You can take it now.

—Let me see what's in the lost-and-found box. Some gear gets left behind on trips.

Looking around the store, Owen made a mental inventory of essential purchases. The salesman returned with a cardboard box and a pole.

—One of your fellow Americans cracked a trekking pole a few

months ago and left the partner behind. Should be tall enough for you as long as you don't go downhill. Here. Try that on.

Owen put on an orange fleece. He kept his arms winged out so as not to split the back.

—That's the only jacket I've got. Take this vest. You can wear it under your sweater. And let's see. You can use this beanie. Ach. None of this other garbage is going to help. People never leave behind the essentials.

—I still need a tent, sleeping bag, water bottle . . .

The salesman reached into the garbage pail and pulled out a plastic Coke bottle.

—Lots more where that came from. What else?

—Water purification tablets.

—You'll be fine as long as you get water from up high; go higher than wherever the sheep are.

—Jacket.

—You need something waterproof. It'll be raining every-where this time of year.

—Then I should grab some packliners for my gear.

—I've got your packliner too.

He pulled out two garbage bags and put them on the counter.

—I don't think I have enough for a sleeping bag.

—Not even close. I've got a wool blanket in my trunk. Not the softest thing in the world, but it'll keep you warm. I'll sell it to you for a thousand krónur.

—I still need a tent.

—Buy a plastic tarp at the hardware store. And a roll of duct tape. I'll give you some paracord. You can use the trekking pole to pitch it, but that won't last in the wind. Am I scaring you off yet? Want to quit?

—I need a good knife.

—For cutting rock? There are no trees. Iceland's all rock.

Provided you aren't trying to stab someone, there's nothing less useful in the Iceland backcountry than a knife. Now let's look at what you do have to buy: a shell jacket or a poncho, since your coat will soak through in less than an hour, two poles for the tarp, boots, ankle gaiters to keep the rocks out, and some kind of backpack. What do you have there? Twelve thousand krónur? Less a thousand for the blanket. Less another thousand for the tarp and duct tape. You have anything to trade?

—I have a book and a sweater. Some T-shirts.

—Any jewelry?

—No, sad to say.

—No watch?

Owen showed his naked wrist.

—No phone? How about the duffel?

Owen set it on the counter and removed his clothes.

The shop owner sniffed it at the same time that he pulled a face at the cardinal S.

—I got my master's in computer science from Berkeley. Tell you what, go to the hardware store, come back here before eight p.m., and I'll get a pair of old boots that'll more or less fit.

Owen came back a few hours later with a tarp—they only had blue—and duct tape. The shop owner outfitted him with a chicken-yellow poncho and a beat-up sixty-liter backpack with a torn hip belt, which he decided to cut off rather than patch since there was no way of getting the belt to rest on Owen's hips.

—You could carry a smaller bag and keep the blanket outside, but this is the only pack I've got. And this way it'll stay dry. What are you doing for food?

—I thought I'd fish.

—No. Next idea.

—Why not?

—You need a permit, for one. The rivers are all privately

owned, and those guys are deadly serious about what rods get on their river. For two, the nearest river to where I'm going to send you is early-run.

He now got out a map and drew a star in the northwest.

—You haven't been to Akureyri yet?

—No.

—It's the start of the Tröllaskagi, the Troll Peninsula. You'll fit right in. It's also my favorite place in Iceland.

—I've heard it's warmer in the north than in the south.

—That's mostly true. But it's all cold come October. When it gets cold, you're going to need to be in a city.

He drew a star on a green field near the fjord.

—You're probably going to be in trouble before it even gets cold.

Owen was still looking at the lures.

—If you've gotta fish, you can go do some sea angling in the fjords. You might be able to get work on a boat if someone moved or died.

Owen folded up the map and put it in his coat pocket.

—Now the boots. Try these on.

Owen could tell on sight that they wouldn't fit.

—That's the largest size you have?

—You'll have to go to Reykjavik to find bigger. Tell me why in the hell anyone would come to Iceland for a hiking trip in a corduroy suit and a pair of loafers.

—This wasn't well planned.

—Really?

—Those aren't going to work. What can I do? Stuff the gaiters?

—That'll work, I suppose. I'll coat the hell out of them with seam seal.

Owen was looking at the thick wool socks.

—Oh. Actually. You can probably fit in a pair of SealSkinz.

The shop owner grabbed a pair of black waterproof socks from the rack.

—Wear these for the river crossings. You're lucky—most people have to hold their pack over their head when they forge a river. You can probably just leave it on your back and walk across.

Owen exhaled loudly, thinking about crossing arctic rivers.

—I'll throw in two pairs of wool socks, long johns, and an expired box of energy bars.

—How expired?

—Just a month. They'll be good for at least four or five more months in the cold.

Owen was doing some mental math and thought he might not be getting such an extraordinary deal. But he thanked the salesman nonetheless and packed up his gear.

—There are trolls and elves in the highlands. Not as many now as there were in the old days, but you should stay away.

—I can't tell if you're being serious.

—No. I'm not. But stay away. There's no water in the highlands, so you'll die.

—Don't worry. Tröllaskagi sounds like the perfect place for a monster to hide.

Twenty-two. Another tree ring. The remark was dark and cryptic enough to make the Icelander smile. Owen thanked him again. He walked through the door into the wide parking lot that blended into the road. He stuck up his thumb and tried to look as friendly as possible. After an hour in the drizzle, he caught a ride with a man in a four-wheel drive headed north on the ring road.

The sales team of hippies in the mountaineering retail chain— after converting Burr's cash into the supplies now compressed into Gore-Tex bags stuffed inside his mammoth water-resistant, fully lined, independently suspended, lumbar-supported, iliac-crest-fitted, twelve-strap tightened backpack—were adamant about the importance of a "shakeout hike." They suggested Burr go to the ancient meeting place, Thingvellir, and test his equipment on the beginner trails before he set off to find Owen. That way, he could come back to the outlet mall if it turned out he needed to buy more gear.

The trail through the Thingvellir Breach, a rift opened up by two tectonic plates pulling apart, trails like spindles anchored by two centrioles, is quite possibly the most in-between space in the world and should have brought his theory to mind. Instead, Burr scanned the landscape for Owen and only occasionally got lost in the colors.

There may have been more, but he only saw three: yellow, purple, and green. Endless permutations of yellow, purple, and green, all reflected back by a mercury-mirror sky. He looked up and saw the top of his head, his jacket's electric blue arms, his black and grey pack, his silver poles dangling from his wrists like puppet sticks. The gravel crunched under his Alden boots as he hiked through the rift of two diverging plates. He was hiking the spine of the Mid-Atlantic Ridge, deep in a vertebral hollow surrounded by stacked sheets of lava lobes.

He wished his car in the parking lot were camouflage silver and not fire-truck red. But the mechanic Burr bought it from, who either had a tic or kept smiling because he had seen Burr on the news, presented him with two options: the beat-up red Escort or a green truck with an unreliable transmission.

The tent's footprint was easy enough to stake down. As he bent a tent pole into the footprint's grommet, the segmented aluminum rod sprung to life, nearly catching him in the face. With more caution, he flexed the other poles in place and fastened the hooks to the frame, creating a third, habitable dimension. With pure joy at his accomplishment, he sat with his thick wool socks out the zip door and practiced two knots in his newly purchased wilderness survival book while twilight swept over the shield volcano to the north.

Nearly every flavor of boil-in-bag food was hiding somewhere in his pack. Burr's next challenge would be attaching the propane canister to the base of the Big Gulp–sized insulated thermos. They told him the device was a prototype, and he balked, thinking he couldn't risk a malfunction. They told him they probably were just using the wrong word, and returned with the same unit, except this time in a cardboard box. Every hiker in the store swore that this was the greatest invention since Gore-Tex, which was good enough for Burr. Once attached, the canister stove promised to bring water to a boil in about a minute, which he would then pour into tonight's dinner: gourmet boil-in-bag beef stroganoff.

He hoped he had correctly screwed in the palm-size canister of highly flammable pressurized gas. He held the device at arm's length. With great faith, Burr clicked the ignition button and dialed a plastic knob like he had practiced in the store. A butane blue flame crackled to life. A strong easterly wind whipped through the vestibule of his tent, making the canister stove hiss like the milk steamer of his cappuccino machine—which he would have to banish from his head if he were going to survive all this camping.

After five minutes of letting the noodles absorb the boiling water, he dug in with his utility spork. *Gourmet* was no exaggeration. This was one of the finest meals of his life—certainly the finest beef stroganoff. He relished every bite. This life was livable.

Owen wouldn't be here. There were too many tourists. He would be somewhere remote—well, more remote. Burr had sparked a debate in the camping store about the most remote part of Iceland. He got three different answers: the middle of a glacier, the middle of the black desert, and the central highlands. Once the word *highland* was uttered, everyone agreed. Too bad the highlands comprised the entire interior of the country.

He cut short the shakeout hike after only a night. He decided his chief problems were arthritis and poor fitness, not the comfort of his inflatable mattress pad. He was wasting time here. After two hours of struggling to fit his camp back into his pack, Burr finally slammed the trunk of his red car. The pack was still too heavy. He had shaken nothing out. As he drove north on the ring road, he smiled at being the butt of their joke: the store had sold him two hundred pounds of ultralight gear, all justified with the mantra "Light is right." He was beginning to understand Icelandic humor.

Ólafur was making lunch when he heard the dog bark. Then whimper. Then stop.

His first thought was that a vandal had spray-painted one of the white polyurethane hay bales. Then the bale moved. Then the bale stood. Ástríður broke for the house. Ólafur pulled open the door and sprinted straight for the charging bear.

Then all went white.

The first ride had taken Owen most of the way to Akureyri. But no one was picking up a backpacker his size until they could get a good look at him. So he walked in a horse trail at the roadside for three hours as cars occasionally blew by. Eventually someone stopped without him asking. Owen assumed this would mean a longer ride than the twenty miles it turned into. After three more rides from three rural men who told him of trolls and elves, Owen could finally see the harbor at Akureyri.

The farmer he was riding with pointed to a cruise ship drifting down the fjord thousands of feet below. Isaak's description of an inverted bowl had so far held. Bright green ice-patched mountains plunged from the smoky heights into the grey sea. The nearest analogy he had was an ice-capped Hawaiian island.

He looked at his map. The Tröllaskagi Peninsula uncannily resembled a hedge maze. The grooves and ridges could pass for the impression of a molar. He dug his tongue into his bottom teeth. Given the fifty miles of visibility, this was one of the only landscapes where he could be out in the open, even wearing chicken yellow, and avoid detection.

—I bet you can see fifty miles on a clear day.

—Depends on your eyes. That's about the only limitation. Clear air and no trees. I'm not sure what it is in miles, but you can easily see a hundred kilometers in the highlands from horseback. Of course when the fog rolls in, you won't be able to see your hand in front of your face.

—Are you stopping in Akureyri?

—I'm pushing on to Reykjavik.

—Do you think you could let me off on this road just west of town?

—Good hiking up there. You'll want to get a trail map in Dalvík. And when you're there, find the grave of Johann the Giant. He was nearly two and a half meters. What are you, two?

—That's about right.

Owen thanked him and shouldered his pack. He started down the road to Dalvík but veered into the mountains at the first river valley.

Owen tramped around the dales for two weeks in freezing drizzle before he learned to pitch a tarp sturdy enough to make it through the night. The day he acquired this skill, he found a rock shelter in the side of a mountain a thousand feet above human habitation with a cold stream fed by a melting ice cap. His diet was still expired energy bars. The only dietary supplement he found in any of the valleys that he trekked was a seemingly endless field of crowberries. The big ones were delicious and helped lessen the torpor that followed eating a protein brick. His stomach wouldn't last more than a few weeks if he didn't find something else to eat. Even though he knew he needed to move, he was pleased enough with his shelter to settle in.

He pitched his tarp to extend the overhang and then camouflaged the iceberg blue with clumps of moss. Sheep tracks, his only reliable way of making it through the overgrown rock without breaking an ankle in a hidden hole, extended all the way to the rear of the cave. Two immovable slags of rock blocked the mouth of the cave. Crawling was the only way to enter the shelter; it was no more than four feet high at any point, and barely deep enough for him to fit his pack. On the rear wall he mounted his imaginary stereo system to listen to the albums in the empty jewel cases.

Free of his possessions, Owen was able to wander the whole of Tröllaskagi with his trekking pole and a water bottle. In less than a month he had explored all the valleys he could find a way to access. And at the end of each day's ramble, he returned to his cave.

■

Burr thought back to the *Zebulon*, the diving well, and Zuma. He was fairly certain Owen would be camping, but at some deep level Owen associated boats with freedom, and he might be working on a fishing vessel—or at least that was the best Burr had. The list of fishing villages was long but manageable, with a month of driving. Fortunately, there were no harbors in the south. He couldn't see Owen in the agricultural south, so for now he was willing to write off half the country. Burr drew stars over the towns that best fit Owen's inclinations and needs: Breiðavík in the remote Westfjords, and Raufarhöfn in the far northeast. But there was a fair deal of guesswork involved. Owen had been wandering around Iceland since, what, July? Stevie put him on a boat in mid-June. It couldn't have taken more than a week to get to Iceland from the Netherlands by sea. That meant Owen had been stamping around somewhere for two months. In a country this small, someone had to know how to find him. But, as Burr soon discovered, there was no one place to talk to people. What appeared to be towns on his map turned out to be surnames of individual farmers.

Burr had enough boil-in-bag meals in the car to last him three months. Which was a break, because food was expensive and his remaining funds would have to go for gas. He told himself that bars and coffeehouses were the best bet for finding Owen and not mere rubble of his old life, which he combed only because it was familiar. Bars were a good place to start. That was an undeniable fact. Cold and hot beverages thusly justified, he now faced the problem of finding a single bar or café outside of a tourist area.

The Snaefellsnes Peninsula jutted out like a forearm with a balled-up fist to the North Atlantic. Burr drove through a cold rain that he was thankful he wasn't hiking in. His first stop was Stykkishólmur. He asked the man in the gas station–cum–

restaurant if he had heard anything about a one-eyed American giant working on the fishing boats. The Icelandic laugh, he was quickly learning, could easily be mistaken for derision. He produced a photograph of Owen from the Basel show. This laugh was even shorter and harsher.

—You need to get some sleep, my friend. There is a guesthouse just up the road.

Finding Owen was going to be a lesson in mortification. He was going to have to make a fool of himself to a far larger and far more hardened audience than the one he shocked in Athens. One by one every Icelander would have the chance to snort and shake his head. He thanked the man and located the guesthouse on his map.

He turned on the car radio and tuned in a station. A pop song ended and a man came on with a hungover morning growl who sounded like he was reading the newspaper on-air. Whatever this deejay's name was in Icelandic, Burr was positive the translation had to be The Wolfman.

The Escort pulled into the drive. He killed the engine and looked around for a front door or a trace of habitation. Nothing. He walked around the back and found a door. He knocked and rang. Nothing. As he walked back to his car he saw a woman walking across the dirt road from the dale. She wiped her hands and greeted him.

—May I help you? Did you make a booking online? Because I didn't see anyone in the register.

—I'm sorry if I'm interrupting something. To be honest, I'm here on peculiar business. You see, I'm looking for my son.

—Your son? Is he a backpacker?

—Yes. Well, in a way. He doesn't have much experience camping.

—This is not a big hiking region. Have you tried Thórsmörk?

—I'm sorry. Can you show me where that is on the map?

—Thórsmörk is on the south coast. Most backpackers go there or the Dettifoss-Myvatn trek or the Westfjords. Why do you think your son is here?

—He said he would be in the fishing villages in the north. Here, I have a picture.

Burr handed her Owen's senior picture.

—He's very hard to miss. Over two meters tall. He had an accident and wears an eye patch now over his left eye.

She widened her eyes.

His water-resistant insulated jacket was far too efficient at trapping changes in mood. He began to sweat.

—Does your son carry a staff? And have ravens circling his head? And a horse named Sleipnir?

Burr began stammering an apology, but the farmer ignored it.

—They've been talking about the ghost of Odin on the radio. I think they meant your son. The reports have been coming in pretty steady. That's the best I can do.

—Thank you. If you can do me one more favor, will you not tell anyone about this? I'm afraid that if my son feels people are after him, he'll be even harder to find.

—We can appreciate privacy. Best of luck.

Burr wound through the Westfjords for the next three days, sleeping in his car or in the tent pitched next to his car, and listening to the Wolfman or one of the other two deejays, whom Burr dubbed Elaine Benes and Leonard Nimoy. The Wolfman was the only deejay who never drifted into English. Burr tried the doors of farmers and every gas station attendant in the northwest of the country without success. He decided the reticence might be due to the language barrier and memorized the first stanza of an old Icelandic poem in a guidebook as a way of ingratiating himself,

"Thó thú langförull legðir/ sérhvert land undir fót,/ bera hugur og hjarta/ samt thíns heimalands mót . . ." (Though you wander far ranging/ Every land underfoot/ Your heart has been stamped/ with your homeland's mark(?) . . .) He couldn't quite get the last word, *mót*; it was a meeting point, a liminal intersection. The irony wasn't lost on him that the one word he lacked was an Icelandic word for liminalism. According to his map, there was a chapel just ahead. He figured he'd try the poem on the caretaker and, if the man was a scholar, he'd make a joke about *le mót juste*.

He got as far as "Thó thú" before a snapping Doberman on a long leash bolted past the old man who answered the door. The dog snapped out years of pent-up aggression and caught Burr's cuff. He kicked free, and the Icelander didn't say a word. He let out more leash until Burr was running back to his car with the dog howling after him. With windows rolled up, he listened to the dog bark back all Burr's quotations, all his puns. He decided that was it, no more pedantry. No more grave robbing. No more obfuscation. No more association. It was up to him and the radio.

He had cash for maybe two tanks of gas. He stayed west of Akureyri, chiefly because that was the radio station's range, and Nimoy, Elaine, and the Wolfman were his only friends in this world.

Then a break. So far as Burr could tell, it was Nimoy who broke the story. Burr could understand about a quarter of the proper nouns they said, half when he was parked and looking at a map. All he understood from Nimoy's broadcast was "Odin," "Dalvík," and "Tröllaskagi." Two of those were places and one was a Norse god, which was why Nimoy chuckled. Several hours later, the Wolfman laughed through a report of the same story, this time with a recorded interview from an eyewitness. It wasn't until Elaine told the story in English—there were dozens of reported sightings of the Norse god Odin wandering through valleys just outside the town of Dalvík—that Burr headed farther north to the troll's peninsula, Tröllaskagi.

Ástríður recollected the events for her father while he dressed his wounds in the kitchen and later for the national news. At first Ólafur attributed her account to an unhealthy obsession with the Sagas, but the carnage outside was real and a reminder that these stories came from Icelanders living in the same wild land.

Ástríður first thought the bear was another bale of hay. She looked past it and chased the sheep until it lifted its head and sniffed the air. It shambled over like an old cat. The sheep, always skittish, bolted for the highlands. Most got snared by the barbed wire fence or fell in the cleft separating the pasture from the road. The bear jogged toward the densest mass of sheep and struck four dead in as many seconds. He then batted sheep caught in the fence, but appeared to have no interest in them once they were dead on the ground. The bear bit into the loin of the shorn sheep and tore off its leg. It plunged back into the animal and soaked its white coat red.

Their black dog had been sniffing the air and barking furiously. Now that the bear turned his attention to Ástríður, the black sheepdog sprinted between them, snapping at the bear. With one swipe, the bear flung the dog farther than she could throw a stone. Seeing the dog in the air unfroze her. She sprinted for the door.

Ólafur, eyes completely white, ran right by her directly for the bear. He lowered his shoulder to bowl it over. He was still five feet away when the bear hit him with a furious right paw, clawing through his jacket and tearing open his chest. Ólafur's neck snapped back when he hit the ground, knocking him unconscious. The bear sunk his canines into Ólafur's calf and dragged him toward the sheep carcasses.

Ástríður ran upstairs to the painting studio and carried a chair to the wall. She pulled down her grandfather's shotgun from the mount. She breeched the gun. Both barrels were empty. In his desk drawer she found different boxes of shells, one black, one red, and grabbed a handful of each. She ran back downstairs and saw the now red bear dragging her father by the leg not twenty feet from the porch.

She put two black shells into the still-breeched gun and took aim from the rail of the front porch. They hadn't shot since last year because she was simply too small for their only gun. The weakest shot had almost taken her arm off. She had been warned that the black shot did the same thing to her father's arm that the birdshot did to hers. This was going to hurt. She might not be able to take a second shot. She aimed for the biggest part of the bear, the part farthest from her father.

The report echoed up over the scree slopes. The bear sat down before letting go of Ólafur. Then it stood back up and returned to the ram it had been picking at earlier. The slug thumped squarely in his rear leg, in the biggest part of the bear, but the fur didn't redden with blood. The bear shrugged the shot off like a bee sting.

The gunshot was the first thing Ólafur heard. He imagined that he heard a thump as the bullet lodged in the bear's leg, but he didn't tell that to the press. He scrambled to a crawl, his right leg shattered, and hobbled to the house. Ástríður was crumpled against the wooden wall, holding her collarbone and whimpering.

Ólafur took the gun from her feet and the two huddled in the house and locked the door. He called the police. Twenty SUVs were in his drive within the hour. Two police cars were right be-hind. The bear was slinking around the scree mountain, a stone's throw from the decimated pasture.

Burr had hiked himself into a dilemma. The scree slope he'd slid down was too shifty for him to scramble back up. He stood on a moss-grown ledge that looked like a reef at low tide. Before him, a valley that stretched into the walls of two mountains. Beside him, a sheer cliff carved by the millennia of ice cap melting into the stream that drained in the dale. He unbuckled his hip belt and dropped the pack on the gravel embankment. The pack was stuffed with all of his gear, then stacked so high with boil-in-bag meals and fuel canisters that it didn't close properly and extended above his head. It weighed even more than when the employees had stuffed it with sandbags to get a fit. He massaged his shoulders. After a few breaths he peered down the cliff. The stream was at least thirty feet down and littered with boulders that could tear him in two.

The paracord in the lid of his backpack was designed for this very situation. Burr unspooled it all, knotted it to the handle of his pack, and paid out rope, inching it down one rope burn at a time. Halfway down it snagged on rock. He tried to free the cord, but almost lost his footing. Until now, the descent had seemed reversible. He would have to let it drop. Burr dropped the pack and realized he would have to follow it down the wet rock.

He didn't hear anything crack, but it was stupid not to house the canister stove and, more importantly, the canisters of fuel. The whole pack could have exploded. Burr had seen enough of that sort of thing.

He looked over the edge he was about to descend without ropes. Does one face forward or backward when climbing down a rock? How foolish to have wasted his lifeline lowering a bag he could have easily carried, or dropped.

He looked down again and tried to plan a route.

It was no use. The rocks that looked stable obscured the rocks behind them. He dropped to his knees, looked around at the melting snowcap, the stretching greens of twilight, the slick black rocks, and thought, if one had to, this would be an acceptable place to die. But it would be a legendary place to *not* die.

He rolled onto his stomach and tapped his feet for the first rocks. After deep breaths, then quick breaths, he transferred his weight to his legs. He traded his grip on the ledge for a grip on the rock and was thus attached at four points. His short-lived rule for Owen on playground ladders was three points of contact at all times. Had he made that up? There had to be an underlying truth there. It was canonical today, because that was the first and only thing he knew about climbing: three points of contact at all times.

He found a ledge for his left foot. Four points of contact with the rock face. Now he could free his right leg. As soon as he transferred his weight to his left foot, the foothold crumbled away. A divot of moss dropped to the black rocks below. Burr quickly kicked for a new foothold and realized that he would have to test each purchase before abandoning his holds. This entire rock face was covered in moss from ledge to slick slope before the stream. It was impossible to tell what was an untouched clump of moss and what was a millimeter skin over a solid grip of rock.

Shaking with the strain of every grip, Burr picked his way down until he was faced with a completely smooth rock wall. He was out of footholds. In the past half hour he had descended about fifteen feet and was still another ten, at least, from the streambed. He didn't have the energy to climb back up. Spidering along the side was beyond his level of competence, and besides, the smooth black U extended the length of the wall. He would have to slide and hope that he was able to slow himself enough to avoid the jagged rocks in the streambed. He assessed the situation. Rolling an ankle would be a fatal injury in a place like this. He could see fifty miles, and there was no one. The moss suggested that no one had climbed this rock for quite some time, if ever. If he rolled an ankle and couldn't hike out, it would be decades before someone found his body. He breathed deeply. His hands were shaking from stress and from strain. If he didn't do something, his muscles were going to give out, or his heart was. He let go.

His toes skidded down the smooth black wall, his fingers clawing for anything, his nose never more than an inch from the rock while his forearms protected his head, down to the bottom of the slope and stopped, less than a foot from a crippling black rock.

It took him a minute to realize he was stable. He hyperventilated. He was light-headed. That could have cost him his life, and it was over in a blip. It was past. Shaking, Burr looked out at the flooded valley below. Hundreds of sheep on the grassy slope echoed the ice caps. The smoke over the fjord caught the long waves of twilight. What a place to survive. And what a story for his son.

Across the stream, cantilevered stone shaded the wet grass. Burr removed the scuffed trekking poles strapped to the side of the pack, hoisted his backpack, and picked his way over the three-foot stream from slippery rock to slippery rock, taking a series of delicate steps where a leap might have sufficed. He collapsed on the far side, his pack his pillow. Looking up at the weathered rock, he spotted a cave. He knew Owen would have done the same.

This was the second valley he had hiked into and the first cave he had seen. Burr climbed up the opposing rock until he could see the back of the empty cave, which was no more than a rock shelter.

Burr made a thankful camp next to the stream. His wrist alarm woke him at six the next morning. By seven he was eating trail mix, his boots were laced, and every stitch of gear was ready for his hunt for more caves.

By noon he was hiking into the third valley on the eastern side of Tröllaskagi. It cut deeper into the mountain and wound away from the lowland pastures. There were no outcroppings here, only glacier-worn scree. As he turned the final bend, he heard the report of a gunshot. He took off his electric blue jacket and pulled the grey rain cover over the red accents of his backpack. He doubled his pace over the rocks. After a half hour of scrambling, he turned to see where the shooter could be positioned. It sounded as if someone had fired at him from the next valley; the shot was certainly from a long way off. And there was only one. He scanned the heights.

The only anomaly in the uniformly grey talus was a small black mouth in the mountain at the end of this valley. He hiked another hundred yards to get a different angle and saw that the mouth of the cave was much larger, but camouflaged by a blue tarp weighed down with gravel and moss.

He stopped to think. There had been no follow-up shot. Only the one. There was nothing to hunt up here, so the shot must have been meant for him. It sounded too faint to have come from the camouflaged cave. The cave seemed no more than sixty yards away, but in Iceland he had no sense of perspective. He'd be exposed on rock the entire time. But the only way was up. He chanced it.

Burr scrambled up the scree and grabbed a rock when it got steeper. He took a big step and slid. He settled a few feet lower, hands gripping the slab that had just been under his feet. He ground in the toes of his boots an inch deeper, to the firmer rock beneath the gravel, and pulled himself back to the slab. He angled into the rock and listened for another shot.

His approach had been too direct. The rock threatened to

crumble with every step and take him hundreds of feet down. To get up, he'd have to kick steps and take a switchback route. His trekking poles were more of a liability than an asset—whenever he put weight on the uphill pole, the rock slid down and threatened to sweep him away from the cave in an unfightable riptide. He telescoped down his aluminum poles and lashed them to his pack.

Inch by inch, kicking in his boots and testing each step, Burr angled up the hill, certain at this point that if the shooter was in range, he would have been hit by now, or at least heard a shot. He heard nothing but his breathing.

Every tenth step a slide.

After a half hour, he'd completed the forty-foot scramble to the surety of boulders. He sipped from the dromedary attached to his pack and looked down on the runnels of black rocks each of his slides had upturned.

Burr looked up again to the cave. There was no motion, no sound in the bunker. He pushed hard with his upper legs on the tested holds, certain that if he missed a grip and skidded back down, he wouldn't have the energy to repeat the ascent.

The ledge was no more than a foot wide and at eye level. He reached high and caught the ground with elbows like axes. Gravel bits burrowed into his fleece and hands as he hauled up his stomach, then his hips, then tilted forward and dangled his feet in the air.

He found his knees in well-worn gravel. Grooves cut from traffic back and forth.

He pulled back the tarp at the mouth of the cave. Rock bits rained down and settled between his shoulders and the pack. A stream of light edged into the cave.

Dawn on his son, asleep.

Burr ducked in and unharnessed his pack without waking

Owen. He wanted to collapse and grovel, but summoned the strength to breathe and hold himself up. He had never seen Owen with a beard. He had never seen Owen gaunt. Burr dropped at Owen's feet.

He tugged Owen's toe.

Owen rolled on his felt blanket, turning to face Burr and wiping away sleep with the base of his palm.

He looked at his father: backlit shoulders, a golem in grime and chalk, two streaks of mud across his brow. Owen reached out and took his father's hand.

Burr crawled to Owen's side. He swept back Owen's crisp curls and looked at the bad eye, no longer covered by an eye patch. He placed a firm hand on Owen's shoulder and then tilted his son's chin to the light, making sure this wasn't the inflamed mess the doctor had prepared him for. He squinted back tears.

—Thank God you're okay.

Owen sat up and embraced his father, not quite sure what he was seeing. Head on his father's shoulder, he caught sight of the pack in the corner and realized this was real.

Burr buried his cheek in his son's chest, then patted Owen's cheeks with his gravel-chalked hands.

They sat in silence, laughing and shaking their heads.

Owen hadn't spoken in weeks. He was only able to find one word:

—Dad?

Burr unlaced his boots and dumped out a fishbowl's worth of gravel. He filled his stainless steel canteen, handed it to Owen, and collapsed at his son's side.

—You're safe. We're safe.

They sat in silence until helicopter blades snapped the sky. The rotors whistled toward them, then away.

After a minute:

—You heard the shot? I think that was meant for me.

—What? What the fuck, Dad?

—I'm in some trouble. But we're fine, because you're fine.

They sat together on a bench Owen had constructed from drift-wood and blue jugs of sun-bleached plastic he'd collected from the black beach of Heðinsfjörður. If there was anything redeeming about the travesty of one of the most remote beaches in the world littered with ghost nets, bobs, and nurdles, it was how salt, sun, and grinding through the gyres had tumbled these plastics into colors faded richer than their machine-pressed brightness, now turquoise where once they were industrial blue, now coral where once fuel-can red. Owen's father looked the same, weath-ered and blanched, but with a glow amid the scratches.

Burr looked around the cave at Owen's tiny home.

—I don't think I brought anyone to your cave.

—It's more of a lean-to.

Burr's enthusiasm dropped.

—No, no. It's a cave.

Owen took his eye patch from the trekking pole. It was now so overstretched that it sagged across his brow.

—North Iceland was a hell of a landing spot. You know half the farmers in the country think you're the ghost of Odin.

With the lone trekking pole, eye patch, and battered suit, complete with gaiters stuffed and bound to his shins, Burr saw how his son could be mistaken for the ghost of a pagan god.

—That's not why they're hunting me. That sounds like an-other helicopter making a pass.

They listened to a chopper buzz the cliff and then circle back to the sea.

—That's not for you.

—Whatever you heard isn't true.

—I am positive that you're not a fugitive. You're not guilty of anything, not anything that would make helicopters chase you, at least. I, on the other hand—

—That's not in any way reassuring.

Burr wanted to impress Owen with his celebrity and daring, but he needed to comfort his son. He placed a hand on Owen's back.

—No, you're fine. Kurt didn't . . . die. He was severely hurt, however. He cracked his T-4.

—*He* didn't do it. *I* did it. How can I be even remotely fine?

—It's gonna be all right.

—No, it's not.

Burr spoke in a low, even voice:

—If they pressed charges, Kurt and Altberg would have to answer kidnapping charges of their own. There's also international jurisdiction involved, since this whole work was a process initiated in Berlin and executed through Basel, also encompassing the entirety of your flight to Iceland, I suppose. You running away and disappearing made the piece even more valuable. The actual event will get buried and forgotten, in the name of art—or commerce. You made Kurt a very rich man.

—I don't care about that. I doubt he does either.

—He sold one sculpture for twelve million dollars. You got nothing. In a sense, that's the settlement. Kurt even titled it *Settlement*. No one is after you. They're after me.

—What? Why?

—I burned down the Parthenon trying to find you.

—The Parthenon? In Athens?

—On the Acropolis. Athene's high-built hill itself. I threw a Molotov cocktail at the Odeon of Herodes Atticus.

—Why in the hell would you do that?

—It was the only choice. I was in Athens because that was all I had to go on. Since you've left I've, well, I've made quite a name for myself among activists.

—I leave for six months, and you become an anarchist?

—More or less. But we can talk about that later. You're alive! Not only alive, doing well. You don't know.

Burr was now whispering, exhausted, repeating "You don't know."

—We should rest. The only thing we need to do is keep quiet and still. You did a great job of disguising the cave.

—Rest.

Father and son woke to a dense fog misting into the cave.

—I don't suppose you have a hot shower back there?

—Sure. Just push that rock on the left and the secret entrance opens.

—Aren't there hot springs?

—Not in this part of Iceland. Those are all in the nameless places near the Mid-Atlantic Ridge.

—I hiked through it! Just last week.

—You flew into Reykjavik?

—I think it was my last international flight.

—Because of the anarchism?

—I think they're calling it terrorism. Jean Baudrillard says they'll throw me in Guantanamo if they find me.

—What?

—He may have been kidding. He's a friend. We spoke together in Athens. During the Olympics. Before the riots. Well, I think the State Department is now calling them my riots. Hence Guantanamo.

—You're not kidding.

—No.

—Jesus, Dad. Seriously?

—I'm afraid— No. That's not true. I'm not afraid at all. I'm perfectly content to stay right here. The only trace I left was a flight record. And a few people have seen me in the north. I stopped at a croft, looking for you. But when's the last time you saw someone in this valley? I'm guessing I could live out the rest of my life and no one would make it up here.

Owen peeked out from under the tarp to see if he could spot any more helicopters.

—I met your girlfriend in Berlin.

Owen rubbed his brow and blinked.

—Dad, I'm a little weak. You've got to keep things slow.

—No rush. I'll unpack.

Burr unloaded all eighty-five liters on the floor opposite the bench. A white canister filled with at least ten gallons of water dwarfed Burr's two aluminum water bottles. Burr washed the grit from his hands and face.

—How did you carry that jug up here?

—I nearly fell when I tried to carry it all at once. Now I add to it a few liters at a time. What do you mean, you met my girl-friend? Stevie?

Burr unzipped the lid extender of his pack and handed a silver flask of whisky over his head.

—One and the same. At the Pergamon Altar. I've never met anyone like her.

—If what you said about Kurt's true, I'm going back to Berlin for her.

—You'll have to hurry.

Owen looked quizzically at his father.

—If Gaskin kept his word, she should already be at our place. Possibly even taking classes.

—He admitted her to Mission?

—As you get older, you lose the wonder of youth. And when

you find even a flicker of that old light, you're very nearly brought to tears—not by the beauty of what you see, it's more selfish than that, but by the fact that you can still see beauty. You aren't this rheumy broken thing. You have the capacity for wonder and beauty and light and are not yet dead. Gerry heard that in my voice. He's heard it before. You try not to press a friend, because then it gets weepy real quick, but you hear it in his voice and you nod and you realize that we are all these perfect broken things, holding a thimbleful of light.

Owen nodded. They drank. Owen smiled.

—Or a Molotov cocktail.

Burr coughed.

—That actually happened. This guy comes running down the center aisle . . . Wait, let me back up. I'm giving a talk on Liminalism in *Scarface*—

—When did you get an -ism?

—Baudrillard gave it to me. So Baudrillard's backstage. I'm at the Herodes Atticus at twilight, giving a talk on *Scarface*.

—*Scarface*?

—I don't know. It was on the TV at the hotel. I'm talking about how Tony Montana is great. How we need to refuse constraints of the binary. How anticapitalism is doomed so long as it remains nonliminal. The crowd is finally starting to laugh at my jokes and whoop and cheer and just be young, you know, have fun on this beautiful night in Athens. Everyone is feeling alive, maybe even a touch of wonder, definitely a sense of self-satisfaction veering on smugness because they're listening to an academic talk about Aristotle's law of noncontradiction when there are blue funnel glasses and sports just a stone's throw away. And then this guy in a black shirt and a mask comes running down the center aisle with a Molotov cocktail in his hands. He's not in a particular hurry, considering he's holding a bomb. He just sort of stands there, like he's delivering a pizza. Torchlight is flickering off the crowd. This thing's going to explode and take out the first three rows of my wonderful laughing crowd, so I throw it as far away from them as I can.

—Into the walls of the Odeon?

—I was hoping it would make it through one of those arched windows behind the stage, you know what I'm talking about?

—Yeah, I know those windows. But it didn't?

—Not so lucky. It explodes on the side of the wall. Glass shards, flame spittle, people screaming—everyone's fine, but the people who aren't sitting there totally stunned are vaulting over the top row and running up the slope of the Acropolis. And I'm more than a bit flustered. Then I see Baudrillard striding over to the podium, like he's going to calm everyone down. He adjusts the microphone, everyone is totally silent at this point, and he lifts his arms and says: "Go," like Moses or something. So everyone runs toward the lights of the Parthenon, but the Greek riot police are waiting. They're wearing gas masks with respirators and thumping their shields with truncheons.

Spittle, respirators, truncheons. Owen realized that all of his words, all of his sounds, came from his father.

—Someone throws a jag of rock, and you hear it thump off the shield. The police fire off tear gas. Missiles launch, and they start swinging clubs at the students clinging to their jackboots. I don't know. I've seen pictures since then, and I can't remember what I actually saw. Baudrillard and I ran down the southern slope and booked it for the airport. And that's how I got to Berlin.

—Where you found Stevie?

—I went on a talk show to send up a flare.

—Athens wasn't enough of a flare?

—You know, all of this could have been avoided if you would have just answered your fucking e-mail.

—I was indisposed. I'm sorry.

—Before then. I mean before then.

—I didn't have anything to tell you. I mean, what was I going to write? "Hey Dad, everything's great. I'm really making a difference in the world. Think this art thing is going to take." You realize you're impossible to disappoint.

—You could *never* disappoint me.

—That's what I mean.

—You've never failed at anything. Whereas I've been a disappointment to us both. And to the memory of your mother.

Owen tried to dismiss the thought. Burr put on his faux severe paternal face:

—Don't interrupt. Hear me out. I'm willing to face the bad decisions I've made as a father because, at the end of the day, I got Stevie to California. That seemed right.

—It was.

The report of four gunshots cut short Owen's question. Five, six, seven more shots. Owen spoke:

—It sounds like a firing squad. But those shots don't sound close.

—Close enough.

—Close enough. Look, we'll both stay in the cave until things calm down out there. Let's hope this fog lasts. Although it means we need to be more quiet. As long as the helicopters don't see us wandering around, we should be fine. I'll hike down to Dalvík and figure out what's going on, maybe also clear up the whole Odin thing.

They passed the flask back and forth while Burr described scaling down a cliff and how he nearly died. Owen laughed with his dad until he saw that a couple of the scrapes were pretty bad. Burr raised his eyebrows and trickled whisky on his palm, even though he had hand sanitizer in his first aid kit. Owen winced, then drank.

—Do you remember that time you fell in a great ravine in Iceland, never to be heard from again, the anarchist professor from California, on the run from the law, lost to the world forever?

They were both glowing from the Scotch. Burr had to echo his son's words before he caught the meaning.

—Aha! Actually, now that I think about it, I remember dying at sea.

—It was a cold day in what, November?

—I think it was October.

—That's right. It was October. You had taken a little skiff out by yourself down the fjord and into the Greenland Sea.

—Then my boat capsized.

—That's right. And you were swept away in the freezing water.

—A horrible death.

—No one would wish that on anyone, not even an international terrorist.

—No. They'd wish worse on an international terrorist.

Owen laughed. His father continued:

—But the people on the shore saw my face. And it was calm. And if that's how the international terrorist met his end, no one will be able to object that it wasn't justice served.

—Amen.

They drank more Scotch.

—Real history now: Do you remember when you were five years old and ran away, swam away, at Point Dume?

—I remember thinking that I was fine the whole time and I couldn't understand why you were making such a big deal about it.

—Well. It was the second worst moment of my life. A son has a right to expect his father to be there for him. I should have outswum the lifeguards.

—I was fine. I was always fine.

—I just mean to say . . . if you do end up scattering my ashes, real or staged, I want them to drown in the water off Point Dume, and let the fathoms have the memory of the one time I wasn't there for you.

—The *one* time?

—Ach! You're impossible. Hand me that Scotch.

Over the next week, helicopters swarmed the maze of Tröllaskagi, proving to both father and son that Burr was a wanted man; proving that the investiture of world interest in Joseph Burr was so great that tireless aviators would stare down rain and gusting winds for a glimpse; proving that the striking stipple portrait in the the *Wall Street Journal*, the crown jewel Burr eventually handed off to Owen for safekeeping, was an etching in history and not an error to be retracted. Beset from above, Burr would need to remain in this cave for at least a month before he could return to the lowland coast and join the outlaws of northern Iceland in braving the winter.

On the morning of Owen's departure, they ate boil-in-bag stroganoff and taco chili noodles and finalized the plan for Burr's disappearance from human ken.

—We may not have to stage anything if you don't cut back on the meals, Dad. These things have sodium levels off the charts and about a thousand calories a bag. They're assuming that you are exerting yourself severely, not sitting around all day outlining a manifesto.

—It takes serious effort to maintain body temperature at this latitude. What is the equation, one calorie heats one gram of water by one degree? Your math is far better than mine, but I certainly weigh more than a thousand grams, and I'm positive that it hasn't topped eight degrees centigrade in the past week.

—That's not how it works. Look at your gut. You're the first hiker in history to gain twenty pounds in two weeks.

—I appreciate your concern.

—I'm serious. I'm going to tell whoever agrees to come for you to bring shock paddles.

—Would you suggest we eat more of those expired energy bars?

The bars were a disaster. The Burrs' ideological support of Leave No Trace camping, coupled with helicopters shuffling the sky as compulsively as a convict with a deck of playing cards, meant digestive issues were no joke.

—No more bars. Ever. But you need to get some fish or something without so much salt in it. Seriously.

—They eat whale here. Do you think my diet is going to improve in the winter?

—It has to. You can't eat these boil-in-bags forever. And I don't think that's true about the whales. Regardless. I'll find someone to come up here and signal to you. If nobody comes, go to the post office in Dalvík—I'll leave a package for you with instructions. But listen, you have to come down for winter. Seriously.

—I have a lot of writing to do—*Liminalism and Seinfeld* will make a killing. I mean, the Kramer chapter alone—

—But you're staying on a farm through winter?

—Do you think I want to freeze to death?

—I'm worried you're going to get some poor landowner killed when he has to hike all the way up here to rescue you. Or when they raid his croft and find your anarchist cookbook.

—Find someone with a large fireplace and a whisky still.

—And a hot tub. I got it.

—You'll be back here, when, next fall?

—I'll be back here every year. Two weeks before classes start at Mission.

The Burrs parted with a back-clapping, neck-pulling, head-shaking embrace.

No more bullets cracked the valley after the first day's salvo. For over a week the helicopters had chugged through their conversations, scrambling clear words to turbulent noise knuckled into the cave's back wall. They'd chopped up the streams and vacuumed the mountainsides until five days ago, but found nothing. From any elevated angle, the Burrs' cave was invisible. Only by hiking in would someone discover their camp. It was too late in the year for hikers and too early for skiers, which gave Burr an undisturbed month before he would come down from the highlands.

The sky, stratospheric blue with wisps of cirrus in aurora-like sweeps. Owen, crabbing along the scree and hopping over river stones whenever the notion struck him. A month ago, he would have seen wet feet as life-threatening. Now he was two hours from Dalvík and could afford to be a touch careless. Four empty CD cases rattled in his bag with every step. He tried to hear the music, but didn't know it well enough. He dipped cupped hands into the stream, slurped like a child, and looked upward to the curl of the clouds and the tuning of the sky.

Owen entered Dalvík weightless. Long grass scrubbed the grit from his gaiters as he descended from the higher country to the acreage just south of the town. A light snow beaded his long hair and hung in his brow. The first building he saw was an outdoor swim complex, complete with two-storey curlicue waterslide. He walked the perimeter, realizing his dad was right about the hot springs. Steam twisted from pool to air like soft-serve ice cream. He smiled through the front door and was able to find a suit and swim cap in lost-and-found.

He soaked for hours in the ceramic-tiled hotpot, listening to everyone abuzz with the latest about the little farm girl who shot the bear and saved her father's life. Round after round of women soft scissor-kicking from the hot tub steps, squatting to their chins with arms outstretched and hands in salute, repeated the tale, each adding a new twist, but all marveling at the poise of Iceland's endangered heroes.

A polar bear had been lumbering mere miles from his camp. He asked if there was still any danger. The villagers told him it was a rare enough occurrence that he needn't worry: a group of six local hunters, all of whom they named and counted on fingers, had shot and killed the bear. The helicopter sorties had been a precaution against more bears. The old women lunging in bathing caps clucked their tongues at the extravagance; the grey-chested man chewed his cigar and never stopped sizing up Owen.

Toweled off, wrapped in a robe, Owen sat in front of a computer in the swim facility's solarium. It took him less than a minute to discover that animals were not the greatest threat to his father's welfare.

Athens was no exaggeration. This had all happened. The conservative media compared his father to a drunk vagrant raving in a park, which didn't seem to undercut their other message that Burr was a fearsome terrorist who must be brought to justice.

Owen winced at the world he would have to rejoin. The world of opinion-poll decisions and parceled attention. The binary world where you're either with us or against us. The world where men of nuance are neither known nor respected, wandering the world until they retreat to the maw of a mountain.

No one reproduced the text of the speech. Thousands of photos of the spectacle, but not one word of the speech. Owen thought of his father's pride at the hedcut portrait and the *New Yorker* caricature, which Burr kept in a zipped pocket of his down vest, and decided to let his father have his infamy. He let him have his helicopter chase.

Owen found the breathless dispatches from Athens and the

sober op-eds in the international press. His father had made the front page of the *Times* international news section. They called Burr a provocateur. One of the *Economist*'s anonymous writers alighted upon the word *firebrand*, and from that day on, the stories echoed or permuted the epithet: the firebrand professor, the firebug professor, Professor Fireburr. In an article entitled "The Wannabe Socrates," the *Post* gleefully reported Burr's addition to the National Security Threat List. The *International Herald Tribune* said his dad might be an election issue.

And then in three days, Burr was no longer news.

On the blank side of an activities calendar, Owen wrote a letter to his father transcribing the paragraphs and phrases that he thought would elicit a chuckle or a beam of pride. He quickly ran out of room on the first sheet and grabbed three more from the counter. Owen could find no evidence of an exhaustive manhunt; it appeared Burr had been a punch line for a few days, then an afterthought. But amid the late-night jokes, there was the rather serious consequence of being on the terrorist watchlist. Owen found no confirmation that his dad was on the no-fly list, a much more exclusive database. But he did read that Senator Ted Kennedy had apparently been added to the list in August, right around the time of Athens. By page four of his letter, staring at a dozen bricks of vitriolic block quotes Owen had copied out by hand, he realized his father was better off in this frond of the world, in the shadow of a great rock, fighting the barbarian hordes from his cave.

He read about the famous Icelanders, the man and his daughter who fought off a bear, and realized they were his best shot at finding his father an ally.

After getting a jump start for his dad's Ford Escort, Owen drove to the Sigurðsson homestead to ask the father and daughter for a favor. He waited half an hour to get an audience with the father; the daughter shuttled from call to call in the other room. Ástríður, and to a lesser extent Ólafur, were national heroes. It was just a matter of time before she got a postage stamp. Her dad might even get one too.

Every news crew in Iceland had managed to make it to the Sigurðssons' corner of Tröllaskagi. After a week, the international press got wind of the story and sent field agents from London. These were the journalists who passed while he waited on the front porch, leaning on the rail where Ástríður had rested her gun. The family had seen all manner of foreigner in the past two weeks, but no one like Owen. And never had they expected anyone to ask for more than an autograph. Owen explained the situation.

—I'm the guy who was inspired by your story and is here to ask you to do something you don't want to do.

Owen waited for a reaction. No smile. No sign the father even understood. Then the man took a chair.

—Go ahead. You're off to a great start. Don't let me stop you.

—Do you mind if I sit?

The man said nothing. Owen sat.

—I suppose the worst thing a child can do to his father is run away without a word. Either that, or spend years making his father feel irrelevant. I did both. And my father, Professor Joseph Burr, did what he had to do to bring me back to the fold.

—What do you want, man?

—My father was speaking to a large crowd in Athens when a protestor stormed the stage with a Molotov cocktail. In an attempt to protect the crowd, he threw the bottle away. But it exploded. And chaos erupted. And he became a political pawn. The conservatives made him into an outlaw.

—I'm indifferent to politics.

—So is he. He is a world-class scholar and a kind-hearted

man. He can teach English, Latin, and Greek. It's probably best to keep him away from philosophy.

—In exchange for what?

—A story. In a few months, I want you to say you saw him take a rowboat out into the fjord and get swept away.

—So your father is a fugitive, living where?

—In a cave just on the other side of this mountain.

—And you want me to say I saw him drown.

—I don't want to undercut your heroism. If you saw him drown, people might ask why you didn't try to save him. I'm thinking something like, you met this odd fellow named Joseph Burr sometime in September. In October, on the other side of the country in Egilsstadir, a friend of yours saw the same man pushing a rowboat into the fjord.

—My friend told him a storm was coming, but he went anyway.

—Perfect.

—Understand, your father really will die if he tries to last out winter in a small cave. There's no fuel for fire.

—That's an interesting point. And I'm sure it would be much easier to have your daughter's tutor living in the house, or even in the barn, provided it's warm.

—Ah. Jesus. Does he bring any real skills with him? Do you have a picture of the man?

Owen set a printout of the *New York Times* article on the dining table. This was the only one to include favorable quotes from his former students. Ólafur leaned forward and scanned the piece.

—But will he be eager to clean sheep all winter? Does he have the hands for it?

—Are you kidding? He'll get giddy at the thought of checking that box on the US Immigration form that asks "Have you handled livestock recently?"

—So he will be returning to America eventually.

—That depends on who wins in November. Honestly, I have no idea when he's going to be able to return to the States, if ever. I need to talk to a good lawyer. I'm not sure he's actually guilty of anything.

—And if he can't go back?

—I suppose he will keep living in the cave and come back down every winter that you'll have him to help you on the farm and teach your daughter. At least for a few years, until things calm down. I'll be here every year in early September. I'm hoping that by this time next year I have a check for an advance on one of his books.

—He would be content to live in a cave for eight months a year?

Owen thought of mentioning their missing garage door in California, but decided to let it go.

—My dad's an outdoorsman. He loves camping. And the valleys of Tröllaskagi are the most beautiful place I've ever seen.

—When does this need to happen?

—If you are willing to help, I'll leave a small package poste restante with the post office in Dalvík; inside will be a map and your contact information. He should be hiking down in a month. After he finds the message, I'd guess it'll be a few days before he makes it here. He thinks all those helicopters were after him and not the bear, so he'll be taking his time to get my package. You know the timeline better than me. If a cold front comes in, you might want to tell him to get the hell out of here.

—Why us?

—You're the only people I can think of whose word would never be questioned. If you, or one of your friends, saw Joseph Burr climb into a boat, then Joseph Burr climbed into a boat. You're heroes. And you're a family. You know the absurdities that come with the territory.

Ástríður had been on a phone call with the BBC. She paused halfway down the staircase, surprised to find a giant in her living room.

—Who's this?

—The son of your new tutor. He's just leaving.

Owen asked a final favor of them both:

—Oh, and if it comes up, don't tell him the helicopters were for the bear. Let him have his Saga.

Later that night, parked on the shoulder of the Ring Road with his hazards blinking, flopping back and forth in the reclined passenger seat and waking every hour to turn the heater on high, Owen thought of blackout curtains, a bed that was almost long enough, and a hot cup of coffee. He should have learned by now to avoid exhausting himself, but his thoughts were tumbling to California and Stevie. After a few hours he rejoined the desolate road.

He drove into Reykjavik at dawn and waited in the mechanic's parking lot, tracing H's with the gearshift until the shop opened. Owen hoped to get enough for a plane ticket. Lacking leverage, he was given enough for a bus ticket to Keflavik Airport, a few meals, and a few magazines. He took it.

A sales agent for Iceland Air patiently secured authorization for the one-way fare to SFO from President Gaskin's office. Owen felt like a recruited athlete when she added that the university would have someone waiting on him when he landed.

■

White sandals dangled between her fingers, sleeves of the oatmeal sweater she found in his dresser curling away from the blue finch-feet of her inner wrist, the wrist he kissed before he left. Before he had to leave. The sea, a fluted column rolling to her feet.

She wasn't exactly disappointed, but she had been so sure that the sand would be white and smooth as a shell's interior or, if not white, starfish orange. Instead the beach was dark enough to camouflage the hauled-out seals and pooled with cold lakes mirroring the clouds. She swam only once, as Gaskin had predicted, and now felt daring when the water lapped over her bare ankles.

A shared delusion made this California. It was no warmer than Berlin. Here the wind rose with purpose, capable of eroding a cliff, content with shivering a pool. And yet the people here wore shorts. Tenured professors wore shorts to lecture—not many, but some, and some was something. She followed their lead. Despite the cold, the sun had etched in flip-flop tan lines, a white gull drawn on the top of each foot.

Her introduction to Mission could have been more graceful. On her first day, in a hemisphere of grad students, she offhandedly remarked that the quality of the prose in *Phenomenology of the Spirit* was no better in the original German, but still wasn't as mind-numbing as deejaying five nights a week. She was just angling her plumage in the sun, but they heard *deejay* and her comment met with silence. No one heard the gratitude. She wanted to add that she loved it here in the cloisters, but just walked away. And from that moment on, most of her program labeled her conceited and potentially a weak scholar; a handful of guys referred to her as Deejay Stevie. She tried to be good humored about the sobriquet. Word must have reached the professors because they began squinting whenever she spoke up in seminars. Given time, the work would win out.

Kelp bulbs at her toes. She picked her steps carefully, thinking she might have heard somewhere that kelp is poisonous. She stretched her neck until her shadow darkened the lace ribbon of a surging wave. She imagined him doing something virile, scooping up the ocean and gargling the sea.

The horizon was navy corduroy, a steady swell of waves holding more and more of their breath. She set her sandals on the black rocks. The rocks were a paradise for the shore crabs dodging barnacles and darting through the glistens. She curled her toes and whisked her feet a few times in a cold pool on the rock, then stepped into her sandals and climbed up the cliff to the house.

The screen door squawked on its rusted hinges. She wiped her feet on the bristle mat then dipped them in the blue plastic bowl of warm water she'd filled earlier. Inside, shadows from the blinds plaited the floor slats. The house was warmer than when she left it. Beams of light pulled to unfinished wooden trim, bent as if by magnets.

Her doubts, she was okay with. But she hoped he left his doubts in Basel. She felt like a little girl waiting for a total eclipse, holding her little pinhole device—not sure how the contraption was supposed to work, but trusting that it would.

She sat on the tatami mats in the den combing the frays, watching rushes catch sun. In slants of light, rare colors visible: soap-bubble green and cyan. His Post-it note, which she peeled from the pencil-marked doorframe of the study and stuck to the forehead of her collected Auden, now curled up into the light from the arm of the sofa. The note had been a surprise, a reminder that she wasn't the first person he'd left.

But today he was coming home.

He looked for her as soon as he was in the terminal. If anyone would know to ask for a gate pass, it was her, which meant she had something else planned. On the other side of customs, baggage claim, and security, he scanned the crowd. She wasn't there. But still he smiled. He had always wanted to clear customs and see a driver holding a card with his name. There it was: OWEN BURR. The driver, wearing gloves and a cap, was initially taken aback by Owen's height. Closer, he thought the young man was more skeletal than advertised and had trouble believing that his passenger arrived with no luggage, just a white plastic sack.

Owen swung the sack into the backseat of the towncar, four jewel cases rattling and the November issue of *SURFER* magazine sliding free, and stretched out on the black leather seats. He kicked off his shoes and rubbed his arches on the carpeted center hump. The driver had taken off his hat. He looked at Owen in the mirror.

—You have enough room back there, man? I'm guessing those long-haul flights are hard on the knees.

Owen agreed.

—You came in from Iceland?

—I did.

—Short vacation?

—I've been in Europe awhile.

—I did a Europe trip when I was your age. Hostels. Foreign girls. Rome. Did you make it to Rome?

—Almost made it to Athens.

He dangled the city's name in front of the driver to see if it would get a response. Nothing. Apparently his dad wasn't an election issue after all.

He lowered the window and let the salt-stained wind sculpt his fingers. The sun warmed his cheek and the back of his hand.

Like a magician dancing a coin over his knuckles, he played with the different weight of the California air, trying to have faith that she would be there and that this was right. But he had been losing memories of her like a tree losing its leaves—he was a little colder, less capable of transforming air by fixing the sky, less green against the clouds.

They pulled up to the Burrs' house. His hands were sweating. He thought of asking the driver to honk a few times, but decided to walk around to the garage.

Earlier in the week had been perfect: rain running down the wooden eaves and crinkling off the stepping stones, every hundredth drop heavy and snapping with the suddenness of a plastic bottle refinding its form. She initially thought the sharplined eaves and the total absence of curvature inside the house would fence her rounded thoughts, wasting space, like a circle inscribed in a rectangle. Instead, she imagined the house harnessing the flood outside. The lines became chutes for rain to weave back and forth. Every bookshelf a channel where water rushed, then dropped a level, then rushed back the other direction. She still saw the run of flumes and the home now had the humid quiet of a forgotten garden. Today's shadows were dry. She looked at the light fringes of her outstretched hand, the penumbra a memory of touch.

She thought she would wait for Owen in the master bed, maybe at the top of the stairs, make him open a few doors and call her name. Her deliberations vanished when she heard the car idling outside. She walked downstairs to the front door then saw him heading around to the garage and was there to meet him in the laundry room when he opened the door.

She had a few wry comments ready for this moment, but when she saw him her arms simply shot around his neck.

Joined lips joined laughs and they wove away.

He was worried that his return would mean gluing the leaves back on branches, his trembling fingers guessing at depth, holding each memory in place until it dried and was reattached. Instead, everything shot back at once, a live crown of memories: the shadow of her pulled-back hair just behind her ear, her almost hidden smile when she was being serious, the insistence this was serious whenever she laughed, her searching timbre, the skipped beat of each quick reply, skimming fingertips on his collarbone before she collapsed at his side, her breath against his eye, the voltage of her softness, the first beads high on her forehead, her hair falling over her left shoulder every time she let it down, her chin to her chest and her hair as a veil, first her veil then covering them both, curling then stretching awake with arms over her head in a dive, ordinary smells like soap and skin, the trust in her eyes and how she smiled when she watched it make him buckle, her warmth to his touch, clasped hands unclasping and rippling wrist and arm, the windmills of Nijmegen, Netherlands, the city where they parted.

The memory of their meeting, drawn on a transparency and sealed in a manila envelope, waited on the nightstand. Three corners with molar bites of travel, one corner beaked up like a paper swan.

She saw him looking.

—We could open it. And retrace Berlin. I found the projector in the garage and it works. But the Gaskins have planned a homecoming reception. And he's been implying that he has news.

Owen was too indebted to protest. She traced his rack-ribbed chest. He imagined her hearing xylophone notes, sometimes singular, sometimes paired, as the mallets of her first two fingers percussed his side. She listened, a finger suspended for a second then finding the next rib. He sat up, resolved:

—We'll eat, shake some hands, then come right back here.

Despite his resolution, it was dark before they began getting ready. He opened the window. Night lacquered black and a rustle of the trees. He imagined how their room looked to someone walking by: amber proving out against the dark, a warm glow from the petal-thin panels in the wall. The white noise of night was cut by distant car horns and a radio, faint enough to be deck music from a ship anchored at sea.

The occasion called for a jacket, but he only had one, corduroy, and since he had nearly transformed it into a murder weapon, he dressed down in a barn jacket left in his closet since high school. She dressed up in a sleeveless emerald dress. She took her leather jacket from the counter and squeezed his hand.

He led her through his shortcut to campus. Quiet stars and the still of expectation. The eucalyptus branches heavy with evening dew, their feet shuffling woodchips, braiding eights in the silver grass, and edging hillocks from the first mulch of fall. She walked up the cement balance beam of a culvert, climbing just inches above him, as she had been when they met.

The porch light spread into the salt-stained air. A crowd was shaking hands at the threshold, lumbering indoors like a creature eager for domestication.

They waited, enjoying the moment before they were discovered.

The porch light haloed a shuffling couple in hats. When Mrs. Gaskin opened the door to receive them, she spotted Owen and Stevie. She took Stevie by the hand and introduced her to friends, leaving Owen to grab a glass of wine and settle on the couch.

Without the rugs, wood polish, and white linen, the president's residence would have resembled an exclusive fraternity house at a university in the south. Every stick of furniture was Mission: drum-tight leather, heavy oak planed by thick hands.

People nodded, but kept their distance, presumably because of Berlin. And Basel. It would have been worse had he worn the jacket.

A crystal rocks glass rested on the arm of an adjacent chair. Owen watched a cold droplet roll over the glass's pineapple cuts, snailing ever closer to the polished grain. Over the din, he heard the ice snap and resettle. He heard the wood creak at the cold warping of the drink. He took the glass. The professor sitting next to him turned:

—I believe that's mine, dear boy.

Owen handed it back. Without taking a sip, the professor replaced the drink on the wooden arm, chaining the waterstain with a second ring.

President Gaskin had been watching. He approached:

—Owen, I see you've met Professor George Hill.

Owen stood. Gaskin shook his hand firmly and clapped his arm a few times.

—Professor Hill is currently advising your better half on her independent study.

She stood on the far side of the room under crystal pendants, two champagne glasses in her hands fizzing the incandescence and burning down like sparklers.

Hill spoke to Gaskin, but for Owen's benefit:

—Ms. Schneider is a gifted reader and picks up subtle rhythms of the texts that other students miss. The department would be lucky to retain her.

—I couldn't agree more. If you'll excuse us a moment.

At six-eight with an eyepatch, he didn't need to raise his hand to get his date's attention—standing gave them a private line of sight. But when he stood, he also raised his hand, and in the course of doing so, stopped conversation. The entire reception watched Owen follow Gaskin to the adjoining study.

Hundreds of volumes of poetry lined the shelves. This was very different from his father's version of Gaskin, the same president who was now pinching silver tongs and talking about the special whisky they would soon be tasting.

—Are these books yours, or Mrs. Gaskin's?

—When your father and I were younger, we had fierce debates at the Tilted Wig about Paul Celan and Georg Trakl. Your mother could recite poetry by the yard. She was friends with my first wife, but that's not why we met. I'm not sure your father ever knew this, but our friendship wasn't coincidental.

Gaskin now had Owen's attention.

—No. Not a coincidence at all. The academy stands on two pillars: theory and fundraising. Even as a grad student, I bristled at the word *thesis*. I was never going to come up with a theory—I'm too allergic to paradox. I did Frost, not the dark Frost of Brodsky, mind you; I read the apple orchard Frost, the walking for a think Frost. My Whitman was asexual, which is to say doomed. I latched onto the brightest star I could find, your father, and confirmed my private suspicions that I was no theorist.

—But you're here.

—But I'm here. Which speaks to the power of ambition meeting self-awareness. Unlike the legions of unsuccessful academics, I knew who I was and found another way to make myself indispensable. So I campaigned for a seat on the faculty senate and spent my day trading faculty grievances for favors. The provost was impressed enough to appoint me his special assistant. I played golf with the pioneers of Silicon Valley and squash with fund managers. When time came for a change, the Board of Trustees, maybe for the first time, saw someone who understood the business of education. For all your father's lecturing on *know thyself*, I think he's just recently learned his value. Which is to say, there are two ways you can continue living the academic life, but you have to know what value you bring to Mission.

Gaskin offered Owen a Scotch. Owen set down his wine and took it, uncertain what Gaskin was implying. He faced the problem:

—How bad's the fallout from Athens?

—Fallout? You mean *windfall*. I'm hearing from college counselors all over this great land that Mission University is the new Berkeley. That's because of your father. Now we have an edge. Only our name can hold us back. It sounds religious; there's no escaping that. I tell you this in confidence, but this year I'm going to put it to the trustees that we change the name to Big Sur. It has a valence to it, no?

—Big Sur is better.

—"Where did you do your undergrad?" "Big Sur." Much better. It's less . . .

—Normative.

—I was going to say *snotty*, but yes.

They drank. Owen smacked his lips and nodded in appreciation of the drink. Both men waited to draw serious remarks. Gaskin won:

—Could you see yourself as an associate professor at Big Sur?

Owen coughed, whisky fumes laughing out his nose.

—I don't even have a degree.

—Three and a half years at Stanford . . .

—Three and a third.

—You have real-world experience as a contemporary artist. That's who kids want to listen to. That's the lecture alumni want to attend when they come back for homecoming. It sends a message. *You* send a message. And your connections will be a boon to fundraising if we build a museum of contemporary art.

—You've read the wrong CV. I'm no artist.

—And your legacy extends back to the richest days of Mission

University. A clutch of professors like you will make Big Sur the most exciting school in the country.

—I appreciate the compliment, but I can't be a professor; I have nothing to profess. Especially about art.

Silence indicated Gaskin's displeasure at being handed back a gift.

Owen crunched ice. Owen guessed that if this silence lasted another moment, he was going to hear that his ninety-nine-year lease was less than iron-clad. He had an idea:

—You're focusing too much on my first name and not enough on my last. There's no one with a better grasp of Liminalism than me. My dad left behind one big manuscript, which I could edit in a year. You're going to have an influx of students looking for progressive theory and, no offense to anyone out there in the parlor, but it looks like you're lacking in that department.

They met eyes and sealed the proposal with a toast.

—We'll try to get you a course for the spring semester. Start putting together a lesson plan that I can show to the provost.

Gaskin rose. Gripping the door handle he asked a final question.

—You never told me. How the hell did he find you?

—By looking in every cave.

Gaskin looked puzzled, giving Owen an opening.

—Actually, do you mind if we have another? I have some bad news about my father, which shouldn't hurt our plans.

Gaskin tilted his head. He refilled Owen's glass, then his own. He sat on the bench in front of the casement window, crossing his legs and enjoying his role as spectator. Owen smiled then assumed faux solemnity.

—I'm afraid my father is going to meet a dreadful end next month.

Owen pinched his lips with another drink of scotch and shook his head.

Gaskin grinned.

—Oh really. How will this transpire?

—The Greenland Sea is vast, cold, and capable of capsizing any small craft on any given day.

—Why on earth would Joe be rowing a boat in the Arctic?

—Hunger. He was on the run. Had no money, I'm afraid. He had the idea he would catch a fish—two rural Icelanders will see him sneak into a rowboat with fishing gear. They'll say they saw the boat flip over, just on the other side of the fjord—too far for them to reach him in time. The boat was sucked up in the foaming cold then dashed down by a frozen slab . . .

—Okay. I get it. And when exactly is this going to go down?

—It should happen within the month. At that point, we negotiate the sale of a manuscript he left behind.

—The manuscript you're talking about is real?

—He left behind several. I'm going to be editing all winter to piece it all together, but he's been writing about this stuff since before I was born. He's writing his magnum opus as we speak.

—You're going to need to hold off on your negotiations for at least a year. The university will recognize the tragedy at once. We will help the authorities in whatever way we can. On your end, you'll hold out hope that your father is still alive. As far as you're concerned, he's a missing person and you would *never* look for a payout from the insurance company. You can get away with just about anything in this world until it costs people money. So. No insurance claim. I know the attorney who can handle this.

—We'll keep it small. He wants the ceremony at Point Dume.

Owen caught sight of Stevie through the glass door. She raised her eyebrows. Gaskin saw how eager Owen was to get back to her side.

—Shall we join the others, Professor Burr?

■

Burr stood in longjohns and camp shoes, rubbing his arms and yawning out steam. He grabbed the keystone of the cave, stretched his back, and then looked down on the full sea. The cave faced northwest. He could almost see Greenland. He imagined his stare wrapping around the world a few times until it settled upon his son and Stevie in Big Sur. A light fan of arctic air rose up. He caught his foot to stretch his swollen knees. His hands still smelled of menthol and his Achilles burned from the camphor balm he knuckled into his frayed tendons first thing after waking. His beard was scratchy, his shoulders a knotted cordage, each day brought rain, but here he breathed down all the way to his pelvic floor and exhaled all the waste that had accumulated in his fifty years of sedentary life. He could feel all the cowardice he had crammed down under his diaphragm now lift to the thin air until his body was weightless and empty, his chest open, the best definition he had of what it meant to be a brave man.

He distilled each day's best thought or experience until it was no more than a cliché: while watching gulls circle the sky, he missed a step and slipped in a hummock field—head in the clouds; his desiccated hands now cracked in tire treads—you are what you eat; ebullient at the realization that he was finally making no claim to originality—nothing's new under the sun.

He decided he would dictate the status of his own freedom. Sunrise started calling him to the basalt beach a few miles away. And each morning on the black shore, grinding his way over egg-shaped stones, he swung his trekking poles overhead in great aluminum loops to keep the arctic terns from diving at his head. He walked over stones in a riffle of tide and a roil of squawks, untouched by talons and tracing bracelets over the dark earth with his poles. From above, he was one man with a revolving ensemble of birds, one man conducting the sky.

ACKNOWLEDGMENTS

Eric Groff was the most talented of all of us. He invited me up to Montana and listened patiently to my early ravings about this book. He was the first person to take me seriously as a writer and told me to emphasize the undeveloped character of the father—which ended up being the key to the story. Eric was a brilliant reader, writer, and person. I've never met anyone as vital. He inspired his friends and his students to live bigger. I picture him with his massive arms crossed, red goatee jawing the sky, laughing that those typewritten rambles amounted to this. Thank you, Eric. Man, you're missed.

There's no way this book would exist in any form without Kevin Jaszek. As a reader, he's both brilliant and savage. As a friend, he kept me sane and focused on the book. Thank you for having the patience to suffer me—who knew how much trouble could come from a game of hangman? _ _ _ _ _ _ _ _

Thank you to my daughter, Vivian, born with a fierce love of yellow, for teaching me to see the world in new, brighter ways. I hope you always carry with you a world steeped in color, wonder, and hilarity. All my love.

Thank you to my parents and my family for unwavering, unconditional—and totally unwarranted—trust and support.

Thank you to Jonathan Burnham and Michael Signorelli for the rare gamble they took on me and on this book. And to Barry Harbaugh for really loving books.

This novel took a long time to write. I've leaned so heavily on my friends that *Brave Man* should really be published as three pages of story and three hundred ninety-seven pages detailing all of the amazing things the following people have done. I am forever indebted to:

Erwin Cook. Jon Jackson. Billy Hart. Noah Lit. Jenny and Tom Terbell. Damian Loeb. Daniel Subkoff. James Fuentes. Alex Adler. Viktor Timofeev. Chris Arp. Miranda Ottewell. Ben Okaty. Paul Lynch. Dina Pugh. Brian Heifferon. Paolo Resmini. Kevin Shaffer. Alex Auritt. Brendan Jones. Atisha Paulson. Thomas McEvilley. Tim Carey. Chien Si Harriman. Dez Croan. Maria Wade. Casey McMahon. Alaska McFadden. Louis Epstein. Akiva Elstein. Lindsay Welsch. Aaron Zubaty. Igor Ramírez. Marcello Pisu. Peter Murphy. Matt Bardin. Michael Englander. Marc Englander. Matt Abramcyk. Jared Kushner. Rune Hedeman. Josh Cody. Barry Crooks. Chris Kartalia. Jackson Wagener. Jay Wagener. Chad Schafer. Steffen Angstmann. Kyra Barry. James Killough. Bill Beslow. Gianfranco Galluzzo. Stanley Bard. John Kule. Jon Jonisch. Van Rainy Hecht-Nelson. Drew Machat. Borut Grgic. Chris Stein. Matt Witte. Kate D'Esmond. Gabe Saporta. Tom Russotti. Russell Kerr. Josh Griffiths. Marek Berry. Josh Wyrtzen. Armin Rosencranz.

ABOUT THE AUTHOR

Will Chancellor lives in New York City. This is his first book.